SULFUR SPRINGS

This Large Print Book carries the
Seal of Approval of N.A.V.H.

SULFUR SPRINGS

WILLIAM KENT KRUEGER

THORNDIKE PRESS
A part of Gale, a Cengage Company

Farmington Hills, Mich • San Francisco • New York • Waterville, Maine
Meriden, Conn • Mason, Ohio • Chicago

Thorndike Press® Large Print Thriller.
The text of this Large Print edition is unabridged.
Other aspects of the book may vary from the original edition.
Set in 16 pt. Plantin.

LIBRARY OF CONGRESS CIP DATA ON FILE.
CATALOGUING IN PUBLICATION FOR THIS BOOK
IS AVAILABLE FROM THE LIBRARY OF CONGRESS.

ISBN-13: 978-1-4328-4105-8 (hardcover)
ISBN-10: 1-4328-4105-x (hardcover)

Published in 2017 by arrangement with Atria Books, a division of Simon & Schuster, Inc.

Printed in Mexico
3 4 5 6 7 8 21 20 19 18 17

For Paul and Becky. The lost
treasures have been found.

ACKNOWLEDGMENTS

My heartfelt thanks — and also my deep admiration — to those who work as volunteers with Los Samaritanos and Humane Borders. These are courageous, good-hearted people who risk a great deal to offer assistance to the thousands of refugees crossing the border every year in the hope of finding sanctuary. Their knowledge, personal experiences, and insights, which they shared so generously with me, proved extraordinarily helpful in my understanding of the difficult situation — political, economic, and humanitarian — that currently exists along our border with Mexico.

Thanks also to the U.S. Customs and Border Protection agents who were willing to talk to me and who offered their own perspectives. I have nothing but the greatest respect for law enforcement and for the men and women who put their lives on the line every day, believing in their hearts that they are *ogichidaa.*

And finally, my thanks to the people who live in southern Arizona and who feel the impact of the undeclared war being waged there. Over coffee and over beer, they helped to open my North Country eyes in many useful ways.

CHAPTER 1

In the balance of who we are and what we do, the weight of history is immeasurable.

When I was thirteen years old, my father, who was sheriff of Tamarack County, Minnesota, was killed in the line of duty. Five years later, at the height of the Vietnam War, I graduated from high school. In the first draft lottery since 1942, the number I drew was well above 300, high enough to ensure that I would never be called up. But I saw my friends entering military service, by choice or not, and although I had my doubts about that conflict, its legitimacy and its ultimate goal, I felt I should do my part. My widowed mother begged her only child not to go. We argued, sometimes bitterly. In the end, I agreed to a compromise. I would not go to war; instead, I would go into law enforcement, as my father had. In that way, wearing a little metal shield, I would fight the battles I believed were im-

9

portant.

The weight of history.

I completed an associate's degree in criminal justice at the community college in my hometown of Aurora, Minnesota, then applied for and was accepted to the Chicago Police Training Academy. Why Chicago? It was where my father had been born and had trained and had been a cop before marrying my mother and moving to Tamarack County.

The weight of history.

The morning I headed off, just before I stepped onto the Greyhound bus idling blue exhaust in front of Pflugleman's Rexall Drugs, my mother kissed me good-bye. She put her hand on my chest over my heart. The last thing she said to me, this woman who'd been trained as a teacher and had been inordinately fond of gothic romances, was this wonderfully melodramatic parting: "Wherever you are, there I am also."

A week before I completed my academy training, I received word that my mother had died unexpectedly, felled by an aneurysm, a burst vessel in her brain. I missed the graduation ceremony, returning home instead to bury her in the O'Connor family plot next to my father. Into the granite marker above her grave, I had chiseled her

10

final words to me: "Wherever you are, there I am also."

I served eight years with CPD, working mostly the South Side, before I met and married Nancy Jo McKenzie, a smart woman attending the University of Chicago Law School. When our first child was born, I brought my family back to Aurora, deep in the beautiful North Country of Minnesota, and took a job as a Tamarack County deputy. In a few years, I was elected sheriff and wore the badge my father had worn.

The weight of history.

I lost my wife in the same way I'd lost my father, to mindless violence. I used to blame myself for these tragedies, though they were events I could never have foreseen and could not have prevented. I've let go of this blame and others, not an easy thing, but I've had help, mostly from my second wife, a lovely woman named Rainy. She's Native, full-blood Lac Courte Oreilles Anishinaabe, member of the Grand Medicine Society, a Mide, a healer. When we married, she kept her family name, Bisonette, because it has been hers for nearly half a century and is part of the way in which she thinks of herself.

Again, the weight of history.

I haven't worn a badge or uniform in the

11

last ten years, yet I still often find myself in the middle of situations in which my law enforcement experience and training have proven invaluable. The story I'm about to tell you is one of these. Like many of the stories from my history, stories that have so shaped my life, it begins with murder.

Rainy wears her hair long, often in a single braid that sways across the middle of her back as she walks. Her skin is light tan, but deepens in the summer. Her eyes are dark jewels, like brown topaz, and even in dim light they sparkle. She smiles often, and her laugh is exactly the sound my heart needs to hear.

Naked, as she was that evening in our bed, she was all I needed to know of heaven. She glanced at the clock on the nightstand. "Almost time for the fireworks to begin."

I kissed her shoulder, wet and salty from our lovemaking. "I don't know about you, but I've already seen them. In spades."

She laughed, nestled against me, and I felt her heart still beating fast and strong. "We promised the kids we would join them in Grant Park. Waaboo's looking forward to his grandfather being there. He'll be awfully disappointed if you don't show."

"Duty," I said.

"Duty," she echoed.

The cell phone in her purse, which lay atop the dresser, began to ring. She tried to get up but I held her to me.

"Cork," she said laughing, "I have to answer it."

"You don't have to do anything but give me five more minutes."

"Cork." Her tone made it clear our time together, at least for the moment, was at an end.

I let her go, but the cell phone had stopped ringing by then. Rainy got up, pulled the phone from her purse, and checked the display.

"It was Peter," she said, speaking of her son. "He left a voice message."

Peter was living in Arizona, where he'd completed a drug rehabilitation program that had worked wonders for him. He'd become a substance abuse counselor himself and was now employed in the rehab center where he'd gotten clean, located in a town called Cadiz, south of Tucson. I'd met him only once, the previous April, when he'd come to Aurora for our wedding. I liked him, liked him a lot. A young man who'd been through the wringer, he'd come out straightened and determined, and I thought he had a great deal to offer those in need of

13

his kind of help.

Rainy listened to the message, and I saw her face darken. She lowered the phone and stared at it, as if it were a snake in her hand, a snake about to strike.

"What is it, Rainy?"

She lifted her eyes to me. "He killed someone, Cork."

I swung my legs off the bed and was up and beside her in an instant. "Killed who?"

"I couldn't hear very well. The connection was terrible. Someone named Rodriguez, I think."

"Why?"

"I don't know."

"Where is he now?"

"He didn't say." She was punching in his number, her hands trembling.

"Tell him to get himself a lawyer, stat."

"He can't afford a lawyer." She put the phone to her ear.

"We can. And even if we couldn't, he needs legal counsel and he needs it now."

She looked at the ceiling while she waited, as if praying, then looked at me. "He's not answering." She waited another few seconds. "Peter, it's your mother. Call me back. Now."

I held out my hand for the phone. "Let me listen to his message."

14

She was right. It was scratchy and broken, but the name Rodriguez and the words "killed him" and "they'll be looking for me" were all discernible.

"Okay if I try him?"

She nodded.

I called him back. On his end, the phone rang and rang and then went to voice mail.

"Peter, it's Cork. Your message was garbled, so I don't know exactly what's happened. It sounds like someone's been killed. Rodriguez maybe, whoever that is. And it sounds like you believe you're responsible. You also said they'll be looking for you. That much came through. I don't know who's looking for you, but if it's the police, get a lawyer and get one now. We'll be there just as soon as we can."

Rainy signaled for the phone back. She took a deep breath and said, "It's Mom, Peter. I love you. I believe in you. Whatever is going to happen, I'll be there for you."

She ended the call and stood staring at me, stunned. For a moment, there was not a sound in our bedroom, in our house, in our whole world. Then the first explosion of the Fourth of July fireworks in Grant Park made us both flinch.

"You'll go with me?" she said. Some women might have been crying. All I saw in

Rainy was an iron resolve.

I took her in my arms and we stood together, naked, and I felt once again the weight of history settle on my shoulders.

"Wherever you are," I told her, "there I am also."

CHAPTER 2

I made a phone call to a guy named Ed Larson, who'd worked as a deputy for me when I was sheriff in Tamarack County. He'd retired to Green Valley, south of Tucson. I told him what was up and asked if he could check things out in Cadiz, which wasn't all that far from where he lived. Ed was only too happy to help. Rainy insisted I book a flight for us as soon as possible. The first plane out of the airport in Duluth was at six-thirty the next morning, and I bought two seats. Rainy had been trying to connect with Peter, but still no answer. She'd thrown on her robe and paced the room. Every few minutes, she punched in her son's number on her cell phone, tapping the display screen hard as if squashing a bug there.

"Why isn't he answering, Cork?"

"I have no idea, Rainy. It may be that he's already been arrested, and they've taken his phone away."

17

"They have to allow him one call, right?"

"That's protocol, more or less, but it doesn't have to be immediately. It depends on a lot of things."

"Like what?"

"Where they picked him up, whether they actually intend to arrest him, whether it's a custodial interrogation or they're simply probing for information. Or maybe his phone just ran out of juice."

"The moment after he called us?" She shook her head.

She was right. That would have been a huge coincidence, and I don't put much stock in coincidence. His silence concerned me, too, but I've been in enough bad situations to know how to keep a rein on my worst fears. And I know how callous this sounds, but the reality for me was that he was my wife's son, not mine, and so once removed from that place in my heart where a parent's deepest fears are locked away. For Rainy, of course, it was different.

"He said they're after him." She gave me a dark look. "That doesn't necessarily mean the police."

"Let's not assume anything until we know more. Maybe Ed can find out something helpful. In the meantime, do you know anyone down there you could call?"

18

She thought a long time. "He's never talked about people, his friends." It seemed a revelation to her, one that disturbed her, and the hard front she was putting up cracked a little. She closed her eyes. "It's possible he's using again."

"Don't do this to yourself. He got clean and he's stayed clean. This is about something else."

I said it as if it were an absolute. There are no absolutes, but sometimes, to keep fear at bay, you have to insist that there are.

My cell phone rang. I hoped it was Ed getting back to me. But it was my daughter Jenny calling.

"Dad, you and Rainy missed the fireworks. Where are you?"

I did a quick explanation, and she said, "We'll be right there."

Rainy stood in the middle of the room, and I could tell she'd come to some decision. "I have to talk to Uncle Henry."

Henry Meloux is Rainy's great-uncle, a man as old as time itself. For several years, Rainy had lived with Meloux in his isolation on Crow Point, a finger of land that juts into Iron Lake far north of Aurora. Like Rainy, he is Mide and was her mentor as she learned the ways of the Grand Medicine Society. After we married, Rainy had come

19

to live in the house on Gooseberry Lane where I'd been raised and where I'd raised my children.

"He knows even less than we do about Peter's situation," I said.

"That's not what I want from him." She threw off her robe and began to dress.

We were both downstairs when the rest of the family returned home. It was hard dark by then, late. Five-year-old Waaboo, always in a rush of energy, came storming in. His legal name is Aaron Smalldog O'Connor. He's half Ojibwe, Red Lake Band. His nickname is Waaboozoons, which in the language of the Anishinaabeg means "little rabbit." We call him Waaboo for short.

"Baa-baa," he cried, his name for me. Don't ask; the explanation is a long one.

"Good fireworks?" I said.

His response was a terrible scowl. "You weren't there."

"Something came up, little guy." I glanced at Jenny and she shook her head. She hadn't explained.

But it was clear Daniel understood. "Does Peter have a lawyer?"

Daniel English is Rainy's nephew, and like her, full-blood Ojibwe. He and Jenny had been married less than a year. In keeping with the tradition of the Anishinaabeg, and because they were saving money for a place of their own, after the wedding, they'd moved in with us. Daniel was a game warden for the Iron Lake Reservation and understood the necessity of good counsel when navigating all the unpredictable cross-currents that were usually involved in a legal proceeding.

"We don't know," Rainy said. "He's not answering his phone."

"Could be a lot of explanations for that, Aunt Rainy," Daniel said. Calm counsel. One of the reasons I liked him.

"We're flying down first thing in the morning," Rainy said. "But right now, I want to talk to Uncle Henry."

I could see that Jenny and Daniel understood. The old man might not be able to advise on specifics, but Rainy needed grounding, and at one time or another we'd all gone to Meloux for the solace of his company.

"It's late," Daniel offered cautiously. "Dark."

"I can find Crow Point blindfolded," Rainy said, no idle boast.

"Can I go?" Waaboo pleaded.

"The only place you're going is to bed," Jenny said and kissed the top of his head.

We left them to the nighttime rituals and

21

drove north out of Aurora.

If you have never been outside a city at night when there is no moon, then you don't know darkness. Without streetlamps and neon and all the ambient glow in any town or city, night can be impenetrably black. Even a million stars won't illuminate a path through a forest. We drove the county road along the shore of Iron Lake and saw the occasional porch light of a cabin or the dull luminescence from behind a curtained window as we passed, but without the headlights on my Expedition, we'd have been stone blind. Rainy stared ahead and held to silence, deep in her anxious thinking, her own terrible imaginings. I could have tried to ease her worry, but it would have done no good. She needed Henry Meloux.

I parked off the gravel road beside the double-trunk birch that marks the beginning of the trail to Crow Point. The path cuts through thick woods of pine and spruce mixed with stands of poplars. It's well worn. For most of his hundred years, Henry Meloux has lived in virtual isolation. To my knowledge, he's never discouraged anyone from visiting him, but because he's a hell of a lot more difficult to get to than your family physician, you have to want his help pretty bad. That well-worn path was a clear indication that a lot of people did.

By flashlight, we made our way two miles through the woods, crossing at some point onto land that belonged to the Iron Lake Ojibwe. When we broke from the trees onto Crow Point, the whole sky opened before us, and against the haze of a billion stars, I could see the dark shapes of two cabins. The older was Meloux's, which he and his uncle had built more than eighty years before. The other had been Rainy's once, and I'd helped build that one. Rainy's aunt, Leah Duling, lived under its roof now.

There has never been electricity on Crow Point, but I could see light in both cabins, kerosene lamps. I'd expected to have to wake Meloux, but in his mysterious way, he was probably already expecting us. My suspicion was confirmed when, just before we knocked, I heard his melodious old voice call out, "Leah, they are here."

Rainy's aunt opened the door and welcomed us both with a hug. Leah was just into her seventies, and most folks would have called her old, but compared to Henry Meloux, she was a spring chicken. She'd spent her life in difficult places all over the world, the wife of a missionary. She maintained that until she came to Crow Point, she'd never known a place where she felt she belonged. But in Meloux's cabin, which smelled of tea, blackberry, and sage, she seemed beautifully at home.

Meloux sat at the table, one he'd made himself so long ago that he claimed even he couldn't remember exactly when. The walls of his cabin held mementos from his past — a deer-prong pipe, a bear skin, a bow whose string was made of snapping turtle sinew. The old man sat straight and tall, his hair a long fall of white over his shoulders, his face more lined than the shell of a map turtle, his brown eyes bright even at that late hour. Though it was a hot night, a steaming mug sat in front of him.

"He told me a storm is coming," Leah said as she handed us each a mug of tea.

"But not from the sky." Meloux's eyes settled on Rainy. "What troubles you, Niece?"

How the old Mide always knew when turmoil was coming was only one of the many mysteries in the puzzle that was Henry Meloux.

We sat at the table.

"I got a call from my son, Uncle Henry, a desperate call." Rainy gave him the details, and the old man sipped his tea as he listened.

"And you are afraid," Meloux said at the end.

"Yes." Which was something she hadn't admitted to, not even with me.

"What is there to be afraid of?" Meloux asked.

"He's in trouble."

"What is there to be afraid of?" the old man asked again.

"That he'll be arrested, that he'll be charged with murder, that he's alone in all this."

"And are these things really so?"

"I don't know."

"Then you do not know what there is to be afraid of. There is only what you imagine."

"I can guess how these things usually go, Uncle Henry."

"Suppose," Meloux said, "you imagined something different."

"Like what?"

"What would give you comfort?"

"To believe that it's all some terrible mistake."

"Then why not imagine that?"

"Because he was so afraid."

"That is his fear. It does not have to be

25

yours. If you feed his fear with your own, what do you have?"

"It's hard, Uncle Henry."

"I did not say it was easy." He eyed her with great compassion. "You have helped others do this." A gentle reminder of her own training and work as a Mide.

Rainy took a deep, calming breath.

"Leah," the old man said. "Light sage and smudge this room, cleanse the air and cleanse our spirits." He reached across the table and took Rainy's hands in his own callused, wrinkled palms. "You have work ahead of you, Niece. It will probably be hard work, work that will test you. That is one of the things love does. It tests us in difficult ways. But love is also fear's worst enemy. In what is ahead of you, hold to your love and not your fear. And when you imagine, imagine the best of what might be." He smiled and offered a little shrug. "What harm can it do?"

As we walked the long path back, I could tell that Rainy was comforted, and I marveled, as I often did, at the wisdom of Henry Meloux. What had he told her, really, that she didn't already know? This was one of the old Mide's greatest gifts, I thought, his ability to guide people to the place of their own wisdom, helping them see the truths they already knew but had lost sight of. He'd been right. With what little we knew about Peter's situation, what could we do but imagine, and so why not imagine the best? That it was all some great misunderstanding, some terrible mistake. When everything was revealed to us and we knew all the facts, if the situation turned out to be different, we could deal with that. In the meantime, I thought, we would hold to love and to love's companion, which is hope.

Rainy took my hand as we walked, following the light our flashlights threw on the ground.

"Migwech," she said, which is the Ojibwe word for "thank you."

"What for?"

"There are so many people alone in this world, but I have you. Whatever's ahead, I have you." She put her arms around me and lifted her face to mine and kissed me.

It was nearing 1:00 a.m. when we returned to the house. Jenny and Daniel were waiting up, sitting at the kitchen table with mugs of coffee in front of them.

"Annie called to wish us a happy Fourth of July," Jenny said.

Rainy and I joined them at the table. "And you told her about Peter?"

She nodded.

Annie is my second daughter, younger than Jenny by nearly two years. She was living in San Francisco.

"If you need her help, you have it," Jenny said.

"We'll see what happens."

"And she insisted I call Stephen and keep him in the loop."

My son, Stephen, is the youngest of my children. He was in West Texas, helping out on a cattle ranch owned by a family friend. Punching cows was something Stephen had done in past summers. It was that or working at Sam's Place, the burger joint I own on Iron Lake. Given a choice between flipping burgers and pushing around that meat on the hoof, Stephen had often opted for the life of a cowpoke.

"Did you get him?"

She shook her head. "Apparently, he's out driving cattle somewhere cell phones don't reach."

"What did Uncle Henry say?" Daniel asked.

"That until we know the whole truth, it's best not to imagine the worst," Rainy said. "Pretty simple but absolutely true."

My cell phone rang. Ed Larson. He told me he'd made some calls to a deputy he

28

knew with the Coronado County Sheriff's Department, which was located in Cadiz. Peter wasn't on law enforcement's radar there. Ed assured me he'd been discreet in his inquiry, and if I wanted, he could do some more checking, broaden his search. I told him we were flying down in the morning. He offered to help when we arrived. I said I'd call if I needed him.

"We should pack, Rainy," I told her, "and try to get a couple of hours of sleep before we head off."

We left Jenny and Daniel the task of turning out the lights. Upstairs, Rainy and I pulled our suitcases from the closet and filled them. I could tell something was still eating at her, but I waited until we were in bed to ask. She sat with her back to the headboard and drew her knees to her chest as if to protect herself. The streetlamp outside our window threw light into the dark room, and in the glow I studied Rainy's face. For a very long time, she said nothing. Then, without looking at me, she reached out and took my hand.

"What is it?" I asked.

"There are things you don't know about me, Cork."

"I know the important things."

"I hate Arizona," she said.

"Well, that's one I didn't know."

She turned her face to me fully. Despite all the calm Henry Meloux had done his best to offer her, I could see the storm coming.

"Here it is," she said and took a deep breath. "Peter's not the only Bisonette who's killed a man there."

CHAPTER 3

Patience is a virtue that I learned as a cop. I waited a good, long while before Rainy said anything more.

"I know you've killed men," she finally went on. "I know about two of them anyway. Do I know about them all?"

"No."

"Why not?"

"Because it might put you in a difficult situation, legally."

"Was it wrong, whatever the other killing you did?"

"It was necessary. Or I thought it was. I still do."

The streetlamp on Gooseberry Lane seemed glaringly bright that night, and as the light pushed through our bedroom window, it cast shadows of the mullions on the wall, which reminded me way too much of the bars of a jail cell. Rainy stared at them with the same look I'd seen in the eyes of

31

prison inmates. I understood that the past is never really past. We live our history over and over, the worst of our memories right there alongside us, step for step, our companions to the grave. In the dark hours of that long night, with sleep forsaking us, I thought I would hear Rainy's story.

Instead she said, "It's like that for me."

"You can't tell me about it?"

She shook her head.

"Does it have anything to do with Peter, whatever he's involved in now?"

"I can't imagine that it does. It was so long ago."

I wanted to press her for the story she felt she couldn't tell me, but I have my own secrets, so who was I to deny Rainy hers? I simply held her. Together we watched the light through the window give way to a gray that signaled dawn, and we got up and dressed.

We landed at the Tucson airport in the early afternoon. Despite dozens of attempts, Rainy had not been able to reach Peter before we left. As soon as we landed, she tried once more. Same result.

I'd been in Arizona only once, when the kids were young. In late May of that long-ago year, Jo and I had taken them out of school a week early and driven across the country to see the Grand Canyon. On the way, we'd stopped at Mesa Verde and Canyon de Chelly and Monument Valley, places where a sense of the sacred was still palpable. It was easy to understand why the ancient people had made their homes there, but why they'd chosen to abandon all they'd built was a great, lingering mystery. On the way back to Minnesota, we'd stayed north, hitting the stunning parks in Utah, so I'd never been in southern Arizona and never in the depth of summer. Hell couldn't have been any hotter. We walked out of the airport and into a blast furnace. The heat, the glare, the unwelcoming aridness of every breath I took made me want to turn immediately and head back to the cool North Country of home.

We rented a Jeep Cherokee and hit I-10 heading southeast out of the city. I had the air conditioner cranked up to max. The landscape surprised me. I'd expected flat desert, but everywhere I looked, the horizon was dominated by mountains. After half an hour, we turned off on a state road and began to climb into hills that were covered more in grassland and scrub trees than in cactus. I watched the exterior thermometer readout on the dash drop gradually from

108 degrees to a relatively cool 97.

"They call these Los Conejos Hills," Rainy said. "Jackrabbit Hills."

We crested a rise and came out onto a long, flat plateau set against mountains blue in the distance. The ground was covered with short, coarse grass and sectioned with wire. Ranchland, I guessed. This was far from the desert I'd been anticipating, so different from the Arizona I'd seen when I'd driven the family to the Grand Canyon those many years before. We came to a small town, not much more than a crossroads with a gas station, a little convenience store, and a building whose name surprised me as much as anything I'd seen: the Southern Arizona Wine Showroom.

"Wine showroom?" I said.

"A lot of vineyards down here, Cork. The wines are surprisingly good."

We followed the course of a dry riverbed that cut through a valley between two mountain ranges.

"The San Gabriel River," Rainy said. "Cadiz isn't far now."

From the things she'd told me, I had a sense of the town. It was the seat of Coronado County and only a stone's throw from Mexico. Somewhere on the outskirts was the Goodman Center for Recovery, where more than two years earlier Peter had spent three months kicking a painkiller addiction that had threatened everything in his life. Through most of it, Rainy had been there with him, living in a rented place near enough to offer support as a mother and her skills as a Mide.

I had no idea what awaited us in Cadiz, but I could sense Rainy's growing anxiety. She was normally a quiet woman, but quiet in a calming way. Her silence, as we followed the dry bed of the San Gabriel, was different, and her dark eyes, as they considered this landscape so alien to all I knew, were alert, watchful, as if she was aware of some danger here that she hadn't shared with me. I thought again of the killing she wouldn't tell me about. She'd said it was long ago in her history. I was beginning to wonder just how long.

We continued to climb. The outside thermometer crept downward, and by the time we pulled into Cadiz, the temperature was ninety-five degrees, hot by Minnesota standards but pleasant in the middle of an Arizona summer.

The San Gabriel River split Cadiz. The main thoroughfare, Clementine Street, ran along the west bank, with a stone bridge in the heart of the town connecting to the

35

other side. The two blocks of the downtown were lined with shops and stores housed in revamped Old West buildings straight out of a John Wayne oater. The Stagecoach Inn occupied a prominent corner location. Although in its day it had probably served mostly dusty, weary cowpokes and prospectors, it had been restored to a glory I doubted it ever really knew before. Out front, instead of mules and quarter horses tethered to a hitching post, were parked some pricey sets of wheels — a Mercedes sedan, a couple of Lincoln Navigators, a beautifully restored roadster of some kind. With a clear sky above, mountains on two sides, and a moderate temperature, Cadiz was clearly a tourist destination. Banners celebrating the Fourth of July and the Independence Day Rodeo at the county fairgrounds still hung above the main street. All the shops were done up with decorations in red, white, and blue. There were bits and pieces of exploded fireworks lying in the street along the curbs.

"Any idea where the county sheriff's office is?" I asked Rainy.

"Across the river at the far end of town."

We drove along the main street until we came to a second bridge over the San Gabriel, and on the other side, just as Rainy

36

had said, stood the Coronado County Law Enforcement Center.

"Been here before?" I asked.

"Small town. After a couple of weeks, you know where everything is."

It was a relatively new brick structure with an incarceration wing that struck me as surprisingly large for what appeared to be a sparsely populated county. Rainy and I went in together. In the public contact area, several people sat in plastic chairs. All of them appeared to be Hispanic, and only the three children with an older lady, who was probably their grandmother, looked at us directly.

We stepped up to the window. A woman not in uniform spoke to us through the microphone.

"Can I help you?"

"Just looking for a little information," I said. "Have there been any arrests in the past twenty-four hours?"

She was in her late twenties, brunette, with a tight, tanned face, all business. "Yes."

"Was someone named Peter Bisonette among them?"

"Just a moment." She pulled a sheet from several others that lay to her left and scanned it. "No one by that name."

"Have there been any fatalities reported

37

in the past twenty-four hours?"

"Yes."

"Is the information public?"

She almost smiled. "An accidental death. From snakebite, more or less."

"More or less?"

"Most snakebites involve a male between the age of eighteen and thirty-four, with tattoos, who's been drinking. This one fit the demographic perfectly. A biker. Got himself bit by a rattler, tried to ride back to Cadiz, ran off the road and into a fence post. Was actually the fence post that killed him."

"That's it for fatalities?"

"That's it." She considered us. "Is there something we should know about this Peter Bisonette?"

"We're having some trouble finding him."

"He's missing? Would you like to file a report?"

I said, "I don't think that's necessary."

She finally smiled, in a reassuring way. "Cadiz isn't that big and Coronado County isn't that populous. If he's here, I'm sure you'll find him."

"You heard her," I said to Rainy as we left. "We'll find him."

We got into the car, which in just the few minutes we'd been inside the county building, had become an oven.

"Where to now?" I said. I had some ideas, but this was Rainy's show.

"The Goodman Center. Maybe he's working today."

"Point the way."

The Norman Goodman Center for Recovery sat atop a mesa east of town, with a million-dollar view of the mountains and the valley of the San Gabriel River. It looked like an old Spanish mission with white-washed adobe walls, a red-tile roof, and a bell tower. Dotting the mesa around it were a lot of new, expansive homes built in what I thought of as mission style and that probably cost an arm and two legs. We pulled into an asphalt lot, where there were half a dozen other vehicles, all of them high-end. We walked through an archway into a courtyard with a bubbling fountain and flower beds and palm trees. White benches were spaced around, inviting in the shade of the palms, but all were empty. Rainy had told me very little about the time she'd spent here with Peter, and I had no idea what to expect. Against the backdrop of the high mountains, the place looked like a little bit of paradise. A very expensive little bit.

Rainy led the way through tinted, pneumatic doors, which opened with a whish of cool air into a reception area that smelled of gardenias. Behind the reception desk sat a young woman studying a computer monitor. She looked up and smiled as if she'd been expecting us and couldn't be happier that we'd finally arrived.

"Welcome to the Goodman Center. May I help you?"

"Can you tell me if Peter Bisonette is working today?" Rainy said.

"Peter?" The lovely smile faltered. "Peter doesn't work here anymore."

That caught Rainy by surprise. Me, too.

"Are you sure?"

"Quite sure."

"When did he leave?"

"And you are?" Her dark eyebrows arched in a Hollywood pantomime of inquiry.

"His mother, Rainy Bisonette."

The young woman considered this information, still maintaining her smile, and finally said, "Perhaps you should talk to our director, Dr. Saunders."

"Yes," Rainy said. "I'd like that."

"Have a seat, and I'll let her know you're here."

The chairs in the waiting area were arranged around a large glass-topped coffee table on which sat an array of magazines — *Elle, Allure, GQ, Forbes, Entrepreneur.* The chair I sat in was more comfortable than anything I'd ever bought for myself. I looked at Rainy, who'd spent the last several years in a cabin on Crow Point with no electricity, running water, or even an indoor toilet, and I wondered how in the hell she'd managed to pay for her son's treatment in a place that probably catered primarily to the kinds of people who didn't blink at the cost of a new Jaguar.

Rainy sat with her hands in her lap, her back straight, her eyes focused somewhere ahead of her. I wondered if maybe she was visualizing a good outcome to all of this. She reached into her purse and pulled out a photograph I couldn't see. She handed it over to me. It was two kids in swimming suits, standing at the end of a dock, smiling at the camera. On the day it had been taken, the sky was seriously blue and the lake behind the boys looked cool and inviting. One of the boys had dark hair, a dark complexion, and Rainy's dark, beautiful eyes. The other kid's hair was wiry and red, and he had so many freckles his face looked like a bowl of cornflakes.

"Peter with Arweiler Bosch," she said.

"Arweiler?"

"His family was from Germany. His father was an academic, doing some research on Native Americans of the Great Lakes. He

41

brought the family onto the rez when Arweiler was twelve, the same age as Peter. Arweiler was an awkward kid, a loner, spoke with a thick accent, picked on by everyone. Peter took him under his wing, befriended him, got into fights with kids who tried to bully him. Arweiler attached himself to Peter. It got so Peter couldn't go anywhere without Arweiler following him. He was always at our house, under foot. Honestly, I found the kid irritating, but Peter was so patient with him."

She took the photograph back and studied it.

"Arweiler began to show up with bruises. Like I said, he was an awkward kid, and he had stories about falling off his bike, stumbling over rocks, credible stories. Then Peter was at his house one day, and Arweiler's father was stinking drunk. He yelled horrible things at Arweiler's mother. It was all in German, but Peter had picked up a lot of the language by then and he understood. The man began to beat his wife. Arweiler tried to intervene and got beat as well. Peter ran, came straight to the tribal clinic, where I was working, told me what was happening. I called the sheriff's office, but got the runaround, so Peter and I headed back to Arweiler's. The man had beat his wife senseless, Cork, but the boy, his son, Arweiler, he'd beat to death."

She stopped her story and sat staring at the two boys in the photograph.

"Why did you keep that all these years?"

"I didn't. It's Peter's. He kept it pinned to the wall of his bedroom. He blamed himself."

"Why?"

"Because he ran to get me instead of staying to help."

"It was the wise thing to do."

"That's not what his heart told him."

"Why did you bring it with you?"

"I was going to throw it away. But I'm not the one who needs to do that."

She put the photograph back into her purse.

A small woman came from the hallway off the reception area. She wore a colorful, flowing dress, with lots of turquoise on one wrist and about her neck. Her hair was silver-gray and, not unlike Rainy's, hung very long down her back. Her skin was dark, the result, I figured, of a lifetime in the Southwest. It looked soft, not at all like the leathery flesh I'd sometimes seen on people who'd worshipped the sun for decades. I put her at fifty, but she could have been much older, her youthful look the artful

43

work of a skilled plastic surgeon, maybe. The smile on her face at seeing Rainy, however, was all her own and genuine.

"Rainy," she said, sweeping toward us and offering her hand in what struck me as a grand manner. "It's good to see you again."

"Hello, Jeanette. How are you?"

"Busy and content," she said. The blue diamonds of her eyes took me in, then swung back to Rainy.

"My husband, Cork O'Connor," Rainy said.

"New development?"

"April."

"How do you do, Cork?" She held out her hand, and I took it and felt her soft, warm palm. "I'm Jeanette Saunders, the director here." Her attention turned again to Rainy. "You're asking about Peter. Let's go to my office."

We followed her down the quiet corridor. The walls were hung with impressionistic paintings whose bright colors suggested the Southwest. She stepped into her office, and when we followed, I saw that the far wall was all glass, overlooking the azure water of a very large swimming pool. I understood why everything inside the building seemed so quiet. All the action was at the pool. In the shade of umbrellaed tables, a lot of good-looking, partially clothed people sat together, sipping what I presumed, in a facility devoted to recovery, was iced tea or lemonade or soft drinks. Before she sat at her desk, Saunders took a moment with her back to us, admiring the view. The room smelled faintly of patchouli.

"They come estranged from one another and from the world. They find reconnection here, a healthy way of centering." She turned to us. "I wish I could say that they all leave healed. But at least they leave knowing that they can be healed, if that's what they truly want."

I thought three months of iced tea and swimming in a little paradise away from the rest of the world would probably cure a lot of people of what ailed them.

"Please, sit down." She gestured to a couple of cushy-looking chairs on our side of her big, polished desk. She folded her hands and looked sympathetically at Rainy. "Peter," she said.

"The young woman in reception told me he doesn't work here anymore."

"That's true."

"When did he leave?"

"Over a year ago."

"A year?" Rainy sat back, as if struck. "He didn't say anything when I saw him in April.

45

Did he resign?"

"He probably didn't say anything because I had to let him go, Rainy."

"Why?"

"When you saw him at your wedding, how did he seem?"

"Good," Rainy said. "A little intense maybe, but happy."

Saunders nodded. "I'm glad to hear that. When I let him go, he was different. He'd started coming in late, looking exhausted, as if he hadn't slept. It affected his work. I talked to him about it."

"You thought he was using again," Rainy said.

"It was a classic symptom. He denied it. Of course. They always do. He told me he was simply having trouble sleeping. Bad dreams, he said, flashbacks to Afghanistan."

"He's had them before," Rainy said.

"I know. So I asked him to see Dr. Jordan. She's a staff psychologist with extensive experience in dealing with PTSD."

"And did he see her?"

"Only once. She reported that he was sullen, withdrawn, uncooperative. I insisted on a drug test. Instead of complying, he simply stopped coming to work. I had to let him go, Rainy. I'd be happy to help him. We did

46

once. Sometimes it takes more than one stay."

"He was clean," Rainy said. "When I saw him in April, he was clean."

"I'm sure that's what he told you. And you believed him. We love them so much, we want to believe them."

"Did he tell you what he was going to do?"

Saunders shook her head. "But I heard that he was working for Jayne and Frank Harris. They have vineyards on the other side of the Coronados."

"Have you seen him?"

"Not since he left us." Saunders leaned across her desk and put out her hands to take Rainy's. The turquoise bracelet she wore slid over the polished wood with a sound like bone scraping across a dinner plate.

"You're a healer, too," she said. "When you find him, if you can convince him to come back to us, we'll have another go. All of us together."

She saw us out and hugged Rainy in parting.

We stepped outside, into the heat again, and the glare of the sun.

"Just a minute," I said to Rainy and went back inside.

Jeanette Saunders was walking away. I

47

called to her and she came back.

"Yes, Cork?"

"How much does it cost for treatment here?"

Her face betrayed a little concern, in her eyes a clear hesitation. Finally she said, "We charge thirty-five thousand dollars a month." Then, as if to justify, "We're very good and we're very discreet and we're very isolated."

"Of course," I said. "Thank you."

Rainy was waiting in the shade of a palm. "What was it?"

"Nothing important."

We walked out of that little piece of paradise, past the expensive cars shooting arrows of reflected sunlight off their chrome. No medical insurance plan I knew of would cover the cost of rehab in a place like the Goodman Center. I wondered how Rainy, who'd lived in self-imposed poverty on Crow Point for years, could afford to pay over $100,000 for the three months Peter had spent at the center during his recovery. It was only one of the many questions about Rainy that I was beginning to ask myself.

CHAPTER 4

"We should try Sulfur Springs," Rainy suggested. "See if we can find where he lives."

Peter had never been a young man who called or texted frequently. Instead, he preferred to communicate through letters, long, thoughtful missives, a habit from his days in the military, when he used the letters, he'd told Rainy, to get his head clear. The letters she'd received from him for the past year — ever since he'd been let go from the Goodman Center, I now understood — had a return address in Sulfur Springs, a tiny town another ten miles south, toward the border. Before that, he'd been living in Cadiz.

"All right," I said. "Next stop, Sulfur Springs."

We continued to follow the river, winding our way up the valley between the mountains until we came to a cutoff with a sign pointing southeast: SULFUR SPRINGS 8

MILES. The road we followed snaked steeply upward, then crested. Below, along the base of the range, lay a kind of alluvial plain, an apron of high desert with a clear view to the south. We could see for miles and miles. In the distance, unnatural against the pale, washed-out color of the desert it ran through, was a long black line that stretched all the way to the horizons east and west.

"The fence," Rainy said.

I'd read about it. Hadn't everybody by now? But I'd never seen it. The structure was often referred to as a fence, but along the line that separated Coronado County from Mexico, it was a tall, stark metal wall. Like a scar follows the shape of a body, the wall followed the contour of the land. And that's exactly what it looked like — a dark, ugly scar. I thought it was probably not unlike the wall that had once divided Berlin. Except that this one had been erected to keep people out and not in. From what I understood, it wasn't doing a stellar job.

We passed an abandoned ranch house, a weathered, gray derelict with fallen-down fences and a windmill that no longer pumped. Someone had made a go of it, at least for a while, in this desolate country. Then something had happened, harsh enough to drive them away. Or maybe it wasn't a single thing, but the long struggle against a land that, I imagined, received too little rain and too much sun and, day after relentless day, was beset by heat that could bake your brain.

I saw Sulfur Springs long before we hit the outskirts. A gathering of buildings shaded by a few trees, the glint of sunlight reflected off steel and glass, the harsh, unnatural geometry of habitation.

"What do you know about this place?" I asked as we approached.

"Nothing, really. I never came here when Peter was in rehab. No reason to."

"Why does he live here?"

"He told me he liked the simplicity."

"Any idea where he lives?"

She shook her head. "His letters all have a return address with a P.O. box number."

"That didn't strike you as odd?"

"He told me he might be moving around a bit until he really settled in. He said it was easier."

"Maybe we should start at the post office," I suggested.

Sulfur Springs was a cross-hatching of a dozen or so streets. The houses were simple, single-story structures, the yards ornamented with cacti instead of flower beds, every one of them enclosed by adobe walls or metal fencing. The trees, when there were some, were thorny-looking things with sparse leafage, not what, in Minnesota, we would have called a tree at all.

The business section was a single block, old buildings not updated and boutiqued in the way they'd been in Cadiz. The effects of time and weather were evident on every storefront. There was a small grocery store, a barbershop, a little eatery called Rosa's Cantina, a one-pump gas station, a real estate office, a few other businesses that appeared to be not particularly thriving. There was also a little police station, more a storefront operation, it looked like, and next to it was the post office, which was not much bigger than one of the stamps you could buy there.

Inside the post office, set into the wall to our left, was a small bank of P.O. boxes. On the wall to the right was a narrow counter with postal forms. Above the counter hung a bulletin board with both official notices — "Policies for the Apprehension, Detention, and Removal of Undocumented Immigrants" — and also notices of local interest — "Fiesta at St. Esteban's, Wednesday, July 17." Although the hours posted on the door said the office was open from 10:00 until 4:00, the place seemed empty. I could hear Tejano music playing somewhere in back.

"Hello!" I called.

"Just a minute," came a woman's reply.

True to her word, in one minute, she appeared, a dark-skinned woman with a bright, white smile. Her hair was a wild crown of black and gray. Her eyes were dark and shiny in a face full of welcome. She was clearly well fed, though not quite rotund, and was dressed in the blue, short-sleeved shirt of a postal employee. Below that, she wore bright floral shorts.

"What can I do for you folks?" she asked, with a slight Hispanic accent.

"I'm trying to locate my son," Rainy said. "He has a post office box here. His name is Peter Bisonette."

The woman shook her head. "I don't know that name."

"Do you know most of the people who have post office boxes here?" I asked.

"Towns don't get much smaller than Sulfur Springs. Everybody knows everybody."

"But you don't know a Peter Bisonette?"

"Not that name."

Rainy pulled her wallet from her purse and drew out the photograph of Peter she kept there, one taken after he'd completed

53

rehab. "This is him," she said, handing the picture over.

The woman studied it. "I haven't seen him."

"You're sure?" Rainy asked.

"Like I said, small town. We all know each other."

"His post office box is number twenty-seven."

The woman smiled but shook her head. She handed back the photograph. "You said you're his mother?"

Rainy nodded.

"You look worried."

"I am."

"I have a son I worry about, too. I hope you find your Peter."

"Gracias," Rainy said. Then she said a good deal more in Spanish and the woman closed her eyes and nodded.

Outside, we stood a moment in the sun, looking down the main street, which was quiet and mostly empty.

"What did you say to her?"

"Something a mother once told me. That for the sake of her child, a mother's heart has to be like a willow branch, bending but never broken." She looked around her at what she could see of the desolate little town. Not far away, a rooster crowed. "I

54

don't know why, but maybe he goes by another name here."

"He can change his name but not his face," I said. "She claimed not to recognize that either."

"Claimed?"

"Small town. Everybody knows everybody. If Peter collects his mail there, she's bound to have seen him at one time or another."

"You think she lied to us?"

"Let's talk to some more people," I said.

We walked to the police station, which from the outside, didn't look much larger than the post office. A sign hung on the door: ON PATROL. IN EMERGENCY, CALL 911.

Rainy glanced at me. "Peter said someone was after him. Maybe the police here?"

"Maybe," I said. "But jurisdiction in something as serious as a killing is going to fall to the county. The sheriff's people didn't seem to know anything."

A couple of motorcycles roared into Sulfur Springs, loud and fast, and cruised down the main street. The riders, two guys with red bandannas wrapped around their heads and wearing black T-shirts and sunglasses, gave us a good looking over as they passed. They seemed out of place to me in this quiet border town.

We visited every storefront on both sides of the single, rundown block of businesses, asking about Peter and showing the photograph. Everywhere the response was the same. We tried the church on the corner across the street from the *mercado,* St. Esteban's. Empty and locked. The information on a little sign in front indicated that two services were held there on Sundays. One was Catholic at 8:00 a.m., the other Methodist at 10:00 a.m. There was a different name and contact number under each service.

At last we stood in front of the town's eatery, Rosa's Cantina.

"Let's see if Feleena is whirling inside," I said.

Rainy gave me a blank look.

"From a great song by Marty Robbins," I explained.

The aroma of chilies and melted cheese and tortillas on a hot griddle greeted us as we entered. I realized that we hadn't eaten since breakfast during our layover in the Twin Cities airport, and I was starved. It took a moment for my eyes to adjust to the light inside, which was dark compared to the glare in the street. Except for a couple of hombres sitting at the bar, the place was empty. It wasn't Marty Robbins on the jukebox but Kenny Chesney, crooning "All I Need to Know." The two at the bar, who had beers in front of them, turned their heads to stare as we entered. One of them was an old-timer, long beard and all, wearing a red and black Diamondbacks ball cap. The other was dressed in a police uniform.

A young woman, tall, with jet-black hair, came through a door behind the bar. She wore a colorful blouse and tight jeans. Gold hoops big enough for a bird to fly through hung from her earlobes.

"Hola," she said brightly. "Lost tourists?"

"Not lost," I said.

"Mister, nobody who isn't from here comes to Sulfur Springs unless they're lost."

"Not lost," I said again. "But hungry."

"Well, then, you've come to the right place. Take a table, I'll bring you a couple of menus. Anything to drink?"

"Cerveza," I said, one of the few Spanish words I knew.

"Water for me," Rainy said.

"Una cerveza fría," the woman said with a laugh. "And a water."

We sat at a table. Kenny Chesney ended his song, and the juke fell silent. The two guys at the bar went on drinking their beers, not speaking a word, waiting, I was pretty sure, to overhear what we might have to say.

57

Rainy elbowed me and nodded at the uniform.

"In a minute," I said. "The beer first."

It came, and God bless her, our barmaid brought it in a frosted glass. She put Rainy's water down, too, along with the promised menus.

"What's good?" I asked.

"What isn't?" she said. "Let me know when you're ready."

I took a long draw on the beer, and it was every bit as satisfying as I'd hoped.

"So," I said. "If he's not here, where is he?"

"I don't know, Cork." She sipped her water.

"He gets his mail here. That doesn't mean he lives here."

The uniform turned on his stool. "You folks looking for somebody?"

"Peter Bisonette," Rainy said. "My son."

"Bisonette," the uniform said, as if testing the word. "Don't believe I know anyone named Bisonette here."

He was stocky, middle-aged, hair thick and silver. Hispanic. He wore a sidearm, a revolver. I was pretty sure it was a Smith & Wesson .38 Police Special, which was the same weapon I'd worn when I was sheriff, and also my father before me.

"How about a guy named Rodriguez?" I asked.

The uniform laughed. "Mister, in a border town like Sulfur Springs, asking about a guy named Rodriguez is like asking in Minnesota about a guy named Johnson."

"Minnesota? Why Minnesota?"

"If you're not from Minnesota, I'll eat Sylvester's hat." He lightly slapped the ball cap the old-timer wore. "You talk that flat talk I hear every Saturday on *A Prairie Home Companion*. Love that show. You ever met Garrison Keillor?"

"Afraid not," I said. "Any fatalities reported around here lately?"

"Just yesterday. A biker. Snake bit him and he was so panicky driving himself to the hospital that he ran his Harley off the road."

"That's it?"

"That's it. You worried about your son, ma'am?"

"A little," Rainy said.

"And this Rodriguez?" The cop looked at me.

"Not so much about him. You part of the local constabulary?"

"Mister, I *am* the local constabulary." He slid off his stool and came over. "Mike Sanchez."

"Cork O'Connor." I shook the hand he'd

offered. "This is my wife, Rainy."

"How do, ma'am?"

"I'd be better if I could find my son," she said.

"When did you last hear from him?"

"Yesterday. He called. Then nothing."

"Kids," the cop said with a shrug. "They're like that. Call you when they need something, but otherwise about as conversive as a rock. Am I right?" He glanced back at Sylvester for agreement, then said, "Gets his mail here, huh?"

"This is where I've sent all my letters and cards for the past year or so," Rainy said.

"That is curious," Sanchez said. "Does he work around here?"

"He used to. In Cadiz."

He mulled that over. "Tell you what I'll do. I'll ask around. If I hear something, I'll let you know. You have a number where I can reach you?"

I wrote down Rainy's cell phone number on the back of one of my business cards and handed it to him.

He read the card and squinted at me. "Confidential investigations? You're a P.I.?"

"Among other things."

"Any good?"

"I make a living."

"Well, hell, you don't need my help, then."

"On the contrary," I said. "I've always found the cooperation of local law enforcement to be of the highest value. I was a cop, too, for a lot of years. Sheriff of Tamarack County, Minnesota."

The barmaid returned from the kitchen. "Ready to order?"

"Hang on a sec, Sierra," Sanchez said. "Rainy, has your son been known to have a beer now and again?"

"Maybe," Rainy said.

"Sierra, you ever serve a young man named Peter Bisonette?"

She gave it some thought. "Doesn't ring a bell. Why?"

"These folks're looking for him. Gets his mail here in Sulfur Springs, apparently. Got a photo or something?" Sanchez asked Rainy.

She took out the picture she'd shown to the postmistress. The barmaid studied it and shook her head. "Never saw him before. Sorry."

Sanchez opened his hands as if to say, *See? We're all in the dark.* He shook my hand again and returned to the bar.

When we left, Officer Mike Sanchez and Sylvester were still sitting at the bar. The cop called a good-bye to us and promised a second time to let us know if he heard

61

anything. The post office was closed by then. We got into the car, and I thought I was stepping into an oven preheated for roasting a chicken. Heading back down the main street, I looked into my rearview mirror. The postmistress was standing in front of her office, shading her eyes against the sun, staring at us like we were a couple exotic birds she might never see again.

CHAPTER 5

"Someone's lying." Rainy's voice was as cold as the day was hot.

"That's a given," I said. "We saw half the residents of Sulfur Springs, and they all claim to know nothing about a young man who, at the very least, has collected his mail there for the past year."

"Why would they lie?"

"I don't know, but we're going to find out."

"How do we do that?"

"Why don't we talk to Peter's current employers, the Harrises? Maybe they can enlighten us."

I had no idea how to find the Harris property. Saunders had simply said it was on the other side of the Coronados, the mountains to the east of Cadiz. I stopped and studied the Arizona highway map I'd picked up at the car rental office in Tucson. Just beyond the Coronados were a couple

63

of towns — Hebron and Lacabra — little dots on the map, just like the dot for Sulfur Springs. We could get to them by returning to Cadiz and circling north of the mountains or by taking an unimproved county back road that branched off just outside Sulfur Springs and stayed south, which would easily save us an hour of driving time.

We took the back road and almost immediately rounded a hill and came to a barren flat where a community of trailers sat like bricks baking in a kiln. I spotted lots of motorcycles parked there, alongside Jeeps and trucks with oversize wheels, probably designed to help navigate rugged desert tracks. Canvas tarps had been stretched from some of the trailers, shading tables and lawn chairs. There wasn't a human being in sight, no one outside in that intense heat. I recalled the two bikers who'd roared down the main street of Sulfur Springs and who'd seemed so out of place to me.

"Paradiso," Rainy said.

"What?"

She pointed toward a sign made of weathered gray wood that was nailed to a post. The word paradiso had been burned into it in black letters.

"Paradise," Rainy said. "Could have fooled me."

"You seemed pretty fluent with Spanish in your conversation with the postmistress back there. I didn't realize you could speak it so well. Or, hell, at all."

Once we were past the trailer community, Rainy became intent on studying the landscape, her eyes scanning the barren stretch to the south, as if expecting something to come at us suddenly out of Mexico.

"Not much call to use it in Tamarack County," she finally said.

"You learned it while you were at the U of A?"

We'd shared our histories, or I'd thought we had, so I knew that Rainy had been a student at the University of Arizona, where she'd met her first husband. They'd divorced after four years and two children, and Rainy had moved back to Wisconsin, where she'd finished her education as a public health nurse and had raised her kids as a single mother. About her time in Tucson, I knew almost nothing. About her first husband, I knew only that she preferred to discuss him as little as possible.

"More or less," she said, and I could tell from her tone that was the end of this conversational thread.

I tried to tell myself it wasn't important that there were clearly many details of

Rainy's past I didn't know. We'd only been married three months, newlyweds almost. Although we'd known each other for years before that, I was beginning to understand there were depths to Rainy I had yet to plumb. Because of what little she had told me and her secretiveness about the rest, I was beginning to suspect that those depths were quite dark. I could have pressed her, but one thing I knew about Rainy for sure was that until she was ready to share these things with me, I'd just be beating my fists against a hard, closed door.

We were near enough to the wall along the border that as we went into and out of dry washes and arroyos, its tall, dark, flat face loomed and then disappeared from our sight. I watched three vultures circling above the cacti and mesquite, and it made me think of the cartoons I'd seen forever of people dying of thirst in the desert and saying something funny. At that moment, the prospect didn't strike me as particularly humorous.

We came out of a wash, and as we crested the next rise I hit the brakes. A white Chevy Tahoe was parked across the road, blocking our way. Along the shoulder perpendicular to it sat another vehicle, identical. Both had light bars on top and broad green slashes down the rear doors, and as I drew up to them, I saw the writing across the sides: BORDER PATROL. Several uniformed officers stood beside the vehicles, taking a good, hard look at Rainy and me through our windshield. One of the officers separated himself from the others and approached our rental car. When I'd made the travel arrangements, I'd requested a Jeep Cherokee. The one they gave me was clown-nose red.

I lowered my window, and the heat of the afternoon flooded in.

"Afternoon, Officer," I said.

"License," he replied in an even tone.

I pulled it from my wallet and handed it over.

He read it and said, "Minnesota. Long way from home."

"You sound like Texas to me," I said. "Long way from home."

He smiled briefly. I knew I probably didn't fit any demographic he might be concerned about. He bent and looked through my window and studied Rainy on the other side of the Jeep, and any friendliness vanished from his face. He handed my driver's license back and walked around the front of the vehicle to Rainy's side. She lowered her window.

"You have a driver's license, ma'am?"

"Yes."

"May I see it?"

Rainy opened her purse, drew out her wallet, found her license, and gave it to the officer. He looked at it carefully, then eyed her for an uncomfortably long time.

"Is anything wrong?" I asked.

"Are you a citizen of the United States, ma'am?"

"I was born in Wisconsin," she said.

He considered this. "My wife's brother lives in Chippewa Falls. You know where that is?"

"Ninety miles east of the Twin Cities. They brew Leinenkugel's beer there."

He nodded, but didn't seem a hundred percent satisfied.

"Does my skin color concern you, Officer?" she said. "I'm an enrolled member of the Lac Courte Oreilles Ojibwe, the indigenous people in our neck of the woods. I'm an Indian."

"You didn't look Mexican to me, ma'am, but I couldn't quite place you. We have to be careful. I hope you understand." He returned her license. "Where you folks headed?"

"I'm not exactly sure," I said. "Somewhere around Hebron or Lacabra."

"Most visitors take the north road. Safer."

"Trying to save a little time."

"Your business there?"

"Looking for someone. Family."

"Name?"

"Bisonette."

"Is that first or last?"

"Peter Bisonette."

The officer turned and called toward the others in uniform. "Jake, the name Peter Bisonette ring a bell?"

"Nope," one of them called back. "Should it?"

"Can't help you, Mr. O'Connor."

I nodded toward the vehicle blocking our way. "Kind of an odd place for a speed trap."

"Move it," the officer called, and one of his companions got into the Tahoe. "Sorry to have detained you folks. You're free to go on your way."

I raised my window, and when the Border Patrol's Tahoe had moved aside, I continued down the back road.

"Did you see the vultures circling back there?" I said. "What interested them, do you suppose?"

"I don't even want to think about that," Rainy said. "Do I look Hispanic to you?"

"Your skin's pretty dark these days. Black hair and brownish eyes, too. But to me you don't look Hispanic. You look beautifully Ojibwe."

"If I was white, he wouldn't have taken a second look at me."

"Probably not."

"It doesn't upset you?"

"That he scrutinized you a little more carefully because of your skin color? Not really. If he'd harassed you, that would have been different. He was just doing his job, which isn't an easy one, I imagine."

"Spoken like a member of the club," she said.

"Club?"

"Those who wear or have worn a badge."

"Is that really what's upsetting you?" I said.

"Peter is half-Mexican. He looks very Hispanic. What if he was driving one of these roads and was stopped by the Border Patrol?"

"If he was respectful and wasn't doing anything he shouldn't, he would probably be just fine."

"Your Native blood doesn't show, Cork. You don't get looked at twice. To be Indian anywhere, and to be Mexican as well, especially here, can you imagine how difficult that is?"

"I can, Rainy. And I hope you understand

that I can also imagine how difficult it must be to be a Border Patrol officer. A conscionable officer, anyway. Back there, I just saw a man trying to do a tough job. I didn't see any disrespect."

"You were with me, Cork. Isn't it possible that made all the difference?"

"Rainy, if we're going to get through this, we can't fight each other."

"You're right." But when she said it, her words were still hard.

Beyond the Coronados, we entered a broad basin with blue mountains along the far horizon. I turned north, and once again we climbed slowly onto a high plateau that was a mix of grassland and irrigated fields. Soon I began to see, as we had on our way to Cadiz, an occasional vineyard, dark green against all the other colors that had been washed pale by the sun.

The town of Lacabra was little more than a crossroads with a few new-looking homes, a gas station, a farm supply and implement store, a restaurant called the Golden Fork, and a hacienda-style building with a sign out front advertising Arizona wines. I figured we had the best chance of tracking down the Harrises at the farm store. We hit pay dirt inside, got directions, and Rainy and I turned around and headed back the way we'd come.

We arrived at a cutoff that shot east toward vineyards nestled against rugged hills. The sign at the juncture read HARRIS RANCH ROAD. We'd passed it on our way into town, but I hadn't been watching. We followed the road among the vineyards, under a stone arch into which had been etched the words SONORA HILLS CELLARS, and approached a grand home of tan adobe surrounded by palms. A hundred yards to the right, hard against a hillside, stood a large structure that looked like a warehouse. In front sat a forklift, a dusty F-150 pickup, and a motorcycle. Wooden pallets stood stacked against the building, whose broad door was open. We parked beside the pickup, got out, and walked to the opened door.

"Sorry, folks. No tours today," called a voice from the cool shade inside.

"Not here for a tour," I called back.

We stood in the doorway, facing a huge room full of tall silver tanks and racks of wooden kegs. I couldn't see anyone.

"If you're here to help with the harvest, that's not for another month." The voice came from somewhere near the back, behind the silver vats.

"We're looking for Peter Bisonette."

"Just a minute." In less than that, two men slipped from between the tanks. The first appeared to be about my age, mid-fifties, slim but in good shape, with a little brown mustache that matched his hair. He sported glasses and wore jeans and a blue work shirt with the sleeves rolled above the elbows. The guy who followed him was taller, well over six feet, and much older, though hard to say exactly how much, with a full head of white hair, a big nose, big hands, and a big, wistful smile.

"Looking for Peter?" the younger man said, as he approached. He had a rag and was wiping his hands of what appeared to be grease.

I glanced at Rainy and saw relief all over her face. Finally someone who admitted to knowing her son.

"Yes," I said. "We were told he works here."

"What do you want with him?" the older man asked.

Rainy said, "I'm his mother."

"Rainy Bisonette?" The younger man seemed surprised and pleased. "Then you must be Cork. This is a real pleasure."

Rainy said, "We were told at the Goodman Center that he works here now."

"That he does," said the older man.

The younger one finished wiping away the grease and held out his hand. "Frank Harris. And this is Robert Wieman."

"Just call me Jocko." The big white-haired man offered us his hand, large as a catcher's mitt.

"Is he here?" Rainy asked.

"He didn't show up today," Harris said. "Which is not like Peter at all."

"He didn't call?"

"We haven't heard a word from him since he left work yesterday. He didn't say anything about you coming for a visit."

"A spur of the moment thing," I said. "The truth is we're worried about him. He seems to have disappeared."

"As I said, it's not like Peter to miss work without calling, but things come up, you know. Is there a particular reason you're worried?"

"What do you know about my son?" Rainy asked.

"Look, why don't we talk inside?" Harris suggested. "Jayne would love to meet you. She's in her office in the house." He half-turned and opened his arms to the winery fixtures. "The quality of what's in those tanks is up to me. But the business is all Jayne's. Jocko, why don't you go check on those new graftings?"

The older man seemed more inclined to accompany us to the house, but he gave a nod. He mounted the motorcycle, kicked over the engine, and took off into the vineyards.

"His bike?" I asked.

"Jocko's pride and joy. He used to be a crop duster, flew a biplane. Had to give up the job when he hit eighty. But that Honda Hawk of his? Never."

We followed Harris across the yard and through a small, adobe-walled garden with a bubbling fountain at its center. Inside the house, everything was deadly quiet and the air blessedly cool. The place was decorated in a Mexican motif — tiled floors in beautiful patterns, walls and tapestries done in bright, singing colors, furniture of dark wood and leather. I smelled cinnamon.

"Have a seat," Harris said, when we arrived at the living room. "I'll get Jayne."

We sat on a sofa upholstered in soft brown leather.

"Is that a Frida Kahlo?" Rainy nodded toward a large painting of fuzzy fruit, which hung above the hearth of a fireplace that, I suspected, had never seen a flame.

"What's a Frida Kahlo?" I asked.

Before Rainy could answer, Harris returned with his wife. Jayne Harris was striking — tall, ash blond, and lovely. She was dressed in a way I remembered Dale Evans did on the old Roy Rogers television show: cowboy boots, a pearl snap shirt, and blue jeans, except that the jeans were stone-washed and fit so tight I figured she'd had to grease herself to get into them. She beamed a gracious western smile and said, "Howdy."

"Jayne doesn't usually look like this," Harris said.

His wife laughed. "I did a photo shoot this morning for a Phoenix magazine that's featuring our winery in next month's issue. The theme was the Old West meets the New West. You know, beef versus bottle. Corny, I know, but the wine market is competitive and it's important to keep our name out there."

"Would you like some wine?" Harris asked. "We make a really fine pinot gris."

Rainy glanced at me and I could read her eyes.

"Thanks, no," I said. "We're a little anxious to find Peter."

"Let's sit and talk," Harris suggested.

When we'd arranged ourselves, Jayne said, "Frank told you that Peter didn't come to work this morning? He's always been so reliable. One of his many endearing qualities."

76

"What kind of work does Peter do here?" I asked.

"Anything and everything," Harris said. "He's a quick study."

"How is it that you know my son?" Rainy asked.

"Grace Methodist Church in Cadiz," Jayne said. "Small congregation and we all know one another pretty well. After Peter lost his job at the Goodman Center, we gave him one here. We couldn't pay him a lot, not like what he'd been making at the center, but he seemed fine with that."

Rainy said, "You know Peter was in treatment there once."

"Of course. Are you worried he's using again?" Jayne said. "Because if you are, you can let go of that fear. Peter's stayed clean, I'd stake my life on it."

"Do you know where he lives?" Rainy asked.

Jayne seemed surprised. "You don't?"

Rainy explained about the P.O. box in Sulfur Springs.

"We don't have an exact address for him, but he drove to work from Sulfur Springs every day," Frank Harris said.

"How'd he come?" I asked.

"The Old Douglas Road, south of the mountains."

"We came that way," I said. "Got stopped by Border Patrol."

"Doesn't surprise me," Harris said. "There's been a lot of activity along the border here lately."

"What kind of activity? Undocumented immigrants coming in?"

Harris shook his head. "The big wall ends twenty miles west of here. Just low barbed wire after that, pretty easy to get over, so that's where they try most often. Around here it's drugs. They're pretty inventive getting them across."

"We were just in Sulfur Springs," Rainy said. "No one we talked to claimed to know Peter."

"He's a very quiet guy," Jayne said. "Maybe he just preferred to keep to himself."

"Why Sulfur Springs?" I asked. "Did he ever say what made him choose that place to live after he left the Goodman Center?"

"Not really," Harris replied. "I just figured it was cheaper than renting a place in Cadiz, which is a tourist town, so things are more expensive there. Sulfur Springs isn't exactly an oasis."

"Does Peter have any friends? A girlfriend maybe?" Rainy asked.

"Friends among our congregation, I suppose. But a girlfriend?" Jayne gave Rainy a look I couldn't quite interpret. "You're his mother. You don't know?"

"Clearly there's a good deal that Peter hasn't shared with me," Rainy said.

For a moment or two, there was an uncomfortable quiet in the room and a chill that was not from the air-conditioning.

"Does the name Rodriguez mean anything to you?" I asked.

"Lots of Rodriguezes in these parts," Harris said. "Why?"

"Peter mentioned a man named Rodriguez when he called Rainy last night. Not in a good way."

Harris gave a little shrug of innocence.

"We should be going," I said. I handed Harris my card. "If you hear from Peter, please let us know."

"Of course," he said.

They saw us out, and as we stood in the late afternoon sun with our shadows long across the ground, Jayne Harris gave Rainy a hug. "I'm sure there's a reasonable explanation for all of this. But in the meantime, I'll keep you and Peter in my prayers."

I shook hands with Frank Harris, and we got into our oven on wheels and headed under the stone arch and down the road through the grapevines.

"I'm feeling like a terrible mother," Rainy said. "There's so much I should know about Peter and I don't."

"Did you tell your mother everything?"

"It would have just broken her heart."

"Well, there you go. It's not about being a bad parent. It's about children trying to keep their parents from worrying."

"What was it Peter didn't want me to worry about?"

Before I had a chance to consider her question, Jocko stepped from among the vines and waved us down. I braked to a stop, and the old man came to Rainy's window, which she lowered. He leaned his big, tanned arms on the Cherokee and looked into Rainy's eyes.

"Peter's like a grandson to me. You hear from him, you let me know."

"Of course."

He looked back at the Harrises' grand home, where the walls rose high above the green vines. "Don't let anyone tell you Peter's not in trouble."

"What do you know?" Rainy asked. "Tell me the truth."

He shook his head. "In Coronado County, ma'am, only the dead know the whole truth."

He pushed away and walked back into the grapevines.

CHAPTER 6

We headed west, back to Cadiz, taking the longer way, following paved roads. The sun was hanging just above the Coronados. The rays came through the windshield at a blinding angle, and I kept the visor down. It was an empty country, this desert grassland, and one that seemed full of menace — snakes and thirst and cacti and lies. In Minnesota, even as you drove miles with tall evergreens standing close, like ragged walls on either side, you didn't feel this alone or this threatened. At least I didn't. Out here, I had the sense that a person could die way too easily and so absolutely alone that only the circling vultures would be the wiser.

I could feel Rainy's fear. It came out of her love for her son and from a growing sense that there was great reason to be afraid for Peter. I was tempted to give myself over to the same sense of dread. But I remembered what Henry Meloux had advised, that until we knew something different, it was best to imagine what gave us hope. And I remembered his other piece of advice, too, not to feed someone else's fear with your own, so I tried to stay clear and to corral the demons of my own doubts.

"People are lying to us, Rainy, that much is obvious. But it might not be because of Peter."

"Jocko said Peter's in trouble."

"He didn't say what kind of trouble."

"And why didn't he?" She was angry. That was her fear coming through.

"Because he didn't know or because he was afraid."

"We should have made him tell us."

"And how exactly should we have done that?"

I swerved to avoid some kind of small animal that darted across the highway. It was brown and without a tail. In Minnesota, I could have told you exactly what it was. Here, I didn't have a clue.

"I don't know, Cork. But I need some answers soon."

"I understand. When we hit Cadiz, let's track down the minister at Grace Church, see if the pastor has something to offer us that might be helpful. And, Rainy, let's continue to imagine the best — that in the end this is all some kind of terrible mistake."

Rainy inhaled deeply several times, trying, I suspected, to breathe out her fear, her anger. Eventually, she reached out and put her hand gently on my arm. *"Migwech."*

"Thank you for what?"

"For being Uncle Henry when Uncle Henry isn't here."

Which was one of the greatest compliments she could have paid me.

Cadiz, as the day died, was a much less busy place than when we'd been there earlier. I figured the folks from Tucson and maybe Phoenix who'd come to the high country of Coronado County to escape the worst of the summer heat had headed back home. Grace Methodist Church wasn't difficult to find. It was a small square with a squat bell tower, built of gray stone, set on the east side of the San Gabriel River. The little parking lot was empty and the doors were locked. In front stood a stone statue of an angel in the company of a small child. The angel was pointing up, as if directing the child to look heavenward. Beside the statue was a sign that, along with the times of services, gave the telephone number and name of the pastor, Michelle Abbott.

"That's the same number on the church sign in Sulfur Springs," I said.

The sun had set by now, and we stood next to the angel and the child, in the shadow of the western mountains, while I dialed the minister's number. Her line rang several times, then went to voice mail. I left a brief indication of who I was and my number.

"We should get a room for the night," I suggested.

On the main street, we'd passed a nice-looking little inn of white adobe. I drove to it, and we checked in with a pleasant older woman who was delighted to hear that we were from Minnesota.

"My grandparents lived there," she said. "Duluth. You know it?"

"We know it well," I said.

"I remember how cool it used to be by the lake when we visited them in the summer."

"Ever visit in the winter?" I asked.

She laughed. "We weren't crazy."

The Desert Breeze Inn was built around a small cactus garden with a bubbling fountain, which seemed to be such a favorite of folks in the Southwest. I thought that Henry Meloux might look at this as a form of smudging, the cleansing sound of water in a land that had so little of it. There were only six rooms, and we were given the one at the very end. No sooner had we carried in our luggage than my cell phone rang.

"This is Pastor Michelle Abbott. You called about Peter?"

"Yes," I said. "Let me give the phone to his mother. She'd like to talk with you."

"This is Rainy Bisonette. Thanks so much for calling back." Rainy listened and nodded. "I think he's wonderful, too. But I'm concerned that he might be in some trouble, and I wondered if I could meet with you to talk about it." She listened again and glanced at me. "We're free right now." She smiled and said, "I can't thank you enough." She ended the call and handed my cell phone back. "She'll meet us at the church in fifteen minutes."

We walked, following the river, and then across a little footbridge that led right to the church. A few minutes after we arrived, a dusty green pickup rolled up and parked in the lot. A woman with a red bandanna around her head and wearing dusty jeans and a yellow T-shirt got out and came toward us. She was probably well into her sixties, but with a smile that was ageless.

"Hello, folks. I'm Pastor Michelle. But you can drop the pastor part. Just call me Michelle."

We shook her hand. Her grip was strong,

her palm callused.

"Why don't we talk inside?" she suggested and unlocked the front door. "This is an historic church, built when the mines around here were booming."

The rafters and altar and pews were all of dark, heavy wood. The stained-glass windows seemed awfully ornate for such a small sanctuary.

"Built with the same money that built the town — silver, gold, copper, and cattle," she explained. "Now we rely mostly on tourism."

The church was hot and stuffy. We followed her to her office, which was left of the altar, where she turned on a window air conditioner. She sat at her desk, and Rainy and I took the two empty chairs.

"This isn't your only congregation," I said.

"That's right. I have another charge, a small congregation in Sulfur Springs. The Catholics and the Methodists share the church, St. Esteban's."

"Peter lives there," Rainy said.

"In Sulfur Springs?" It was clearly a revelation to her.

"At least that's where he receives his mail," Rainy said. "A box at the Sulfur Springs post office."

"That's interesting. He's always been a

member of the congregation here. I've never seen him at a service in Sulfur Springs, but that doesn't mean he doesn't live there. When you attend a particular church regularly, as Peter does here, it becomes a bit like home."

"We've been to Sulfur Springs. No one we talked to would admit to knowing him."

"That does seem a little odd." Michelle gave Rainy a piercing look. "You said you were afraid Peter might be in trouble."

"Does the name Rodriguez mean anything to you?" Rainy asked.

"Rodriguez? No first name?"

"No."

"Lots of Rodriguezes in Coronado County and south of the border. Why do you ask?"

Rainy glanced at me in a questioning way, and I gave her a nod. Eventually, you have to trust someone. She told the story of Peter's phone call, and his silence since then.

"He said he killed someone named Rodriguez? That doesn't sound at all like Peter."

"It's not exactly clear that he did," Rainy said, holding to the best hope we had. "The message is garbled. Maybe if you listened it would help."

She brought out her cell phone and played Peter's message on the speakerphone.

"You're right, Rainy. It's garbled. How-ever, Peter says something at the end that's a little scratchy, but it's important and scary."

"What is it?" Rainy asked.

"Play it again," Michelle said. As Peter's message neared the end, she said, "Here. Listen. Did you catch that word? *Lagarto?*"

"Was that the word?" Rainy said. "I couldn't quite tell."

"The big Rodriguez in these parts is Carlos Rodriguez. He's the head of Las Calaveras."

"The Skulls," Rainy translated.

Michelle nodded. "One of the cartels in northern Mexico. As I understand, he runs it with his two sons. I suppose Peter's situation could involve some other Rodriguez. Like I said, it's a common surname around here. But Carlos Rodriguez is often called Lagarto. Lizard. He's very tall and very slender and absolutely cold-blooded. I think you have good reason to be worried."

"Why in the world would Peter be involved with a drug cartel?" Rainy said.

Michelle sat for a long moment. "Peter's a Marine," she finally said.

"Was a Marine," Rainy said.

"Once a Marine, always a Marine. I'm a Marine, too. That's one of the first connections Peter and I made, and it's been a powerful one. He's a veteran of Afghanistan. For me it was Desert Storm. My last deployment before I retired from the Corps."

"A chaplain?" I asked.

She shook her head. "Intel, like Peter. I have this thing, a knack for languages. I'm fluent in both Farsi and Arabic. Also Chinese, German, French, and, of course, Spanish, which comes in handy here. When I retired and felt I had the call, I went to seminary. While I was there, I added Greek and Latin to my repertoire."

"Peter's good with languages?" I asked.

"Better even than me. I've always figured that was one of the reasons he attended the U of A in Tucson, their Critical Languages Program. Instruction in languages not normally taught in colleges. His facility was also a big reason he was in intel, I'm sure. But what's more important is that Peter's good with people. They trust him, and he has a real knack for knowing who to trust." She looked at Rainy for confirmation.

"He's always been like that," Rainy said.

"In the Marines, Peter was in the field, working with the locals, gathering intelligence."

"So you understood what Peter went through," Rainy said.

"He was very open with me about it."

I knew what they were referring to. Rainy had shared Peter's military experience with me, especially the part that had led to his addiction. What ended his service was a Taliban ambush in the mountains in which a number of his comrades were killed. Peter had been badly wounded and medevaced out. He'd spent a long time in a hospital, recovering. On discharge, he'd enrolled in the University of Arizona in Tucson. Then the real difficulty had begun. During his hospital convalescence, he'd become reliant on painkillers. In civilian life, he found that he couldn't function without them. That's when Rainy had intervened and had got him admitted to the Goodman Center.

"It's clear that Peter hasn't been so open with me," Rainy said. "About his life in Coronado County anyway. What could he be involved in that would put him at odds with this cartel?"

"All I could do is speculate, and that wouldn't get you anywhere," the minister replied. "But I know someone who might be able to answer all your questions. Nikki Edwards. She manages our local radio station, and is a DJ as well. Five times a week, she hosts a program from ten to midnight called *Nikki at Night*. She's also a member of the congregation here. She and Peter are very good friends."

"Peter never mentioned her to me."

"Talk to Nikki. I think she can tell you some of the things you need to know."

"How can we get in touch with her?"

"Let me check the church directory."

From her desk drawer, the pastor pulled several sheets of paper held together by a staple. She turned to the second page. "I have her cell phone number." She copied it on a slip of paper and handed it to me.

Before we left her office, Michelle took Rainy's hands into her own and gazed with deep concern into my wife's eyes.

"Look, I don't want to scare you, but if this has even the slightest chance of having something to do with Lagarto and Las Calaveras, be very careful who you talk to and what you ask. The brutality of those people is beyond belief." Then she offered Rainy a hopeful little smile and said, *Vaya con Dios.*

CHAPTER 7

As soon as we left the church, I tried the cell phone number Michelle had given us for Nikki Edwards but got no answer. The hour was late and we were hungry. We ate at a café called the Wagon Wheel, on the main street through Cadiz. It was a quiet meal, cheeseburger and beer for me, salad and iced tea for Rainy. There was a lot to think about. Rainy stared out the window at the street, which was mostly empty.

"I felt better when I didn't know Peter might be involved with some death-dealing cartel," she said.

"We don't know the truth yet."

"And we're no closer to it than when we got here."

"We know people who know Peter. If we keep asking, we'll know more. Eventually we'll find someone who can give us the answers we're looking for."

"Or, if Michelle is right, we'll run into

someone who'll slit our throats for asking."

"Then we need to be careful."

"How do we ask without taking risks?"

"I don't think we can. I'm just saying we should anticipate that we're stirring up a hornet's nest and be incredibly vigilant."

"Incredibly scared, too? Because I am."

"So am I, Rainy, but do we give up?"

"Rhetorical question," she said.

"All right, tomorrow we begin by tracking down Nikki Edwards. And then I want to go back to the Harrises' place."

"They didn't seem to know much."

"I got the feeling they knew more than they said. But it's really Jocko I want to talk to. If we get him alone and press him, he might be willing to tell us what he knows."

We left the café and walked back to the Desert Breeze Inn. The air was still uncomfortably hot, though not as oppressive as it had been when the sun was overhead.

"I thought the desert got cool at night," I said.

"Cooler," Rainy said. "It's all relative."

It was a few minutes before ten when we reached our room. There was a clock radio on the nightstand, and I turned it on and found the local station. Our bodies were still on Minnesota time and we were both bushed. We got ready for bed, climbed under the sheets, and *Nikki at Night* came on.

"Hello, night owls, this is Nikki Edwards. For the next few hours, I'll be your guide to music of all things nocturnal. Sit back or lie down, close your eyes, and imagine the night sky, a canopy of stars above you."

Her voice was smooth and smoky.

"She sounds awfully sexy," Rainy said.

"I wouldn't mind going to bed with her every night," I said. Then added, "Listening to her on the radio."

Her playlist, languid and sultry cuts, fit her voice and the theme of her show. She was inordinately fond of offering arcane information about each track.

"Here's a cut from Tommy Roe, singing one of the classics from way back when: 'Stormy.' It might be a hundred and ten degrees outside, but this song'll make you feel like it's a cool thirty-two. It lasts a satisfying two minutes, fifty-one seconds. Enjoy, all you night owls."

A thought occurred to me, and I got up and went to the desk in the corner of the room. I opened the top drawer and found what I was looking for.

"What are you doing?" Rainy asked from the bed.

"Local phone book," I said, holding up

the little volume of yellow pages. "I'm looking up the number for the radio station. If Nikki Edwards isn't answering her phone, maybe Nikki at Night is."

I located the number and punched it in on my cell phone. A tired, male voice answered.

"Could I speak with Nikki Edwards?"

"You want to request a song?"

"No. I'd just like to talk with her."

"She's on air."

"When she has a moment. I can wait."

"Unless you want to request a number —" he began.

"Tell her it's about Peter Bisonette."

There was a deep sigh on the other end. "Hold on."

Nikki at Night had moved on to another number, a long cut from Enya. I waited, and in a moment, it was her voice coming through on my cell, not sultry in the least, but guarded.

"Who is this?" she said.

"My name's Cork O'Connor. My wife is Rainy Bisonette, Peter's mother. We're here because we're worried about Peter. Pastor Michelle at Grace Church recommended we talk to you."

I said it quickly because I wanted to get in as much as I could before she hung up or had to leave to key up the next cut for her show.

"Why are you worried about Peter?"

"We got a call from him yesterday. He told us he was in trouble. We haven't been able to reach him since."

"Where are you?"

"Here in Cadiz."

"I can't talk now," she said. "Can we meet tomorrow morning?"

"When?"

"I have to be in Tucson at eight. Is six too early for you?"

"Where?"

"I pass right by the radio station on my way out of town. How about we meet here?"

"We'll be there," I said.

She hung up without a good-bye. I turned to Rainy and relayed the 6:00 a.m. request. She lay back on her pillow and stared up at the ceiling.

"Maybe tomorrow we'll get some answers," she said.

I woke in the middle of the night. Rainy wasn't beside me. I called her name and got no reply. I left the bed, checked the bathroom, then went to the window that overlooked the cactus garden and the bubbling fountain. The night was moonless and black, but the streetlights threw a drizzle of illumination over the Desert Breeze Inn. I saw Rainy standing near the fountain, talking on her cell phone. Her back was to me. She'd been trying Peter's number frequently since we'd arrived, but I didn't think it was Peter she was talking to. She shook her head and gestured with her free hand in a way that signaled frustration. Or maybe it was pleading. She paced and looked up at the night sky and shook her head again.

I stepped outside to join her. As soon as she saw me, she said something quickly and quietly on the phone and ended the call.

"Chantelle," she said. Her daughter, who lived in Alaska. "I thought she should know about Peter. I hoped maybe he'd talked with her."

"Looked like a pretty lively conversation."

"I'm a little upset is all."

"How is she?"

"Who? Oh, Chantelle. Worried, of course."

"Of course. Want to talk?"

"I'm tired, Cork. I just want to go back to bed."

We lay together, but neither of us slept. One of the things I'd always loved about Rainy was that I'd believed she would never lie to me. Until that moment.

In the morning, we both showered and

98

dressed and said very little. It was early, and when I drew back the curtains, there was only the gray promise of day in the sky. I opened the door and felt the heat, and I thought again how I'd always heard the desert got cool at night. Another lie, I figured.

The Jeep Cherokee I'd rented had a remote starter, which I'd thought would come in handy on those blazing days when I wanted to kick over the engine from our hotel room and get the air-conditioning pumping out a cool stream long before we got in. I grabbed the key from the desktop, where I'd put it the night before, and stepped back into the doorway. The Cherokee was parked thirty or forty yards from our room, beyond the cactus garden, the only vehicle in the small lot. I hit the ignition button.

The Cherokee disappeared in a great ball of flame, and the blast of air against my face was ten times hotter than any Arizona sun.

CHAPTER 8

"Peter Bisonette," Sheriff Chet Carlson said. "Not a name I'm familiar with."

They'd cordoned off the burned-out hulk that had been our rented Jeep Cherokee. Cadiz Volunteer Fire and Rescue had doused the flames ten minutes after the explosion. Although it was still early, a good share of the town's population had gathered on the street to gawk. Rainy and I sat on a bench in the cactus garden, while the sheriff questioned us and a deputy took notes.

"He was here because of the Goodman Center?" the sheriff said. "Patient or employee?"

"He's been both," Rainy said.

Carlson was in his late thirties, slender, dark hair, serious eyes. "Most recently?"

"Employee. A counselor."

"Still employed?"

"Not there."

"Where?"

100

"He works for the Harrises."

Sheriff Carlson thought a moment and shook his head.

"Frank and Jayne Harris," the deputy said. He hadn't introduced himself, but he'd been writing a lot. He was boyishly good looking, with dark eyes and high cheekbones. Around the crown of his tan cowboy hat, he wore a band that was beaded in a colorful design that made me think of the Navajo. Although his name badge read CROCKETT, the same name as that legendary frontiersman and Indian fighter, I thought he might have some Native heritage in him. "They own a winery other side of the Coronados, set up against the Sonora Hills."

Carlson turned again to Rainy. "What's he do for them?"

"I'm not sure exactly," Rainy replied. "Kind of a jack-of-all-trades, as I understand it."

"Have you checked with them about your missing son?"

"They haven't seen him since the day before yesterday."

"So it's been less than forty-eight hours since you've had contact with Peter?"

"That's right."

"We don't consider a person officially

101

missing until they've been gone forty-eight hours."

I said, "When it's your family, you look at it differently."

He nodded toward the wreckage of the Jeep. "I've got to figure, since you just arrived, the car bomb, if that's what it actually was, had something to do with your son. Doesn't that seem reasonable to you?"

"Of course it does."

"So?" He waited to be enlightened.

"I don't know, Sheriff," Rainy said. "I honestly don't know."

"When you talked with Peter the night before last, during your phone conversation, did he give you any indication what kind of trouble he might be in?"

"I didn't actually talk with him," Rainy said. "He left a voice message. And he said nothing about any kind of trouble."

Another lie from the lips of the woman I thought I knew so well. But this lie, I understood.

"Okay, Ms. Bisonette, how about this? He was a patient at Goodman and then he worked there. At the Goodman Center you come into contact with a lot of folks who have a lot to do with drugs. Coronado County shares a long border with Mexico. We do our best to battle the flow of drugs up here, but sometimes it feels like we're trying to hold back a flood with a dam riddled full of holes. You understand?"

Rainy just looked at him.

"You've been throwing his name out to a lot of folks around here," Carlson went on. "I've got to tell you my first thought is that your son might be involved in trafficking drugs, and somebody doesn't want you poking into that. It would go a long way to explaining both his disappearance and that burned-up Jeep of yours."

"Peter got clean. And Peter would never traffic."

"I know you believe your son was successful in his rehab, but sometimes it doesn't take the first time around. And if he's still trying to support a costly habit, I'm guessing what he makes working odd jobs at a winery won't cut it."

"Peter wouldn't —" Rainy began.

"Then explain that Jeep to me, ma'am." He gave her a piercing cop look, one I'd used myself when I wore a badge. A moment later, he turned the look on me.

"Everything you say makes perfect sense," I said. Because it did. And because I didn't really know Peter and had no other facts to offer, I figured at that point arguing with him would get us nowhere.

"You have a photograph of Peter?" he asked Rainy.

"It's in our room. I'll get it."

Rainy headed away, leaving me alone with the sheriff.

The woman who'd checked us in the night before stood in the doorway of her office, speaking with another deputy. Her eyes flicked my way, and even at that distance, I could see how afraid she was.

"Peter's not your son?" Carlson asked me.

"No. He's my wife's son, from her first marriage."

"And you two? Been married long."

"Since April."

"Newlyweds. You know Peter well?"

"Not well, no."

"Could he still be using?"

"He could be."

"I'd like a list of everyone you and your wife have talked to since you arrived in Coronado County."

"All right. Is there a car rental company here in Cadiz?"

"Nope. But even if there was, considering what happened to your last rental, I doubt you'd have any luck there."

One of the firemen approached and said, "Could I talk to you a minute, Chet?" They walked away toward what was left of the Jeep.

Rainy came back with the photo.

"I'll take that, ma'am," Deputy Crockett said politely.

"I'd like it back."

"We'll scan it and return it to you. Sheriff's going to be putting out a BOLO on your son."

Carlson returned. "I'd like you to come down to the office and give us an official statement, and that list I asked for of everyone you've talked to. Do you have that photo?"

"Got it," Crockett said and held it up for the sheriff to see.

We were given a ride in a cruiser, made our statements at the law enforcement center, wrote up a list of the people with whom we'd already talked, then were driven back to the Desert Breeze Inn. The Jeep had been towed away and the debris had been swept up. All that was left on the asphalt of the little parking lot was a big patch of soot, like the print of a black hand.

The woman in the office came out to meet us. She wouldn't look at us as she spoke.

"You can't stay here."

"I understand," Rainy said.

"May we leave our bags in the room until we find other accommodations?" I asked.

The woman nodded and, as she turned to walk away, said quietly over her shoulder, "I'm sorry."

It was midmorning by then. We'd missed our appointment to talk with Nikki Edwards. I was hungry, and Rainy and I needed to sit for a while and consider our options. We went back to the Wagon Wheel. A lot of heads turned our way as we walked in, but no one said a word to us. We sat down at a table by a front window where the morning sun came through in a bright splash of light. Immediately, a young waitress was at our table.

"You're them," she said, handing us two menus. "The folks with the bombed car."

"Guess our cover's blown," I said to Rainy. I scanned my menu. "Could we get a couple of coffees, black?"

"Sure. If it's any consolation, you're not the first."

I looked up. "Oh?"

"Same thing happened down in Sulfur Springs a couple of months ago. That guy wasn't so lucky."

"What do you mean?" Rainy asked.

"Killed him, the bomb. But he was local, not tourists like you."

"Did the sheriff solve that one?"

"Nope." She shrugged. "Nothing new. You live along the border, things like that happen way too often these days. That fence?" She shook her head. "Doesn't do a thing. Be right back with those coffees."

Rainy leaned across the table. "Modus operandi."

"If they're related."

"Why didn't the sheriff mention it?"

"Maybe he didn't want to jump to conclusions. Officially."

"He was sure ready to jump to a lot of conclusions about Peter." She tapped the tabletop with her fingers. "I want to ask him about that bombing."

"Maybe better to ask someone more willing to talk off the record."

"Like who?"

"Her," I said and nodded toward the street outside the restaurant window.

I'd watched as Michelle had parked her truck in the lot of the Desert Breeze Inn, gone into the office, come out, and walked toward the restaurant. She spotted us as soon as she entered.

"Heard the explosion?" I asked.

"Hardly. I live on a ranch ten miles from here. But heard about it pretty quick." She pulled up a chair and joined us. "Mind?"

"I was just thinking of you," I said. "Can we buy you breakfast?"

"I ate a couple of hours ago. But coffee would be fine."

The waitress brought our coffee and an extra cup. "How you doing, Michelle?"

"Real good, Georgia."

"You folks ready to order?"

When the waitress had gone, the pastor said quietly, "Are you both okay?"

"A little shook up," I said. "But all things considered, we're doing okay."

Rainy didn't say anything.

"This is way worse than I thought," the minister said.

"What did you think?" I said.

"Not here."

"We're kind of limited now in our choices of where else to talk." I nodded toward the black spot on the asphalt next to her truck.

"I'll take care of that," she said.

Our breakfast came and we ate, a little on the fast side, because we were both eager to hear what the Marine turned minister had to say. We paid, and as we left, Georgia called, "You folks take care. And I mean that."

We crossed the street to Michelle's truck.

"We've been asked to leave the Desert Breeze," I said. "Not without good reason."

108

"Where will you stay?"

"Not sure. My guess is that the other places in town won't be smiling a big greeting when we show up."

"I've got a place for you. Throw your bags in the back of my truck."

We did and got into the cab beside her. She pulled out of the lot and, a couple of minutes later, parked on the street across from the little church where we'd met her the night before.

"The church?" Rainy said. "That's the place you're thinking of?"

"Not the church," Michelle said. "The parsonage." She nodded toward a small stone house on our side of the street, shadowed by tall cottonwoods. "Like I said, I have a ranch ten miles out of town, so I use the parsonage for guests of the congregation. It's made of the same stone as the church. Somebody wants to blow you up, it'll take a small nuclear device. Not fancy, but it might do until you figure your next move."

We carried our things inside, where the air was blessedly cool.

"I kicked on the AC before I met you this morning, just in case," Michelle said.

The parsonage was small and sunny. We dropped our bags in the tiny bedroom, then sat in the living room with Michelle.

"Georgia told us about the car bombing in Sulfur Springs," Rainy said.

The minister nodded. "Happened a couple of months ago."

"One man killed," I said. "Who?"

"Word is that he was a member of White Horse."

"White Horse?"

"There's a war going on in Coronado County and the other counties along the border," Michelle said.

"A drug war?"

"It's a great deal more complicated."

"Who is White Horse?" Rainy asked.

"A vigilante group, trying to go head-to-head with the cartels. They've taken their name from a passage in Revelation. 'And I saw heaven opened, and behold a white horse; and he that sat upon him was called Faithful and True, and in righteousness he doth judge and make war.' "

"So White Horse against the cartels. Not so complicated," I said.

"Not until you consider the Border Patrol, and the federal governments on both sides of that wall, and local law enforcement, and vigilantes like White Horse, and the wave of refugees trying to make it to the U.S., and the humanitarian groups trying to help them, and on and on and on. In what crosses that border, nothing is simple."

"Do you think Peter is involved in what crosses that border?" Rainy asked.

"I do. But not the drugs. Peter's stayed clean, I'm sure of that."

"If not the drugs, then what?" I said.

"Peter has a big heart and a strong conscience," Michelle said. "Where refugees are involved, the situation is frightening. So many of those coming across from Mexico are women and children. They're preyed on by the *coyotes* who take their money to lead them here. They're sometimes robbed and raped by these men and abandoned in the desert. If they don't have money for their passage, they become mules for the cartels. Imagine the kind of desperation that drives people to take those risks."

"So how does Peter fit in?"

"I think he's helping these desperate people. That's not something we talk about openly here in Coronado County. Feelings run high on both sides of the issue, and honestly, it can be dangerous. I can't say for certain that's what Peter is doing, but I've strongly suspected it for a while."

"And this would bring him into conflict with the cartel run by the Rodriguez family?"

"The cartels don't just traffic drugs. They traffic people. Anything that might bring you into contact with one of the cartels is risky business."

"You told us to talk to Nikki Edwards," I said. "Is that because she's close enough to Peter to be in his confidence? Or do you believe she's involved in helping the undocumented immigrants?"

Michelle considered her words before replying. "Like Peter, she's a person of strong conscience and conviction."

"We were supposed to talk to her this morning. Missed our appointment."

"Have you tried calling?"

"Not yet. Been a little busy. Have you talked to anyone in your Sulfur Springs congregation about Peter?"

"I've called." She shook her head. "I can't tell if they really don't know anything or if they're too afraid to talk. What are you going to do?"

"We're not leaving Coronado County until we know what's going on with Peter," Rainy said.

A smile came to Michelle's lips, one of understanding, and she said, "You'll need a vehicle. We don't have any car rentals in Cadiz. So, how would you like my truck? She's got a lot of miles on her, but she's reliable as the day is long."

"We couldn't," Rainy said.

"Don't worry. Somebody blows her up, she's fully insured."

"Thank you," I said.

She handed me a ring with two keys on it. One was an old skeleton key. She touched the other. "This key's for the parsonage."

"What's the other for?"

"That'll open the church, in case you decide you want to pray there. And one more thing. You'll need to give me a lift back to the ranch."

"If you're willing to risk a ride with us," Rainy said.

She took Rainy's hand. "Wouldn't be here if I wasn't."

CHAPTER 9

We dropped Michelle at her ranch, which was east and south of Cadiz, set among grassland within sight of the border fence.

"I drive my property along that fence almost every day, and almost every day I find something left behind by the mules," she'd told us on the way there. "Mostly backpacks stuffed with marijuana. I always wonder why they've dropped them, what the consequences might be. I call the sheriff's office. They come out, take possession. It's the same for all of us who own property that abuts the fence."

"Do you try to interfere with the trafficking?"

"Are you kidding? That's just asking to get shot. Life along the border," she'd said with a shrug.

We headed back toward Cadiz. Once again, Rainy was quiet in a disturbing way, her focus to the south, beyond the fence.

"What is it, Rainy?" I asked. "What's coming at us from across the border?"

"When I know for sure, Cork, I'll tell you."

"Why all the mystery? We almost got ourselves blown to kingdom come this morning. What aren't you telling me?"

She turned her brown eyes to my face and studied me as intensely as she'd studied that foreign landscape to the south. It occurred to me that Rainy knew almost everything there was to know about my life before we met. I'd shared it with her willingly. But in her own life, there was a great gap, and that gap was the years she'd spent in Arizona during her first marriage. She'd offered me little pieces of information, but never the whole ball of wax. And now here we were, in that territory of her untold life, and I was aware of how much of her was still a mystery to me.

"Do you trust me, Cork?"

"I want to, Rainy."

"Do you trust me?" she said again.

I should have been able to answer immediately. "Yes," I finally said.

Was it the truth? I wanted it be.

"You'll know everything soon, I promise," she said.

"How soon?" I asked. "And what does it depend on?"

115

Before she could answer, I spotted a Border Patrol vehicle coming up fast behind me, the light bar flashing. It pulled close, and in my rearview mirror I saw the officer at the wheel waving me over. I braked to a stop at the side of the road and lowered the truck window. The hot air rushed in and with it the smell of that arid place, which was beginning to seem to me like the distant smell of death, dry and leathery.

The agent got out. His green uniform was smartly pressed, his shoes polished, his metal badge shining in the bright sun. He wore mirrored sunglasses under the bill of his green cap. His right hand rested on the butt of his holstered sidearm.

"Morning Mr. O'Connor. Ms. Bisonette." I recognized him from the day before, when we'd been stopped on the Old Douglas Road.

"Good morning, Agent . . . ?"

"Sprangers. Jamie Sprangers."

He took off the sunglasses. His eyes were like small glistening stones, his face tanned and cut by lines from squinting into a relentless sun. He was handsome, his good looks dark, what, I suppose, a romance novelist might have called "swarthy."

"Heard about the incident with your vehicle this morning," he said.

116

"Seems like all of Coronado County's heard about it," I said.

"Big county, small population. Word travels fast. Especially with something like this. Kind of unusual."

"Not so much, from my understanding."

He nodded. Once. Then looked across me at Rainy.

"How're you holding up, ma'am?"

"Just fine, Agent Sprangers."

"Your son is Peter Bisonette. Correct?"

"Yes."

"Gone missing, I understand."

"We haven't heard from him since the day before yesterday. No one has."

"Lots of kids are uncommunicative. A day or two doesn't seem like much to be concerned about. Any reason you should be worried?"

I said, "Mind me asking what your interest is, Agent Sprangers?"

"That destroyed Jeep Cherokee you rented. That has all the hallmarks of a hit. Around here hits usually go along with the drug traffic. Drug traffic across the border is one of my areas of concern."

"Fair enough," I said.

"Does the name Rodriguez mean anything to you folks?"

I didn't let a thing show on my face. I

117

hoped Rainy didn't either.

"Should it?" I asked.

"Mexican family responsible for most of what crosses illegally along the border here with Coronado County. A cartel, more or less. They call themselves Las Calaveras. The Skulls. Carlos Rodriguez heads the family. Enjoys being called Lagarto. Lizard. Something like a hit, that would come from orders handed down by Rodriguez."

"I don't know that name," I said.

I glanced at Rainy. She shook her head.

Over Sprangers's shoulder, I saw three vultures circling on thermals, in the same way I'd seen the day before when we encountered the agent. He saw me looking and turned.

"Buzzards," he said. "Admirable creatures in their way. They survive in a landscape inhospitable to most other animals, thriving on what dies in that landscape. An interesting fact about those buzzards. They defecate and urinate on themselves, use the evaporation of the water as a coolant. They're all about survival, whatever it takes. I've always seen that as a valuable lesson. Not uncommon for us to stumble across the bleached white bones of someone who ignored that lesson. A lot more of those bones in this desert than we'll ever find. Out here, the lost usually stay lost forever." He turned back to us, reached into his shirt pocket, and drew out a business card, which he handed to me. "In Coronado County, you need to be very careful about who you talk to, and even more careful about who you trust. If you feel you're in any danger, call me."

"And we should trust you because . . ." I said.

He gave us a swarthy smile and put a finger to his cap. "Good day, folks."

Agent Sprangers returned to his vehicle, did a U-turn, and headed south, toward the border.

"Was that a warning?" Rainy asked. "Or was he really offering to help?"

"I'm not sure. Could be he's just trying to read us."

"Like we're trying to read him?"

My cell phone rang.

"Cork O'Connor," I answered.

"This is Nikki Edwards. I heard about this morning. We need to talk."

We met her in a little park on the San Gabriel River south of Cadiz. It sat among cottonwoods and sycamores that grew along the banks and gave welcome shade, and was rendered almost invisible from the road by a thicket of shrubs I later learned were tamarisk bushes. Nikki was waiting for us at a picnic table, the only person there.

"I'm so sorry," she said even before the introductions. "They didn't wait long to target you."

"Who?" I said.

On the radio, her voice had been velvety, and I'd imagined some young, slinky siren. But Nikki Edwards wasn't much younger than I. Her hair was pulled back in a ponytail. She wore glasses and a ball cap with NAMI printed across the bill. She ignored my question, and all her attention went immediately to the woman at my side.

"You're Rainy. Peter's told me so much about you. I can imagine how worried you are."

"Who targeted us?" I asked again.

"Here," Nikki said and indicated the picnic table. "Sit. We'll talk."

The riverbed lay a few yards from where we sat. In Minnesota, I might have heard the rush and tumble of clear water over stones, but here there was only the dry rustle of leaves as a small breeze blew through the trees along the bank.

"When did you last hear from Peter?" Nikki asked.

"The day before yesterday," Rainy said.

"How did he sound?"

"Scared."

"What did he say?"

Rainy hesitated. Dangerous territory, telling someone your son confessed to murder.

"Did he mention Rodriguez?" Nikki said. "Or White Horse?"

"Only Rodriguez. And the name Lagarto."

She nodded as if that made sense.

"We know about him and Las Calaveras," I said.

"A family of reptiles," Nikki said. "A ball of snakes."

"Why would Peter mention White Horse?"

Nikki folded her hands on the tabletop and closed her eyes, as if in prayer. "Where to start?"

We heard a car approaching on the road, and Nikki's eyes shot open. She raised her head and listened intently, in the way deer in the great Northwoods do when they sense danger. The car passed and she relaxed.

"It sometimes feels like a war zone in Coronado County," she said. "Like in any war zone, those who suffer most are the innocents. The Pima County Medical Examiner's Office handles the work of identifying human remains found in the desert in the counties along the Mexican border. There are hundreds of sets of remains still unidentified. That's only a fraction of what probably is out there undiscovered. The most common demographic used to be males between the ages of twenty-five and thirty-five. But that's changed. We're seeing more and more women and children, the majority coming from Central America and the states farthest south in Mexico. Border control has tightened, so the flow is not what it used to be, but more people are dying."

"Why?"

"They're forced to make the crossing in some of the worst country imaginable. And too often, they cross alone and unprepared, or if they come with a *coyote,* they're abandoned or even murdered."

"What does this have to do with Peter?" Rainy asked.

"Peter works with a group who call themselves Los Angeles del Desierto."

"Desert Angels," Rainy translated.

"They do what they can to keep the innocents who are so desperate to come to the United States out of the hands of the predators. They intercept these people in Mexico and arrange safe passage."

"And Peter?"

"Peter was a soldier. He's been trained in

reconnaissance behind enemy lines. He's fearless, but not stupid. When it comes to moving through the desert, he knows how to disguise his presence so effectively that the cartels and the sign cutters have no idea where he is."

"Sign cutters?" Rainy asked.

"That's what trackers are called," I said. "When they're following someone's trail, it's called cutting sign."

"So, Border Patrol?" Rainy said.

Nikki nodded. "Border Patrol."

Rainy put it together. "Peter leads these people to safety."

"At great risk," Nikki said. "Carlos Rodriguez has put a price on the head of anyone who helps Los Angeles del Desierto. And on this side of the border, there's not only the Border Patrol to contend with, there's White Horse."

"Vigilantes," I said.

"They haunt the routes refugees often take, where water jugs and food and blankets have been set out by a broad range of humanitarian groups. They slash the jugs, steal the food and blankets, intimidate the refugees. And although they've never been caught at it, there's good reason to believe they're not above killing. They know about Los Angeles del Desierto, and are no more

123

pleased with it than the Rodriguez family is."

"How often does he lead people across?"

"Several times each month."

"And you know all this how?" I asked.

Rainy said, "Because there's a price on your head, too, isn't there? You're a Desert Angel."

Nikki didn't deny it.

"Did Peter get you involved?"

"Other way around. I drew Peter in." She gave a weak smile. "Several years ago, a number of us in Cadiz who were concerned about the terrible ordeal of those coming across the border began putting out jugs of water, food, blankets. It wasn't much of an organization then. We did it quietly, because we didn't want to draw attention. Two years ago, I convinced Peter to help us. His vision changed everything. With Peter, we became the Desert Angels. There are humanitarians on the other side of the border who've been helping those who want to cross. Peter connected with them, established a network. He began taking as many refugees away from the *coyotes* as he could. These are people so desperate to come here that fences and laws won't stop them."

"Peter keeps them from dying," Rainy said.

"That and more. He keeps them out of the hands of the *coyotes*, who would take everything from them. He keeps them from being caught by the Border Patrol, who would just send them back. He delivers them into the hands of people here who'll see to it that they arrive safely wherever it is that they're going for a new life. He truly is an angel."

Rainy asked, "What happened to him the day he called me?"

"He'd set up a rendezvous that night. The way it always worked was this: He would identify a crossing location along the border, somewhere away from the usual routes, and he would give it to me. I'd broadcast it during my show, work the longitude in with my chatter about the cuts I play."

I thought about the odd information I'd heard her give the night before when I listened to her program, the number of minutes and seconds in each selection. A longitude would be easy to embed in all that arcana.

"The people on the other side use that information and are there to meet Peter with the group he's going to lead," she said.

"He met the group that night?" Rainy asked.

"I don't know. I haven't heard from him."

"Do you have any idea what might have happened?"

"You need to talk to Old Turtle."

"Who's that?"

"I have no idea. When we communicate, we only use cover names now. It protects us all. To everyone else, I'm known as Nightingale."

"Why do we need to talk to Old Turtle?"

"Peter told me that if ever there was any trouble, he's the one to talk to."

"How do we get in touch with Old Turtle?" I asked.

"Send your telephone number to this email address." She wrote it down on a slip of paper and passed it to me.

"Telephone number, that's all?"

"That's all. Old Turtle will contact you."

"When?"

"I don't know. I've never tried it before."

"Do you know where Peter lives?"

"When he left Cadiz, he didn't tell anyone where he was going. But whenever we've met, I've always had the sense that he's come from somewhere south."

"Sulfur Springs?"

"I doubt that. The town's a hotbed for White Horse. But maybe in the area."

"Are you in any danger?" Rainy asked.

"Only if they grab Peter and he talks. Or,"

126

she said, giving us a dark look, "if they grab you."

CHAPTER 10

It was only noon and already so much had happened that day. We drove back to the parsonage in Cadiz and sat at the table in the little kitchen. Rainy pulled out the photograph of Peter with Arweiler Bosch.

"Still atoning?" she asked.

Although she wasn't really addressing me, I answered, "You believe he's doing the right thing, don't you?"

"Of course."

"Then does it matter why?"

She put the photograph back into her purse.

As soon as Nikki Edwards had left, I'd used my cell phone to send a message to the email address she'd given me. Before we parted ways, she'd also given me the co-ordinates she'd broadcast the night before Peter went missing, the coordinates of the spot where the border crossing would take place. I'd used my cell phone to locate the

128

place on a map. It was far to the west, as nearly as I could tell, in the middle of nowhere. I wasn't sure what more there was to do at the moment except wait.

We didn't have to wait long. Within ten minutes of our arrival, my cell phone rang.

"O'Connor here," I said.

"Mr. O'Connor, this is Albert Swanson. I'm a claims representative for Southwestern Mutual, the company that insured the automobile you rented. I wonder if we could meet to talk about that rental. The report I got is a little unusual."

"Someone blew the vehicle up, Mr. Swanson. That's all there is to it."

"This isn't quite like a normal accident report, Mr. O'Connor."

"I suppose not. But I arranged for full coverage. What's the problem?"

"There are details I need."

"Look — Albert, is it? I can't talk now."

"Mr. O'Connor —"

"Later," I said and ended the call.

Rainy gave me a questioning look.

"Insurance," I said.

The phone rang again immediately. I expected it to be Swanson, but it wasn't. The display read MUSTANG PROP.

"Mr. O'Connor, you don't know me, but I'd like very much to talk to you." It was a

129

woman's voice, not what I'd expected from someone who'd taken the code name Old Turtle.

"Who is this?"

"My name is Marian Brown. I'm mayor of Sulfur Springs. I heard about what happened this morning. I believe we need to talk."

"I'm listening."

"I'd prefer to do this in person. Can I meet you somewhere?"

"How about Sulfur Springs?"

"That would be fine. My office is on Main Street, a block south of Rosa's Cantina. Mustang Properties. How soon can you be here?"

"Half an hour."

"I'll be waiting."

"Who was that?" Rainy asked.

"The mayor of Sulfur Springs. She wants to see us."

"Maybe she knows Peter."

"Let's find out."

It was the nicest of the buildings on Main Street in Sulfur Springs, though still ancient. We'd seen it the day before, but hadn't paid much attention. When we pulled into town and parked, I looked up the street at Rosa's Cantina. The old-timer named Sylvester, who'd been drinking with the cop Sanchez the day before, sat on a rocker in front, watching us with great interest.

We stepped into the cool air of the office. A woman stood and came from behind her desk to greet us.

"Ms. Brown?"

"Call me Marian. You must be Cork. And that would make you Rainy."

Marian Brown looked old enough to have been retired many years, but there was nothing retiring about the mayor of Sulfur Springs. Her hair was red, her eyes dark and sharp. Her face was tanned leather, and from the moment I laid eyes on her, I thought she seemed well suited to the desert, where everything protected itself with thorns. She was decked out in jewelry. Not the silver and turquoise I'd always associated with the Southwest. It was all diamonds and gold. We shook hands around and she invited us to sit in the chairs where, I imagined, her clients sat.

"You're the mayor here?" Rainy said.

"For twenty years. Before that, it was my father. Before him, his father. My family goes way back in the Southwest. We've fought Apaches and Pimas and Pancho Villa."

"Is the fighting over?" I asked.

"Between politics, economics, and the

131

weather, is the fight ever over anywhere? So." She folded her hands on her desk as a schoolteacher might have. "That car bomb wasn't about the weather. Maybe a little about politics. But most probably, I think, it was about economics. By now, the name Carlos Rodriguez is familiar to you."

"We know it."

"Did you know it before you came to Coronado County?"

"No."

"Rodriguez. Las Calaveras. Sinaloa. Los Zetas. The Knights Templar. Cartels whose billion-dollar business is to shove drugs and poor people up the ass of this country." She leveled a long, hard look on Rainy. "What is it about your son that makes Carlos Rodriguez want you dead?"

"You know about my son?"

"I know you've been asking about him all over Coronado County. He seems to be missing, yes? No sooner do you arrive to look for him than you almost get yourselves blown to smithereens. So I'm guessing that bomb wasn't really because of you but because of your son. Around here, the only people who blow up other people are the Rodriguezes. The question becomes, then, why do they want you dead? And now we're back to your son."

"If it was Carlos Rodriguez or one of his family, I have no idea why they tried to kill us," Rainy replied. "I don't know what my son might have to do with that. I only want to find him and make sure he's all right."

The mayor of Sulfur Springs studied my wife, and I was pretty sure she wasn't convinced. "What brought you here?"

"Peter called me. He said he was in trouble."

"What kind of trouble?"

"He didn't say."

"I've heard that your son has struggled with drug addiction."

"He's clean now."

"But he probably knows the people around here who deal."

"He came for treatment at the Goodman Center. Before that, he was in Tucson. A student there. And before that, he was a Marine. I don't know why he'd have any information about drug dealers here."

"The people who get treatment at Goodman are usually wealthy, or their families are. Are you wealthy?"

"What's your point?" I asked.

"Just trying to get the lay of the land, Cork. I'd like to understand all the elements at work here."

"What's your interest in Rainy's son?"

133

"I'd like to help you find him."

"Out of the goodness of your heart?"

"We lost one of our citizens to a car bomb a few months back. I'm sure he was killed by the same people who targeted you. The Rodriguezes."

"We heard that citizen of yours was involved in White Horse," I said.

"I can't say one way or the other about that."

"Why did the Rodriguezes want him dead?"

"Maybe for the same reason they seem to want you dead. And that's what I'd like to know. The why of it."

"Because you're mayor of Sulfur Springs and you worry about your constituents?"

"What happens in Sulfur Springs, in all of Coronado County, is my business. When I spit, I hit Mexico. If the cartel wanted to decimate this town, they could do it in a heartbeat. What's to stop them? That fence?"

"So it's up to you? And maybe White Horse?"

"I've got nothing to do with White Horse. I don't know anyone who does. But I do hear things, so I might be able to help you find your son."

"How?" Rainy asked.

"I'll put the word out to watch for him, or for any sign of him."

"Sheriff Carlson said he'd do the same thing," I told her. "And your Officer Sanchez."

"Nobody who knows anything talks to anyone associated with legal authority here. God alone knows who's in the pockets of the cartels."

"So you're the one we should trust?" I said.

"Best to trust no one. But if you want to be sure you're not whispering into the ear of the cartel, I'm the one to talk to. You have my number. And you know how to find me now."

We stood to leave.

"Tell me something, Marian," I said. "Do you sell a lot of real estate in Coronado County?"

"It's not a bad place if you want to get away from the rat race."

"And if you don't mind getting poor people shoved up your ass?"

Which didn't seem to faze her at all. She smiled and said, "Good day."

On the street outside, Rainy said, "Another someone who says trust no one but me."

"A familiar refrain in this county. Hungry?"

"Breakfast was a long time ago. I suppose we should eat."

We walked up the street to Rosa's Cantina. The rocking chair in front was empty now. When we stepped inside, the place seemed empty, too.

"Anybody home?" I called.

The young woman who'd served us the day before came from the kitchen, and her surprise at seeing us was obvious.

"Can we get a bite to eat?" I asked.

"No problem. Have a seat. Something to drink?"

"I'll have a Tecate."

"Iced tea," Rainy said. "If you have some."

"Be right back."

We sat and she brought our drinks.

"Kind of surprised to see you folks. Most people who aren't local stumble in here once and I never see them again."

"We didn't exactly stumble," I said.

"Menus?"

"I'll have the same thing I had yesterday."

"That'd be the enchilada stack." She glanced at Rainy. "Smothered burrito again?"

"Why not?" Rainy said. "You have a good memory."

136

"About food and drink anyway." She vanished into the kitchen.

When we were alone, Rainy said, "This town gives me the creeps."

"This whole county gives me the creeps. It's just like everyone keeps saying, a war zone. But the casualties are kept out of sight."

Rainy stared out the window at the empty street. "Maybe like Agent Sprangers said, they're dead in the desert and good luck finding them."

"That's not Peter," I said.

She took my hand. "That's not Peter."

When the food came, our waitress said, "What brings you folks back to our lovely little burg?"

"We just met with your mayor," I said.

"Marian? Real piece of work, that one. Notice her jewelry? When she dies, I'm betting she'll be buried with all of it. That and her Lexus. Pretty much owns Sulfur Springs. A lot of ranch country around here, too. And some old mine holdings. Her family goes way back."

"So she told us. What about you?" I asked.

"When I'm not minding the bar, I take photographs. I like to think of myself as an artist. I've got some pieces showing in a gallery up in Tucson."

Rainy said, "Do you mind if I ask you something?"

"Nothing to hide. Go right ahead."

"You're Hispanic?"

"Mexican on my mother's side. From Chihuahua. My father's Italian."

"How is it in Coronado County for someone with Mexican blood?"

"The more Mexican you look, or Indian for that matter, the harder it is." She gave Rainy a frank look. "Native?"

"Yes."

"Have you been stopped yet? By Border Patrol or cops?"

"Yes," Rainy said.

"But you were with him, right?" She nodded at me. "So I'm guessing it wasn't so bad."

"They can't stop everyone who looks Hispanic."

"They can try. There are things you do and don't do in Coronado County if you look like us. Learn what they are and you're fine. You just blend in then."

"How is it here in Sulfur Springs?" I asked.

"Sulfur Creek divides this town. Have you been south of the creek yet?"

"No."

"Go south of the creek. You'll see."

"What will we find?"

"The maids, the cooks, the service people for Cadiz, the hired hands for the ranches and the vineyards. People doing the jobs white folks don't want to do for the pay that's being offered. It's a nice little community south of the creek. The housing's not so great maybe, but it's affordable. You'll hear Spanish more than English. And good luck ever catching Britney Spears coming out of a boom box. Folks north of Sulfur Creek call it Gallina Town."

"*Gallina?* Chicken Town?" Rainy said.

"If you go, you'll see why." She smiled at me. "Don't worry that you're the only white faces there. Being white south of Sulfur Creek is a whole lot safer than being Mexican north of the border."

"What about White Horse?" I asked. "Do they cause any trouble here?"

The change in her demeanor was almost imperceptible. "I don't know anything about them."

"How about the Rodriguezes?"

"Lots of Rodriguezes in southern Arizona. You folks enjoy your food."

It was midafternoon when we finished our meal and walked out of Rosa's Cantina. The thermometer hanging on the wall of the post office read ninety-nine degrees. We strolled the street, sweat trickling down my temples like the crawl of flies. I thought about home, about how, when a summer day got too warm, you could just dive into a clear, clean, cool lake, and it was all better. We crossed a narrow bridge in the shade of cottonwoods, and were south of Sulfur Creek. Gallina Town. The main street was paved, but those that cut off from it right and left were all gravel or dirt. The houses along them were small and shabby looking, some built of adobe but more prefabs. A number of mobile homes were set among them, mounted on cinder blocks, and dogs peered out at us from the shadows under them, too tired or hot or disinterested to move as we passed. The reason for the name was clear. The only signs of life were the chickens and the colorful roosters that strutted and scratched in the yards and roamed freely in the dirt streets.

We passed a little taqueria with an old Coca-Cola sign hanging out front. From inside came the muffled sound of music.

"Mariachi?" I said.

Rainy laughed. "White North Americans think it's all mariachi. That's norteño. Hear the polka beat?"

From behind a shade-covered window

came the high laughter of children, and from a distance, insect-like, the buzz of a small gas engine.

"This is the El Dorado so many people risk their lives for?" I said.

"They keep going, Cork, to Tucson or Phoenix or L.A. or Chicago. But bleak as this seems to you, it's better than what so many of the refugees are leaving behind."

We returned to the pickup, but before we got in, Rainy's cell phone rang. She glanced at the display.

"I have to take this." She walked away.

Across the street at Rosa's Cantina, the young waitress stood in the shade of the porch awning, fanning herself with a menu. I walked over to her.

"Took the grand tour of Gallina Town?" she said.

"Pretty quiet place. Didn't see anyone, not even children."

"They're around. Their parents are off working, so they're staying with their *abuelas* or their *tías*. Hottest part of the day now. They're inside, probably napping. Siestas aren't just a quaint joke out here. Me, I could use one about now." She looked south across Sulfur Creek. "You come back in the evening, it's different. People are outside, visiting with each other, catching

141

up. They'll gather in the street in front of the taqueria, play dominoes, music, maybe even dance a little."

"Sounds like a good place."

"People with money, they think wealth is happiness."

"You don't?"

She laughed. "I'm an artist. If I believed that, I'd really be screwed."

"If undocumented immigrants came knocking at a door south of Sulfur Creek, would it be opened to them?"

"Depends on the door. Like everywhere else, there are people whose hearts are great and others, well, not so much." She saw something behind me and her face changed. "Back to work. See you around."

I turned and watched the town's police car pull up beside the pickup. Rainy put away her cell phone and walked to meet the cop when he got out. I headed that way, too.

"Afternoon, Officer Sanchez," I said.

He wore sunglasses and a brimmed hat. He leaned against his cruiser and folded his arms across his chest. "Heard about what happened this morning. Surprised to see you're still around. Still looking for that son of yours?"

"Still looking," Rainy said.

"In Gallina Town?"

I hadn't seen him there, but somehow he knew.

"Just sightseeing," I said.

"You folks sure must've pissed somebody off."

"Maybe somebody named Rodriguez?" I said.

"If that's the case and I was you, I'd skedaddle just as fast as I could."

"You told us yesterday that you'd ask around about Peter," Rainy said.

"True to my word, ma'am. *Nada*. Nobody here knows that name. Sorry."

"You have any problem with White Horse in Sulfur Springs?" I asked.

He removed his sunglasses and wiped sweat from his forehead. "I know about White Horse, sure, but I can't say they've caused any trouble here."

"Maybe they don't cause it, but maybe they bring it. As in a car bomb."

"You heard about that, did you? Then maybe you heard the sheriff's people still don't have a clue what that was about."

"We heard it was about the Rodriguez family and White Horse."

"I'm betting you didn't hear that officially."

"What's your official line?"

143

He shrugged. "Shit happens. Will we be seeing more of you folks around here?"

"We like the food at Rosa's Cantina, so maybe," I said.

"Try the chiles rellenos. To die for." He tipped his hat and put his sunglasses back on. "You folks take care." He left us and headed toward the cantina.

I reached for the handle on the pickup door, and it was like touching a branding iron.

"You learn to be careful," Rainy said. "And to park in shade whenever you can."

I cranked the air conditioner as soon as we were in the truck, but it took a while for the heat to drop below broil. I started out of Sulfur Springs.

"Who called?"

"A friend," she said. "Wondering how things were going."

"I know this friend?"

"No."

I waited, got nothing more.

Then my cell phone rang.

"You left your number," the voice on the other end of the line said.

"Old Turtle?"

"Who is this?"

"My name's Cork O'Connor."

A long pause followed, then: "I can't talk

144

now. I'll call you again later."

"When?"

"Later." And he hung up.

"Old Turtle?"

"Yep."

"What did he say?"

"He said he'd call again later. But I think we'll talk to him before that."

She gave me a questioning look.

"I recognized his voice," I said. "Old Turtle also goes by another name that's not really his own. When we met him yesterday, he told us to call him Jocko."

CHAPTER 11

We took the same road we'd driven the day before to the Sonora Hills Cellars. Outside Sulfur Springs, we passed the barren flat where the trailer homes of Paradiso baked under the sun. The Border Patrol didn't stop us this time. In fact, we saw no sign of them or any other animals, human or otherwise. The only movement was the shimmer of the land all around us as waves of heat rose up. We were both quiet. I didn't know what Rainy was thinking. Me, I was chewing like crazy on the question of her mysterious phone calls.

Trust. An easy word to say. One syllable. Comes readily off the tongue. Also a thing easy to believe in, to advocate for, to hold in lofty regard. But putting it into practice? Good luck with that one. You share your life, your body, your dreams with another human being. You tie your fortunes together with sacred vows. But the truth is that you

146

always keep some deep part of yourself separate from all that. You hold a place inside that's only for you and that you never let anyone else into. Hell, after she died, we found out even Mother Teresa had secrets too dark to share.

That's where I was, driving through the desolation on Old Douglas Road.

"Cork," Rainy finally said.

"I'm right here."

"Do you trust me?"

Like she'd been reading my mind. Or with Rainy, more likely my heart.

"You asked me that same damn question this morning. You're not making it easy for me, Rainy, but the answer is still yes."

She was quiet, her eyes to the south. "There are things I can't share with you, not yet. Other people are involved. It's terribly complicated. And I can't imagine that it has anything to do with Peter's disappearance. I know what's going on is dangerous for us, but this is about my son and keeping him safe. When I can, I'll tell you everything, I promise."

"Could I be dead before that happens?"

She looked at me, her eyes serious and beautiful. "God, I hope not. Because wherever you are, there I am also."

We turned onto the lane that cut through

the vineyards, under the stone arch, and pulled up to the warehouse, with its great stainless-steel vats. The door was closed. No motorcycle, and the F-150 pickup was gone. We got out and walked to the house. The bell, when I rang it, gave out three deep, sonorous chimes. It was almost a full minute before Jayne Harris opened the door, clearly surprised to see us but smiling.

"We don't mean to bother you, Jayne. We're looking for Jocko."

"He and Frank are checking the new plantings in the south vineyard," she said.

"Still expanding?" I asked.

"Diversifying. Adding new resistant varieties."

"Resistant to what? This heat?"

"Would you like to come inside?"

"Thank you," Rainy said.

It was blessedly cool in the house and just as quiet as the first time we'd visited.

"May I offer you something to drink?" Jayne asked.

I shook my head. "No, thanks."

"If you have a moment, let me explain a few things," Jayne said. She indicated the living room, and we all sat down. "To answer your question, Cork, the heat isn't the problem. A few years ago we lost a major part of our vineyard to GLD. That's short for grapevine leafroll disease. A lot of the vineyards in the area suffered. Since then, we've been working with more resistant varieties. It's slow going. Vines take quite a while to produce. This new variety seems to be doing well, but we monitor everything closely. Or Frank does. That's his territory of concern. He's the wine guy."

"And you're all about the business," I said.

"It's what I do," she said. "I'm a Minnesota girl, Cork. I met Frank ten years ago at a conference in Minneapolis. I was there offering advice to small business people on planned growth. Frank was a widower, I was divorced, we hit it off. His family had been in cattle here, but raising beef profitably is tough, and Frank wanted to do something different with the land."

"The vineyards," Rainy said.

"They call this area Napa-zona. The soil here on the plateau is similar to the area around Burgundy, France, and the micro-climate is Mediterranean. It's perfect grape country."

"So this is home now," I said.

She smiled. "For better or for worse, isn't that how the vow goes?"

I heard it as resignation, and I understood. I've always believed that if Minnesota is in

149

your blood, it's hard to be completely happy anywhere else.

Rainy said, "Would it be difficult for us to find Frank and Jocko?"

"Not at all. Just go back to the main road and head south. You'll come to a little dirt lane that runs along the edge of that section of our vineyards. Can't miss it. We planted a row of yews. You ought to see Frank's pickup from there. But I can call his cell phone and have him and Jocko meet you here."

"That's all right. We'll find them and let you get back to your business."

"You wouldn't believe the paperwork," she said and stood to see us out.

We returned to the main road and headed south. At the end of the vineyards, we found the line of yew trees marching toward the hills and the dirt lane that ran alongside them. We saw no sign of Frank's pickup. We stepped out of the truck and stood in the silence of that landscape, the deep green rows of vines on one side of the yews, the pale green-yellow of the grasslands on the other.

"What now?" Rainy asked.

A hot wind blew up from the direction of the border, and carried on it was a peculiar sound.

"Listen," I said.

Rainy cocked her head, then pointed. "There." A black shape cut low across the sky. At that distance, it appeared no larger than one of the vultures we'd seen circling earlier in the day. "A biplane."

We found the landing strip cut into grass-land near a gathering of cottonwood trees in whose shade stood a little ranch house and a couple of outbuildings. The biplane sat at the end of the strip in front of a small hangar. Frank Harris's pickup was there, too. As we drove up, Harris and Robert Wie-man, the man who called himself Jocko, turned and watched us come.

"Well, this is a surprise," Frank said amiably.

"Spotted Jocko's biplane," I said. "I thought you gave up crop dusting."

"I still fly. Just not for money," Jocko said. "Something we can do for you folks?"

"We'd like to talk with you. It's important."

The old man studied my face, then Rainy's, then glanced at Harris.

Harris shrugged, gave a nod, and said, "Looks like they made you, Old Turtle."

We sat at the kitchen table in the cool of the ranch house. Jocko had poured us

151

lemonade, cold from the refrigerator and colder still with ice.

"My father and Frank's grandfather, Gus Harris, were prospecting partners," Jocko explained. "Back when they were young bucks and this was all still pretty wild country. They did a little wildcat mining together, up there in the Sonora Hills. Never got enough ore out of it to get real rich, but Frank's grandfather used his share to buy land around here and started running cattle. My father kept prospecting, never got anywhere. When he married my mother and needed regular money, he hired on with Frank's grandfather. When Gus died, he left my father this section of land so that he could start his own spread. We did okay, but it was a brutal life, hard on us all. My father wanted me to run cattle with him, but at the county fair when I was twelve, I took a flight in a biplane and from that moment on my heart was always in the sky. When we went to war in Korea, I enlisted in the air force, and that was that. After I retired from flying for employment, I came back home. Too old to run cattle, so I went to work for the Harrises, just like my father had."

"You're both Desert Angels?" Rainy asked.

"Old Turtle," Frank said nodding toward

Jocko. "Me, I'm Armadillo. How'd you get the contact email?"

"Nightingale."

It was clear that neither of them could connect the name to a person. Peter's plan.

"So you know all about Los Angeles del Desierto?" Harris said.

"Not all, but enough," Rainy replied. "Is Jayne a Desert Angel, too?"

"For Jayne, putting out water and food is one thing. Helping guide these people through the desert is something else altogether. She knows that Jocko and I are involved, but she doesn't approve. For my part, mostly what I do is give Peter a modest income working for me and give him a lot of time off to do what needs to be done. Small stuff in the grand scheme. I don't think there's a lot of risk involved in any of that, but it makes Jayne nervous." He gave a little, disappointed sigh. "The only risk that interests her is the business kind."

"When we spoke yesterday, you knew Peter was in trouble," Rainy said.

"Not for sure. And I certainly didn't want to say anything that might put you two in danger."

"Moot point now," I said. "Do you know anything about what's happened to him?"

Harris looked to his companion. "You

want to take this one, Jocko?"

The old man put down his lemonade. "You know that Peter is what the refugees call a *guía*?"

"A guide," Rainy said. "Like a *coyote*?"

"Not a *coyote*." The word was clearly distasteful to him. "He takes nothing and he cares about the people he leads through the desert. He brings them across in many different places. Those places are often at a distance. I fly him there, he leads his people to safety, I fly him back."

"Safety?" I said.

"Sometimes to others waiting with vehicles. Sometimes to a safe location, out of the sun and the heat, until arrangements can be made."

"What kind of safe location?"

Jocko shrugged. "Peter's always secretive. In case of a leak. The less any of us know, the better."

"But there was a leak," Rainy said. "Somehow the Rodriguez family knew."

"That's what it looks like."

"We know Peter had a rendezvous set up two nights ago," I said. "Did you fly him there, Jocko?"

The old man nodded. "We had a prearranged pickup time yesterday. When he didn't show, I knew something was wrong."

Harris said, "Then you two pop up asking about him and the Rodriguez family. It wasn't hard to put two and two together."

"We just saw you come in for a landing, Jocko. Where were you?"

"Flew over the area where I dropped Peter. Been at it the last two days, looking for whatever. So far nothing."

"Could you fly us there?"

"I've got a single-passenger biplane. I can fly only one of you."

"Today?"

"Got to fuel up first."

"Okay if I go, Rainy?" I said.

"I'm heading home. You can come with me and wait there," Harris offered her.

"I'd rather wait here," Rainy said. "If it's all right with Jocko."

"*Mi casa es su casa*," the old man said with a grin.

"You men be careful out there," Harris said. "There are a lot of names for that desert. The one that covers it all is an old one. The earliest inhabitants called it simply Desolation."

CHAPTER 12

I've been in small planes before, and choppers, but Jocko's biplane was something else. He'd given me goggles, which helped, because in the open passenger cockpit the wind smacked me around a lot. Jocko had given me headphones so that we could communicate, but between the roar of the engine and the rush of the wind, I couldn't hear very well. We were bounced by sudden currents, and I felt like the ball in a circus act of trained seals. Jocko flew west into the sun and south of the Coronados. I saw Sulfur Springs below us, green tendrils against a canvas that was mostly dirty yellow. Not far away was Paradiso, the trailers like Legos in a sandbox. We dropped low and followed the southern edge of yet another mountain range whose name I didn't know. Then came desert. Real desert. Mesquite and barrel cactus and jumping cholla and saguaro and prickly pear and pipe organ. Most of these things, I knew, were covered with long thorns or short prickles or little hairs whose barbed ends, though delicate, could still drive you crazy trying to get them out of your skin. They gave no shade, no sense of comfort. Nowhere on the hardpan of that desert was there anything that might offer relief from the baking sun. I understood the ancient name for the place: Desolation.

More than an hour after we'd taken off, Jocko circled a landing strip in the middle of nowhere. He touched down, we rolled to a stop, and climbed out.

"What is this?" I asked.

"Got me. This here's Tohono O'odham land. Some kind of old military training strip, maybe. Peter found it. He uses it as a drop-off and pickup point when he's leading groups up from the border near Sasabe. Border Patrol knows about it, so I just drop him and take off quick. Maybe he keeps a Jeep out here or has arranged for transport, I don't know. Could be he just walks."

I turned in a full circle. Like everywhere else in that part of Arizona, there were mountains in almost every direction, hard walls that rimmed the horizons.

"You go far enough north from here, you hit Eighty-Six between Sells and Three

Points. It's plenty walkable, especially if you've got someone who knows what they're doing, knows how to keep the sign cutters from finding their tracks."

"Sign cutters? The Border Patrol, you mean?"

"Exactly. They're damn good at what they do, and what they do is find people who cross that border illegally. But Peter's every bit as good at erasing his trail as they are at cutting sign."

"So that's the only way, walking north?"

"You could also head east, beyond the Santa Margaritas toward Arivaca. Go far enough and you hit I-Nineteen. It's pretty much impossible if you don't know what you're doing, but that wasn't Peter. I don't know if he walked his groups to one of the highways, or crossed the mountains, or if there was a rendezvous point where other Desert Angels were waiting with vehicles. Or maybe he used a safe place somewhere as a kind of way station. He didn't let us in on that part of the operation."

"You dropped him here two days ago?"

"A couple of hours before sunset. Then I flew back."

"How did you know when to return to pick him up?"

"This time it was preset. I was supposed

to be here at noon yesterday. I showed up, Peter didn't. I flew the whole area, a criss-cross pattern. Couldn't see a thing. I went back to my place and took my motorcycle up to the winery to talk to Frank about it. That's when you folks showed up."

"You don't know where along the border he was going to meet his group?"

"Only the general area, and I spent a good deal of today flying that. The truth is, finding a body out here, especially when you don't really know where to look, well, good luck with that one, mister."

"I've got the coordinates for the spot where the rendezvous was supposed to take place."

I could see his surprise. Clearly, he had no idea of Nikki Edwards's part in all this. Peter's wisdom. He took a map from the biplane, laid it on the wing, and found the location.

"How far from here?" I asked.

"No more than an hour's walk."

"You said good luck finding a body. You think Peter's dead?"

"I hope not. But out here, the way things are, it's best to steel yourself."

"When the pickup wasn't preset, how did he communicate?"

"Called Old Turtle's phone."

"Used a cell phone?"

"Coverage is pretty hit and miss out here. Probably a satellite phone."

"What if he didn't?"

"He'd have to be someplace where he could get a signal. Best bet would be east. The Santa Margaritas." He nodded toward a wall of mountains in that direction.

"You know that range?"

"Not well."

"Who does?"

"The Border Patrol. Also some of the old prospectors, I imagine. That area was part of the Oro Rico Mining District. Some big operations there in the day. All closed down now, I believe. And Oro Rico itself is just a ghost town."

"Have you flown over the area?"

"Not yet."

"Could we do that?"

"Not today. Need to get back before the light's gone."

"Tomorrow?"

He looked toward the Santa Margaritas. Since we'd departed Coronado County, the sun had dropped low in the sky. The heat was unchanged, the desert still an oven, and the mountains to the east were a blazing wall of red-orange fire against the hard, blue sky.

"Why not?" He looked at me wistfully and gave a little shrug. "But who knows? Maybe we'll hear something before then."

We took off and flew over the rendezvous point. The border fence there was nothing but strung wire. We stayed low enough that we could scan the desert for any sign of Peter or the people he'd arranged to lead to safety, but like Jocko had said, spotting an unmoving body in that broad expanse would be next to impossible. I had to fight hard against the sense that all this was useless.

We flew south of the Coronados and came up over the high grassland to Jocko's little spread and landing strip. I'd thought Rainy would rush out, hoping for news, but no one met us when we climbed down from the biplane. We walked to the ranch house. It was empty. The pickup truck Michelle had loaned us was still parked in front, but Harris's F-150 was gone.

"She probably took Frank up on his offer and went back to the winery with him," Jocko suggested. "Let me give him a call." He used his landline. "Frank, it's me. You at the winery? Is that little lady Rainy there, too?" He shook his head. "No, she's not. Thought maybe she'd gone with you." He listened and said, "When we know, we'll let you know." He hung up and looked at me as if I'd asked a question to which he had no answer.

I pulled out my cell phone and saw that I had plenty of bars. "Let me try calling her."

I punched in her number. A few moments later it began to ring. Outside the ranch house, I heard the notes of "Natural Woman" playing. Rainy's ringtone. I headed out the door, but the call went to voice mail. The sun had dropped below the Coronados, and I stood with Jocko in the blue twilight and called again. The song played from somewhere in the tall grass that grew beyond the cottonwoods sheltering the house. I followed the sound but didn't nail its location before my call went to voice mail again. I tried once more. The ringtone came from an area just ahead of me, where the grass was crushed and matted in the way I sometimes found in the foliage of the Northwoods where deer had bedded down for the night. The pale green-yellow of the standing grass was splashed with a darker, rust color. But I knew it wasn't rust.

"Jesus," Jocko said quietly at my back.

I'd been in this place before, losing someone I loved deeply. The phone sang to me, but for a moment, I couldn't make my legs move. Then Rainy's voice came on the line, brightly telling me to leave a message, and I walked forward.

Her phone lay in the center of the bloody, matted-down grass. Rainy wasn't there.

CHAPTER 13

"What were you doing in Mr. Wieman's
biplane?" Sheriff Carlson asked.

"Sightseeing," I said.

Carlson looked at Jocko. "Sightseeing
where, Mr. Wieman?"

It was heading toward dark. The sheriff's
people were still going over Jocko's property,
the bloody matting of grass, mostly with the
aid of flashlights now, moving along the
perimeter they'd established for their search.
I'd already checked the area thoroughly and
had found nothing, no sign of Rainy.

We'd been grilled by a couple of investiga-
tors, including Deputy Crockett, who'd
been part of the investigation of the bombing that morning. Now the sheriff was going over the same territory, probably trying
to get the lay of the land for himself and
maybe looking for holes in our story.

"Like I already told your deputies, I flew
Cork over the Coronados, the San Gabriel

164

Valley, showed him a bit of the desert."

"What time did you take off?"

"A little before five."

"And you came back when?"

"Bout eight-thirty."

Carlson looked back at me. "She was here when you left?"

"She was here when we left."

"And when you came back, that cell phone was all you found?"

"Yes."

"Did she try to contact you while you were gone?"

"I was out of service range, and she didn't leave me any messages."

"I understand someone was here with her when you left."

"Frank Harris, but he was going to head home after Jocko and I took off."

The sheriff looked back at the pickup on loan from the minister. "Where'd you get the wheels?"

"A friend."

"I thought you'd never been to Coronado County before, Mr. O'Connor."

"I make friends easily."

"Know your wife's blood type?"

"I don't."

"Can you find out?"

"I can."

He nodded. "We've already got a sample from what's splashed all over the grass. We'll get it typed ASAP. We'll be keeping your wife's cell phone."

I knew they'd do this. So while Jocko was making the 911 call from the ranch house, I'd taken a moment to delete the frantic, garbled message Peter had left his mother in which it sounded as if he might be confessing to killing someone named Rodriguez.

Deputy Crockett came from the search area. His features and colorful hatband continued to make me suspect some Native blood ran in his veins.

"What do you think, Crockett?" the sheriff asked.

"From the blood spatter, looks like the shot came from somewhere over there." Crockett pointed toward the main road. "Probably used a high-powered rifle and scope."

"The body?"

"It wasn't dragged away. From the signs we could find in the grass, looks like somebody carried it off."

"Why take the body?" Carlson said.

"I can't answer that yet." Deputy Crockett looked at me as if he believed I might be able to field that one.

"Who knew you were here?" Carlson asked.

"Frank and Jayne Harris," I said. "Nobody else."

"I've got someone talking to the Harrises right now."

Stars salted the inky blue above us. Beyond the Coronados, the sky was still hazy with a faint lemon glow. Under the cottonwoods, the long fingers of the flashlight beams continued their probing. And I worked very hard at not letting myself believe that Rainy was gone.

When they'd done all they could do for the moment, the sheriff's people climbed into their vehicles and headed back to Cadiz.

Before he left, Carlson said, "Where are you staying, Mr. O'Connor?"

"The old parsonage of the Methodist church in town."

"Grace Church?"

"That's right."

He glanced at the pickup I'd been driving. "Michelle Abbott wouldn't happen to be the friend you mentioned?"

Considering all that had happened, I was reluctant to bring the minister into this any more than I had to. But the evidence was there, all half ton of it.

167

"Christian charity," I said.

His face changed. It didn't soften, but something different seemed to shape his features, something that ran deeper than a concern just for law enforcement. I understood that he was a man who cared about those he was trying to protect and serve. "These people, Mr. O'Connor, they kill anything that smells remotely unpleasant to them."

"These people? They have names?"

"I'd say they all go under the same name. Narco scum." He eyed Jocko. "If I was you, old-timer, I'd make a shotgun my bedmate for a while. I'll be in touch, Mr. O'Connor." He put a finger to his Stetson in a parting salute, started to walk away, but stopped and turned back. "It's pretty clear to me, O'Connor, and it should be to you, that in the bombing this morning your wife was the target and her son was the reason. You? You would just have been collateral damage. If it was me and I really didn't know the whole story here, I'd be asking myself why." He eyed me, but if he expected a reply, he didn't get one. "I'm sure we'll want to talk to you some more. Not planning on leaving Coronado County, are you?"

"Not without my wife."

"Of course," he said. Then more gently

168

and with a note of real sympathy, "Of course."

When we were finally alone, I said to Jocko, "Maybe it's best you find someplace not so isolated to sleep tonight."

"I'm already in spitting distance of my heavenly reward, Cork. I'll be fine here. What about you?"

"I'm going to talk to Frank and Jayne, then head back to the parsonage."

"Who knows what might be waiting for you there? Hang on a second." Jocko went into the ranch house and came back with a rifle and a box of cartridges. "I've had this Winchester since I was sixteen. I call her Lena. Named after my dog, truest-hearted animal ever lived. She might help you get through the night with a little less worry."

Although I'd been a hunter all my life, it had been a long time since I'd carried a firearm as a weapon of defense. That was a part of my life I'd been trying to put behind me. But I was in a war now, in an alien land, and the feel of the Winchester in my hands was satisfying.

"Cork, I got no words to make any of this easier, except that after more than four score years on this earth, the one thing I've found worth believing in is hope."

"Thanks, Jocko. You take care of yourself."

"You find out anything, you'll let me know?"

"That's a promise."

I drove away, leaving Jocko alone. By the time I hit the main road, the lights of his ranch house were little more than fireflies in the night.

Halfway to the Sonora Hills Cellars, I pulled the truck to the side of the road and got out. The moon wasn't up yet, and even if it had been, the only thing visible would have been a sliver offering no illumination at all. The stars, there were billions of those, more than I'd ever seen in the sky above Minnesota. The dryness of the air, I figured. The dark outline of the Coronado Mountains stood black against the faintest blue along the western horizon, which was mostly the memory of light. All around me was silence, absolute and oppressive.

You hold it off as long as you can, and then it hits you. The crushing weight of history.

I slammed my fist on the hood of the pickup.

"Goddamn it!" I howled. "This will not happen again. I will not lose Rainy."

I wanted to hold to the hope that Jocko

170

had advised, which was exactly the advice I knew Henry Meloux would have given me, but strength failed me. Even my body failed me. My knees buckled and I slid to the ground and sat in the dust and gravel on the shoulder at the edge of the road and gave in to despair. How could hope stand against the evidence, all that blood and Rainy's abandoned cell phone? I knew Sheriff Carlson was right. If I'd been killed that morning, it would have been because of my proximity to Rainy. Whatever the truth she'd been hiding from me, it was a lethal one. Maybe she'd been trying to protect me. Or maybe she simply didn't love me enough to trust me. Didn't matter now. Nothing mattered.

When you begin to wallow in self-pity, you have two choices. You slide into it like you would quicksand and drown. Or you pull yourself out.

Me, I had help that night. Headlights on the road. They came from the north. I stood up and thought about the Winchester Jocko had given me. I didn't know if there were cartridges already in it. If not, I knew I wouldn't have time to load any before whoever was coming was on me. I simply waited. Still as a man wrapped up in barbed wire.

The vehicle slowed as it approached. The headlights kept me blind. I'd be a liar if I didn't admit that my heart had crawled away from my chest and taken up lodging in my throat, which was as dry as the dust I stood in. The vehicle, a pickup, drew abreast of me, the headlights no longer glaring in my eyes, and I could see again. The driver's window slid down. A man who was probably my own age, wearing a red ball cap, studied me. In the backsplash of the headlights, I could see that his skin was shades darker than mine and the irises of his eyes were large, black seeds on white pillows.

"You okay, friend?" he asked.

"Fine, thanks."

"Just enjoying the night sky?"

"Something like that."

He peered up at the heavens. "Makes you believe in God, don't it? Lived here all my life and looking up at that sky never gets old. Also never ceases to make me feel small and humble and grateful all at the same time, know what I mean?"

I did. And I told him so.

"You're not from around here," he said.

I told him no.

"Just a heads-up, friend. Truck like yours stopped along a back road like this, well, it might be interpreted by a lot of folks as an invitation to a particular kind of trouble."

"You stopped."

He said something to me in a language I didn't understand, but from the tonal quality and cadence I figured was Native.

"What's it mean?" I asked.

"It's Apache. Roughly translated, it means "Though I walk through the valley of the shadow of death, I will fear no evil." He smiled. "Didn't mean to interrupt your reverie. Just wanted to offer a hand if you needed it. Have yourself a blessed night."

He drove on.

I got back into the pickup and returned to my journey.

Angels come in many forms.

CHAPTER 14

The Harrises' home was a blaze of lights in the great dome of night. Frank came out to meet me long before I reached his doorstep.

"Saw your headlights," he said. "Thought it might be you or Jocko. Cork, I'm so sorry."

A long shadow crossed the glare from the porch. I looked up and saw Jayne coming from the house. When she reached me, she threw her arms around me in a warm hug.

"Oh, Cork, I don't know what to say. How are you doing?"

"Holding up."

Around us, illuminated in the porch light, were a thousand winged creatures, darting or hovering. The desert might have looked dead by day, but by night, it was insect Grand Central.

"Come inside," Frank said, batting at something in front of his face. "We can talk there."

In the house, Jayne said, "Can I get you something cold to drink?"

"Nothing, thanks. The sheriff's people were here?"

"Just one deputy," Frank said.

"What did you tell him?"

"The truth. That a few minutes after you flew out, I came back home. Everything was fine when I left Jocko's. I worked on the winepress for a little while. I want to make sure we're ready to go for harvest. Then Jayne and I had dinner and settled down to watch a video. That's when the deputy came knocking on the door. He didn't give us a lot of details. What exactly happened, Cork? All we know is that Rainy has disappeared."

"She was gone when Jocko and I came back. All we found was blood and her cell phone."

Jayne closed her eyes, as if trying to block out the image, and put a hand to her mouth.

"Did you tell them why Jocko took me up?" I asked.

"Told them you wanted to get a better sense of the lay of the land."

"Good. Pretty much what we told them, too."

Jayne's eyes shot open, and she gave me and her husband a suspicious look. "But that wasn't the real reason you were up there?"

"Part of it," I said.

She hesitated, as if not sure she should ask what was next on her mind. "And the other part?"

Frank didn't jump in — his reluctance, I remembered, to bring his wife into the business of the Desert Angels — so I did. "It had to do with Peter."

She appeared to consider asking more, then must have decided against it.

"Whoever it was that took Rainy knew we were at Jocko's," I said. "Did either of you mention it to anyone?"

"I was glued to my computer," Jayne said. "I didn't even get any phone calls, which is unusual but always welcome. Lets me work uninterrupted."

Frank shook his head. "Except for Jayne, I haven't talked to anyone." He looked beyond me. "By the way, where is Jocko?"

"His ranch house. I told him staying there might not be safe, but he insisted."

"Stubborn old coot," Frank said.

"These people probably know that I've talked with you two. And they certainly know that you employed Peter. How secure is this house?"

"It's not just coyotes roam the hills at

176

night," Frank said. "We're pretty well bunkered here."

"Do you own a firearm?"

"This is Arizona," he said as answer.

"All right. If you hear anything or think of anything, let me know."

"Absolutely," Jayne said. Then offered, "Would you like to stay here tonight?"

"That's kind, but no thanks."

"You'll let us know if you find out anything?"

"Sure," I told her.

I left them together in the cool of their big house and drove down the lane to the main road. I killed the engine and stared back at the glow from the Sonora Hills Cellars. Against the hard, black night, which was the natural state of affairs in a moonless desert, it seemed a terrible and somehow menacing brilliance. About Rainy's disappearance, Frank and Jayne Harris claimed to be ignorant. But someone had let the bad guys know where Rainy was. I thought then about what everyone in Coronado County had been telling me from the beginning: Be careful who you talk to and even more careful who you trust.

Things were quiet when I rolled into Cadiz. I cruised down the main street. Only the bars were open, and judging from the vehicles parked in front, the business they were doing that night was just so-so. I drove past the church and the parsonage, keeping my eyes open for anything that might stand out on my radar. Both structures were dark and seemed no more threatening than empty pews. I drove down side streets, looking for someone who might have parked in walking distance. Or rifle range. Although I was satisfied that no one was waiting to ice me from the dark, I parked one street east and approached the parsonage from the rear. I unlocked the back door and went in. I didn't switch on lights but used the flashlight app on my cell phone to find my way around and drew all the shades. Only then did I turn on a lamp.

I hadn't eaten since Rosa's Cantina, but I wasn't hungry. Thirst was something else. I set the Winchester on the kitchen table and pulled ice from the refrigerator and a glass from the cupboard. I stood at the sink, taking a long, cold drink, and thinking.

If Rainy had been the target of the bomb that morning, I wasn't just collateral damage. The people who'd planted it were the kind of people who killed not only their targets but everyone connected with their targets. *Killed.* There I was, thinking that word again and trying my damnedest not to connect it to Rainy. Trying to hold to hope. Trying to walk through the valley without fear.

I remembered a poem Rainy had taught me. She called it a lovers' prayer and said it was from the Pueblo people.

Across the dark night, we are not afraid.
Our love is the star that guides us.
Through the empty desert, we do not thirst.
Our love is the water that refreshes.
On the long journey, we do not weary.
Our love is the truth that offers strength.
As the mountains rise before us, we are not
    discouraged.
Our love is the hope that waits on the other
    side.
When we are together, let us hold hands.
Our love is the promise that is never
    broken.

I lay down for the night with that prayer in my heart and the Winchester at my side.

I woke suddenly. The bedroom was in absolute darkness. I felt around on the mattress and touched the metal of the Winchester barrel, cooled by the breeze from the window air conditioner. I wrapped my hand around the rifle and slowly sat up.

I listened. Nothing. Still, I jacked a round into the chamber and slid from the bed. I had a good sense of the room, and I crept to the wall next to the door and pressed myself there.

The parsonage was silent.

There is something that happens to you when you have steeled yourself for violence. It's like an embrace. You want it. You want to do the violent thing so that it's done and you can let it go. That's what I wanted, standing by the door, waiting for whatever was coming.

Five minutes I stood there, barely breathing, and nothing came. But something had brought me out of my sleep. I finally eased myself through the doorway into the small living room. There were streetlights outside, not many but enough to cast a faint glow against the drawn shades. My eyes had long ago adjusted to the dark, and that glow was enough for me to see dimly but clearly. I carefully went through the parsonage, checking every corner, every closet. I finally accepted that I was alone.

If what had awakened me wasn't inside the parsonage, it had to have come from outside. The bark of a dog? A distant backfire? I tried to call up the dreamy memory of sound, but it was gone. I went to the back door, opened it slowly, just a crack. The hot night air came through the narrow gap. I opened the door a little more and risked poking my head into the heat. The backyard was dimly lit from the distant streetlamps and loosely outlined with paloverde trees and low desert shrubs. Nothing moved. If someone was there, they were more patient than I was. I slipped from the house and crouched low, the Winchester cradled and ready. I hadn't undressed before I lay down, except for my boots, so I stood sock-footed in the dirt of the yard. I began to make my way around the house, sliding along the wall, until I came to the front yard.

Inside the church across the street, I saw a light, of a sort. Not incandescent; it moved. A flashlight? No, not powerful enough. A candle, I decided. I studied the street, empty except for an old Buick parked in front of the little house next door. I darted to the parked car and studied the church for another minute. The candle had stopped moving but still burned. I crossed the street like a deer dodging headlights and pressed myself to the stone of the church wall, which was still warm from the day. I crept to the front door and listened. Voices, too soft to hear clearly. Pastor Michelle Abbott? I tried the knob, turned it ever so slowly, eased the door open.

The voices were clearer now. A male, angry. And a woman's voice. Wonderfully familiar.

I made my move and was inside the church, the Winchester stock cradled against my shoulder, the barrel pointed toward the altar rail, where Rainy stood holding the candle.

She turned, her eyes huge with surprise and fear.

The man behind her stepped forward. In the flickering candlelight, I saw that he held a big pistol in his raised hand.

"Wait!" Rainy shouted. "Don't shoot."

"Quién es?" the man demanded.

"Mi esposo," she said.

The hand holding the pistol didn't drop. I kept the sight of my Winchester on the stranger's chest.

"Who's that with you, Rainy?" I called.

"Cork," she began but faltered. She held her empty hand out to me as if begging.

"Who is he?"

I saw her body, which had been held so tense at my appearance, go limp. Her hand fell to her side. She glanced at the man beside her, then turned her dark eyes to me.

It was the man who answered for her.

"I'm her husband," he said.

182

I eyed the man who'd spoken for Rainy, feeling a great urge to pull the trigger of the Winchester, and not just because of the threatening gun in his hand.

He was tall, powerfully built, with a face so damn good-looking it could have been taken from a Hollywood movie poster. His hair in the candlelight was black and shiny, polished onyx. He wore a black T-shirt stretched across the kind of chest that would have made a weight lifter proud. His pants and running shoes were black as well, as was that pistol he still held trained on me.

"Husband?" I said.

"Ex-husband," Rainy clarified.

"In the eyes of the church, *mi amor,* we are married for eternity."

"What about Consuela?" Rainy said. "In the eyes of the church, wouldn't that make you a bigamist?"

He shrugged. "Solomon had hundreds of wives."

"Are you all right, Rainy?" I asked.

"Yes," she said. "You can put that rifle down."

In the candlelight, I studied the face of this man who was a stranger to me, but far from a stranger to Rainy. At the same time, he was studying me. At last he nodded, and I returned the gesture, and we both lowered our weapons.

"This is Gilbert Mondragón, Cork," Rainy said. "Berto, meet Cork O'Connor."

"I've heard about you," Mondragón said.

"You're one up on me there."

"Let me talk to him, Berto. Explain things."

He thought it over, leaned to Rainy, and kissed her hair. "I'll wait outside, *querida*."

When he'd left, Rainy said, "Let's sit."

She set the candle, which was secured in an antique brass holder, on the altar rail, and we took the first pew. For a moment, Rainy just sat there, her head lowered, her face a flickering of shadows in the inconstant light.

"This is the drug-addicted, low-life ex-husband you never talk about? A man so loathsome to you that you've never even mentioned his name in my presence? Ancient history, you've always insisted."

"There are things you didn't need to know before, Cork. That's changed."

"Clearly. So what's the real story?"

"I met Berto when I first enrolled at U of A," she began.

"Berto? You said his name is Gilbert. What kind of name is Gilbert for a Mexican?"

"He'll tell you he's Spanish, not Mexican. And he's only half Spanish. His mother was an American citizen, which makes him a citizen, too. She loved Gilbert Roland. Some old movie star. Do you remember him?"

"Maybe," I said. "Vaguely."

"So that's what's on his birth certificate. But he prefers the Spanish name Gilberto. Or Berto. I was eighteen when we met. He was twenty. We fell in love. I became pregnant with my first child, Chantelle. I thought when you were pregnant, getting married was what you did. So we married."

"Catholic wedding, apparently."

"A quiet one. He didn't want his parents to know."

"Why?"

"They had another bride picked out for him. His family is powerful, Cork. They wanted him to marry the daughter of another powerful family."

"A political union?"

"Something like that. For a while, we lived a quiet life. Peter came along. Berto finished his undergraduate degree. Then we entered hell."

"Your husband and a drug habit. That's what you've always said."

"That's how I've always explained it to people. It's easier than the truth."

"What's the truth?"

"The marriage his family had in mind was to have been a union of business interests, Cork. Not the kind of business you'd find listed on the New York Stock Exchange."

"Drugs?"

"And everything that goes with drugs. But that wasn't Berto. Do you know what he majored in at U of A? Social work. He wanted to help people, not prey on them."

"So what happened?"

"While he was in graduate school, he began to get a lot of pressure from his family to return to his home in Mexico."

"Which was where?"

"Outside Hermosillo."

I gave her a blank look.

"It's in the state of Sonora. A hundred and fifty miles south of the border. Things were getting difficult. The family was under attack from groups who wanted control of those particular business interests."

"Berto resisted the pressure?"

She nodded. "But he kept being called back. First for short visits, then longer. He'd return looking grim. He never shared the details of what was happening. Which was fine with me. I had enough to worry about. I was practically raising the children alone. Then one night a man showed up at our door. A stranger to me, but Berto knew him. The family *rancho* had been attacked. Some of Berto's family had been killed. His father had been shot. It didn't look like he was going to make it. Berto had to go. The situation down there was dangerous, so I stayed with Chantelle and Peter. The stranger, a man whose name I only knew as El Perro, remained behind. For protection."

Rainy sat back and breathed deeply. It was stiflingly hot in the sanctuary, and I watched sweat trickle down her temple and fall drop by drop onto the white blouse she wore, turning the fabric there a wet gray.

"Berto was gone all the next day. I heard no word from him. That night, El Perro told me he'd received instructions. He was to take us into the desert, where Berto would meet us. I asked him what was going on. Revolution, he told me.

"I gathered the children and we left with El Perro. I wasn't sure what we might run into, so I took the Ruger Berto had given me."

"What? An anniversary present?"

"When he began making his trips back to Hermosillo, he insisted on taking me out to a gun range. He taught me how to use firearms. First a handgun, the Ruger. Then rifles. He made me practice until I was very good."

"Thoughtful of him," I said.

"I wasn't happy about it. But . . . it was a good thing in the end. El Perro drove us south and west, far into the desert. Then he stopped and told me we should get out and wait for Berto. The children were asleep in the backseat. I asked if it was all right not to wake them. He said to let them sleep. Nothing about this felt right. I couldn't understand why Berto hadn't contacted me directly. Why had the message come through El Perro? As I got out, I slid the Ruger from my purse. El Perro walked ahead of me. I remember there was a full moon that night. The whole desert was silver and cut with black shadows. I saw El Perro's right hand move up toward his chest, where he wore a shoulder holster. He had a big silver ring on his pinkie, and I still remember how it flashed in the moonlight as his hand rose. He turned around suddenly. His gun was in his hand. But I'd had the Ruger aimed on him from the moment we left the car. I fired that gun until it was empty."

She stared at the candle awhile. I waited.

"The children slept through it. I took his wallet so that he couldn't be identified. There were a thousand U.S. dollars in it. I drove the car back to Tucson, directly to the bus station. I bought us all tickets to Hayward, Wisconsin."

"And Berto?"

"It was, as El Perro said, a revolution. Berto and his father, who, in fact, survived, along with two of Berto's brothers, somehow managed to hold out and hold on. It took him a while to find me. I'd already started divorce proceedings. He didn't fight it. My safety, the safety of our children, he put those things first, I'll give him that."

"You haven't seen him since?"

"We've communicated over the years. I've sent him photos of the kids. He stayed out of our lives, remarried, began another family. But I needed his help when Peter went through treatment."

"Ah," I said, finally understanding how Rainy could afford to send her son to a rehab center that charged $35,000 a month. "And what did that buy him with you, Rainy?"

She lifted her eyes to mine, and the deep despair I saw in them made me ashamed of my words.

"I'm sorry," I said. "That was uncalled for."

"The Berto I married, he was such a good man, Cork. This Berto I hardly recognize."

The church door opened. Mondragón stepped in.

"So, *preciosa,* does he know all now?"

"Not all," I said. "I'd like to know what happened at Jocko's."

Rainy's first husband sat on the altar rail, next to the candleholder. Only a couple of years must have separated us in age, but he looked a decade younger than I felt. Except for his eyes. There was something old and tired about them.

"After Rainy's call last night, I came as quickly as I could," he said. "I caught up with you in Sulfur Springs."

"I didn't see you," I said.

He smiled, perfect white teeth. "I'm good, huh? I followed you far enough back to keep off your radar. When you pulled into that old-timer's ranch, I found a good place to watch with my binoculars. After you took off in the biplane, and the other man left in his pickup truck, Rainy was alone. I was going to show myself and discuss Peter's situation. But I caught sight of someone sneaking through the tall grass south of the ranch house. He surprised Rainy. I could see he had a gun on her. When they started off in the direction he'd come from, I called Rainy. She talked him into letting her answer. I told her to drop the cell phone and bend to pick it up. When she went down, I took him out."

"With that?" I nodded toward the pistol he still held.

He shook his head. "A scoped Weatherby."

"Had he followed us, the way you did?"

Mondragón shook his head. "He might have been tracking Rainy's cell phone."

I understood now why it had been left behind in the bloodied grass.

"What did you do with the body?"

"I dropped it in the burial ground of the great Arizona desert, where the vultures and coyotes and ants will reduce it very quickly to nothing but bone."

"Who was it?"

"No identification. That's how it's done. I'm sure it was one of Rodriguez's men."

Grudgingly I said, "Thanks."

"I love her, too, Cork." Then he smiled and shrugged. "Mother of my children."

"What do you know about the Rodriguezes?"

"Jackals," he said. "They operate crudely. In the grand scheme, they're nothing. They like to believe that they control this area of the border and what crosses over it. The larger, more powerful interests allow them to go about their business here, but at a price."

"Larger, more powerful interests? Other cartels?"

"Think of it as a feudal system, Cork. There are those who operate below the cartels but only with their blessing. Like the Rodriguezes. And below that are those who live on the scraps the Rodriguezes throw them."

"What about your family?"

"We need no one's blessing, and we live on no one's scraps."

The candle was burning low. It was becoming more and more difficult to breathe in the hot, dead air of the sanctuary.

"You came alone?" I said.

"This is my business. My family — my family in Mexico — have no interest in my family here. In fact, if they knew what my son was up to, they might add to the bounty the Rodriguezes have already placed on his head. I didn't know anything about Peter's involvement in the Desert Angels until Rainy called me last night. Had I known

192

earlier, I would have put an end to it my-self."

"He's helping people who need help," Rainy said.

"He's interfering with a number of enter-prises."

"I remember a time when you would have applauded what he's doing. Probably you would have helped."

"That time is long past, *querida.*"

"So what now?" I said.

"It's safest that Rainy stay with me. Those *buitres* will try again if they know she's still alive."

"What about Peter?" Rainy said.

"Until Peter makes his presence known, there's nothing we can do."

"Where will you go?" I asked.

"Best you don't know, don't you think?" Mondragón said. "They may still come after you to get to her. If nothing is what you know, nothing is what you can tell them."

"Why do they want me?" Rainy said.

"I thought at first it was just pure revenge. That car bomb this morning. But I believe they understand now that you would make a good bargaining chip. They might be able to use you to lure Peter into the open."

"What is it about Peter that's so threaten-ing to them?" Rainy said.

193

Mondragón shook his head. "I don't know. But the fact that they're still after you is an encouraging sign that he's alive and probably in hiding. Let's go, *querida.*"

"I'm not leaving Cork," Rainy said.

"Think about it," Mondragón said. "You stay with him, he continues to be a target. Is that what you want? If you remain missing, along with that *pendejo* I shot, I think it will take them a while to decide what to do next. So we've bought some time."

"If what everyone says about the Rodriguezes is true, they'll kill Cork just because he was with me."

"They may try." Mondragón gave me and the Winchester at my side a frank look of appraisal. "But I think Cork is a man who can take care of himself."

"I'm not going," Rainy said. "Not without Cork."

I hated the thought of putting her into the keeping of Mondragón, but he was right. It was safest for her. Still, I knew it would be a hard sell.

"I can't stay with you and help Peter, too," I argued gently. "If I'm not worried about you, it will be easier for me to do what I have to do."

"And what exactly is that, Cork?" she said, clearly not convinced.

Mondragón laughed. "*Corazón,* this man is a detective. He will detect." His eyes nailed me. "And he will share with us what he discovers in his detection, yes?"

"What seems appropriate," I agreed. "Rainy, this really is the best way."

She looked at me, then at Mondragón, who said, "For our son, *querida.*"

Finally, she gave a grudging nod.

"A suggestion, Cork," Mondragón said. "Get rid of your cell phone. They may be tracking you, too."

"I'll disable the location services. That should do it."

"I'd prefer to be absolutely certain," Mondragón said.

"How do you suggest we communicate?"

"An antiquated system. Let's leave notes."

"Where?"

"Why not here?"

"The door's always locked. You don't have a key."

He laughed again. "It's an old lock. It opens with a skeleton key. No problem at all."

"Where do we leave the notes?"

He got up from the rail and went to the small altar. He lifted the cross, which was heavy and looked gold but was probably just brass.

"How about under here?" he said.

"All right. And how do we know when a note's been left?"

"The angel statue out front. We'll tie a little ribbon on her uplifted finger. It will be easy enough to see. We remove the ribbon to signal that we've received the message."

"Might be a little conspicuous, tying that ribbon."

"It'll take all of three seconds. And this isn't exactly a busy neighborhood."

"All right. For now."

"We should go, *querida.*"

I stood and Rainy with me. She stepped into my arms and laid her head against my chest. "You be safe."

I kissed her hair. "You, too."

I glanced at Mondragón for assurance. The best he could do was give me a nod.

CHAPTER 16

I lay in bed in the cool of the parsonage, the weight of history once again pressing down on me. I have often felt deeply alone in my life. After my father died. After my mother died. After Jo died. There are always people around me, family and friends, but I tend to isolate myself, at least for a while. It's how I deal with hard things. Although Rainy wasn't gone in the same way, I still felt alone. As if I'd lost something as essential as my heart.

I finally got up. I was going to disable the location apps on my phone, those I was aware of that might help someone who was interested to know exactly where I was, but I realized that I hadn't communicated with my children since Rainy and I left Aurora. I called Jenny, explained all that had happened and where we stood, and told her I needed Rainy's blood type. She promised to get on it first thing in the morning. I asked

197

her to call Annie and to let Stephen know what was up when he was back from driving cattle. I told her I loved her and to pass my love along to the others. Then I spent some time disabling the apps and turned the cell off. I thought I might buy a throwaway when I had an opportunity, just to be on the safe side.

I checked the old Winchester. It was a 30-30, model 94. Jocko had done a fine job of keeping it clean and oiled and in good working condition. Like a human being, every rifle is a little different from every other. You have to spend time getting to know it. I decided that first thing in the morning, I would head out somewhere away from civilization and acquaint myself with the peculiarities of this particular firearm, in the event that I needed to trust it and to trust my aim with it.

I slept fitfully and rose at first light. There was nothing in the parsonage, food-wise, so I showered and dressed, checked the pickup for any sign of explosives, and went to a convenience store/gas station called Cadiz Corners, where I bought coffee, a breakfast burrito, and the six boxes of Arm & Hammer baking soda stocked on the shelf. I wolfed down the burrito, sipped the coffee as I drove south out of town. I climbed the saddle in the Coronados and passed through Sulfur Springs, which was only just waking up. I spent a little time getting a further feel for the town, driving up and down the streets north of Sulfur Creek, then across the bridge to the south, in the area known as Gallina Town. Although they were separated by a creek no more than ten feet across and physically were not all that dissimilar, they were two very different communities. Except for the name Rosa's Cantina, there was nothing north of the bridge that even hinted at a heritage that wasn't white American. There were ceramic deer in some yards, just like in Minnesota. The wagon wheel motif seemed very popular. There was a dull consistency to everything. South of the bridge was almost like another country. The yard decorations were brightly colored — ceramic roosters and chimineas and bathtub Madonnas. Things looked a bit more run-down, maybe, but alive. Almost all the signage was in Spanish.

I kept driving. Outside Sulfur Springs, the road turned to dirt and gravel and began to climb. I followed it into an area wild with mesquite and prickly pear cacti. I came to a junction where a hard, narrow track cut to the right. The track snaked up into the desolate-looking mountains, where I could see an old structure high against a wall of rock.

I took the cutoff and climbed the switchbacks until I came to a flat area at the base of the wall. The structure I'd seen from below had probably been part of a transport system for a mine operation — water or maybe the ore itself — but it didn't look as if it would carry the weight of a fly these days. The flat was strewn with old detritus from the enterprise. I remembered Michelle talking about how mining had been an important part of the heritage of Coronado County. I parked and got out. Looking back, I could see the narrow track I'd followed up from the main road, and not far beyond that the fence along the border. I could also see where that dark fence line ended a few miles to the west. I thought I remembered the minister telling me that along much of the border there was still nothing but barbed wire, which presented almost no barrier at all.

The mine entrance, a huge hole in the rock wall, looked to me like a dark, open mouth. A few yards in front of it, where tracks must have once run, sat an old ore car. Rusted piping lay tumbled on the ground around me like pickup sticks. A great piece of machinery that I thought might be a pump stood covered in cancerous-looking, orange splotches that, had I been in the Northwoods, I would have figured were lichen. In this alien environment, God alone knew what was feeding on that metal. To my right was a pile of creosoted railroad ties and to my left a mine building of some kind that had fallen in on itself. I walked to the mine entrance, which was framed by old wooden beams. Barbed wire had been loosely strung across the opening. A sign hung from the wire. A big skull and crossbones dominated the middle of the sign. The text, which ran above and below the skull, read: ABANDONED MINE. WARNING! DANGER! STAY OUT! STAY ALIVE! I could feel cool air on my face, a fine respite from the heat of the morning, which was, again, more intense than on the worst summer days in Minnesota.

I walked back to the truck, loaded half a dozen cartridges into the Winchester, took the six boxes of baking soda I'd purchased at the convenience store, and set them up on a flat rock fifty yards away. I returned to the truck and jacked the first cartridge into the chamber. I've been a hunter all my life, and the feel of the rifle stock against my shoulder was old and familiar. I sighted on the box farthest to the right and squeezed off a round. A chip exploded off the rock just to the side of the box. I levered in the next cartridge and adjusted my aim. When I fired, the box spun like a crazy ballerina and fell. I sighted on the next box, adjusting my aim just a hair. This time the box of baking soda flew straight back off the rock.

I sensed rather than heard someone behind me. I spun around. Sitting on the pile of railroad ties, watching me with great interest, was the old-timer from Rosa's Cantina. He nodded to me, and the brim of his worn hat put his face in shadow for a moment. I walked to him. He didn't seem at all inclined to get up to greet me but looked at the Winchester in my hands with great interest.

"Sylvester, right?" I said.

"That'll do."

"What are you doing here, Sylvester?"

"Right back at you, stranger."

"Just a little sightseeing."

"Kind of far afield from where most tourists go."

"I'm a little more than a tourist."

"Figured. Still looking for the boy?"

"Young man," I said.

"When you're my age, mister, they're all boys." His eyes shifted to the mine entrance. "Lots of old diggings just like this one in these mountains. Somebody puts something in there, good luck ever finding it."

"You know where these old diggings are?"

"Been prospecting here since long before you were born. I know them all."

He pulled a pack of cigarettes from his shirt pocket, drew one out, and lit it with a wooden match that he scratched to flame with his thumbnail. He blew smoke and watched it rise in the dry air above him.

"Them Mexicans who come across the border, sometimes I find them holed up in the old mines. If I was to say anything about that in town, there's folks would come up and use those poor souls for target practice." Like blackflies, his eyes lit on my Winchester.

I set the rifle down, leaned it against the stack of railroad ties. "Who would do that?"

"Just folks," he said.

"So you don't say anything. Why not?"

"Maybe because lots of people in this part of the country got some Mexican blood in them somewhere. Or Indian. It's far enough back you don't see it in their faces. Because of how sentiments run way too often out here, you don't advertise that fact." He took a drag off his cigarette. "Or maybe I don't say anything because having a cold, white face don't mean you have a cold, white heart."

"Do you know something about Peter Bisonette?"

"I know you keep looking for him, you're asking for trouble."

"That's not news."

"I suppose not." He studied the tip of his cigarette. "You know the story of the optimistic kid? Always seeing the bright side of things? One day his old man decides to wise him up to the way the world really is. So for the kid's birthday the old man gives him a big pile of horseshit. Figures that'll do the trick. Well, the kid dives into that pile of horseshit with a big smile on his face and sets to digging. His old man says, 'What the hell are you doing?' Kid says, 'With all this horseshit, there's got to be a pony somewhere.' " He laughed. "The kid you're looking for, he's like that. Strikes me, you probably are, too. World needs people like you folks. Hope you find your kid, mister."

"You can't help with that?"

We both heard the sound of the vehicle coming, the grind of the engine up the hard track I'd followed. I picked up the Winchester, walked away from the old-timer, and stood near my truck, looking down from the flat where the mine had been dug.

I could see the dust in the vehicle's wake, rising up amid the mesquite, and in a moment, I could see the vehicle. Border Patrol. I turned around and found that I was alone again. Sylvester was nowhere to be seen.

I set the Winchester in the bed of the pickup, out of sight but within reach. I still didn't have a feel for which way the winds blew in these parts. The SUV rolled to a stop behind my pickup and two men got out. One of them I recognized. Agent Jamie Sprangers. The other was a stranger, Hispanic in his features.

Sprangers said, "I've been looking for you, Mr. O'Connor."

"Interesting that you were able to find me way out here."

"It's what Border Patrol is good at. I'd like you to meet a colleague of mine. Jesús Vega." He pronounced the first name *Hey-soos.*

The man was big, professional wrestler big. He offered his hand and nearly crushed my own when he shook it. I couldn't help thinking about the Mexican wrestlers who wore masks in the ring. "Folks call me Jessie," he said.

"You Border Patrol, too?"

"DEA. A lot of jurisdictions involved out here along the border. It's kind of like a jigsaw puzzle."

Sprangers picked up the empty cartridge casings from the dirt beside the pickup. "Thought I smelled gunpowder."

"A friend loaned me his rifle. Just getting used to it. Came up for a little target practice." I pointed to the baking soda boxes still sitting on the rock. "Something I can do for you gentlemen?"

Sprangers said, "I'm sorry about your wife."

"Thank you."

"It was my understanding, when I spoke with Sheriff Carlson, that you would get your wife's blood type to him so his people could compare it with the blood type of the sample they took from Robert Wieman's ranch last night."

"Yes."

"You haven't done that."

"No."

"You felt it was more important to come way out here for target practice?"

"I contacted my daughter in Aurora, Minnesota. She's working on getting me what we need. As soon as she gets back to me, I'll let the sheriff know."

He digested this, and it seemed to sit all right with him. He glanced toward the mine entrance. "You know about this place,

O'Connor?"

I shrugged. "What's to know?"

"A year ago, we found the bodies of four illegals in that mine. They were Guatemalans. Two men, two women. They'd all been shot." He waited for that to sink in. "Just a coincidence you're up here?"

"Just a coincidence," I said.

"Mr. O'Connor," Vega said, "we know there's a significant pipeline of drugs running through Coronado County and we're pretty certain the Rodriguezes are running it."

"The Guatemalans who were killed here, were they mules?"

"We think it's possible. What often happens with the illegal immigrants from Central America is this: They come with their children. They've already paid for the passage, but when they get to the border, their children are taken from them, kidnapped. These people are told that they have to work for the Rodriguezes, as mules or in other ways, if they ever want to see their children again. In our investigation, we discovered that the people we found here had, indeed, come with children."

"What happened to the children?"

"Unfortunately, your guess is as good as ours."

"Who killed the Guatemalans?"

"We don't know," Agent Sprangers said. "It's still an open case. It could have been the Rodriguezes. It could have been one of the other drug interests. It could have been locals fed up with the drug traffic and the illegals."

"Why did you come looking for me?"

"I want to know what you're not telling us."

"Peter Bisonette," Vega said. "What's his connection with the Rodriguezes?"

"I don't know that there is one."

"What is it about him that would make the Rodriguezes go after his mother?"

"I've been told they're just those kinds of people. They kill you right down to the last member of your family, cut down the tree to the roots."

"Even they have reasons. Revenge?" Vega offered. "Leverage? Information?"

"I have nothing to give you," I said.

Sprangers stepped to the back of the pickup and peered into the bed, where I'd laid the Winchester. "Nice old piece. But Las Calaveras use AK-47s and Uzis and M16s." He looked up at the sky. "I know it feels hot already, O'Connor. Trust me, if Carlos Rodriguez has his sights set on you, it's only going to get worse. When you finally decide it's too hot, let me know. You have my card."

The two agents returned to their SUV and headed back the way they'd come. I watched until they hit the main road and turned toward Sulfur Springs. Then I went over the pickup very carefully. Under the rear bumper, I found a transmitter, a tracking unit, which I decided to leave in place for the moment.

I picked up the Winchester and, with my next four shots, sent the final boxes of baking soda flying. I climbed back into the truck and headed down the mountainside.

CHAPTER 17

I drove slowly through Sulfur Springs. The place had awakened. Cars and trucks were leaving Gallina Town, heading north toward Cadiz, probably to jobs there. I came to a little open area near the taqueria where a couple of kids were kicking around a soccer ball. They stopped as I passed, seemed to recognize me, and took off running as if I was El Diablo himself. I crossed the bridge and rolled down the main street past the Mustang Properties office, where I caught a glimpse of Marian Brown inside, her back to the window. She didn't see me. The post office hadn't opened yet. The parking space in front of the little police department was empty. Up ahead, I saw the barmaid Sierra standing in the shade of the front porch of Rosa's Cantina. I can't say that she beckoned to me exactly, but I got the feeling that she'd been watching for me. She glanced up and down the street, then stepped back inside as I parked.

When I walked in, the place was deserted, but she was waiting with a menu. She nodded toward a table at the back, and I sat down. Without a word, she dropped the menu in front of me, turned around, and vanished into the kitchen. She came back a minute later with a cup of coffee.

"The huevos rancheros," she said. "Best thing we serve this time of day."

"Over easy," I said.

"Saw you come through town earlier. Then saw the Border Patrol follow a little while later."

"I was up at an old mine in the mountains."

"Which one?"

"Don't know its name. Place where some undocumented immigrants were killed last year."

Her face looked pained. "The El Dorado. I heard about your wife. Is it true?"

"What did you hear?"

"That she's missing, too."

"You heard right."

She looked like she wanted to say something but thought better of it.

"What?" I said.

"I don't want to shoot down your hopes, but when somebody disappears around

211

here, they usually stay disappeared."

"It's happened before?"

"Yeah."

"Who?"

"The Suazo brothers. From Gallina Town. Everybody pretty much figured they were involved with the Rodriguezes. That was the word anyway. They never tried to deny it. Then they just vanished. No trace."

"When?"

"After the car bombing."

"Nice peaceful little community you've got here."

"It was, once."

The door opened and a man walked in. He wore a Stetson. Or a cowboy hat, anyway. To me, they're all Stetsons. He glanced our way.

"Billy," Sierra said. *"Qué pasa?"*

The man took a stool at the bar. "Nuthin' a drink won't solve."

She gave me a wink. "Be right back with those eggs."

She slipped behind the bar. Without a word to Billy, she poured a shot of Jameson and set it in front of him, then went into the kitchen. Billy tipped his head back, and the whiskey went down in one big gulp. He got up from the stool and walked to the men's room.

212

Sierra came back with silverware and a napkin.

"You know the old-timer?" I asked. "Sylvester?"

"Everybody knows Sylvester."

"Know where he lives?"

"Up on the hill above town."

"Walkable from here?"

"Sure. Head out, take a right, go two blocks and take another right on Palomino Street, then just keep going."

"Which house?"

She laughed. "Believe me, you'll know it when you see it."

Billy came from the men's room. Sierra poured him another shot, went back to the kitchen, and returned in a few minutes with my breakfast.

"Gracias," I said.

She gave me a thin smile. *"De nada."*

When I'd finished eating, I left the truck parked in front of the cantina and walked to Palomino Street. I turned west and followed between desert willows and Russian olives and other trees that lined the fences and walls erected around every home. They were small, these things they called trees here, fragile compared to the great, graceful beauties in Minnesota. Like everything else in the desert, they were covered with thorns.

213

Past the last house, the road climbed above Sulfur Springs. A quarter mile farther, nestled into a little cup of rock, was a small, flat-roofed house built of adobe into which had been pressed pieces of brightly colored glass, ceramic tiles, seashells, God knows what else. Scattered among the cacti in the yard and set into the rocks on either side of the house were bleached cow skulls, a whole herd of the dead. A wooden animal shed with a corral stood off to one side. Through the open window of the shed I could see movement. I walked that way. When I peered through the window, I came face-to-face with a mule, staring at me with his big, brown eyes.

"His name's Franklin."

I turned and there was Sylvester, once again popping up behind me without a sound.

"Franklin cuz I bought him with a hundred-dollar bill. Worth that to me and a whole lot more."

"Use him in your prospecting?" I asked.

"More reliable than a vehicle and lots better company. What can I do for you?"

"How'd you know I would be at the El Dorado this morning?"

"There's a movie I never saw but the title fits this area, mister. *The Hills Have Eyes.*

Got ears, too. The El Dorado, it's not far from here the way the crow flies. Is that all you wanted?"

"You said you've prospected most of the mountains in southern Arizona. You know the Santa Margaritas?"

"Know 'em well. The Oro Rico Mining District."

"Think you could pinpoint some old mines for me?"

"Lots of excavations there. Any one in particular?"

"A place someone coming from the west might use for shelter."

"Someone coming illegally?"

"Maybe."

He stepped up next to me and, while he thought that one over, reached through the window and ran his hand gently down the long, broad face of the mule.

"Or maybe a place somebody might want to dump something where nobody'd ever find it?"

"That's not what I'm hoping for," I said.

"There you go. A pile of horseshit and you're digging for a pony. Come on into the house."

It was dark inside and cool, but not unnaturally so, the way it probably would have felt with air-conditioning. The shades were drawn. I had trouble seeing at first, but my eyes adjusted quickly. Unlike the outside, where the walls were a mash-up of everything under the sun, the inside was Spartan, clean, organized. The furniture looked handmade. What few items hung on the walls were all framed photographs, desert shots, some in black and white, some in color. They belonged in a gallery.

Sylvester saw me noticing. "Sierra's work. Has a real eye for beauty, that girl. Have a seat." He nodded toward a small table, where there were only two chairs.

I sat down, and he opened a cabinet made of fine polished wood. Inside was shelving that held rolled documents. He ran a finger along a shelf and pulled down one of the rolls. He closed the cabinet and brought the roll to the table, where he spread it out. A contour map.

"I'm thinking that the area around Oro Rico itself might be too popular for something like you're thinking of. Lots of folks get back in there to explore the ghost town. So maybe a bit farther north. More rugged and less visited, even by the Border Patrol. They figure it's too rough for illegals. But three old claims were worked there for a while. I know, cuz my father worked one of them and I helped him in my youth."

He put a finger on the map. I knew how to read a contour map, and I could tell from the close proximity of the lines that the spot he indicated was high up on a steep rise.

"He called her the Lulabelle, after a girl he was sweet on before he married my mother. It was hard getting in and hard getting out. But we pulled enough gold from the Lulabelle to make it worth our while. Least ways back then. No way I could do that kind of hard packing in and out these days."

"A lot of people know about the Lulabelle?"

"My secret as far as I know. But who knows what a desperate man coming out of that desert to the west might stumble onto? Especially if he's savvy to begin with and maybe got a desert angel sitting on his shoulder to boot."

"Los Angeles del Desierto?" I said.

"Got no idea what you're talking about," Sylvester said. "But I'll give you the coordinates for the Lulabelle, if you want them."

He wrote with a pencil on a slip of paper.

"How do you keep so cool in here?" I asked.

"Adobe," he said. "There's a reason the people of this desert been building with it

217

for centuries. And them rocks behind the house, they give shade all afternoon. At night, I open the place up and let it cool down, then seal it back up in the morning. Kind of like living in a cave. Or a mine. Feels pretty familiar to me. I gave you something, mister, but I want something in return."

"What?"

"A promise. When you find who you're looking for, you keep him safe."

"Done," I said and held out my hand.

I walked down the hill into Sulfur Springs, through the sparse shade of what in the desert passed for trees. The heat made me tired. I wouldn't have minded just curling up somewhere for a nap until things cooled off. But there was much to do.

I'd had my cell phone off all morning. I turned it on to check if I'd had any messages. I saw that Michelle Abbott had tried me, twice. I called her back.

"You tried to reach me," I said.

"I heard about Rainy," the minister said. "I'm so sorry, Cork."

"Thanks."

"Is there anything I can do?"

"A prayer wouldn't hurt." I meant it, but it probably didn't come out that way.

"I'll do that. Look, I know you must be

218

worried. Would you like some company?"

"I'm fine, really. And thank you."

"Any word?"

"Not yet." I hated lying to a woman who'd been kind to us and in doing so might even have put herself in harm's way, but what could I say that wouldn't put her in more danger?

"Promise me you'll call if you need anything. Or if you hear anything."

"It's a deal."

She was quiet a long time on her end.

"Michelle?" I said. "You still there?"

"Just saying that prayer I promised you. Please, please be careful, Cork."

The sun was well above the Coronados now. The turnoff for the Old Douglas Road was another quarter mile north. I punched in a number on my cell phone. When the line picked up on the other end, I said, "Old Turtle, I need wings."

CHAPTER 18

I'd become familiar with the back road out of Sulfur Springs, a snaking byway that rose and dipped among the desert swales. Beyond the trailer community that called itself Paradiso, it became a solitary stretch. I hadn't seen any sign of life along there at all, except for Sprangers and the other Border Patrol agents we'd encountered on our first day in Coronado County. And the circling vultures.

I glanced in the rearview mirror and saw a black pickup truck a couple of hundred yards back, coming up on me fast. I'd turned off my cell phone, but because of the transmitter I'd found, that didn't mean I wasn't being followed. I made sure the Winchester and the box of cartridges were in easy reach. I maintained my speed, mindful of the curves and dips in the road ahead, and keeping a watchful eye on that approaching vehicle. As it neared, it pulled to the left to pass. The sun glared off the windshield so that I couldn't see inside the cab. The pickup didn't slow as it came abreast, and I finally saw the driver and the single passenger. They were both Hispanic, with thin black beards carefully sculpted along their jawlines. They paid me no attention at all as they passed and then disappeared over the rise ahead. When I crested that hill, I caught sight of the tail end of the pickup vanishing over the next.

I let myself relax and returned to thinking about the flight I was going to make with Jocko. I figured we'd buzz Sylvester's Lulabelle Mine. Although he hadn't said it outright, I was pretty sure the old prospector considered the Lulabelle a good bet if Peter had been seeking sanctuary.

I was deep in thought when I came over the next rise. Blocking the road ahead was the black pickup. I hit the brakes and came to a stop fifty yards shy of the truck. The two men were no longer inside. They stood in front of it with what looked like assault rifles cradled in their arms.

I shifted into reverse and started to back up fast. Over the rise behind me appeared a black SUV, blocking any retreat in that direction. I killed the engine, grabbed the

Winchester and box of shells, and lit out for cover.

An upthrust of yellow rock lay north of the road, maybe fifty yards. High ground. I made for it as fast as I could. I expected the assault rifles to open up on me any second, but nothing happened. I clambered up the rise, lay flat, and took stock. The SUV had come to a halt behind my pickup. The two men inside met up with the guys from the first vehicle and held a little war council. I took the opportunity to fill the Winchester's magazine with cartridges.

The four men separated, one flanking me far to the left and one to the right. The other two stayed central. Those two came slowly up the rise, staying to cover as much as possible. They stopped a good thirty yards out, behind thick cactus cover. The men on the flanks kept moving.

"Hey, mister," one of the men below me shouted in a heavy accent. "We only want to talk."

"So talk."

"Give us the answer to one question, and we will leave you alone, promise."

"What's the question?"

"Where is he?"

"Who?"

"Where is he?"

The two men on the flanks were drawing even with me. I took aim and sent a round near the man to the right, and then did the same with the guy to the left. They both hit the ground. I saw movement behind the cactus in front of me, but couldn't see exactly what that duo was up to.

"You come any nearer, any of you, and I'll put a bullet in you," I called. "That's my promise."

I saw the man to the right leap up and dash for higher cover. Prone as I was, I couldn't get a good shot off quickly. I glanced east. That guy rose to make a run. I swung around, took aim, and caught him just as he started to drop for cover.

"*Carajo!*" the spokesman from below shouted. And in the next moment, the whole area around me exploded.

The shots came fast but wild. My immediate concern was the man still trying to take the high ground to my right. If he got behind me, I was in trouble. The biggest advantage I had over him at the moment was that the sun was in his face. It's hard to take good aim when you're blinking against that blinding glare. Instead of patiently moving himself to a good vantage, he stood recklessly and hit my position with a spray of bullets, chipping away at the little hump

223

of yellow rock that gave me modest protection on that side. I focused on him, and when he let up on his trigger, I laid the Winchester barrel atop the rock hump, took aim, and squeezed off a round. He staggered back and fell. I levered in another cartridge and swung toward the two guys below me. They were already in the black pickup leaving dust behind them as they sped away. The first man I'd shot was up and trying desperately to hobble toward his SUV, his weapon no longer in his hands. He stumbled and was reduced to crawling. I thought about putting another round into him, but his agenda, at least as far as it concerned me, had clearly changed.

I saw another rooster tail of dust rising in the west, the direction of Sulfur Springs. *Lord, give me a break,* I thought.

Then, in that quiet after gunfire which always seems so immense, I heard the sirens.

"You actually had the presence of mind to note the license plate on the pickup that took off?" Sheriff Carlson's brows met each other in a deep V of consternation. Or, more probably, doubt.

"I made a mental note of it as they passed," I said. "Kind of a habit, especially in circumstances like these."

He sat back. We were in his air-conditioned cruiser.

"Sheriff once yourself, I understand," he said. "Back in Minnesota. I talked to a colleague of yours this morning. The current sheriff there, Marsha Dross." His tone had changed, taken on a note of collegiality. Two guys who'd worn the same kind of badge, chewing the fat. "She said you go by Cork. Okay if I call you that? She vouched for you. Lucky. Because from where I've been standing, you've looked ass deep in the business of the Rodriguezes."

"Just in the wrong place at the wrong time."

The paramedics were carting off the two men I'd shot. They weren't dead, but neither was in good shape. I'd explained in detail what had occurred. The assault rifles, the expended shell casings, the torn-up yellow rock that had given me shelter, all lent credibility to my story.

"How'd you know to come running?" I asked.

"Got a call from Border Patrol." He nodded toward my pickup; Agent Sprangers and the DEA agent Jesús Vega were carefully searching the vehicle inside and out. The sheriff laid his arms over his steering wheel and peered up at a couple of vultures that were circling high above us. "Where were you headed, Cork?"

"The Sonora Hills Cellars," I said.

"Business there?"

"Peter Bisonette worked for them. I just wanted to ask a few questions."

"We already interviewed them."

"I'm sure you know from your own experience it pays to cover the same ground more than once. Given a little time, people remember things."

He nodded, as if allowing that could be true. "I was thinking you might be headed to Robert Wieman's place. Maybe for another sightseeing trip."

"I might have been considering it."

"And where, if you might have been considering it, would you have had him fly you?"

"Big county. Lots to see, Chet." I gave him a collegial smile.

Agent Sprangers walked to my side of the cruiser. Vega stood looming huge beside him like a wrestler waiting to be tagged into the ring. I slid the window down. Sprangers held out his hand. In his palm was the tracking transmitter.

"Somebody was very interested in where you might be going, O'Connor," he said.

"Where'd you find it?"

"Under your back bumper. No telling how long it's been there. But it explains the men who ambushed you." He eyed me from the shade his hat brim cast across his face. "And you say all they asked you was 'Where is he?' "

"That's it."

Sprangers looked past me at the sheriff. "Peter Bisonette."

"Lucky you had that Winchester," Carlson said.

"And that you were so accurate with it," Vega added.

I knew that tone, all deep and weighty with cop incredulity. I understood the why of it completely. But the thing was this: If that transmitter wasn't planted by Sprangers, how the hell had he tracked me to the El Dorado Mine? And if it was true, as Carlson had said, that Border Patrol had alerted him about the ambush, how did Sprangers know?

Suspicion and secrets. We were mired in them.

"If I were a betting man," Sprangers said, "I'd bet the men you shot are Las Calaveras. They work for Carlos Rodriguez. And I'd also bet they're responsible for the tracker under your bumper."

"Am I free to go?" I asked.

"After a shooting? Oh no, Cork," the sheriff said. "You're following me back to the department. We've got paperwork to do."

CHAPTER 19

They kept me at the Coronado County Law Enforcement Center until well after noon. We went over the same territory again and again. One of the things they hammered on was Rainy's cell phone. The last call she'd received had come around the same time she vanished. It was a number that appeared several times on her call log since she'd arrived in Arizona, both incoming and outgoing. Did I recognize the number? I swore to them I knew nothing about it.

"This new wife of yours seems to have kept a lot from you, O'Connor," Sheriff Carlson observed.

Agent Sprangers said, "Chet, if you ever get married, you'll probably keep secrets from your wife. All married people do. What's important is the nature of the secret." He gave me a pointed look. "Some secrets can get you killed."

Amid all the questions, they offered me a

piece of information. They'd found an abandoned Jeep parked south of Jocko's ranch. It had been reported stolen in Nogales. They didn't know what it might have to do with whatever had happened at Jocko's place, but they worked me pretty hard to find out if I might. When they got tired of asking, they finally gave up, and let me go.

The first thing I did was drive past Grace Church. No ribbon on the angel's uplifted finger. I was hungry, so I pulled into a little drive-in joint called Burger Billy's and ordered a cheeseburger and fries. While I waited for the food, I turned my cell phone on and tried Old Turtle's number. When he answered, I explained my delay. He said he'd be waiting for me when I arrived.

I also had a text from Jenny with Rainy's blood type. I called Sheriff Carlson and let him know.

I ate on the road. The food wasn't nearly as good as what I served my customers at Sam's Place back in Aurora. The fries were limp and greasy, and the burger tasted like grilled leather. It made me homesick, the thought of Sam's Place, of Aurora. I wanted to be somewhere that I understood and that understood me as well. But because I had no idea what the hell was going on in Coronado County, I had no idea when I'd get home.

After a lot of discussion, Sheriff Carlson had allowed me to keep the Winchester, which was near at hand. I'd shot two men that day. They weren't going to die, but it was a form of violence that I'd tried to step away from a long time ago. In Aurora the night Peter called, Rainy had asked me about the men I'd killed across the course of my life. I didn't tell her, because the truth was that I'd been involved in a slaughter once. In one terrible moment, I'd been part of the killing of a lot of men. I wasn't wearing a badge then, and it was an action completely outside the law. I'd like to say that they were men who deserved to die, but in truth I knew none of them. I'd told myself it was necessary, but it had sickened me. It had sickened my soul. I'd put away my firearms. Forever, I thought. Now the Winchester sat at my side, and there was blood on my hands again.

There is a word in the Ojibwe language: *ogichidaa*. It means "one who stands between evil and his people." Long ago, Henry Meloux had told me I was born *ogichidaa*. It was my purpose and my fate. I couldn't escape it. As I drove toward Jocko's ranch house, with one eye constantly on the

231

rearview mirror, I knew in my heart I was prepared to kill again, if it came to that, not just to defend myself but to protect the people who were my family, the people I loved.

I was also thinking about that damn tracking device Sprangers had blamed on Las Calaveras. It explained the ambush well enough, but left the question of Sprangers's uncanny awareness of my location and situation a mystery. Unless, of course, he'd been lying and had had a hand in planting the device and had pulled it only because he suspected that, as a result of the ambush, I would check the pickup myself. Which left the possibility that, now I believed I was safe, another device had been planted somewhere else.

As soon as that thought hit me, I pulled onto the next side road and scoured the pickup thoroughly. I found nothing, which meant either that I was safe or that they'd been more sophisticated in planting it this time around. Either way, I didn't have much choice except to continue to Jocko's place.

He wasn't alone when I arrived. Frank Harris was with him. They came from the little ranch house and Frank shook my hand. "Glad you're still with us, Cork."

Jocko slapped me on the back. "Nice

shooting, pardner. You and my Lena, a match made in heaven."

"Lena?" Frank said.

"The Winchester I gave him. Still got it, Cork?"

"In the truck."

Frank said, "Jocko told me you might have a lead on Peter."

"It's just a possibility, Frank. Probably a remote possibility. But it's worth checking out. You still okay with flying me, Jocko?"

"I've got her all gassed up and ready to go."

"Where exactly?" Frank said.

"I'm going to hold on to that piece of information," I told him. "I think Peter was right. The less those involved know, the safer they are. I'd feel bad if I thought I put you and Jayne in any more danger than I probably already have."

"What about Jocko here?"

"Don't worry about me, Frank. I was a pilot in World War Two. Been itching for a good fight for sixty years."

"Just a sense of where you're headed, then," Frank said. "If things go south, I'd like an idea where to start looking for you two."

I weighed the advisability of telling him against what I felt was his sincere concern for our safety.

"I think Peter may have made for the Santa Margaritas," I finally said. "It's a long shot but the only lead I have at the moment."

"How'd you come by it?"

"Turned over enough rocks until I found something. It's what I do."

I grabbed the Winchester and cartridges from the pickup, and we walked to Jocko's waiting biplane.

"Be careful, you old coot," Frank said and gave Jocko a gentle slap on the back. "Jayne would kill me if I let anything happen to you." He shook my hand. "Good luck, Cork. Call me when you're back. Let me know that you're both safe and how it went."

He returned to the ranch house, and I watched until he headed off in his F-150. Then I pulled out the slip of paper on which Sylvester had written the coordinates for the Lulabelle Mine. Jocko took a look at them, climbed into the cockpit, and came out with a map, which he spread on the wing of the plane. He checked the coordinates, studied the map, and finally laid a finger down.

"Got it," he said. "But what the hell is it?"

"An old mine where Peter might be holed up."

Jocko nodded as if that made sense. "These mountains along the border, they're all riddled with old tunnels and shafts. The drug smugglers, they know about 'em."

"This is one they might not be so familiar with."

"Well, then, let's give 'er a shot."

Jocko climbed into the plane again, stowed his map, and when he came back out, carried a pair of field glasses, which he handed to me.

"I fly. You look," he said.

He took his place at the controls, and I settled into the seat behind. We put on our headsets, he got us rolling, and once again we headed west.

As nearly as I could tell, we followed the same route we'd taken before. We edged past the Coronados and flew just south of Sulfur Springs. Because I knew what to look for now, I used the field glasses and spotted the abandoned El Dorado Mine. I wondered just how many more old diggings might riddle those mountains and what, in this struggle along the border, they might hide.

We stayed north of Nogales, and I could see the suburban streets spreading out into the desert like tendrils from some greedy plant. We skirted more mountains and flew over rolling desert hills empty of any sign of habitation, and kept flying west. The sun was dropping in the sky, and I knew time and darkness would eventually become a concern. We passed yet another long ridge of mountains, Jocko banked north, and we dropped and flew a few hundred feet above the western foothills. I understood these were the Santa Margaritas and now Jocko was working on locating the Lulabelle Mine.

At last he gave me a thumbs-up, and we began to circle.

Although I trusted Jocko's navigation, I could see nothing below that was as easily identifiable from the air as the workings of the El Dorado. The hillsides were covered with scrub, desert growth, and great rock outcroppings like red carbuncles. Even with the field glasses, I couldn't make out anything remotely hopeful. Jocko circled half a dozen times, widening the arc of our search a little each time.

"Anything?" he asked over the head-phones.

"Nothing," I said.

The sun was touching the tops of the next range of mountains to the west when Jocko held up a finger.

"One more time around, Cork," he said. "That's all I can give you."

The constraints of fuel and time, I figured.

He banked, and we made a wide loop.

Then I saw it. The flashing of sun off a mirror. Three flashes, separated by three short spaces. Then a flash, and a long lapse before the next. Then it was gone. Not random. An attempt at an SOS, I was certain.

"There, Jocko," I said.

He turned and saw where I pointed, and he banked and circled back.

Again the flashing, and this time Jocko spotted it, too. It came from a tight fold between two steep ridges, a place Jocko couldn't possibly fly into. If this was, indeed, the Lulabelle, I could understand why Sylvester, at his age, wouldn't want to try mining it. Getting in and out looked rough. But it might be a reasonable sanctuary, a good place to hide if that's what you were after. I scanned the spot with the field glasses, but couldn't see anything definite.

We made another high pass. This time there was no flashing of light.

"Where'd it go?" Jocko asked.

"I don't know. But it was there and it was definitely a signal."

"Peter?"

"That would be my guess."

"Why did he stop?"

Jocko made a wide loop for another pass.

Against the sun, low in the west, I saw a hovering vulture. But there was something not right about it. I used the field glasses and could see that it wasn't a vulture or any other bird.

"Chopper, Jocko. At three o'clock."

He turned his head and nodded.

"Border Patrol?" I said.

"Got me. But I'm guessing that's why whoever's down there below us stopped signaling. I think we've seen all we're going to see here today."

We cleared the southern end of the Santa Margaritas and headed east. I tried to spot the chopper again, but either it didn't follow us or it was so far back that even with the field glasses I couldn't get a visual.

When we touched down on Jocko's landing strip, Frank and Jayne Harris were there to meet us.

"Jayne figured you'd be back before sunset," Frank explained. "She insisted on having supper ready for you. It's warming in your oven, Jocko."

"Well?" Jayne said as we walked to the ranch house. "Anything?"

"Something," Jocko said. "But what exactly we can't say. Border Patrol helicopter chased us away before we could confirm anything."

I told them about the mirror signal.

"Who else could it be but Peter?" Jayne said.

"That's pretty much my thinking, too," I said. "I need to get over there and check it out."

"If it's in the Santa Margaritas," Frank said, "you'll never make it before dark. And you don't want to get lost in that desert at night."

"When was the last time you ate a decent meal?" Jayne said. "Have some supper. It's lasagna. One of my specialties. And some of our best wine."

We stood at the door to the ranch house. I could smell the lasagna, and my stomach was making a pretty good argument for staying. But I had to get back to Cadiz and tie a ribbon on the angel's uplifted finger. Rainy needed to know.

CHAPTER 20

It was dusk when I hit Cadiz and drove past the church. The angel's finger was bare. I stopped at Cadiz Corners to fill the tank of the pickup truck. Inside the convenience store, I bought a pen, a notepad, and a little spool of red ribbon. I parked on the main street across from the Wagon Wheel Café, cut a small section of ribbon, tore a page from the notepad, and wrote on it: *I found him.*

To be sure I wasn't being followed, I walked a winding route back to the church. Inside, I put the paper slip beneath the cross on the altar. I left the church, spent a few seconds tying the little red ribbon around the angel's finger, returned to the pickup, and drove to Burger Billy's. I took the leathery cheeseburger I bought, and the greasy onion rings and the grainy milk shake, back to the parsonage and settled in to wait.

Which is always the hardest part.

The demons that plague you are patient horrors. You may think that you've dealt with them, driven them out with logic, put them to rest with prayer, but they're never really gone. They're always with you. And why? Because they're not things separate from you. They are you.

I chewed on the idea of Rainy with Gilberto Mondragón. There was history between them, significant history, a life they'd created together. And children. There'd been love, fire, passion, dreams, everything that melds two souls, makes two people marry, compels them to commit to walking one road together for the rest of their lives. When Rainy fled Arizona, it hadn't been because she wasn't in love with Mondragón. She'd run for the safety of her children and herself. The separation afterward and the divorce hadn't come because they'd fallen out of love. Over the years, they'd remained in touch. Rainy had shared photos of the children as they grew. Probably she'd shared stories. When she'd come to Cadiz to help in Peter's rehab, she'd asked Mondragón to be a part of that, to share the burden of its great cost and perhaps the emotional burden as well.

And now, in the long wait, the demon

deep inside me, which was the voice of the worst part of me, kept whispering: *Did she share more with him?*

Who was this man with all his *queridas* and *mi amors* and *preciosas*? Wealthy. Way too good looking. With an easy bearing that suggested he was used to wielding power and accustomed to the deferential treatment that came with great authority.

And the demon whispered, but not for the first time: *Who is Rainy? Do you really know this woman you married?*

She'd kept secrets from me. For important reasons, she believed. Or said she believed.

And then the demon whispered: *If she kept these things from you, things you had a right to know, what else has she kept from you?*

The food sat heavy on my stomach. I was tired, weary right down to my bones. I laid myself out on the couch with the Winchester on the floor beside me and the map Jocko had given me on the coffee table, and I stared up at the ceiling. I could tell from the cobwebs in the corners that the parsonage wasn't often used. I rolled my head and saw that there was dust on the coffee table, disturbed by the map I'd put there. Michelle Abbott had offered the little house to us with no time to prepare, and there was dust everywhere. Except, I noticed, in the center of the shelf of the bookcase next to the couch. I got up and looked more closely. As on the coffee table where I'd put the map, the thin layer of dust had been disturbed. Books had recently been moved. I carefully slid them out one by one until I found the bug.

The Rodriguezes? Border Patrol? The Coronado County Sheriff's Department? DEA? Who could say?

And then the demon spoke up, whispering: *Why not Mondragón?*

Why not Mondragón, indeed. What was his interest in the situation as it stood? Making sure that his son and Rainy were safe, certainly. But what beyond that? Why should he care about me at all? What was I to him but the man who'd stepped in to fill his place? Did it matter that the place had been empty for years? It might, especially if what he and Rainy had shared in those months of helping Peter to heal was more than just parental concern.

I wondered if this was the only device that had been planted in the house. It didn't matter. I knew now the parsonage wasn't safe. I could have destroyed the bug but, in doing so, would have played my hand. Better, I thought, to wait and to use it to my advantage, if that was possible.

The text came a short time later. It read simply: *Goodman.* I took the Winchester and slipped quietly out the back door. I walked up the road to the mesa top where the Goodman Center stood among the scattering of new, expensive homes. So late at night there was only one vehicle in the visitors' lot, a dark SUV parked as far back from the glow of the overhead lights as possible. I started across the lot. As I approached, the doors of the SUV opened and two figures got out. Rainy and Mondragón. They came toward me together, so close to each other they might as well have been holding hands.

Rainy suddenly broke from her ex-husband and ran to me. She threw her arms around me and laid her head against my chest. "Oh, God, Cork I was so worried about you. And you found Peter. Thank you, thank you."

It felt good to have her back in my arms, but as I held her, I saw Mondragón approaching, looking as if he thought I was going to rob him.

Rainy looked expectantly into my eyes. "Where is he?"

"Not here," I said. "But I'm pretty sure I know where."

"He's safe?"

"He's alive. At least, I believe he is."

"I don't understand," she said.

I explained about the Lulabelle Mine and the mirror flashes.

"It could have been anything," Mondragón said, clearly unhappy with what I'd brought him. "The reflection of the sun off something."

I shook my head. "It was purposeful. It was meant for Jocko and me."

"We need to go to him," Rainy said.

"We'll leave before first light. By the time we reach the area, we'll be able to see where we're going."

"We leave now," Mondragón said. "I don't want to risk being discovered before we have a chance to get to Peter. We can wait out there in the desert until sunrise."

Which made sense. But I didn't like the way he said it, as if there was no room for objection, as if his word was somehow law. And I felt the demon stirring deep inside me again.

Rainy said, "I'd feel better if we left now, Cork. I'm not sure I could stand just waiting here."

In the dim light, I thought I saw a smug look of satisfaction on Mondragón's face.

"All right," I said. "But I left the map at the parsonage."

"Let's get it," Mondragón said.

"I'll get it and meet you," I said. "Safer for Rainy."

He absorbed that and didn't object. "Where?"

"Cadiz Corners. A gas station and convenience store at the north end of town."

"Twenty minutes," he said.

I kissed Rainy, longer than was strictly necessary, then headed off again on foot.

The moon had risen, a quarter full, delivering enough light for me to see my way easily. Which was good because my head was with Rainy. Rainy and Mondragón. The longer the two of them were alone together, the less I liked it. I entered the parsonage through the back door, still arguing with Mondragón in my head. I wasn't completely in the moment, completely focused. A big mistake.

The blow, when it came, caught me from behind, and I fell into a blackness that no moonlight could penetrate.

I came to with a splash of cold water on my face. Everything was dark, and I realized I'd been blindfolded. I tried to move and discovered I was bound to a chair, hand and foot.

"Where is he?" said a voice I'd never heard. It was like gravel rattling in a tin pan.

"Who are you?" I said.

"Where is he?"

"What are you talking about?"

"You know what I'm talking about. Where's Peter Bisonette?"

There was no Hispanic accent to this voice. Although that didn't necessarily mean he wasn't Latino, my first guess was that he was probably white.

"I put a couple of bullets into the last guys who asked me that," I said.

The blow came to my ribs, left side. It caught me off guard and shook me hard. But not so hard I didn't register the thought that whoever it was, he was probably right-handed.

"Where is he?"

He spoke close to my face. I registered the smell of whiskey on his breath, of marijuana on his clothing.

"Why do you want to know?" I said.

"If we get to him before those Rodriguez shits do, he might still be alive when we deliver him to his mother."

"What do you want with him?"

"That's between him and us."

"I need a little information before I drop the dime on him."

"I don't think so. I think all you need is a little more of this."

Another blow to my ribs, same spot. I was going to have an ugly bruise there in the morning.

"So, where is he?"

"You make a persuasive point," I said, trying not to let the pain affect my voice. "But mostly you're persuading me of what a bad idea it would be to give you Peter. Even if I could. Which I can't."

The next blow connected with my cheek near my ear. It rattled me good, but what hurt most was the cut it left. I could feel blood running down my jaw. So — my brain registered — whoever he was, he was wearing a ring big enough to cut a canyon across my cheek.

There'd been only one speaker, but I'd had a sense from the beginning that he wasn't alone. Now that suspicion was confirmed because I heard whispering that involved several voices.

"You're a stranger here. You have no idea what's going on." A different voice this time, but one that seemed familiar, though I couldn't place it yet. "It's a complicated situation, a very bad situation, which your Peter is only making worse."

"How about this?" I said. "What if I convince him not to do whatever it is he's doing that's pissed you off?"

"I think we can convince him better," said the first voice, the gravelly one I didn't recognize at all.

I picked up something now, a subtle but pleasant fragrance. Something both floral and cinnamon. A cologne or perfume maybe.

Some more whispers, then another blow, this one directly to my stomach. It punched the air right out of me, and for a long moment, I couldn't breathe.

When I finally gasped and sucked in air, the vaguely familiar voice said, "This will only get worse, O'Connor. You don't want that. We don't either. You're not a part of this. So just tell us."

"I can't tell you what I don't know."

"Burn him," said a third voice, hushed, whispery. Female?

Hands ripped my shirt, tearing off the buttons. I heard a match struck and smelled cigarette smoke.

"You sure about this?" said the voice I could almost recognize.

"Burn him," whispered the third voice.

I tensed, trying to prepare myself, but the sear of the cigarette ember was more painful than I'd imagined. I cried out.

"Tape his mouth," the familiar voice said.

"He can't talk with tape over his mouth,"

said the whispery voice, definitely female.

"He screams like that again, the neighbors'll come running." The gravelly voice.

"We're going to burn you until you talk, O'Connor," said the whispery voice. "We can do this all night."

No idle threat, I knew. I steeled myself.

Then I heard the shatter of window glass, and a deep cry of pain.

"Jesus!" The gravelly voice. "I'm hit."

"Out of here. Now." The woman's voice.

I heard a furious scrambling, and the front door was thrown open. A moment later, a big engine turned over and tires squealed, painting the street, I imagined, with black lines of rubber.

I waited in the dark behind the blindfold. My head hurt. My chest and ribs hurt. My stomach hurt. I was as confused as I'd ever been.

I heard the back door cautiously open, felt the air stir as someone moved past me. I held my breath.

Then Mondragón said, "It's clear, Rainy." And she was all over me.

CHAPTER 21

"No talking," I whispered, as Rainy removed the blindfold.

Mondragón had a pocketknife in his hand and bent to cut the duct tape that bound me to the kitchen chair. He opened his mouth to speak, but I shook my head furiously and made a shushing sound to silence him. His response was an angry look. But he said nothing.

Rainy stared at my face in horror. She touched my gouged cheek, then put her fingertips near the cigarette burn on my chest.

"Oh, sweetheart," she whispered.

I laid a finger to my lips. When Mondragón had cut me completely free, I stood up and signaled for them to follow. I went to the living room and from the bookshelf pulled the book that hid the bug. I gave Mondragón a pointed look. He shook his head.

I mouthed *Outside,* and put the book back.

I snatched the rolled map from the coffee table. Jocko's Winchester was on the kitchen table, where my assailants must have laid it, and I grabbed that as well. We left quietly by the back door. I trailed Rainy and Mondragón to the next street, where he'd parked his SUV.

"Do you have anything for first aid, Berto?" Rainy asked.

"Glove box," Mondragón said.

He'd been carrying a rifle, the one he must have used to put the bullet through the kitchen window and into the gravelly voiced man who'd been torturing me. Probably the one he'd used to kill Rainy's assailant as well. It was fitted with a suppressor, which explained why I hadn't heard a shot. He laid it in the back of the SUV and hurried into the driver's seat.

Rainy spent a moment rummaging in the glove box, then slipped into the backseat with me, and Mondragón took off. In the first aid kit, she found a small tube of antiseptic ointment, which she applied to the burn on my chest and the cut on my face.

"You should have stitches," she said, but she settled on a sterile adhesive bandage, huge on my cheek.

"What happened back there?" I asked.

From the front, Mondragón replied, "We agreed twenty minutes. You didn't show. I figured trouble. How did you bumble your way into that situation?"

"They jumped me as soon as I walked into the parsonage."

"Who were they?"

"My best guess is White Horse."

"The vigilante group," Rainy said. "What did they want?"

"Peter."

"Why?"

"Same reason the Rodriguezes want him. To stop what he's doing. And probably to get the names of the other Desert Angels."

Mondragón said, "Did you get a look at them?"

"Just heard their voices."

"Recognize any of them?"

"Not sure. But give me some time and maybe it'll come to me."

We left Cadiz and drove north into the night.

Any landscape under moonlight is a beautiful mystery. The high desert of southern Arizona, with its hills and black mountains silhouetted against a star-salted sky, was no exception. I stared out the window thinking that in the great Northwoods of Minnesota the roads were walled with thick forest in a way that made you feel as if you were passing through one long, verdant tunnel. Here, the land was wide open, and in the far distance I could see the little embers of yard lights that glowed outside the isolated ranch houses of Coronado County. In the dark, too, were snakes and lizards and spiders that could kill you with poison. And cacti just waiting to pierce your skin. In the washes, sometimes, crept men with guns and drugs who might shoot you without thinking twice. And also, there were women and children lost in so many ways, desperate to be led to safety. I thought about Peter and how much I admired what he was attempting to do. And I wondered, if I were in his place, would I have the courage to do what he did?

Mondragón, as if reading my mind, said, "When I find Peter, I'm going to make sure I put an end to this stupidity."

"Not stupidity, Berto," Rainy said. "I'm scared for Peter, and I don't like at all the idea that he's put himself in danger this way. But, oh, God, I do admire our son for it."

"What's the point, Rainy?" Mondragón shot back. "The people he helps, more often than not, get picked up later by Border

Patrol or ICE and end up right back where they began, but only worse because now they have nothing. Hell, less than nothing. What good does that do them?"

"You don't know that, Berto." She was quiet a moment. "There was a time when you would have understood. Maybe even have helped him."

"You stick your neck out only for family, Rainy. Everyone else is on their own."

"Your world is so small, Berto," Rainy said. "You must be so afraid inside it."

"I'm afraid of no one," Mondragón snapped. "As for my world, it's a very comfortable place. Not like that hovel you lived in out there in Who Gives a Fuck, Minnesota. If I'd raised our son, he'd be a man feared and respected."

Rainy said, "Better, I believe, to be loved."

"You think he doesn't love me? That I don't love him? Then what the hell am I doing here?"

Squabbling like an old married couple, I thought, but held my tongue.

We pulled into a truck stop outside Tucson that sold everything: CBs, cell phones, audiobooks, clothing, knives, souvenirs, medicines, an array of drinks and snack foods. While Mondragón filled the gas tank, Rainy and I went inside. I needed to replace the shirt my tormentors had ripped, and I picked out a long-sleeved T-shirt with a big coiled rattlesnake on the front. Rainy gathered some medical supplies: sterile gauze, bandages, adhesive tape, antiseptic.

"When we find Peter and the people with him, they may need tending," she explained.

We also picked up several gallon jugs of water. When we went to pay, the clerk, a kid with spiked hair the color of cotton candy, eyed my torn shirt and the blood-soaked bandage on my cheek.

"I'd like to see the other guy," he said.

Before we rejoined Mondragón, I asked Rainy, "Where you're staying, is it safe?"

"Berto arranged for a house in Nogales. We're less than half an hour from Cadiz. Don't worry about me, Cork. It feels very safe." She glanced outside, where her ex-husband was seeing to the SUV, and she shook her head. "But I'm remembering now all of Berto's bad habits." She smiled and kissed my cheek. "I'd rather be with you."

Outside, we put the supplies in the back of the SUV. Under the bright glare of the truck stop lights, I rolled out the map on the hood, and Mondragón and Rainy flanked me.

"Here," I said and pinpointed the Lulabelle.

Mondragón studied the map for a couple of minutes, then, without a word, walked away and made a call on his cell phone. When he came back, he leaned over the map and said, "There's a jeep trail off the Magdalena Road this side of Sells. It will take us to the base of the Santa Margaritas within a stone's throw of the mine."

"Who'd you call?" I said.

"Friends," he answered. "Who know the area well."

We took a highway west toward the desert once called Desolation. After half an hour, Mondragón's cell phone rang and he answered.

"Sí," he said. "Muchas gracias, amigo." Over his shoulder, he said, "There's a rolling Border Patrol just after we turn off Eighty-Six. You looking decent back there, O'Connor?" Then he said, "Doesn't matter. You're white. But probably best we hide your Winchester and my Weatherby."

He pulled over, and I handed him my Winchester. He opened the back of the SUV, lifted a panel in the flooring, laid both weapons inside, then dropped the panel back into place.

"You should come up front with me, Rainy," he said. "A little more natural looking."

257

She patted my hand and climbed into the passenger seat.

A short while later, we turned onto the Magdalena Road, a dirt and gravel track, and almost immediately hit the checkpoint, a couple of wooden barricades manned by several Border Patrol agents. One of them held up a hand signaling us to stop, and Mondragón complied. The agent approached us with a flashlight in his hand. Mondragón slid his window down. The agent shot the light into his face, then across to Rainy, then in back, where I was sitting.

"Where you folks headed?" he asked.

"Ali Molina," Mondragón said. "But when I was growing up we called it Magdalena."

The agent moved around to the rear of the SUV and shone the light into the back, which looked empty. He continued circling and, when he came to the window beside me, studied my face carefully.

"What happened?" he asked.

"A little surgery," I said. "Had a skin cancer removed. Looks worse than it is."

He grunted, maybe in acceptance of my story or maybe in sympathy. Hard to tell from the stone of his face. He moved to Rainy and took a good look at her. She smiled and said, "Good evening, Officer. Beautiful night on the desert."

"Yes, ma'am, it is. You folks wait here a minute."

He returned to the barricade and spoke briefly with one of the other agents.

"What's the holdup?" I said quietly to Mondragón.

"I don't know, but I don't like it."

The agent returned. "Where you folks coming from?"

"Phoenix," Mondragón said.

"What's your business?"

"Family reunion," Mondragón said.

"In Magdalena?" The agent didn't hide his skepticism.

"The family reunion is in Phoenix. We came down to visit my uncle, who's too old to travel."

"Kind of late for a visit, don't you think?"

"Our plane was delayed. We got to Phoenix much later than we'd expected."

"Got lots of water in the back."

"Our relatives have warned us plenty about being in the desert without water."

The agent nodded, then looked into the dark beyond the barricades. "I need to caution you, there's been significant drug activity reported in this area. One of our agents was attacked out here this morning. I can't stop you, but if you come across a vehicle off to the side of the road or see anything that looks suspicious, I'd advise you to just keep moving, don't stop. If it's something you think needs to be looked into, give 911 a call."

"Thank you, Officer," Mondragón said. "We'll be careful."

"All right, then. Night, folks. Drive safely." The agent returned to the barricades, moved one of them aside for us to pass, and we drove on.

"Rodriguez," Mondragón said, the name like something foul he'd spit from his mouth. "He conducts his business with all the finesse of a pig in a sty."

I said, "His business is drugs and trafficking in human misery. How do you expect him to operate?"

"Quietly," Mondragón said.

"Like you?"

"We are legitimate businesspeople, O'Connor. The holdings of my family, our investments, are international. We have interests in manufacturing, transportation, real estate, electronics."

"All from laundered money, I would guess, that came originally from the same kind of work Rodriguez is doing. Am I wrong?"

"Carnegie's money or the money of the Rockefellers, where do you think that came from? The sweat and labor and even the sacrifice of the lives of small people, and from a manipulation of the law and authority. Do you know the story of the Ludlow Massacre? Coal miners in Colorado striking for fair wages and safe working conditions in 1914. John D. Rockefeller owned the mine. What did he do? He had the governor send in the Colorado National Guard to break the strike. They killed twenty-six people, mostly women and children. And now in the United States, the name of Rockefeller is revered. What my family does, what we aspire to, is simply the American dream."

"And what is Rodriguez to you but competition?"

"Rodriguez has threatened my family," Mondragón said in a low voice. "I will make Rodriguez pay."

We turned onto what was little more than a faint track through the cacti. As soon as we were off the Magdalena Road, Mondragón stopped.

"We wait here. If we tried driving any farther, our headlights would give us away. We'd be visible to Border Patrol or Rodriguez's people, if they're out there."

"I want to get to Peter as soon as possible," Rainy said.

"We'll move at first light, *querida*."

I was beginning to hate that word.

CHAPTER 22

I slept fitfully in the backseat. Rainy had insisted that I lay myself out, try to rest. She'd given me ibuprofen from a container she carried in her purse, but everywhere still hurt like hell.

In my sleep, I dreamed that she and Mondragón were walking on a beach along the ocean somewhere. The sky behind them was a blazing red, as if from either a sunrise or a sunset. Or maybe even from a huge fire invisible except for the glow of its flames. They were talking.

You have always been beautiful, Mondragón said.

Rainy replied, but I heard only the last part: *I loved when you did that.*

This? Mondragón said.

He turned to her and cupped her breasts in his hands and kissed her. Then they were lying naked on the beach, red in the glow of the sunrise or sunset or flames. And I woke

263

with a start.

The desert was on fire with a red dawn. Rainy and Mondragón were in the front seat, talking quietly. I lay for a moment, listening.

"Those of us with dual citizenship, we hope our daughters marry American men, because they're not so macho and won't hit our daughters. Our sons, we hope, will marry Mexican girls, because they know how to be good wives."

"And Consuela, is she a good wife?"

"She is an obedient wife."

"Do you love her?"

"We have a life together. But I have loved, truly loved, only one woman, *querida*."

They were both quiet. I heard the grating caw of a crow in the still of the morning air outside. Then Rainy said, "There's plenty of light now. We should go."

I sat up slowly. Both my cut cheek and the cigarette burn on my chest felt on fire. My ribs were tender where I'd been punched. I pulled up my rattlesnake T-shirt.

Rainy turned in the front seat. "Oh, Cork. It looks awful."

"I've hurt worse." Which even to me sounded way too macho.

"If we were on Crow Point, I'd put together a poultice for that bruise."

"I'll take some more ibuprofen."

I swallowed four tablets and followed them with a lot of water from one of the gallon jugs in back.

"If you're through with your patient, we should be going," Mondragón said. "Here." He handed a GPS device to Rainy. "Cell phone reception out here is pretty iffy. I've keyed in the coordinates for the Lulabelle. Should take us right to Peter."

In a short time, the sun was above the horizon, and for a while we drove with it glaring in our eyes. When we entered the shadow of the Santa Margaritas, Mondragón turned south, following the foothills along the western face of the range. The jeep trail was barely a trail at all, and he took it slow.

After forty minutes, Rainy said, "We're close." She pointed toward the mountains. "Up there."

Mondragón braked to a stop and said, "Let's take another look at that map."

We stepped from the SUV. The air hadn't cooled much in the night, and as the sun climbed, I could feel the day heating up, the blast furnace of the desert being stoked. I unrolled the map and laid it on the vehicle's hood. I studied the contours, then the mountains themselves. I've spent a lifetime in the Boundary Waters Canoe Area Wilderness, reading maps of all kinds, including contour maps, but the shadow of the mountains and the distance and the twisting terrain here made it difficult to locate the fold high up where Jocko and I had seen the mirror flash. The one thing I could tell absolutely was that it was going to be a rugged climb.

"Where is it?" Mondragón said with impatience.

I shrugged. "Hard to say."

"Un momento."

He opened the back of the SUV, lifted the panel where he'd hidden the rifles, rummaged for a moment, and returned with field glasses and a satellite phone. He gave me the field glasses, and I studied the mountains.

"There," I said and pointed. "Beneath the big outcrop that looks like a buffalo head."

Mondragón took the glasses. He eyed the place, nodded to himself, then handed the glasses to Rainy. He walked away from us, far enough that we couldn't hear, and made a call on the sat phone.

When he returned, Rainy said something to him in Spanish. He answered tersely, and I could tell that she wasn't happy with whatever he'd said. But she accepted it.

Mondragón studied the mountains. "I can't get the SUV up there. We walk from here. Let's get our things."

He opened the rear door again and lifted the panel. I stood beside him this time and saw that beneath the panel lay a small arsenal of rifles and handguns.

"What's that Winchester of yours?" he asked.

"A thirty-thirty."

He handed me a box of cartridges, pulled out his Weatherby and then another rifle, a fine looking Mauser with a scope, and held it out to Rainy.

"No," she said.

"It might save Peter's life, *querida*."

"I won't exchange another life for Peter's."

"You've killed for our children before."

"I'm not taking the rifle, Berto. I'll carry water instead. And the first aid supplies."

He gave her that hard look, which, I'm sure, wilted the backbone of those who served him, but Rainy stood firm. Mondragón shook his head slowly. He put the Mauser back and produced a backpack, which he handed to Rainy. She loaded it with the water jugs and the supplies we'd purchased at the truck stop. Mondragón added the sat phone. The pack was heavy, and I offered to carry it.

"The shape you're in, O'Connor, you'll be lucky to make the climb at all," Mondragón said.

Rainy said, "I'll be fine, Cork."

Mondragón put the compartment cover back in place and locked the SUV. Rainy shouldered the pack, and we began our walk into the desolate hills toward the Lulabelle.

Mondragón took the lead. There was no trail. We wove our way among the cacti and scrub desert growth. The slope steepened. We began to slip on the loose rock and had to go more slowly. The ribs on my left side were throbbing. I could hear Rainy breathing hard above me, occasionally gasping as she made her way over difficult rock outcroppings.

"A rest," I finally called to Mondragón, who was getting ahead of us.

He paused and waited. We caught up and sat.

I could see the desert spread out below, stretching toward another hump of mountains to the west. The ground between the ranges rolled gently. The soil that covered it was yellow, and against that backdrop, the succulents — chollo, yucca, saguaro, pincushion, and God knows what else — and the mesquite and occasional acacia trees were a rich and striking green. I saw, maybe for the first time, that this land, in its way, was not unlike the Northwoods of Minnesota. What grew in Tamarack County was exactly what should be growing there, the kind of life that could thrive in that soil and that climate. The desert was a forest of a kind, a community of life perfectly suited to its home. I'd viewed it as alien, but that was only because I didn't understand it. There was danger here, but hell, people got lost and died in the Northwoods, and I still cherished the place. I thought I could understand how someone who knew the desert could love it deeply despite the dangers and the difficulties.

"They come looking for sanctuary," Rainy said. "And this is what greets them."

"Unforgiving," Mondragón said. "Deadly if you don't know what you're doing."

"Peter knows what he's doing," Rainy said.

"We'll soon see. We need to be going."

Mondragón stood and began again to lead the difficult climb.

It was well over an hour before we reached the fold where the opening of the Lulabelle Mine lay in the shadow of the buffalo-head outcrop I'd seen through the binoculars. When the entrance came into view, Rainy started for it quickly, but Mondragón held her back.

She pulled herself free. "Peter's there," she said angrily.

"Maybe," Mondragón said. "We should be very careful."

"He's right, Rainy," I said. "A few minutes of caution won't make a difference to Peter now."

"I'll go first," Mondragón said. "You any good with that rifle, O'Connor?"

"I hit what I aim at."

"Cover me."

Mondragón walked slowly, his attention jumping from the dark mouth of the mine to the walls of rock that rose around us. All the way up the long climb, I'd heard the calls of desert birds. Here there was no sound. Like Mondragón, I scanned the rock walls, but spotted nothing that moved. I could feel Rainy, tense beside me, her eyes riveted to the mine entrance.

Mondragón reached the Lulabelle. He stood a moment, off to the side of the opening, listening.

"Peter!" he called. He received no reply and called again.

"I can't wait any longer," Rainy said. She loped toward Mondragón, the weight of the pack making her gait awkward.

I had the Winchester to my shoulder, a round already chambered, just in case, but nothing happened. She reached her ex-husband and they slipped into the mine. I saw a flashlight blink on, illuminating the dark inside. Then Mondragón stepped out and waved me to join them.

We could see no evidence of anyone having been in the mine recently, at least near the opening. The excavation appeared to go deep, but it wasn't inviting. Rainy called Peter's name several times and got no reply. Mondragón shone his light over the scarred rock walls and floor. The beam hit a little stash of cans and debris, but it was clear the trash was old.

"Wild-goose chase," he said and gave me that stony glare.

"We should go deeper," Rainy said. "We should make sure."

"It's too dangerous, an old mine like this," Mondragón said. "If Peter were here, he would have answered."

"Maybe he can't."

"He isn't here, *querida*. Whatever O'Connor thinks he saw, it wasn't Peter."

Rainy unshouldered her pack, grabbed the flashlight from his hand, and started deeper into the throat of the mine.

I agreed with Mondragón about the danger, and I called out sharply, "Rainy, no farther into the drift."

"Drift?" Mondragón gave me a puzzled look.

"Mining term for a passage like this."

I didn't have time to explain to him that I'd grown up on the Iron Range of Minnesota, where anybody who knew anything about underground mining understood what a drift was.

Rainy stopped, but not because of me or Mondragón. She shone the light behind a fallen piece of rock the size of a doghouse.

"Look," she said.

We joined her and saw what the beam illuminated — a stain the color of rust on the mine floor.

"Blood?" Rainy said.

Mondragón knelt and touched the stain. "It's dried, but I'm sure it's blood." He stood and looked into the black that went deep into the mountain. "I can't believe he's in there. Why would he go deeper?"

"Maybe something scared him," Rainy said.

"Maybe," Mondragón said. "I need to make a call on the sat phone."

He went to the pack Rainy had set near the mine entrance, pulled out the satellite phone, and stepped into the sunlight.

The first shot came like a crack of thunder.

CHAPTER 23

Mondragón spun back into the mine. The rocks around him exploded in fragmenting lines as a steady stream of bullets followed him in. The rounds ricocheted off the walls, and the roar of the gunfire from outside sounded like Armageddon had arrived. It was automatic rifle fire, and I had no way of telling how many shooters there might be.

"Behind there!" I shouted at Rainy, pointing toward the doghouse rock where we'd found the bloodstain.

Mondragón grabbed the Weatherby he'd brought, and I pressed myself into the questionable protection of a slight indentation in the wall with the Winchester in my hands. I could see most of the thirty yards of open ground in front of the mine and spotted one of the shooters in a tier of rocks on the far side. He was laying down a steady lacing of bullets into the floor near where Mondragón had flattened himself against the wall opposite me.

"You okay?" I called in a momentary lull in the gunfire.

"Not hit. Where's Rainy?"

"Here," she called from behind us. "Don't do anything stupid."

"Any suggestions?"

"Just sit tight," Mondragón offered.

"And then what?"

If he gave an answer, I didn't hear it. The storm of bullets came again, chewing up the rock all around us. I thought that if they kept that up long enough, they'd run out of ammunition eventually. They must have thought so, too, because in the next moment the gunfire died away.

From the rocks came a voice with a Hispanic accent: "You in the cave. We want Peter Bisonette. Tell us where he is and we'll leave you in peace."

"Chinga tu madre!" Mondragón shouted.

A few shots came in return, but not the hail of bullets that had been fired before.

"We can blow you up, if that's what you want," the voice informed us.

Mondragón responded in Spanish. I couldn't understand the words, but the tone needed no translation.

I could still see the man who'd laced the floor with fire from his automatic. I was deep in the shadow of the mine and pretty certain he couldn't see me. I cradled the butt of the Winchester stock to my shoulder and sighted carefully. If he behaved as he had before, in the moment in advance of his firing, he would rise just a bit above the rock, exposing half his chest. I prepared myself mentally to take him out.

Rainy said, "Negotiate."

"What?" Mondragón said.

Rainy came up behind me, into the negligible protection of the rock indentation. She called to the men outside in Spanish. In all that she said, I understood only Peter's name and the name Rodriguez.

In the long quiet that followed while our assailants considered her words, Mondragón said, "They'll never buy it, *querida*. They think they're holding all the cards."

"What did you tell them?" I asked.

"That Peter's not here. That we don't know where he is. That killing us gets them nothing."

"Not much of a negotiation, Rainy," I said.

"That's not all," Mondragón said. "She told them to tell their *patrón* Rodriguez that she will meet with him to discuss her son. That will never happen, not as long as I'm alive."

Which, in the next moment, seemed to be

275

not long, because an explosion shook the mountain face outside the mine, and the wall I'd pushed myself against shivered. Dust and grit rained down on us.

"RPG," Mondragón said.

"Rocket-propelled grenade," I told Rainy. "They want us to know they're not bluffing."

From outside, the voice spoke again in Spanish.

Rainy translated for me. "He says in one minute, they'll seal our tomb."

I tried to think, to come up with a rational plan. We could move farther into the mine, where the explosive might not harm us, but that might simply end in us dying slowly in a sealed-up tomb. We could make a dash for it outside, splitting up so that they might not get us all. But they'd get some of us.

The seconds were ticking away, and nothing reasonable came to mind. The only real concern I had was for Rainy. Whatever else, I wanted Rainy safe.

I said to Mondragón, "When I sprint out there, you cover me. I'll make for that first big rock on the right."

"No," Rainy said.

"There's no time to argue. When I get set there, I'll cover you both."

"I'll go," Mondragón said. "You cover me."

I was about to argue, but he pushed himself away from the wall to make his run.

He didn't go any farther, because outside the mine it suddenly became the Fourth of July. We could hear the pop and rattle of gunfire, but no rounds came into the drift.

"What's going on?" Rainy called out.

"The cavalry has arrived," Mondragón said.

I remembered the calls he'd made on his satellite phone and understood why, when the attack first came, he'd advised us to just sit tight. He knew help was on the way. If it hadn't been for the RPG, he'd have been content to do nothing.

The gunfire died out. Mondragón waited. Rainy and I waited.

Amigo came the call from outside. Then more in Spanish.

"It's safe now," Mondragón said. He took Rainy's hand and led her into the light.

There were a half dozen of them, men dressed all in camouflage, looking very military. The one who'd called to Mondragón saluted him when we emerged. They spoke to each other in that language I was beginning to wish to God I'd studied in high school.

"What are they saying?" I asked Rainy.

"He's explaining to Berto what happened. They killed four men in the rocks."

"Who are these guys?"

Rainy shrugged. "He keeps calling Berto 'Jefe.' "

One of the few words I knew. It meant "boss."

Two men in camouflage came from the rocks shoving before them another man, who wore jeans, scuffed boots, and a western shirt with snaps. They forced him to his knees at Mondragón's feet.

"*Mírame,*" Mondragón said.

The man looked up. Man? He was just a kid, not even twenty. Fear whitened his eyes, shortened his breath, poured off him as if a foul scent. He bled from a nasty cut where the skin lay open on his cheek, the result, I could imagine, of a blow from a rifle butt.

Mondragón barked at him. The kid shook his head. One of the men who'd dragged him from the rocks kicked him in the spine. Mondragón spoke again, even more harshly.

The kid began to babble, his words mixed with saliva and tears. He shook his head again and again, and although I couldn't understand a word, he was plainly pleading for his life.

278

Mondragón knelt, took the kid's chin roughly in his hand, and forced him to look directly into Jefe's eyes. Mondragón said something low and quiet. The kid began to cry in earnest, deep sobs.

"What did he say?" I asked Rainy.

"Berto says he's going to gut the kid and leave him for the vultures to feed on."

Mondragón stood up and nodded toward a camouflaged man, who reached to his belt and pulled out a long military blade.

"No," Rainy said.

She stepped between Mondragón and the kid. She addressed her ex-husband, her words, whatever they were, spoken fiercely. Mondragón snapped at her, and she gave it right back at him. They stood eyeing each other, Rainy smaller, her face upturned and as hard as any rock in those mountains. I saw Mondragón's eyes shift from her to the men who surrounded us. This wasn't just about Rainy and him. This was also about El Jefe now.

I said, my voice as reasonable as I could make it, "If you value your relationship with Rainy and you want to work with us to find Peter, you'll do what she asks. Otherwise she will shut you out completely. You know this. Peter is what's important here."

Mondragón considered my words. Finally

he said to Rainy, *"Sí."*

She turned and knelt before the kid. His head was down, his eyes on the ground where his tears were turning the dust to little spots of mud. She took his face in her hands and lifted it, so that he could see her. She spoke to him gently.

"Cómo se llama?"

"Pedro," he replied.

She talked to him quietly for a while. The only word I heard and understood was *madre*. Mother. The kid listened and nodded and then began to respond to her. They conversed for some time. Mondragón listened, and it was clear from his face that he was learning much from the conversation.

At last, Rainy stood.

Mondragón spoke in English, probably for my benefit. "We have everything we need." He nodded to the man who'd kicked the kid in the spine. "Shoot him."

Rainy said, "You will release him."

"He tried to kill us."

"Because those were his orders. He's barely more than a child, Berto. And his name is Pedro. Peter. He goes free."

"Then he goes back to Rodriguez, and we face him again someday."

"He's from a small village. He swears he will return home."

"He's lying."

"Maybe. I want to give him the chance I promised him. Do this thing, Berto. For me, for Peter, for the good of your own soul."

The sun was above the mountains, and Mondragón's shadow fell across the young man and Rainy. At his nod, Pedro would be dead. But I knew what Mondragón was weighing. On one side of the balance was this present moment, and on the other the rest of his life and quite possibly the deep-seated hope that somehow, someday he might win Rainy back. Because the one thing I understood absolutely in all of this was that he still loved her.

"All right, *querida*," he said. "But he goes with nothing and he goes barefoot."

"Berto, that's so cruel."

"If he's truly a man, he has a chance. It's the same chance those people Peter helps are willing to take."

He spoke to Pedro, who said not a word but began removing his boots and socks. When he'd bared his feet, he stood. He said to Rainy, *"Gracias, señora."*

Rainy took his hands in hers. *"Vaya con Dios,* Pedro."

He looked at me, and I saw what Rainy saw, a kid way over his head in something that he regretted now because of the present consequences but that, if he survived and grew wise, he might regret later for all the right reasons.

"You understand English?" I asked.

He gave a nod.

"An old friend once told me the place we walk, wherever we lay our feet, each step of the journey is one we have always been meant to take. From the moment you were born, Pedro, this is a journey that has always been before you. Do you believe in God?"

"Yes, *señor.*"

"Put yourself in those hands. And keep your feet pointed south."

"Gracias, señor."

"Desaparece," Mondragón commanded.

Pedro turned and walked away, disappearing among the rocks. Mondragón gave a gesture to one of his men, who followed.

"Berto," Rainy began.

"Just to make sure that he goes," Mondragón said, then called out, *"Muchachos,"* and delivered his orders in Spanish.

They carried the bodies of the dead men deep into the mine and, while there, searched for more signs of Peter. They found nothing. While this was going on, Rainy removed herself and sat high on the rocks. I finally joined her there.

She didn't look at me. Her dark eyes were

282

taking in the desert far below. "So many deaths. It wasn't supposed to be this way."

"Everybody here calls it a war, Rainy," I said. "And you didn't start it."

"I haven't done anything to stop it. *We* haven't done anything to stop it."

"We? You and me?"

"All of us, Cork. We erect fences. We build walls. And what does that invite? Hostility breeds hostility. Fear breeds fear."

"And love breeds love," I said, because I knew where she was going. "If you'd stepped outside that mine and offered those men love, do you know what would have happened?"

"How many of them were just like Pedro, do you suppose?"

"That's not a question I ask myself when someone's shooting at me."

I looked back toward the Lulabelle. Near the entrance, Mondragón was counseling with the man who seemed to be in charge of the others. The man gave a sharp whistle, and all those in camouflage followed him into the rocks in the same direction Pedro had gone.

Mondragón climbed to where we sat. "We're done here. Get your pack, Rainy. It's time to go."

She left the water, just in case Peter or

someone else came and needed it. Then we started down out of the mountains, putting the Lulabelle behind us. Riches had come from the mine once upon a time. Now, for a while, all that would be coming out was the stench of rotting flesh.

CHAPTER 24

"What now?"

We were returning to Cadiz, Mondragón at the wheel of his SUV, Rainy in the seat beside him, me in back. We'd been a quiet crew since leaving the Lulabelle. So much death behind us. I'd seen it on that scale only once before, an incident I'd told no one about, not even Rainy. In that profoundly disturbing circumstance, I'd killed several times over. I didn't know exactly what the events of our morning had done to Rainy. She stared out the window at the desert streaming past us. She was one of the best, one of the kindest, spirits I'd ever known. In all this, she'd wanted only to find her son. But that search had brought terrible death. And there was no guarantee that the dying was over.

"What now?" Mondragón repeated.

"How did they know we'd be there?" I said.

285

"I asked Pedro that," Rainy said. "He didn't know."

"Rodriguez has eyes and ears everywhere in his little kingdom," Mondragón said.

"No one knew where we were going except Jocko and Sylvester," I said. "And your people. Who are they anyway? They looked like real military."

"Perhaps they are," Mondragón said. "Mexico is no different from any other country. Money buys everything."

"Loyalty?"

"Anyone can be bought. That is why you trust no one but family," Mondragón said.

"So maybe one of those men?"

"I will have someone look into that, but I think not. The price of betrayal is very high. I think it would be better to talk to your Jocko and Sylvester."

Which I'd already decided to do.

"What else did Pedro tell you, Rainy?"

"He said there'd been bad trouble a few nights ago. Lagarto — Carlos Rodriguez — and his oldest son, Miguel, went out with some of their men. Lagarto came back badly wounded, but Miguel didn't come back at all. Many of the men who went with them also didn't come back. Those who did were ordered not to talk about what had happened. Pedro thought maybe it had been a skirmish with another cartel."

"Not another cartel," Mondragón said. "Peter."

"Peter wouldn't have shot men," Rainy said.

"He called you and confessed, *querida.*"

"I don't know what he confessed to."

"Don't know or just don't want to accept? He is not your little boy. He is a man. A man does what he must."

"Oh, Berto, give me a break. What movie did you lift that from?"

It was just after noon when we reached the outskirts of Cadiz. Mondragón dropped me at the side of the road. Before I left her, Rainy lowered her window. I saw such a shadow over her face that it nearly broke my heart.

"He only wanted to help people," she said. "Now all this."

"Not his doing, Rainy."

She surprised me with a faint smile. "What you told Pedro about his journey always being before him, was that from Uncle Henry?"

"Almost verbatim."

"I hope Uncle Henry's spirit is with that child."

"Henry would probably say that we never

walk our journey alone." I reached in and held her hand. "Are you all right?"

"I need to process." She leaned to me and kissed my lips briefly. "And you need to be careful."

"Enough," Mondragón said. "Someone will see us."

"Where are you going?" I asked him.

"I've told you before, best you don't know. Just in case. It's safest for Rainy."

"Bye, love," she said to me.

"You find out anything, tie a ribbon."

Mondragón pulled away, and once again, I watched Rainy disappear with him.

I started for the parsonage, carrying my Winchester down the streets of Cadiz, surprised that no one seemed to take particular notice. But this was Arizona. I was feeling pretty low. Some of that was because of my worry about Rainy and Peter. Some of it was because I felt a little sick. My cheek was inflamed. My ribs felt as if they'd been kicked by Sylvester's mule. I had a headache. I was famished, because I hadn't eaten in a good long while. The heat was blistering, and I was probably dehydrated. But my body was only part of the reason for my dragging ass. I was sick in my soul, exactly the way I'd been after the long-ago slaughter I'd taken part in myself. Men had died. I didn't know them. As Mondragón's minions had carried the bodies into the dark of the mine and dumped them, I'd tried not to think of the dead men as human beings. But Pedro had had a profound impact on me. He wasn't much younger than my own son, Stephen. He'd come from a small village, and God knows how he'd gotten himself mixed up with people like the Rodriguezes. Maybe those who'd died were no different, driven by terrible circumstance into a life no one would willingly choose. I'd seen that when I was a cop on the South Side of Chicago, dealing with gangs. Every child is born a clean sheet of possibility, and no mother dreams of her beautiful baby ending up dead in an alley or rotting in the black of a forgotten mine.

On the main street, a couple of men were taking down the Fourth of July banners. The patriotic red, white, and blue decorations were gone from the store windows. We'd given our annual nod to the battle our founding fathers had fought, and it was back to business as usual. When I reached the parsonage, I was careful on my entry. I checked every room thoroughly. No one was waiting to jump me. The place was a mess. Mondragón's shot through the window had left glass scattered on the kitchen floor, shards lying in the blood that the wounded man, whoever he was, had lost. The chair my assailants had bound me to was still festooned with severed pieces of duct tape. I cleaned up the mess, locked the door behind me, and headed to my borrowed pickup.

It was the middle of the afternoon when I arrived in Sulfur Springs. I stepped into Rosa's Cantina and found Sierra all alone, watching some talk show on the television above the bar. She turned to me and her eyes got big.

"Jesus Christ," she said. "What happened to you?"

"Nothing a cold *cerveza* and a good burrito wouldn't cure," I said, bellying up to the bar.

"You've come to the right place." She gave me a draft from the tap and said, "I'll put in that order." When she came back, she leaned against the bar. "Honey, you look like hell."

"I saw some of your photographs at Sylvester's place. Nice work."

"Thanks. Sylvester's a sweetheart."

"What can you tell me about him?"

"An institution. Knows these mountains and the others around here better than anyone. He's been prospecting in them all

290

his life. That's why Marian hired him, I'm sure."

I set my beer down. "He works for your mayor?"

"Sure does."

"Doing what?"

"Helping her locate old mining claims."

"What for?"

"From what everybody says, mining's coming back to the Coronados. Apparently, they've got all kinds of new techniques for extracting the ores."

"And your mayor is going into the mining business?"

"Word is she's involved with some deep-pocket enterprise out of Phoenix. She owns practically everything around here. Probably figures it's time she played with the really big boys."

"Where's her money come from?"

"Her family settled here way back when, owned one of the big spreads along the border. The truth probably is that they stole it from the Mexican landholders, who'd stolen it from the Apaches. The story around here is that they ran guns, liquor, you name it across the border. Their legitimate enterprises were ranching and mining, then the mines gave out. When Marian took over the operation, she gave up running cattle and took to land speculation. Like I said, she owns most of this town. Have you seen those big houses up on the mesa above Cadiz? Million-dollar-plus places? Marian built those."

"So, bringing big mining back, that's probably right up her alley?"

"Wouldn't surprise me."

"Have you seen Sylvester today?"

"Not so far. You never said what happened to your face."

"Got kicked by a white horse."

She gave it a beat then said, "Those bastards."

The burrito and the beer almost did the job. I left the cantina feeling much fortified. When I walked into the cool of Marian Brown's real estate office, she was scrutinizing a map laid out on her desk. She looked up, then folded the map.

"Afternoon," I said.

"You look like you were in a car accident."

"I don't think there was anything accidental about it."

"What can I do for you?"

"Nothing."

"Why are you here?"

"Just wanted to hear the sound of your voice. It makes my day. And, by the way, I love that fragrance you're wearing. Cinnamon and something else. Jasmine? Smells expensive."

"It is. I have it custom made." She gave me a puzzled, then slightly irritated look. "I'm rather busy."

"Buying up old mining claims?"

"I buy lots of properties."

"You own most of Sulfur Springs, as I understand it."

"Your point?"

"I guess I don't have one. Just thinking that in my experience, the more you have the more you want. Kind of a vicious circle."

"I really don't have time for this, Mr. O'Connor."

"Found the young man we were looking for, by the way."

She didn't blink. For a long time. "I'm happy for you. Where is he?"

"Been nice talking to you, Marian." I turned and left her office.

I walked up the hill to Sylvester's adobe house. I knocked on the door and got no answer. An old, dust-covered, red jalopy of a pickup was parked nearby. It was a quiet place, this small cove in the rock where Sylvester had built his odd little home. In that quiet, I heard a strange sound, a low keening. It came from the animal shed with the attached corral where, on my first visit,

I'd met Franklin, Sylvester's mule. I walked to the open window of the shed and peered in.

The mule lay on a bed of straw. The straw was splashed with blood. The blood had come from a great slash across the animal's throat. Sylvester sat beside his dead mule, his back against the shed wall, a bottle of Old Crow in his hand. He looked up at me.

"You think it's ridiculous to cry your heart out over a dumb animal?" he said.

"It's not ridiculous to cry your heart out over a friend." I ducked between the rails of the corral fence, walked into the shed, and sat beside Sylvester. "What happened?"

He took a long draw off the bottle. "Came back from a run into Cadiz, found him like this. You know, there's people in this world don't come near a mule for the quality of company they provide. Franklin here, he was one hell of a companion. Never complained. Never asked to borrow nothing. Never talked behind my back."

"Any idea who did this?"

"Could be anybody for any reason. Warning. Punishment. Maybe just purely for the mean hell of it. This is the wild west, mister. Out here, reason don't always apply."

"Is it because you helped me?"

"Maybe. But I don't see how anybody

would've known that. Less you told them."
He gave me a look that would have been
more penetrating had he not been halfway
through the bourbon.

"I told no one, Sylvester."

"The hills have eyes," he said and drank.

"I understand you work for Marian
Brown, helping her locate old mining
claims."

"Not no more."

"What did she want with the claims?"

"The old leases, if they were ever filed,
lapsed a long time ago. She wanted to file
new leases on the land. Thinks mining's going to come back to Coronado County in a
big way. Who knows, maybe she's right.
There's ore in these mountains yet."

"Is she planning on entering the mining
business?"

"Not directly, I don't think. When I
located a mine and verified that the lease
had lapsed, she would file in the name of
Southwestern Geotech. It's a drilling and
mineral exploration company out of
Chandler."

"What's that get her?"

"Search me. Maybe a share in the profits,
if there are any. Maybe she's just working
on commission, kind of like I was with her."
He took a swallow of bourbon. "You find

him? The young man you were looking for?"

"I found the Lulabelle. If he was there, he's gone now. Tell me, how'd you come to know Peter?"

"While I was scouting the lapsed claims for Marian, I stumbled across him squatting in one of the old diggings up in the Coronados. He'd made himself quite a home there. Nothing new in that. A lot of hippies did the same thing back in the day. Got to talking to him and over time, well, he grew on me. He told me he was interested in the old excavations. He wasn't the prospector type and it wasn't hard to figure out what he was up to. He was looking for places to give those poor folks coming across the border some shelter on their way to whatever they hoped might be a new life. You don't meet a lot of people like him, who are doing what they're doing just because they believe it's the right thing."

"So you quit working for Marian and started helping Peter?"

"Least I could do. A lot of wildcat mining went on in most of the mountains down here. No legal claim ever filed. No way to know where they are, unless you understand this country and have spent a good deal of time wandering the mountains and hills here."

"Like you have."

"I gave him some leads. He filed the claims."

"So he was competing with Marian in a way."

"She rules the roost around here. Made her hopping mad."

"The Lulabelle, was that a wildcat operation?"

"Yep."

"You told me there were a couple of other old diggings near the Lulabelle. No official claim filed on those?"

"That's right."

"Did Peter know about them?"

"I might have mentioned it."

"I'm thinking that if he decided the Lulabelle wasn't safe for some reason, he may have gone looking for one of those others."

"Reasonable speculation."

"Did he know where they are?"

"Not sure anyone knows exactly where they are."

"Not even you?"

"It was a long time ago I worked the Lulabelle. I knew about the other diggings only in general. The men who worked them were pretty secretive. Near as I could tell, one of them was somewhere south of the Lulabelle, maybe seven miles or so. The other was north a few miles. Back when I was a young buck, I did some drinking with the man worked that particular dig. We were both operating out of Ark."

"Ark?"

"Arivaca. Little town way to the west. When he was two sheets to the wind once, he told me he called his diggings the Jesus Lode. Told me it was because there's this big rock formation above the mine looks just like Jesus wearing a robe."

"What about the one to the south?"

"I got nothing." He looked at me, focused. "You know anything about hunting?"

"I've stalked deer all my life."

"If I was you, I'd go back to the Lulabelle and do like the Border Patrol. Cut sign. Maybe you can track him."

Which seemed to me an excellent idea.

He finally noticed my face. "You look like you tangled with a wildcat. What happened?"

"Some people asked me about that young man we've been discussing. Asked if I knew where he is."

"Didn't ask very politely. And I'm guessing they're still in the dark. Any idea who they were?"

"They blindfolded me, so I only heard voices. But I've been going over it again and again in my mind. I just confirmed that one was Marian Brown, your mayor. That expensive perfume she wears was a dead giveaway. And if I were a betting man, I'd lay down good money that your town cop Mike Sanchez was another."

Sylvester capped the bourbon bottle and threw it on the straw. "Shoulda guessed."

"Don't quote me until I confirm it," I said. "Look, I'll be happy to give you a hand here, if you need it."

He shook his head. "My responsibility. You go see to yours."

CHAPTER 25

Something strange was going on with the sky to the east, black clouds piling up along the horizon. If I'd been in Minnesota, I'd've sworn there was a storm brewing. But this was Arizona in July, the desert in the middle of a blazing summer. Did rain ever come to this country, and did it ever come in summer?

On my way to the Lulabelle, I'd hit an outdoor store at the edge of Tucson and had bought a good topo map of southern Arizona and a handheld GPS. Because I didn't know how long I might be searching the Santa Margaritas, I also picked up a hydration pack and two gallons of water, a thermal blanket, a pair of field glasses, a hunting knife, a Maglite, a ton of jerky, and some protein bars. I had plenty of ammo for the Winchester.

I was driving the same road Mondragón had followed the night before. I was thinking about the ambush that morning, going over in my mind how Rodriguez's men had known about the place and that we would be there. I didn't believe Sylvester was the leak. If Mondragón followed up with his own men and was able to vouch for them, that left two possibilities. One was Jocko. I hated to think that I'd misread the man. I couldn't imagine what might have motivated him to be working with people like Rodriguez. I considered the other possibility — the Border Patrol helicopter that had been hovering over the desert when Jocko and I spotted the mirror flashes from the Lulabelle. Was it possible someone in Border Patrol, Agent Jamie Sprangers maybe, had struck a deal with the devil? The Border Patrol had been tracking me. How, I wasn't sure. I'd gone over the pickup once more and hadn't found a transmitter. That didn't mean there wasn't one, so well placed or so sophisticated that I couldn't see it. I figured that when I reached the Santa Margaritas, Sprangers probably wouldn't be far behind. So I had to do whatever I did quickly and carefully. If that was possible.

As soon as I turned south onto the Magdalena Road, I came to the checkpoint we'd hit the night before. The barricades had been pulled off to the shoulder, where a couple of BP agents leaned against a parked truck. As I drove up, they glanced my way. One of them raised his arm and, with a couple fingers, waved me on. I was a middle-aged white guy. No visible threat. If Mondragón or Rainy had been with me, I probably wouldn't have been given such an easy pass. I understood that. What other criteria would you use to enforce such racially motivated fears? I'd seen it in Minnesota all my life. If you looked Native, if you looked like Rainy, you caught the eye of white people, and many, many white people thought things about you that were absolutely untrue. Often, the laws that white people ignored without a second thought were the ones that got flashing lights and a siren on the ass of someone of color.

I'd keyed in the coordinates of the Lulabelle, and when I came to the place where Mondragón had parked his SUV, I got out. I filled the hydration pack with water and loaded it with the supplies I'd bought, locked the pickup, and started quickly into the mountains.

The Santa Margaritas blocked my view of the eastern horizon, and although the sky above me was perfectly blue, I knew those black clouds I'd seen earlier were on the march. I climbed as fast as I could, as fast as my beat-up body would allow me. My ribs were still sore and there was a little fire burning along my cheek, but I pushed myself. I'd left Cadiz without communicating to Rainy or Mondragón what I was up to. I didn't have time to leave a ribbon tied to the angel's finger, and I probably wouldn't have anyway. I still didn't know where the leak was, and I thought it was best to go on this particular expedition alone.

I made it to the Lulabelle much faster than I had that morning, not only because I knew the way now, but also because I knew that I had to stay ahead of both those storm clouds and whoever might be tracking me. Although we'd found blood in the mine, there was no telling if it was Peter's or that of someone who was with him. There was no guarantee I wasn't on a wild-goose chase. But it was the only lead I had, so I followed it. I began, as I often did when hunting deer, moving in a careful spiral outward from the mine entrance, looking for sign. The firefight that morning had disturbed the area a great deal, and it took me longer than I'd hoped to find what I was looking for. Fifty yards north of the mine entrance, I spotted a partial print left in soft dirt. It looked as if it had been made by the sole of a cheap athletic shoe. A child's shoe. I had my sign.

Nikki Edwards had told me that Peter was good at covering his tracks, making it difficult for the Border Patrol to follow him. If that was true, something was terribly wrong. The trail Peter, or the people Peter was leading, left when they fled the Lulabelle was not hard to follow. Even in the rockiest of terrain there's loose dirt, and I found multiple prints leading north. Some were small, some larger, but none as large as a man might leave. Although I couldn't tell how many were with him, Peter was leading a group of women and children. Either they were moving too fast for him to cover their tracks or he was not able to. I tried not to think about the large bloodstain on the floor of the mine.

I'd gone maybe three miles, most of the way listening to the growing rumble of thunder, when a raindrop finally hit my face. I'd been focused on the ground, and when I looked up, I was startled to see that the great black chest of the storm had appeared over the Santa Margaritas. The temperature, I realized, was dropping rapidly. Something big was coming, and it was coming fast. I took the field glasses and scanned the rugged landscape in front of me.

Henry Meloux was a man surprised by almost nothing. The old Mide had once told me, "When you open yourself to spirit — of the land, of the creatures, of other human beings — what comes to you is always what's to be expected." When I'd asked him what that was, he'd smiled, had spread his arms wide, and said simply, "Bounty."

Standing with the field glasses to my eyes, I understood the truth of my old friend's words. Because what I saw, maybe half a mile ahead, glowing in the sunlight not yet eaten by the storm clouds, was a singular rock that stood tall above all the others and that, to those who were spiritually inclined, might resemble the blazing figure of a robed Jesus.

"Find what you're looking for?"

The voice at my back was as startling as a clap of thunder, and I jerked in response. I'd been so intent on the ground and then on the scene in front of me that I'd paid no attention to what might be coming at me from behind. I turned and faced the four men who'd trailed me.

"Agent Sprangers. And it's Vega, right?" I said to the hulking man beside him. I glanced at the other two and waited for them to identify themselves, but they were mute.

"Just out for a stroll?" I asked.

Sprangers looked up at the sky. "All hell's about to break loose, O'Connor."

"In the middle of summer. Go figure," I said.

"You don't know about the monsoons?" Vega said. He was sweating bullets, the underarms of the khaki shirt he wore dark and wet.

A crooked finger of lightning hit the mountains uncomfortably close to us and the thunder that followed was deafening.

"They always come this time of year," Sprangers said when the din had died away. "We should find some shelter and have a talk."

The shelter we settled on was a narrow overhang of rock facing west. From our precarious little perch, I could see the desert below stretching toward the next range of mountains miles and miles distant. The land turned dark as the clouds gobbled up the last blue of the late afternoon sky. No sooner had we pressed ourselves beneath the little eave of rock than, as Sprangers had predicted, all hell broke loose.

I've been in my share of storms, but what rushed at us down the western slope of the

Santa Margarita Mountains was truly amazing. The lightning became almost constant. Like a violent hand, thunder shook the rock at our backs and the ground beneath our feet. In the sky, a battle between gods seemed to rage, the charcoal-colored clouds lit from within by great explosions of white light. The rain came in sheets, and the sheets were pushed nearly horizontal by the wind. A waterfall gushed over the eave just above our heads, and we pressed ourselves against the rock. Below us, a thousand liquid snakes invaded the desert. If Sprangers and his cohorts had hoped to question me, the storm put their intentions on hold for nearly an hour.

The battle of the gods moved southwest and the rain let up gradually. The waterfall eased to a trickle, and we stepped into the open.

"Quite a coincidence, running into you guys out here," I said.

"Where were you headed?" Sprangers asked.

"Headed? Nowhere. I heard the Santa Margaritas were a lovely area to hike. Gotta tell you, I haven't been disappointed."

"I've been doing a good deal of digging in the last day or so, O'Connor," Sprangers said. "I've found some interesting things.

Your son, Peter Bisonette, for example."

"Not my son," I said. It came out harsher than I'd meant. "My wife's son."

"Exactly," Sprangers said. "His birth certificate lists his last name as Mondragón, not Bisonette. His father's name on the certificate is Gilbert Mondragón."

"His birth father," I said. "Mondragón and my wife divorced after Peter was born. My wife legally returned to her maiden name, Bisonette, and changed her children's names as well."

"Gilbert Mondragón is the son of Santiago Mondragón. Does that name mean anything to you?"

I gave him a blank stare.

Vega took it from there, using his huge hands in surprisingly graceful gestures to frame the points he was making. "Santiago Mondragón is the head of a powerful cartel, operating for the most part out of Hermosillo, Mexico, in the state of Sonora. Carlos Rodriguez also operates out of Sonora. Rodriguez wields a good deal of power in the area just south of the border along Coronado County, but we understand that he'd like to extend his power. That's where he bumps heads with Santiago Mondragón."

"We thought your Peter Bisonette might

308

be involved in the drug trade that we know Rodriguez conducts here in the States," Sprangers said. "But we're beginning to believe there's something else going on."

"Like what?"

"We're hoping you might enlighten us," Vega said.

"That's what you followed me up here for?"

"The Santa Margaritas are part of the historic Oro Rico Mining District," Sprangers said. "They're honeycombed with old excavations. We suspect that Rodriguez has used these abandoned mines to hide his drugs. He might also be using them to hide someone he's kidnapped. Your wife, for example. The blood that was found at Robert Wieman's ranch house was not your wife's blood. We're not sure whose blood it is, but we think she might have been taken as a pawn in this power struggle between Rodriguez and Mondragón. Same with her son."

They didn't seem to realize Peter's true part in all this, and I was not about to enlighten them.

"If you're right," I said, "that means Rainy is still alive somewhere. That's wonderful news. But if it's true, why haven't I been contacted by Rodriguez?"

"That she's your wife means nothing to him. If there's communication taking place, it's probably between Rodriguez and Mondragón."

"Why don't you talk to Mondragón?"

"If we could, we would," Vega said, unconsciously clenching one of his hands into a fist as big as a sledgehammer head.

"What do you want from me?"

"We need answers, and you're the only visible lead we have," Sprangers said.

"Which is why you've been tracking me?"

"You wore a badge once," Sprangers said. "What would you do if you were me?"

I studied the four men. They stood together, their backs to the storm still raging in the distance. The lightning, white in the black clouds, gave them an occasional halo.

"Border Patrol. DEA. What about you?" I said to the two men who hadn't yet spoken a word. "FBI? State cops?" I turned to Sprangers. "You're all part of some kind of multiagency task force?"

"It's a big enemy we're fighting," Sprangers said. "Their crimes cut across all kinds of jurisdictions."

"I wish I could help you fellas, I really do. But . . ." I gave them only a shrug.

"That's the way it is?" Sprangers said. "In that case, you'll be coming with us."

"Where?"

"Back to Cadiz for some more questioning."

"If I refuse?"

"That's not an option, O'Connor."

I was half a mile from Peter. If I led them to him, and if he had, indeed, killed someone, I had no idea what the legal consequences might be. I also wasn't absolutely convinced that I should trust any of these men. Still lingering out there was the question of who'd leaked to Rodriguez the location of the Lulabelle. Mondragón might have been right when he told me that anyone can be bought. And the one piece of advice everyone had so far given me ran in a loop through my head: In Coronado County, trust no one.

"One more thing maybe you should know," Sprangers said. "Your pilot friend, Robert Wieman? Somebody beat him up last night."

"Who?"

"He couldn't say." He nodded toward my bandaged face. "Maybe the same people did that to you."

"Where is he?"

"The hospital in Sierra Vista. He's in pretty bad shape. You probably want to see him, and you can. Just as soon as we've had a good long talk. So, what'll it be?"

The storm was distant but still battering the sky above the land called Desolation.

"Back to Cadiz," I said.

CHAPTER 26

In an interview room in the Coronado County Law Enforcement Center, they worked me over with their questioning. Sprangers and Vega did all the heavy lifting. Deputy Crockett was there, too, although he said almost nothing. He'd taken off his tan cowboy hat, the one with the colorfully beaded band, and I saw that his hair was jet black. I figured he was another member of the task force, maybe representing the local jurisdiction, and maybe a part of it because of his Native heritage — Apache? Tohono O'odham? — and the unique perspective that might offer. God only knew who else might have been watching from the other side of the mirror on the wall. It was clear they thought Rainy had been kidnapped, although they didn't have an explanation for all the blood at the site where they believed she'd been snatched. They thought the same thing had happened to Peter. Their working assumption was that Rodriguez was using both Rainy and Peter as leverage in some kind of power play against Santiago Mondragón. I didn't disabuse them of the notion. Mostly, I played dumb. About my face, I told them that I'd cut myself shaving. Which was probably a line I'd picked up from a Humphrey Bogart movie.

"You and your friend Bob Wieman flew over the Santa Margaritas yesterday. Shortly after that, in the same general area, one of our agents was attacked." Sprangers leaned toward me across the bare table. "Coincidence?"

"I don't have another explanation," I said.

"Tell me you weren't up there looking for your wife or her son."

"Believe whatever you want to believe. It's a free country."

"Has Rodriguez or his people contacted you?"

"No."

"No? They didn't give you that shave?" Vega said. He'd been pacing the little room like a caged animal with a great deal of pent-up energy.

"A lot on my mind these days," I said. "My hand's a little unsteady."

"If Rodriguez has your wife and her son, why lean on you? What can you give him?"

314

"No one's leaning on me."

"Are you some sort of intermediary?"

"I'm some sort of nothing."

"Then maybe you have something they want," Sprangers said.

"What could that possibly be?"

Sprangers glanced at Vega, who stopped his pacing. Vega gave a nod of approval.

Sprangers said, "We know that Carlos Rodriguez has been moving a significant amount of drugs through Arizona. We believe that he's been caching them somewhere this side of the border until he ships them out. Maybe he's been using one of the old mines as a storage depot. We thought it might be in Coronado County, there are so many of them here. But maybe it's in the Santa Margaritas. And just maybe your Peter Bisonette knows where that is."

"And why would Peter know something like that?"

"We've been aware for some time that a humanitarian organization calling itself Desert Angels has been operating across the border. They've been good at keeping a low profile, so we don't know much about them. Peter Bisonette wasn't even on our radar until you showed up. Since we've started looking at him, he's become more and more interesting to us. We're pretty sure now that he's a Desert Angel. Because a lot of the illegals function as mules for the cartels, Peter has quite possibly dealt with some. Maybe they told him something about Rodriguez's operation, maybe something he passed along to his father or his father's people. And maybe his father saw a way to take a bite out of the competition. Maybe Peter was going to help his father steal that cache. Maybe he already has."

"And Rodriguez has grabbed him and Rainy as leverage to get the drugs back? That's your theory?"

"One of them. Look, we don't really have a problem with Peter. We're after the big players here."

I'd handled interviews on that side of the badge for a good long while, and although I figured some of what he'd told me was true, there was probably a lot more to this than he was saying. He was giving me a nugget of truth, maybe so I would overlook what was not true.

I decided to give him my own nugget.

"I can't imagine that Peter's involved in drug trafficking. I do know he's been helping guide undocumented women and children safely across the Arizona desert. That's his only interest in all this. We'd been told, Rainy and I, that Peter often used the old mines as temporary sanctuaries for these people. That's what I was looking for. One of the mines."

"What mine?" Deputy Crockett asked, his first and only question.

Now my own untruth. "The Vermilion One." Which was actually the name of a mine on the Iron Range in Minnesota.

"How'd you hear about the mine?" Sprangers said.

"Rainy had heard of it. I don't know how. Maybe from one of her conversations with Peter at some point. That's why I asked Bob Wieman to fly me over the Santa Margaritas."

"And then he gets beat up and you get that bad shave," Vega said. "If I was you, I'd be thinking there's a leak somewhere. Someone's been giving inside information to Rodriguez. Who did you trust that you shouldn't have?"

"You think I haven't been asking myself that same question?" I wanted to use my fist to wipe that smug look off his big face.

"We're not the enemy, O'Connor," Sprangers said. "We're just trying to do our jobs, which is to enforce the law. You wore a badge once. You get that. Do we always agree with the laws? Did you? So cool down for a moment and think. Who sold you out?"

Once again, I gave them names, the list of people I'd talked to: Michelle Abbott, who'd loaned me her pickup; the Harrises; Jeanette Saunders from the Goodman Center; even Marian Brown. When they figured they'd got everything from me they could possibly squeeze in the interview room, they told me I was free to go.

"The two men I took down yesterday with the Winchester. You get anything out of them?"

"Nothing yet," Vega said.

"No IDs?"

"They were clean, carrying nothing. Their prints aren't in the system. We've traced the vehicles they were driving to a leasing company in Nogales. Company claims the vehicles must have been stolen, that they didn't know about them being missing until our people contacted them. We'll lean on them, but it'll take a while to get anywhere, if we ever do."

As I left, Sprangers said, "Unfortunately, that monsoon downpour this afternoon washed out any signs that might lead us to this Vermilion One Mine. But BP agents are scouting the Santa Margaritas even as we speak. If we find the mine, and if Peter Bisonette is there, we'll let you know."

I had a parting comment for him as well.

"Let me ask you something, Sprangers. Could the leak be coming from your own people? I don't know who all is involved in this big operation of yours, but it seems to me you ought to be asking yourself the same question you asked me. Is there someone you trust but shouldn't?"

Although his face remained stolid, I saw in his eyes that I'd struck home.

It was near dark when I left the law enforcement center. It was cooler, too — the effect of the monsoons. I drove to the parsonage and parked in front. I went directly through the house and paused only long enough to cut a short length of red ribbon and pencil a note that read: *May have found him again.* I left by the back door, circled the block to the church, quickly tied the ribbon to the angel's finger, and put the note under the cross on the altar. Then I retraced my steps to the pickup.

I headed to Sierra Vista to locate the hospital where they'd taken Jocko. The whole way I went over everything I knew at the moment. It was a confusion of information in which I couldn't see any pattern yet. My movements were being tracked. Certainly by Sprangers, who claimed to be interested in bigger fish than Peter. Perhaps by Rodriguez, who had a bounty on Peter's head. Maybe even by the vigilante group called White Horse, whose interest appeared to be either misplaced patriotism or, more probably, simple racism. Much of the information I was operating on had been leaked to others besides me. Two good things: No one seemed to know that Rainy was safe and with her ex-husband, and they seemed to be as clueless as I was about Peter's current situation.

I found Frank Harris sitting in the hospital hallway outside Jocko's room. Harris looked beat to hell himself, emotionally anyway. He was drinking from a vending machine coffee cup.

"How's he doing?" I asked.

"He'll live. But, God, did they work him over. If I hadn't showed up when I did, they might have killed him."

"Tell me what happened?"

"After you left last night, Jocko came to our place for dinner. We ate, drank some good wine, talked about Peter and Rainy and this whole mess. Then I took Jocko back to his ranch and dropped him off. I didn't see anything unusual. When I was almost home, I realized that he'd left his rifle in my truck. With everything that's going on these days, he's been pretty careful to keep it with him. I figured the wine had made him forgetful. I turned around, and when I pulled up to the ranch house, I saw some men take off running through the pasture to the south. I found Jocko, beat to hell and unconscious. I called 911."

"Has he been able to talk?"

"They've had him pretty sedated. He's mostly been out."

"You get a decent look at these men?"

He shook his head. "Just caught a glimpse of them in my headlights. How about you? Any luck finding Peter?"

Who have you trusted that you shouldn't have?

"No," I said. "I spent much of the day talking to law enforcement. Where's Jayne?"

"She couldn't take it, seeing Jocko this way, the waiting. She had to go home. She has no stomach for this kind of thing." He laid his head back against the wall. "I should never have brought her out here. She's a businesswoman. To her, this is all the wild west."

"You both seem to be doing all right," I said.

"Thanks to her."

"What do you mean?"

"We lost more than half our vines to disease two years ago. We weren't alone. The other vineyards on the south end of the

321

plateau got hit, too. They sold and left. But Jayne's made some really savvy investments that have kept us afloat. Sonora Hills is coming back. Some of it's me, sure. I've been working with some guys in California, and I've got new vines growing now. More disease resistant. But it was Jayne's doing that bought me the time." He closed his eyes and took a deep breath. "It's not just God we fight with out here. It's people like Rodriguez."

A nurse passed us and went into Jocko's room. She came out a few minutes later. "He's awake, Mr. Harris, and asking for you."

"May we see him?" Harris asked.

"Just for a minute or two. He needs to rest."

Jocko's face was swollen. His eyes were at the centers of purple circles. Both lips had been stitched. Above the sheet that lay over him, I saw white bandaging across his chest. An IV ran into his left arm. Monitor wires had been attached to him like the strings of a puppet.

"Jocko, I'm so sorry," I said.

When he spoke, it was little more than a mumble. "They tell me I'll live."

I think he tried to smile.

"What did they want?" Harris asked.

"To know where I flew Cork yesterday."

I could barely hear him, his voice was so soft. I leaned closer. "Did you tell them?"

He was quiet, then his head rolled a little. "Don't remember. Sorry, Cork." His eyes focused. "Find him?"

"He wasn't there, but I think I know where he might be."

"Good," Jocko said. "Bring him home safe." He closed his eyes and I thought he was out again. But he said one more thing: "Hate to think I got beat to hell for nothing." His lips twitched, and this time his smile was definite.

Out in the hallway, Harris said, "Where do you think he is? Peter, I mean." When I didn't answer, he raised his hands. "That's okay, I get it. Better I don't know."

While I drove to Cadiz, the moon rose at my back. It had been filling since I'd left Tamarack County and was beginning to look like the belly of a pregnant woman. For some reason, I found that promising. I parked a block from the parsonage, walked a roundabout way past the church, and checked the finger of the angel. The ribbon was still there. I wanted to get back to the Santa Margaritas as quickly as I could, but there was nothing I could do in those mountains at night. It had been a long day, and I was tired and needed sleep.

I returned to the parsonage and checked it carefully. No one was waiting to jump me. I brought the hydration pack in from the truck, then propped chairs beneath the knobs of the front and back doors and made sure the windows were locked, although there was nothing I could do about the pane in which Mondragón's bullet had made a big hole. I thought about showering. I hadn't cleaned up good in a couple of days and figured I smelled pretty ripe. But bed sounded better, so I lay down with the Winchester for company.

I wondered where Rainy was laying her head that night and tried to trust that she was safe in Mondragón's keeping. I wondered what they were up to in their long absences, but tried not to wonder too hard. Before I drifted off, I whispered a part of the Pueblo prayer she'd taught me, "Across the dark night, we are not afraid. Our love is the star that guides us."

And then I was asleep.

CHAPTER 27

I woke early, still in the dark, and with an idea in my head. Sleep does that sometimes, clears the fog so your brain, which never really shuts down, can see things more clearly. I'd been trying to figure how Sprangers had been able to track me, and now I had a speculation. I knew Customs and Border Patrol in Minnesota were using drones to patrol our border with Canada, which often ran through long stretches of remote wilderness. It made sense to me that they were probably using drones along the Mexican border in the same way. If that was true, it wasn't outside the realm of possibility that Sprangers had one monitoring me. It seemed extreme, yet the sense I'd got from Sprangers was that he and everyone else in law enforcement in Coronado County were desperate to net Carlos Rodriguez. If they thought I was good bait, they might well figure the allocation of a drone

325

to track me was justified. I didn't know much about drones, so I turned on my cell phone and Googled them. There was a lot of technical information, but it took some time to find what I was looking for, which was how to elude detection.

Drones flew at great heights, I read, and a primary method of tracking was thermal imaging. Several websites devoted to foiling government plots suggested trying to mask my thermal image.

Along with the other supplies I'd got on my way out to the Lulabelle, I'd bought a thermal blanket in case I was forced to spend the night in the desert. Although it was a long shot, I thought that if I covered myself completely with the blanket, kept all my body heat from escaping, I might be invisible, or nearly so, to a drone. Worth a try, I figured.

The other possibility was that if they'd actually put a drone on me, they couldn't keep it in the sky 24/7. Maybe in the dead of night, the thing returned to base.

I left the lights off. If someone was watching the house, I didn't want them to know I was stirring. I shouldered the hydration pack, wrapped myself in the thermal blanket, covering everything head to toe, grabbed my Winchester, and slipped out the back door. I felt a little ridiculous, like a character from Lord of the Rings in some sort of cloak of invisibility. I'd continued parking the pickup a distance from the parsonage, in case someone had staked out the little house, and I made a dash for it. The streets were empty, no one to spot a crazy man wrapped up in what probably looked like Christmas foil. I drove to the main drag of town, parked, then walked back to the church and checked the statue. The ribbon was still on the angel's finger.

Where the hell were Rainy and Mondragón? Why hadn't they visited the statue?

I didn't have a lot of time to consider those questions. There was a vague suggestion of light along the eastern horizon, the promise of dawn still an hour away. I returned to the pickup and left Cadiz to the last of its slumbering.

An hour later, I hit the truck stop south of Tucson where Rainy and Mondragón and I had stopped a couple days earlier. I gassed up and refilled the hydration pack with water. I still had the power bars and jerky I'd picked up the day before, but I bought four gallon jugs of water and the same medical supplies that Rainy had purchased. When I hit the road again, the sun was just about to bubble up over the horizon.

I had no idea if my speculation about the drone was correct and if I'd slipped away from Cadiz unnoticed. I decided it was best to skirt the Border Patrol checkpoint on the Magdalena Road, in case they'd been alerted to watch for me. I left the highway just shy of the turnoff and carefully maneuvered the pickup cross-country, between cactus and mesquite, until I came to the jeep trail that led to the Santa Margaritas.

I stopped when the GPS indicated I was three miles north of the coordinates for the Lulabelle, which was how far I'd gone the day before when I'd spotted the Jesus-shaped rock and then Sprangers had surprised me. I pulled the truck off the trail and parked in a little swale that gave it some cover should a Border Patrol vehicle or anyone else just happen along. I put the medical supplies I'd bought into the hydration pack, shouldered it, and walked fifty yards away to where I had a good 360-degree view of the desert. The air felt fresh and was still cool from the monsoon rains the day before, and it carried the faint, pleasant scent of sage. The only sound was the chatter of small desert birds. I used the binoculars to scan the sky. It was absolutely clear of clouds and, as nearly as I could tell, of drones. But I knew if one was up there, it was hovering so high my binoculars would never spot it.

I walked into the foothills of the Santa Margaritas, making my way up the slope. Every time I looked to the west, the dark shadow of the mountains had shrunk and more and more of the desert lay yellow under the rising sun. With the dawn, the air had begun to heat up quickly. I thought about Peter and the people who were with him. They'd been in the desert five days. Even if they'd had water when they began, it had to be gone by now. Once again, the desperation of the people Peter was trying to help, their willingness to risk everything in the hope of finding sanctuary, overwhelmed me.

As I climbed, I paused periodically to scan the mountains for what I'd begun thinking of as the Jesus Rock. In the vast wilderness of Minnesota's Boundary Waters, unless you know the territory well, you absolutely need a map, since the many lakes and the terrain around them look so similar. It was the same in the desert, at least to me. This was alien country and I hadn't learned how to read it. I used the GPS to guide me back to the coordinates where I'd ended my search the day before and where, moments before Sprangers had surprised me, I'd spotted the

Jesus Rock glowing in the long, golden slant of the sun. The light was different now, everything in shadow, and I couldn't distinguish it. The heavy rain had washed away any sign that I might have found to help me track Peter. I stood for a while, trying to decide on the best course of action.

I thought about the advice I'd given Pedro before he started barefoot on his journey through the desert, which was the advice Henry Meloux had once offered me. *Wherever we lay our feet, each step of the journey is one we have always been meant to take.* Trust. That was the message. I decided to put myself in the hands of the spirit of that place and to trust the journey, and I began in the general direction I believed the Jesus Rock to be.

I found the shoe half an hour later, a child's canvas sneaker. There was so little of it left that I could understand why it had been discarded. Or maybe it had simply fallen off and the child was too tired or injured to care. The inside was stained with blood. As I knelt on one knee, holding that little piece of some child's hope in my hand, I lifted my eyes, and there it was. The Jesus Rock. Catching the first gold rays as the sun mounted above the Santa Margaritas. I was no more than half a mile from it.

The rock might have been a guide, but the entrance to the Jesus Lode was a bitch to locate. Unlike the El Dorado, there was nothing in the area to indicate an old excavation. There was no clear flat in front of the entrance as there'd been at the Lulabelle. What gave the mine away was the child dipping her head to drink from rainwater gathered in the shallow depression of a stone shelf. She was so intent on drinking that she didn't see me until I was almost upon her. Then her dark eyes grew huge and she turned and fled into the rocks at her back. I followed. And there in a small fold was the opening to the mine, so well hidden that you would have passed right by it unless you had a good sense of what you were looking for or were just incredibly lucky.

The girl was nowhere in sight, but I knew where she was, and I figured that whoever she was with, they were watching me from inside the black throat of the mine.

I called out, "Peter Bisonette, are you there?"

No sound at all came from the darkness.

"Peter, it's Cork O'Connor."

I heard something then, a very low murmur, and a moment later, the little girl appeared again, stepping carefully into the light. She was small, emaciated, dirty, no more than ten years old. Her hair was black and cut raggedly short. Her features looked more Native than Mexican. She wore khakis and a yellow T-shirt that, at the moment, looked as if they'd never been washed. She had canvas shoes on both her feet, so I figured she wasn't the child who'd lost the sneaker. There were probably other children inside. She approached me slowly, and when she was very near, reached out for my hand. I gave it to her, and without a word, she led me into the mine.

The tunnel was a low, narrow dig, not nearly so well or artfully worked as the Lulabelle. The little girl still held my hand, but waited patiently for me as I paused to let my eyes adjust to the dim light inside. As the details began to emerge, I saw several women crowded together, and behind the protection of their bodies were the other children. As tired and beat up as I felt, these women and children looked to be in far worse shape. They were all so very thin, and the clothing that hung on them seemed held together only by threads. Like the little girl, they were Native in their features, and their eyes, when I could finally make them out, were dark wells of weariness and fear.

"Peter Bisonette?" I said to them quietly.

From behind them came a man's voice speaking in a tongue I didn't understand. The women parted, and the little girl guided me through.

"The last person on earth I expected to see," Peter said from where he lay. "How in God's name did you find us?"

He'd been hit in his right thigh. When I cut away his pant leg, I saw that the wound was a through-and-through and seemed to have struck no bone. There were entrance and exit wounds, which had bled significantly. He'd bound them with a strip of cloth one of the women had torn from her blouse. Blood had completely soaked the binding, and when I removed the cloth, I saw that the bullet holes were festering. I took the iodine from the first aid kit I'd bought at the truck stop, cleaned the wounds, and bound them with sterile gauze.

"Mom?" Peter asked as I worked.

"She's with your father. I'm not sure where they are right now. We were all at the Lulabelle yesterday, but you'd left."

"Jocko must have told you he'd seen my signal."

"I was in the plane with him."

"I would have kept signaling, but I saw the chopper hovering off to the west."

"We figured," I said. I finished the bandaging and sat back. "What happened at the rendezvous with these people?"

"Someone gave us up to Carlos Rodriguez," he said.

"Who?"

"I don't know. But Rodriguez and his people were waiting for us after we crossed the border."

"They shot you?"

"Maybe. Or it might have been the others."

"The others?"

Peter lay back against the rock of the tunnel wall. At twenty-nine, black-haired, tawny-skinned, and slender, he looked little different from those he was helping. I could see Rainy in him, in his eyes especially. They were like hers in color and in the compassionate spirit that shone through them. But Mondragón was there, too, in the handsome face and the hard set of his jaw. The women and children — I'd counted eleven in all: six women and five children — had crowded near and had watched as I'd worked on Peter's wounds.

"A bunch of men jumped us but didn't fire their weapons. They were suddenly there, all around us, coming out of the dark. I thought we were done for. Rodriguez identified himself and told me he was going to kill me. He said he was going to take the women and make prostitutes of them and sell their children. Then all hell broke loose. Someone started firing at Rodriguez and his men. I have no idea who it was. I saw him go down. I called to the women and the children, and they followed me out of the firefight. It was only after we were away that I realized I'd been hit. Thank God I was the only one.

"I patched myself up as well as I could and took everyone to the Lulabelle, a full night's walk from the border. On the way, I called Mom. Or tried. I had only one bar and my cell was in the process of dying on me."

"You have a sat phone though, right?"

"Had. I lost it in the firefight."

"Why call your mom? What could she do? Why not call one of the Desert Angels?"

"So you know about us?" he said. "I understood we'd been compromised, and I had no idea who'd sold us out. I thought if I could explain to Mom, she'd rope you into helping. Which, it looks like, is exactly what happened. She must have called my father to enlist his help, too."

He paused a moment and squeezed his face in pain.

"You okay?" I asked.

"I'll live. You didn't happen to bring water, did you?"

"I have some in my hydration pack and four gallons in the truck."

"Could you share what you have with the folks here? That rain yesterday gave us some relief, but they're all still pretty thirsty. And hungry. If you hadn't come along, I was ready to head out, see if we could find some Border Patrol and turn ourselves in."

"Head out? With that leg? You wouldn't get far."

The water in the hydration pack went quickly. I gave out the jerky and the power bars, and they went down fast. Peter asked me to tend to the feet of several of the women and children. They'd walked from Guatemala. Some had worn the shoes nearly off their feet, and their soles were cut and blistered. That they'd kept walking spoke in a heartbreaking way of the depth of their desperation.

"Maybe it would have been better to give them up to the Border Patrol," I said as I worked.

"Last resort," Peter replied. "None of them have family here. Do you know what would have happened? After all they'd been through, they'd have been sent back to

Guatemala. And do you have any idea what they ran from? So many of them have seen their husbands, fathers, brothers slaughtered in the violence there. If you could talk to them, they'd tell you that dying in the desert is no worse."

"Why did you leave the Lulabelle?"

"I'd posted some of the women and children as sentries. They spotted men coming into the mountains. These men weren't wearing uniforms, so I knew they weren't Border Patrol. I figured Rodriguez's men. Or maybe whoever it was who'd attacked Rodriguez. We left quickly and set out for the Jesus Lode."

"You knew where it was?"

"Approximately. I have to tell you, though, it was a stroke of luck actually finding it."

"I know a man who would say you were always meant to find it."

"I know him, too," he said with a laugh. "How is Uncle Henry?"

"Hopeful, as always."

I finished tending the final woman whose feet needed care, and she said something shyly to me in a tongue I didn't recognize.

"She says thank you," Peter translated.

I began to put away the medical supplies. "We were ambushed at the Lulabelle yesterday. By the same people you ran from, I'm sure. Rodriguez's men. We'd have been toast except your father called in the cavalry."

Peter looked pained, and not from the wounds in his leg. "Who knew about the Lulabelle?"

"Jocko. Somebody beat him up, and maybe the intel came from him. He was still in bad shape when I talked to him, and he couldn't say for sure. I also talked to your friend Sylvester. But somebody killed his mule, so I'm thinking he wasn't inclined to be cooperative. It's possible whoever was in the chopper that was hovering out here spotted your signal and relayed that information to Rodriguez."

"I figured the chopper was Border Patrol."

"Could have been. Like your father said to me, anybody can be bought. What now?"

"First, we cart that water up from your truck. Then you get me to Ark."

"Arivaca?"

He nodded. "I have friends there who'll help us. I need to arrange to get these people to safety."

He spoke to the women in a language that wasn't Spanish, and three of them followed me down to the pickup. We carried the water back to the mine. Peter talked with them all for some time, then he said to me, "They understand that you and I have to

338

leave, but that I'll be coming back. I've promised them. If I can't come back, for whatever reason, you have to make sure that someone does."

I looked at the faces of those women and their children, who'd traveled God knew how many miles and had endured God knew how many different kinds of hell. I understood why Peter would do his best to move heaven and earth to help them. What human heart was stony enough to refuse?

"You have my word," I said.

CHAPTER 28

Peter knew the desert. He directed me along a network of jeep trails south of the Santa Margaritas that kept us off main roads as we headed toward Arivaca. It was clear his leg was giving him a lot of grief. The rough ride didn't help. He listened as I filled him in on all that had happened since the night he'd left the message on Rainy's phone. I told him that in the firefight in the desert, Carlos Rodriguez had been wounded and his son Miguel had been killed.

"I tried to be so careful," Peter said. "I didn't want anyone getting hurt because of what I do."

"You've set yourself a pretty difficult task."

"Somebody had to." He shut his eyes for a moment, against the pain, I thought. When he opened them, he said, "A little over a year and a half ago, I was hiking in the desert, scouting safe routes. I came across a skeleton, very small. A child. There

340

was nothing around it, nothing to tell me how it had got there. Lost, abandoned, murdered? However it had happened, I couldn't help imagining that child, dying alone and afraid." He looked at me with those dark eyes that reminded me so much of his mother's eyes. "If it was in your power to prevent it, could you let that happen to one of those children back at the Jesus Lode? I've done all I can to keep children like them, and their mothers, from falling into the hands of a *coyote* who might leave them to die in the desert. Or worse, sell them into a life that's so bad they might as well be dead. But I never wanted killing to be a part of it."

"Unless we can figure out who's been feeding intel to Las Calaveras, the killing probably isn't over. I think they may be playing two sides against each other."

"What do you mean?"

"Whoever started the shooting in the firefight that night in the desert knew about the rendezvous location and probably knew Rodriguez would be there."

"Yeah," Peter said, nodding. "I've been thinking about that. At first I wondered if it might have been Border Patrol. But they opened up without giving any warning and without a lot of regard for the fact that there were women and children in the line of fire. It was just lucky I was the only one hit."

"What do you know about White Horse?"

"They're not happy with what I do, or the others trying to help the refugees crossing into the desert."

"Have they ever threatened you?"

"Not me personally. I've tried to keep a low profile."

"I think you haven't done a bad job. If it was White Horse who started that firefight, I don't think they necessarily knew it was you guiding the Guatemalans. I'm pretty sure you didn't pop onto everyone's radar until Rainy and I showed up. That includes the Border Patrol. They believe Rodriguez has been stashing drugs in one of the old mines down here, and they think you might know where that is."

"Jesus, are they barking up the wrong tree."

"They've put together some kind of task force — DEA, the Coronado Sheriff's Department, probably FBI, among others — with Carlos Rodriguez especially in their sights. They'd love to get their hands on him. You too, now."

"I'm compromised. My work with the Desert Angels is finished. I just want to get those women and children we left at the mine somewhere safe, get them to sanctuary. After that, I don't care what happens to me."

"Your mother cares. Your father, too."

"Mom would understand. My father?" He shook his head. "Who knows?"

I'd known Rainy for years and loved her deeply, but her two children were grown and had been away all that time. I'd met them only once, all too briefly, at our wedding in April. I'd liked them well enough, but they were Rainy's family, not mine. Peter had simply been a smart, handsome young man with a tough history. I hadn't made a place for him in my heart.

That was changing. What I knew of him now, his passionate willingness to risk everything to help all these desperate people who were strangers to him, struck a deeply familiar chord in me.

We entered Arivaca, a ramshackle little town nestled among hills with mountains to the east and desert to the west. Peter directed me to an old ranch house off the highway just north of town. When I pulled up and parked, a border collie leaped off the front porch and began to bark. Although it wasn't a big dog, it set up one hell of a ruckus.

"That's Duke," Peter said. "We'll stay here

343

until Papa Doc comes out."

A moment later, a tall man with a long, white ponytail and a substantial paunch stepped outside. He stood eyeing us but made no move in welcome.

Peter rolled down his window and hollered, "It's me, Papa Doc. Peter Bisonette. Call off your bodyguard."

The man gave one sharp whistle, and the dog returned to the porch and sat down beside him, quiet but still watchful.

I got out of the truck, helped Peter down, and gave him my shoulder to lean on as he hobbled to the house.

"Don't suppose you shot yourself," the man said when he saw the bloody gauze bandaging on Peter's thigh.

"Papa Doc, meet Cork O'Connor. Kind of saved my ass."

The man barely acknowledged me. "Come in before God and everybody spots you here. Last thing I need is Border Patrol swarming all over my place."

Papa Doc, whose real name turned out to be Dave Salisbury, was a retired veterinarian. He'd moved to Arivaca years before to escape a world he'd become pretty disgusted with.

"Out there, it's all about money and fame. We're a culture of celebrity. We bow down before the gods Kardashian. Fuck Wall Street and fuck Hollywood. The only real people left in the world are the ones standing on street corners with a sign asking for a handout."

I wasn't sure what he meant by that last comment, but he had a needle in his hand and was sewing up the wounds on Peter's leg and I wasn't about to argue some vague point with him. He gave Peter a shot of something and then some pills to fight infection.

"I need to use your phone, Papa Doc," Peter said. "I've got folks in the desert that need help."

"My kind of help?"

"Nothing that serious. I just need to get them to sanctuary."

"I'm not sure what's going on, and I don't think I want to know the details, but there's been a shitload of Border Patrol activity around here the last few days. You have anything to do with that?"

"Maybe. About that phone?"

While Peter made his calls, I stepped out onto the ranch house porch and turned on my own cell phone. I found that I had three bars. I texted the number Mondragón had used to set up my meeting with him and Rainy at the Goodman Center. The text read simply, *Got him.*

The phone rang moments later.

"Where are you?" Rainy sounded a little breathless.

"Arivaca."

"We'll be there in a couple of hours."

I told her how to find the ranch house, ended the call, and turned off the phone. Peter joined me. He was wearing different pants, a little big around the waist, but with both legs intact.

"A pair of Papa Doc's," he explained.

"Why do you call him Papa Doc?"

"The Doc part's pretty obvious. Papa because, despite the gruff exterior, he's got a heart of gold. He says he moved out here to escape the crass, modern world and maybe that was part of it. But for the last fifteen years, he's been instrumental in helping refugees survive their ordeal in the desert."

Papa Doc came out with tuna sandwiches and cold beers. We sat on chairs in the porch shade, while Duke lay down beside the old veterinarian. When I'd handed out the jerky and power bars at the Jesus Lode, Peter had refused any food. He wanted to be sure the others had plenty. Now he downed his tuna sandwich in a few quick bites, and Papa Doc brought him another.

346

"Got transport squared away for your people?" the vet asked.

"We'll have to spend another night at the Jesus Lode."

"We?" Papa Doc said. "You should stay off that leg for a while."

"I've got people counting on me. I need to get food back to them. Cork's power bars won't sustain them long."

"I'll take the food," I said. "You wait here for Rainy and your father. You still want to get back to your people, Mondragón can bring you. In the meantime, I'll do what I can up there."

Peter started to object, but Papa Doc said, "Don't let your stubborn nature get in the way of clear thinking, kid. It's a reasonable compromise."

Peter gave in with a reluctant nod. "We'll follow you this afternoon. If anything goes wrong . . ." He didn't finish, probably because there were so many things that could go wrong.

"Nothing will go wrong." I stood up and offered my hand to Papa Doc. "A real pleasure."

"One question for you."

"Shoot."

"You happen to know Garrison Keillor? I love listening to that guy on the radio."

■ ■ ■ ■

I bought food at the mercantile in Arivaca, which I put in a big backpack Papa Doc had loaned me. I set out for the Jesus Lode a little after 2:00 p.m. The jeep trail was a rough drive, and I took it easy with the pickup. In the rearview mirror, I could see those dark clouds mounting, as they had the day before, building toward another monsoon downpour. I was doing fine until I cleared the southern end of the Santa Margaritas. That's when the chopper picked me up.

I caught it out of the corner of my eye, a dark flicker across the sun. At first, I thought it was a vulture, that bird whose biological adaptation to the desert Agent Sprangers so admired. But it tracked me, and I finally stopped and pulled out the binoculars, and knew I'd been made. I had no idea if it was Border Patrol or one of the other interested parties in all this, but I was certain if I kept going, they'd follow me right to the Jesus Lode.

I considered my alternatives. I could stop and let the storm overtake me. The clouds were rolling in fast, lightning alive inside them, spitting bolts at the ground. I figured the violence of what was coming would probably drive off the chopper. But if the day before was any indication of what to expect, I'd have to make my way in a torrential downpour, into and out of swales that might be flash-flooded. I could simply wait where I was until the storm had passed, but I had no idea how long that might be. And if there was flooding, I couldn't even guess how long it would take for the swales to become passable.

The other possibility was simply to continue moving until I neared the Lulabelle, since both the Border Patrol and Rodriguez's people already knew about my visit to that area. I wouldn't be far from the Jesus Lode.

In the end, I went on.

The storm overtook the Santa Margaritas about the same time I came abreast of the Lulabelle. As I'd anticipated, the chopper retreated, swung off to the south, and disappeared. I picked up speed, hoping I didn't crack an axle on a high rock. Just as the rain began, I reached the place where, according to my GPS, I'd parked the truck that morning. I stayed out of the swale where I'd hidden the pickup — didn't want to risk it getting washed away — but pulled off the jeep trail behind a gathering of mesquite that provided some cover. I got out, shouldered the food pack, grabbed my Winchester, and started into the Santa Margaritas, leaning into the violence the storm had begun to throw at me.

In that monsoon rain, the desert became a liquid thing. Water poured off the rocks in sheets. The soil was viscous and slippery, and as I struggled up the slope, I knew I was leaving deep prints that, unless the rain washed them away completely, would easily lead anyone who was interested right to the Jesus Lode. But I didn't have much choice. I kept moving, soaked to the bone, with lightning slashing at the hills around me and thunder shaking the ground under my feet.

They were all gathered at the entrance to the mine, watching the storm from behind a little waterfall that leaped from the rocks above. They moved aside to let me through. I sloughed off the pack and opened it. At the mercantile in Arivaca, I'd selected food that would require no cooking, since a fire, or the smoke from it, could be seen from a great distance. I pulled out the bread, peanut butter, jam, canned fruit, and trail mix I'd bought. In that narrow tunnel, with the storm raging outside, the women and their children ate, while I parked myself behind the waterfall and watched to be certain they were safe.

The storm passed in the late afternoon. I went outside and took up a position in the rocks that gave me a good view of the desert. With my binoculars, I could see where I'd parked the truck a mile or so distant. I waited for Peter and Rainy and Mondragón to show. I heard a noise at my back, and found that one of the children, a boy of eleven or twelve, had left the mine and climbed to where I sat.

"Hi," I said.

"Hi," he replied.

"You speak English?"

"A little."

"Have a seat." I gestured to a place next to me.

He sat and stared at the desert, where the storm still battered the sky far to the west.

"What's your name?" I asked.

"Juan."

"Cork," I said and offered my hand.

He took it easily. His palm was rough, heavily callused.

"You've worked hard," I said.

"Strong." He flexed his arms to show me his muscles. "I cut cane."

"Sugarcane?"

He nodded. "Until the men came."

"What men?"

Juan shrugged. He wore a beat-up Dodgers cap. I tapped the bill and said, "Where'd you get the hat?"

"It was my brother's."

"You like baseball, Juan?"

"Yes. Most of the boys, they play soccer. But I want to be a pitcher, like my brother."

"Where is your brother?"

He looked out across the desert. "The men who came, they killed him. My father. My uncle. They burned the sugarcane." He was quiet, then said, "I want to pitch for the Dodgers someday."

"You like the Dodgers?"

"Hugo Pivaral pitched for them."

He reached into the back pocket of his dirty jeans and brought out a worn baseball card. Hugo Pivaral, a player I'd never heard of. According to the card, Pivaral played for the Dodgers' minor league team in the midnineties. He was from Guatemala.

I handed the card back. "It's a tough road, Juan. I hope you make it."

Other children drifted out and joined us. Juan introduced them, but it was clear that he was the only one who understood English. The women wandered out, too, and the sun went down, and the stars began to appear, but Peter and Rainy and Mondragón did not come.

CHAPTER 29

The night was clear, the stars like white dust against the black heavens, the moon a lopsided, yellow balloon. The vehicles came just before dawn.

I'd been sleeping fitfully among the rocks. It was Juan who shook me awake.

"Lights," the boy said.

They came from the south, following the jeep trail, three sets of headlights. I studied them with my binoculars and watched them stop on the desert floor directly below the Jesus Lode. The moon gave me some light, but not enough to see details. The interior lights came on as the passengers exited, but I couldn't tell who they were or how many.

Once the headlights and the interior lights were out, I couldn't see anything. It could have been Peter and his people. It could have been Mondragón's men, the same ones who'd saved our asses at the Lulabelle. Or even, I supposed, Border Patrol. The worst-case scenario was that it was Rodriguez's goons. I had no way of knowing. If they came up, it would take them less than an hour to reach us.

"Wake up everybody," I said to Juan. "Tell them we have to move."

The boy left me and went among the others, who'd found places to sleep on the rocks outside the narrow tunnel of the Jesus Lode. I continued to scan the folds of the hills that led up to where we'd thought we were safe, but I couldn't make out anything useful.

"They are ready," Juan said at my back.

The moon, what there was of it, dimly illuminated the ground. It was enough, if we went carefully, to see our way. I considered waiting until the sky lightened a little with predawn, which was not that far off, but I couldn't take the chance. Whoever it was below us might already be on the move.

"Follow me."

"Where?" Juan said.

"Where you were before."

"The other mine?"

I nodded. "The other mine."

I did my best to remove any evidence that anyone had been in the mine, put all the food and the waste from what had already been eaten into the pack. Four of the women each took one of the gallon water jugs. Then I led them away single file from the Jesus Lode.

I cursed myself silently, knowing that the prints I'd left in the mud on my climb during the storm could lead anyone directly to where these people had been safe. I tried to think. If they weren't Peter and his people, or Mondragón and his, how did they know where to come looking? The chopper? That would have given them only a general idea. But maybe that was all they'd needed, and then they'd spotted my truck. So it could well have been either Rodriguez's men or Border Patrol.

Christ, I was getting sick of playing at this guessing game. There were too many sides in this struggle, too many unanswered questions, too many threatening possibilities.

The sky began to lighten, and we could see more easily and move more quickly. I picked up my pace, wanting to put as much distance as I could between us and those people behind us. When I calculated that we were roughly halfway to the Lulabelle, I stopped.

"A rest," I told Juan, and he spoke to the others.

After they'd all sat down, I pulled Juan aside.

"Do you think you can find your way to the other mine from here?"

The boy turned and studied the steep slopes and folds of the hills to the south, all of it gray in the dim morning light. "Yes," he finally said.

"You're sure."

"Yes. But why?"

"I'm going back. I want to find out who those people are and make sure they haven't followed us. Do you understand?"

He nodded.

"Will you explain to the others? I don't want them to think I'm deserting you."

He spoke to the others in the language he'd used all along and that I'd heard Peter use. The women talked among themselves, and then to Juan, and then stared at me.

"They are afraid," Juan said. "But we have been afraid before."

"I'll come back to you just as soon as I can."

Juan said, "I believe you."

I unshouldered my pack, which contained the food. "Can you carry this?"

"Yes."

"Five more minutes of rest, then go."

I turned and headed back the way we'd come.

I moved fast now, with the early morning

light illuminating the Santa Margaritas. When I was near enough to the Jesus Lode to use my binoculars, I found a tall, flat outcropping and lay myself down on it. I could see the Jesus Rock, but not the mine opening. I scanned the hillsides below the mine. I saw them coming, like ants swarming.

They were spread out and it took me a while to count them. Fifteen men, all carrying weapons. They weren't dressed in the military fatigues Mondragón's men had worn, nor did they wear Border Patrol uniforms. They were Rodriguez's people. As I watched, I realized that there was one man in the lead, moving slowly, studying the ground. A tracker. He led them to the rocks surrounding the entrance to the Jesus Lode, and they all disappeared where an hour earlier the women and children had been sleeping.

I considered my options. I could slide from the rock and return to Juan and the others, who, if they weren't already at the Lulabelle, would be there soon. Or I could maintain my position until I knew what Rodriguez's people would do next. If the man in the lead was a good tracker, he'd probably find signs that would lead them all to the Lulabelle.

I was torn, but the decision was taken from my hands.

Four men passed below the ledge on which I'd flattened myself. I recognized them. Agent Sprangers and DEA Agent Vega, Sheriff Carlson, and Deputy Crockett. They were headed directly toward the Jesus Rock, but not moving quickly because Sprangers was cutting sign. It was clear that he didn't know exactly where he was leading the others, and that he had no idea what he was heading into.

Trust no one in Coronado County. The advice everyone had been giving me since I'd arrived in this desert place.

Trust only family. Gilberto Mondragón's advice.

Then I heard another voice speaking, that of a wise old man: *Trust your heart.*

"Sprangers. Carlson," I called out.

The men stopped, spun around, and looked up.

"You're heading into a firefight," I said from my perch. "Rodriguez's people. They have you outnumbered and outgunned."

"What are you doing here, O'Connor?" Sprangers said.

"Are you really surprised to see me?"

Carlson said, "Where's Bisonette?"

"Not up there ahead of you. Keep going

358

and in ten minutes you'll run into fifteen heavily armed men."

"Come down and we'll talk," Sprangers said.

I left the ledge and made my way to where the others stood. "Just the four of you? This is all the manpower of your task force?"

"Are you on the up-and-up?" Carlson said. "About Rodriguez's people?"

"God's truth."

"Is the Vermilion One up ahead?" Vega said. "Is Rodriguez finally making his move?"

"It's a mine all right, but there aren't any drugs there."

"And you know this how?" Sprangers said.

"I'm betting Bisonette told him," Vega said.

"Peter has nothing to do with Rodriguez and his drug trade. Look, here's the story. Six nights ago, Peter rendezvoused with a group of Guatemalan refugees. His intent was to guide them safely across the border and to sanctuary. I'm pretty sure somebody in the Desert Angels sold him out. Carlos Rodriguez and his son Miguel and a bunch of Las Calaveras gunmen set up an ambush. But they weren't the only ones waiting out there. Someone opened fire on Rodriguez and Las Calaveras. If I had to guess, I'd say it was members of White Horse."

"Those goddamned vigilantes." Carlson spoke with such vehemence I thought he might throw down in disgust the gray Stetson he wore.

"Peter and his people were caught in the middle of the firefight," I explained. "But they got away. Carlos Rodriguez was wounded. His son was killed. It may be that Carlos blames Peter for Miguel's death and wants very badly to get ahold of him."

"How do you know all this?" Sprangers said.

"Does it matter? It's all true. And now Rodriguez's men are a few minutes ahead of you, looking for Peter and the Guatemalans. I'm willing to bet they wouldn't mind killing some law enforcement officers instead."

"Call it in," Sprangers said to Crockett.

The deputy was carrying a small pack. He took out a sat phone and stepped well away from us.

"Why are you here?" I asked.

"We lost you in Cadiz yesterday," Sprangers said. "This was where we found you before, so I sent a chopper to keep an eye out for you. They spotted you last night before the monsoon came in. Because of the storm and the dark, we didn't get a start out here until first thing this morning." He looked toward the Jesus Rock. "Apparently a little bit later than the others."

"Why just four of you?" I looked at Carlson. "And aren't you a little out of your jurisdiction, Chet?"

"There's something big going on west of here," Carlson said. "All of Sprangers's people have been called in to help."

Sprangers said, "You ever hear about the Yuma Fourteen?"

I shook my head.

"In May of 2001, a couple of *coyotes* led a group of twenty-six illegals across the border. They all got lost, spent way too long wandering in the desert before they were found. Fourteen of them died. It was pretty big news. We got word last night that another group was lost out there. Women and children this time. We've got agents and other law enforcement scouring all of southwest Arizona looking for them."

Crockett returned. "Backup on the way. ETA forty-five minutes."

Vega had a pair of binoculars to his eyes. "I see them."

I used my own field glasses. Rodriguez's men were climbing down the yellow rocks around the Jesus Lode. I figured they'd ascertained that the mine was empty, and I hoped maybe they'd leave. They gathered, palavered, then one of them separated from the others and began to scout the ground. He found something and even across the distance that separated us, I heard him whistle. He signaled the others and began to cut sign, leading them toward us.

We all stepped behind the blind of the outcropping on whose flattened top I'd been lying when Sprangers and the others showed up.

"We need to leave," Carlson said. Wisely, I thought.

Sprangers said, "Let's just make ourselves scarce. I want to keep an eye on them."

I said, "If that guy in the lead is any good at tracking, he could find sign of us all. Then it probably won't matter where we hide. There'll be a firefight."

Vega said, "I'm with Carlson. Let's get out of here."

"Ditto that," Crockett said.

"If they have field glasses, they'll spot us." Sprangers scanned the area where we'd gathered. "Up there." He pointed above us to a little overhang in a rock face maybe a fifty-yard climb away. "We position ourselves there. Then, even if they get wind of us, we'll have the advantage. We can hold them off until help arrives."

"Maybe," Vega said. "And maybe not. It isn't worth the risk. We go. We keep low. And even if they spot us, we've got distance. Let them try to catch us."

"We go, we could lose them," Sprangers argued.

While they fought among themselves, I stepped away and checked on the progress of Rodriguez's men.

"Guys," I said. "They're running."

"Which way?" Sprangers said.

"Away."

Sprangers and the others joined me, and we watched as Rodriguez's men made their way back toward the desert floor, moving fast.

"Something must've spooked them," Vega said.

"Get on the sat phone," Sprangers said to Crockett. "Get a chopper out here ASAP to track those men."

Crockett stepped away to make the call.

It took them less than half the time to reach their vehicles than it had taken them to climb to the Jesus Lode. We watched the black SUVs turn around and head south, toward the border.

"Let's go see what there is to see," Sprangers said. "You mind leading the way, O'Connor?"

The Jesus Lode was empty, as I knew it would be. Vega used a flashlight and went deep into the tunnel, Sprangers and Carlson with him. I stayed outside with Deputy Crockett.

"Gotta see a man about a horse," I said. "Okay?"

Crockett nodded. "Make it quick."

I stepped behind a rock that blocked me from the agent's view and took the opportunity to send Mondragón a text: *Lulabelle.* I turned off my cell phone, put it away, and rejoined Crockett just as the others emerged from the mine.

"Nada," Sprangers said. "He was here though, wasn't he, O'Connor? Where is Peter Bisonette now?"

I was happy he'd asked in that way, because I could tell him the truth. "I have no idea."

"Maybe if we cut sign, we'll find him," Sprangers said.

"What you would find is women and children who ran away from hell looking for nothing but a little peace. You want the big fish, right? I'll make a deal with you. You call off your agents, we go back to Cadiz, and I'll tell you everything I know."

"Will it get me Rodriguez?"

"It will get you closer than you are now."

Sprangers thought it over. Finally, he held out his hand to me.

"Deal," he said.

CHAPTER 30

Sprangers was in the interview room with me. Vega was there, too, practically filling the small room all by himself with his great size and his restless pacing. I figured Sheriff Carlson and his deputy were watching the proceedings on a monitor in another room.

I explained about Peter's phone call that had brought us to Arizona, about Los Angeles del Desierto, about Rainy still being alive. Although I told him about Mondragón, I left out the part about him shooting Rainy's assailant.

"Whose blood was all over the ground at Robert Wieman's place?"

"I have no idea." Which was the truth. I knew no name.

"Where's your wife?" Sprangers asked.

"I don't know. We all thought it best to keep me in the dark about that, in case Rodriguez got ahold of me."

"How do you communicate?"

"I'd rather keep that to myself."

"I thought we were going to trust each other."

"I trust you. I don't trust your whole organization."

"Any particular reason?"

"For starters, Rodriguez's men out there this morning. How'd they know where to look?"

"Bugged your pickup. They did it before."

I shook my head. "I checked that pickup top to bottom. You were there because of the Border Patrol helicopter that spotted me. Rodriguez's men were there because somebody in your organization leaked that information."

Sprangers didn't argue. Instead he said, "How did you know about Bisonette and his Guatemalan refugees and about the ambush in which you claim Carlos Rodriguez was wounded and his son killed?"

"I have better current intel than you. I'm not going to tell you how I got it, because I don't want to put lives in danger. But I'll tell you this. I think the other people involved in that ambush were White Horse."

Vega, who'd been pacing at my back, paused.

"How would White Horse have known about the rendezvous?" he asked.

"Good question. Maybe whoever leaked that information to Rodriguez also leaked it to White Horse."

"To what end?"

"I think they were hoping to decimate Las Calaveras," I said.

"White Horse," Sprangers said. The name clearly left a bad taste in his mouth. He looked at Vega behind me, and some unspoken communication must have passed between them. "A man in Sulfur Springs was killed by a car bomb a few months ago."

"I heard."

"He was one of ours, working undercover. Like I told you before, there's a lot of drug product moving through Coronado County. We're pretty sure that Las Calaveras is the supplier, and we think that a good deal of it is being handled by the trailer community north of Sulfur Springs."

"Paradiso?"

"Right. Our man infiltrated Paradiso. Someone made him, blew him up in his truck."

"I heard he was White Horse."

"He was trying to work his way into the group when he was killed. We're pretty sure that a lot of the residents of Paradiso are White Horse. These guys are bikers, disaffected vets, men who want to live off the grid for all kinds of reasons. Bitterness and disappointment are pretty much what they all have in common. They're disposed to disliking everyone, but their hatred seems to be fixated on the illegals and the government."

"A lot of them use?"

"A lot of them. But the product is distributed way beyond Paradiso and Coronado County."

"So why would they want Rodriguez dead?" I said. "If his organization supplies the product they use and someone there is moving it?"

Behind me, Vega said, "Maybe somebody hired White Horse to ice Rodriguez."

"Who?" Sprangers said.

"Somebody who offered a better deal. Somebody who wanted to eliminate the competition and take over Rodriguez's territory."

The room was quiet for a long moment.

Then Vega said, "Mondragón."

Sprangers looked at me. "Mondragón," he echoed. "A man whose family has dealt in every form of illegal trafficking across the border. And now he just happens to be here, in Coronado County. Along with his son, who knew the location of the rendezvous."

I felt as if we'd just moved back to square one.

"His son was wounded in that firefight in the desert," I said, trying not to sound as frustrated as I felt. "Why would Mondragón put his son in that kind of danger?"

"Maybe it didn't go down the way you think it did," Vega said. "Who told you about the firefight? Bisonette?"

He was right, but in his current state of mind, I didn't want to confirm his thinking. Instead I said, "What kind of man would lead a group of women and children into an ambush knowing there would be gunfire?"

"What kind of man is Bisonette?" Vega asked. "All we really know about him is that he's a drug addict and the son of a man whose family runs a powerful cartel. As for the women and children, we've seen no evidence of that. Maybe it's all part and parcel of some wild story to placate you and your wife."

"Look," I said. "I understand the need to question everything. I was a cop, too. But at some point, you have to trust someone. I trust Peter. I saw the women and children he was leading. I've spoken to Mondragón. He has nothing to do with whatever it is that's going down in Coronado County. He's here because he loves his son, and his son is in trouble. If you want to know why White Horse might have been involved in ambushing Rodriguez, I think I know someone you should talk to."

"Yeah?" Vega said. "And who's that?"

"Marian Brown."

"Brown?" Sprangers said.

"Mayor of Sulfur Springs. She's White Horse, or working hand in glove with White Horse, I'd bet my life on it. And you might talk to the town cop in Sulfur Springs. I'm pretty sure he's White Horse, too."

"Mike Sanchez?" Vega said, incredulously. "His family came from Mexico."

"Okay, maybe he's not actually White Horse. Maybe he's just a partner in what they do in Paradiso."

They asked a few more questions, but I'd already given them all I was going to for the moment. Before we left the interview room, I said, "One more thing."

"What's that?" Sprangers said.

"Take the drone off me."

I could tell from the look on his face that I'd hit home.

"I can do us all a lot more good without you constantly looking over my shoulder."

Sprangers said, "We'll be in touch."

Outside the law enforcement center, I

turned my cell phone back on. I had two missed calls. One was from the car rental insurance guy, who'd left me a message requesting in no uncertain terms that I call him back to discuss the blown-up Cherokee. The other was from Michelle Abbott, just checking in to make sure I was okay. I also had one text message, which had come from Mondragón. It read: *Safe. Everyone.* Which was a relief on so many fronts.

I headed first thing to the hospital in Sierra Vista to check on Jocko. I felt responsible for the beating he'd taken, although I knew it was something he wouldn't blame me for. It was just one of the risks of doing the good work of the Desert Angels, which I understood. The faces of Juan and the women and the children stayed with me. Maybe they weren't innocent in the eyes of the law, but there's something more important than the law, and that is simply compassion. That might sound strange coming from a man who's spent a good deal of his life behind a badge, but laws are made by human beings and human beings are not infallible. We make laws for all kinds of reasons, and not always the right ones. One of the most powerful motivations for the enactment of legislation is fear, and when you act out of fear, you risk becoming exactly the kind of monster you're trying to bar the door against. I couldn't help thinking that we were putting those women and children — and the men, too, who came looking for nothing more sinister than a job and a quiet life — through a monstrous ordeal. And I understood why Peter and the other Desert Angels were willing to risk everything to help them.

I found Jayne Harris at Jocko's bedside, which surprised me. Frank had led me to believe Jocko's condition was too difficult for her to deal with. Clearly, she was stronger than either of us had given her credit for. She was reading to him. When I came in and she closed the book, I saw that it was *West with the Night*.

"Bush pilot," Jocko said, looking and sounding so much better than the night before. "If I had it all to do over again, that's what I would've been. A bush pilot."

Jayne hadn't seen me since I'd been worked over. She studied my face. "Frank told me you'd had a run-in with someone."

"I survived."

"Who was it?"

"I can't say for sure. Out here, the possibilities are numerous."

"Rodriguez?"

"I'll know soon enough."

That intrigued her. "You're onto something?"

"I've got a better handle on a few things."

She nodded toward my face. "I hope you get there before someone kills you."

There was another chair in the room, and I sat down. "Where's Frank?"

"Seeing to the vineyards. Harvest isn't far off and there's plenty of work to be done. Especially now that both Peter and Jocko are out of commission. Any word on your wife or Peter?"

"Nothing official," I said.

"I'm sorry." She looked down at Jocko, lying beat up on the white hospital sheet. "I told you and Frank that getting involved with those people would end up badly."

"Those people?" I said.

"The Desert Angels."

"You knew?"

She laughed, but there was a brittle edge to it. "You can't keep secrets from someone you share a bed with."

Which hadn't been true for Rainy and me, but maybe Jayne and her husband were different.

"I've known about Frank and Peter and Jocko from the beginning. I just didn't want to get involved. One of us needed some dispassionate distance."

374

"You don't sympathize with the people they're trying to help?"

"Of course I do. Who doesn't? But just look what's happened." She held out her hand, indicating the bandaged Jocko.

"I'd do it all again," Jocko said. "You close your heart off, Jayne, and you're as good as dead."

"You go right ahead then and get yourself killed."

He smiled weakly. "Not dead yet."

"Just remember who's minding the store while you and Frank are off playing Mother Teresa. You think it's easy? If it wasn't for me, we'd be no better off than those people sneaking across the border."

Although she'd addressed this to the man in the bed, I had a sense it was a conversation she'd probably had with her husband on more than one occasion.

"In this hard country, Jayne darlin', we all gotta stick together."

"Family, Jocko," she said. "I'll do everything I can for family. Everyone else is on their own."

Which seemed to me to be almost an echo of Mondragón's outlook.

"I'll leave you to your reading," I said. "I just wanted to make sure you're doing okay, Jocko."

"Don't waste your worry on me, son. You got enough on your shoulders. But I appreciate your concern. *Vaya con Dios, amigo.*"

I said good-bye to Jayne, and her response was bitter and enigmatic.

"You've wakened sleeping dogs in Coronado County. I just hope to God you find your wife before they tear her apart." Then she echoed Jocko's final words, *"Vaya con Dios."*

But like an echo, they sounded distant and unfelt.

CHAPTER 31

On the way back to Cadiz, I paused at a little wayside, and spent a moment looking at the mountains to the west, the south, the east, the north. The blue sky was mottled with white and gray clouds, and along the horizon the buildup had begun for another monsoon rain. The whole rolling plateau was spotted with stunted, desperate-looking trees and covered with yellow grass rippling nervously in the breeze. In so many ways, this was a different country than I'd anticipated. I didn't know how to read this land. I didn't understand its people. And I gave myself over to a terrible homesickness for the North Country of Minnesota.

In the months since our marriage, Rainy and I had settled into a comfortable routine. Breakfast together in the early morning, sharing so much in that quiet hour before Jenny and Daniel and Waaboo were awake. It wasn't that we talked a lot. Rainy says

I'm about as talkative as a rolling pin. But sharing isn't necessarily about words. I missed her. Missed us. I felt desolate and alone in Coronado County.

When I thought of Rainy, I couldn't help thinking that she was with Mondragón, that together they'd worked to rescue their son. This sharing of effort was something I was sure would bridge whatever divide had existed between them, something that couldn't help but lace their hearts together.

Trust, I tried to tell myself. In Coronado County, trust was the rarest of commodities. And if I didn't trust Rainy, who could I trust?

As if in answer, the words from the Pueblo prayer came to me: *Our love is the promise that is never broken.*

I got back into the truck and drove on.

In Cadiz, I cruised past the church. The ribbon I'd tied the night before was still there. I headed south out of town and, a few miles later, took the turnoff to Sulfur Springs. As I came over the saddle in the mountains and down onto the desert below, I took careful note of Paradiso, the trailer community that lay north of town, built on a barren stretch of earth with no trees at all. It seemed to me that staying off the grid came at a high cost if it meant living like a reptile baking under a hot sun. I turned off on the Old Douglas Road so that I could take a closer look at Paradiso. I lowered the windows of the pickup, and as I passed the trailer community, I could hear music blasting, something heavy metal. I saw a gathering of motorcycles, and in the shade under a nearby awning, a few bikers in T-shirts lounged in lawn chairs with beer cans in their hands. They eyed me in the way they might a desert snake they couldn't quite identify.

I turned around and continued to Sulfur Springs. Sylvester's empty red pickup truck sat in front of Rosa's Cantina, right alongside what I believed was the only law enforcement vehicle owned by the town of Sulfur Springs. I parked and went inside.

They sat together at the bar, Sylvester, lean and long-bearded, the Arizona Diamondbacks cap crowning his head. Which made me think of Juan and his dream of pitching for the Dodgers. Sanchez sat heavy on his own stool, resting his chunky forearms on the bar top. Each had a beer in front of him and they were staring at the television, where a ball game was in progress. Neither man looked my way when I entered. I sat down next to Sanchez. He turned his head, but not his body, and the swivel of his neck reminded me of an owl eyeing prey.

"O'Connor," he said. The moment he spoke I knew absolutely he'd been at the parsonage the night I'd been beaten. "You look like hell. What happened?"

"Ran into a door," I said.

"A door with a good left hook looks like to me." He barked a laugh.

Sylvester didn't seem to notice my arrival at all. His eyes stayed riveted to the television screen.

Sierra came from the kitchen and stepped behind the bar. "You're getting to be a regular. What'll you have?"

"I'll have whatever the chief here is having."

"One Corona coming up."

"And a cheeseburger," I said.

"Can do."

When the beer was in front of me, I took a sip and asked, "Who's winning?"

"Giants," Sanchez said. "Our bullpen sucks today. Any luck finding that young man you've been looking for?"

"As a matter of fact, yes."

Sanchez nodded, gave it a few seconds, then said, "That so? How'd you manage it?"

"I told you when we first met that I'm a private investigator. I'm good at what I do."

"Where is he?"

"Safe," I said. "By the way, Chief, you know anything about an organization called White Horse?"

"Heard of 'em, sure."

"I understand they have a big following in Paradiso."

"What's your source?"

"I also heard drugs are being run out of there."

"Whoever told you that, mister, doesn't know his ass from nuthin'."

"Because you'd know if that was true."

"Damn right."

"But if it was true, what would that mean?"

"I told you it's bullshit."

"Seems to me that would mean one of two things. Either you're really a terrible cop. Or you're just looking the other way."

He turned slowly on his stool until the whole bulk of his body confronted me.

"You want to speak plainly?"

"I thought I was plain enough."

"You know that door you ran into? You're just about to run into it again, mister."

Sierra came from the kitchen and took quick stock of the dynamic going down at her bar. "Guys," she said. "If you've got something to settle, how about you settle it outside."

"I've got nothing to settle," I said.

Sanchez gave me the kind of stare he must have given kids he caught drinking beer underage. "You go spreading accusations, O'Connor, you're just asking for trouble."

"I'm already in trouble, Chief. But I'm not there alone. I intend to take White Horse down. You might want to pass that along to your friends in Paradiso."

He spoke like a man whose jaw had been wired shut. "I'm going to leave, because like Sierra said, this should be taken outside. O'Connor, next time I see you on the streets of Sulfur Springs, I'm going to arrest your ass."

"What for?"

"I'll have something. And by the time you come out of my jail, you'll think walking into a door was a picnic."

He stood up, squared his shoulders, and strolled out of Rosa's Cantina, affecting the kind of swagger he must have seen in a dozen John Wayne westerns. I followed after him to the door and watched him cross the street and enter the office of Marian Brown.

When I returned to the bar, Sierra said, "I hope you know what you're doing."

"You ever hunt quail?" I said. "You've got to flush them before you can shoot them."

She shook her head. "Let me see about that cheeseburger." She vanished back into the kitchen.

"True?" Sylvester said without looking at me.

"All of it," I said.

"You found him and he's safe?"

"Yep."

"Good."

Sierra brought my cheeseburger, and I watched the Diamondbacks lose as I ate, and Sylvester and I exchanged not another word.

When I left the cantina, Sanchez's cruiser was gone. I crossed the street to Marian Brown's real estate office. It was dark inside and the door was locked. On the glass of her big front window were taped photographs of the properties she represented, along with descriptions and prices. Judging from the listings, there was a good deal of land available for purchase in Coronado County. I wondered what was motivating the sellers. The war along the border? Or maybe they were just worn down from fighting the desert to scrape out a living. I stepped back into the street and scanned the sky, looking for a drone. I had no idea how high those things actually flew. If Sprangers decided to put one on me again,

I didn't know if I'd be able to spot it. The truth was that I didn't trust him. Not yet. Was there anybody in that county I trusted completely?

I remembered that I hadn't returned Michelle Abbott's call. I turned my cell phone on and punched in her number.

"I tried to call earlier," she said when she answered. "I just wanted to check in, make sure you're doing all right."

"I've been better," I said.

"Any word on Rainy?"

Although she might have been the one person I could trust, I knew that telling her anything could put her in danger.

"Nothing yet," I said.

"Peter?"

"Same," I said.

"I don't know if this is important, but I heard something today that you might want to know."

"What's that?"

"A member of my congregation in Sulfur Springs is the housekeeper for Marian Brown. Marian is the town mayor, and she also operates a real estate business."

"I'm familiar with Mayor Brown."

"A man came to Marian's house this morning. A hard-looking man with lots of tattoos. Maria called him a *cabrón*. He went into Marian's office to talk with her. Maria said they began to argue, raise their voices so that she could hear them. At one point Marian shouted, 'Kill him. Just kill him.' "

"Kill who?"

"Maria didn't hear. She was scared. She moved to another part of the house so they wouldn't know she'd been listening."

"Why didn't she go to the police?"

But as soon as I said it, I knew the answer. The same reason someone who was Ojibwe wouldn't go to the police in Minnesota. A history of harassment. A history of distrust.

"I've known Marian all my life, and I hate to say this, but I believe there's not a compassionate bone in her body." Michelle was quiet a moment. "Ah, hell. The truth is, she's a ruthless bitch, and I wouldn't put it past her to be involved in something as coldhearted as murder."

I turned around and stared at the dark real estate office, wondering where Brown and Sanchez had gone.

"Why are you telling me this?" I said.

She laughed, but it was more in disbelief than in humor. "Are you kidding? Ever since you arrived here you've been like a lightning rod. If it's not you, I thought it might be someone you've talked to. I don't know what any of this is about, but if you ended up vulture food and I hadn't said anything, I wouldn't be able to sleep nights. You be careful, Cork."

"Still praying for me?"

"My knees are callused."

I walked back to the cantina. Sylvester was alone at the bar, watching another ball game, drinking his beer. I took the stool next to him.

"Your former employer is on the warpath, looking for blood," I said.

"Whose?" His eyes didn't leave the television screen.

"Not sure. Maybe mine, maybe yours."

"Maybe that young man you thought was safe?"

"Maybe."

"What're you going to do about it?"

"Frankly, I don't know. I just wanted to make sure you're keeping your guard up."

Sierra came from the kitchen carrying a box of limes. "Didn't hear you come back in. Still thirsty?"

"I'm good, thanks. But I do have a question about that little trailer community north of town."

"Paradiso?" Her face clouded, just like a sky expecting a storm.

"Who's the toughest son of a bitch out there?"

"Why would you ask a question like that?"

"Do you have an answer?"

She put the box of limes down behind the bar and shook her head. "You get yourself killed, I'm not taking any responsibility for it."

"Fair enough."

"Royal Diggs," she said.

"Royal?"

She nodded. "Royal. Fits him. Rules the roost out there."

"Mean bastard," Sylvester said.

"Lots of tattoos?"

"They all have lots of tattoos," Sierra said.

"Wouldn't happen to wear a big ring on his right hand?"

"Silver," she said. "Face of a skeleton on it." She eyed me suspiciously. "You're not going out there."

"I haven't decided yet."

"Take a gun if you have one," she said. "Better yet, a bazooka."

She headed back to the kitchen. The door opened and two men walked in, their laughter harsh and loud. They took chairs at a table and one of them called out, "Sierra, where the hell are you, darlin'?"

I said quietly, "We need to talk, Sylvester."

He gave a nod and said, "The El Dorado."

CHAPTER 32

I drove south out of Sulfur Springs, up to the El Dorado, and parked shy of the mine itself, on a high, cactus-covered flat where I could see the land sloping down into Mexico and the long, dark line of the border fence.

A lesson from my earliest memories of my grandmother Dilsey, who was true-blood Iron Lake Ojibwe: Land is not insentient; it is possessed of spirit. Gazing down, I couldn't help feeling that the fence and all it represented was a great violation of the spirit of the land. The mind-set that gave rise to the fence was a great folly, the idea that a thin wall of steel and the imaginary line it demarcated could stand against the tide that swept across the desert, which was the tide of time and changing circumstance. Politics were of a moment. Sentiments shifted. Nations rose and fell. Steel rusted and crumbled. But the desert and the flow of life across it would continue after that fence was nothing but scattered rubble among the cacti and the fear that built it was long forgotten.

The clouds in the east had turned black and boiling. Far in the distance, lightning stabbed at the ground. Sylvester's truck turned onto the winding road up to the El Dorado, and I watched it approach and park next to mine. The old prospector got out and joined me where I stood surveying the country below.

"Better make it quick," he said, nodding toward the coming monsoon storm.

"I thought the people that beat me up were after Peter," I said. "I thought they were White Horse. And maybe they are, but I'm beginning to think that's not why they wanted Peter." I waited a moment, watched the lightning throw white pitchforks. "You said you stopped working for Marian after you stumbled across Peter in one of the mines. What changed?"

"He asked for my help. He wanted to file on the old claims himself and he wanted me to help him locate them."

"To what end? He wasn't interested in mining, was he?"

"Mining? Naw. His only interest was in keeping the people he brought across the

389

border safe. He was hoping to string to-gether a whole slew of sanctuaries, places only he knew about where he could bring people and keep them out of harm's way while he put together more permanent places for them and arranged transport."

"Did Marian know he was filing on those old claims?"

"Not much goes on in this county that Marian doesn't know about."

"So he was competition for her?"

"He has more old claims in his name now than she does."

"And you helped him. You're lucky you're not dead."

"Right back at you," he said.

"There's another thing. The authorities think Rodriguez has been stockpiling drugs. They think he might be using an old mine for that. And I think, like you say, that not much goes on in Coronado County that Marian doesn't know about, which would include the drug traffic."

He was quiet a moment. "Drugs and Marian? I suppose that could be true."

"I'm beginning to wonder if maybe part of the reason Marian's interested in those old diggings is that she thinks she might find more than just ore in one of them."

Sylvester nodded, as if accepting the possibility. "That woman's got a streak of greedy in her wider than the Rio Grande."

"I'm thinking that if she's actually involved in the drugs already moving through Paradiso, she might have the contacts to distribute a lot of product."

"Hell, if Rodriguez got wind of that, she'd be dead in a heartbeat."

"Unless Rodriguez was dead."

"I don't follow."

I told him about the ambush in the desert in which Miguel Rodriguez had been killed and Carlos Rodriguez and Peter wounded.

"I'm thinking maybe that ambush was just as much about getting rid of Rodriguez as it was getting Peter out of the way," I said. "She eliminates Rodriguez, she can move the product he's got stockpiled."

"If she finds it. Big if." He tugged at his long, gray beard. "That beating you took must mean she's still gunning for Peter."

"I think she's still mighty interested in getting those old claims that are in his name, still banking on big mining coming back to Coronado County. But I'm also thinking more and more that it's possible she wants to make certain Peter doesn't file a claim on the mine where Rodriguez has his stockpile. She might even be thinking that maybe

Peter's already stumbled onto the cache of drugs."

"You say you found Peter. Did he say anything about that drug stash?"

I shook my head. "But Marian doesn't know that."

Sylvester pulled at his long beard and thought awhile. "Might be she'll never find those drugs. Might be Rodriguez didn't stash nothing in the claims she or Peter filed on. That's all public land. Anybody could wander in. But there's plenty of mining was done on private property, legal and illegal. A lot of those workings, just small operations, even I don't know about."

I could hear the distant rumble of thunder now and knew that Sylvester and I would have to break up our little war council soon.

"So, somebody tipped off Rodriguez to the rendezvous Peter had with them illegals, and somebody tipped off Marian and White Horse, too," Sylvester said. "Same person?"

"I don't know."

"Got a speculation who that might be?"

"I'm working on it."

Sylvester said, "We better get our asses off this high ground before that storm hits. Do me a favor. You come up with any answers, you let me know. I got myself a score to settle, too."

He headed to his own truck. I waited until he was well out of sight, then started down out of the mountains just as the first big drops of rain began to splat against my windshield.

I drove to Cadiz in a downpour. With each flash of lightning, the mountains around me jumped out in a blaze of white. I cruised past the church and slowed to a crawl. I had to lower the window to make out the statue through the rain. The ribbon I'd tied was gone and in its place was a different ribbon. I kept going, parked a couple of blocks farther on, then hoofed it back to the church on foot. I was soaking wet, but I didn't care. The ribbon meant news of Rainy, and I wanted that like a man dying of thirst wants water. I untied the ribbon and used the skeleton key Michelle had given me to open the church door. Inside under the cross on the altar, I found a note. I read simply: SAME TIME. SAME PLACE. They were block letters, but even so I could tell they hadn't been written in Rainy's hand. It was Mondragón who'd left the note.

I sat in the first pew, relieved that Rainy was safe, and that Peter was, too. Also Juan and the others who'd walked a thousand miles looking only for freedom from violence and constant fear. I hoped that they'd finally found a permanent sanctuary. But I also felt empty and alone. Self-pity, I knew. I missed Rainy, missed her terribly, missed her smile, her laugh, her touch, her warm, dark eyes, her long braid that fell across my chest when we made love. She was with Mondragón now, a man who'd shared everything with her in exactly the same way I had, and then some, because he'd fathered her children. When you'd given your heart deeply to another person, even if things didn't work out, did you take your whole heart back? Or did you leave a part of it with the other? I wanted to ask Rainy what she still felt for this man who was movie-star handsome and rich as Croesus and who'd come to the rescue of us all.

A bit of ancient, Native wisdom that has always stood me in good stead: In every human being there are two wolves constantly battling. One is love and the other is fear. The wolf that wins the battle is the one you feed. Always the one you feed.

I was feeding the wolf of fear. I knew that. And I knew that the best way to end this wallowing in doubt and self-pity was action. I called Jamie Sprangers.

"I want to talk," I said. "But only with you."

"Where and when?" he said.

"Now. I'm at the parsonage in Cadiz."

"I'll be there in ten."

"Bring beer," I said.

I walked across the street, unlocked the parsonage, and went inside. The air conditioner was running, and wet as I was, it chilled me. I changed into dry clothing, then took a towel to my dripping hair. I'd just finished when Sprangers knocked on the front door. He'd brought beer, Leinenkugel's.

He held up the six-pack. "From your neck of the woods, right?"

We sat in the kitchen and drank brew.

"I've got a significant dossier on you now, O'Connor," Sprangers said. "You've got some Indian blood in you."

"Ojibwe," I said. "One-quarter. My grandmother Dilsey was true-blood Iron Lake Anishinaabe."

"And your father was a cop. A county sheriff. Died in the line of duty. Is that why you wore a badge?"

Rain channeled down the panes in gray streaks, and the thunder outside was a relentless cannonade.

"Part of the reason," I said. "But I believe

the things he believed, and that's also part of the reason."

"My dad was a cop, too. Texas Ranger. Thirty-five years. He's retired, but ask him and he says retirement feels more like a prison sentence. He'd love to be back in uniform. There's something about the badge, you know?"

"I know." I sipped my beer. It was ice cold. Perfect. "Why the Border Patrol?"

"My grandparents are from Chihuahua. Moved to Texas when my mother was a little girl." He saw me studying his features. "I know. I look as Mexican as you do Indian. But I think you'll understand this. I'm Border Patrol because I want the people who are trying to get into this country, people like my grandparents, to be treated fairly. I'm not CBP to keep them out. I'm CBP to keep them safe."

I believed him, trusted him, and it felt good. "That's all Peter wants, too," I said.

"I understand. But he's still tied up with Rodriguez somehow."

"It's all a ball of snakes."

He put his beer bottle down on the kitchen tabletop. "I'm listening."

I explained how I saw things: Marian Brown's connection with White Horse and her part in the drug trade through Coronado County; her desire to be rid of Rodriguez; the control she wielded over the town cop Sanchez; her manipulation of Royal Diggs to get White Horse to do her dirty work; the old claims she'd been filing and the stashed drugs she was probably hoping to find in one of the diggings. He listened without interrupting.

When I finished, he looked away and studied the rain-streaked windows awhile. "It all fits," he finally said. "We've had a good idea that Royal Diggs is behind the dealing out of Paradiso. He's the cock of the walk out there. We've also had our eye on Sanchez, figuring that unless he was stupid — and I'm not convinced he isn't — he knew about the drugs being trafficked and was probably on the take. Brown, she's a new wrinkle."

"If you suspected Diggs, why didn't you move on him?"

"Not enough evidence. And he's not the kind of guy who's going to break if you sweat him. With Sanchez, we figured at some point he might become useful to us and we didn't want to tip our hand. Rodriguez is the one we really want to nail." He tapped the tabletop with his fingers, thinking. "But Brown." He nodded, as if the idea appealed to him. "We know that Rodriguez has been diversifying, financially. We think some of the money is being laundered through Coronado County. Maybe Brown's responsible for that. She's a woman used to dealing with large sums in her land transactions. The last couple of years, she's put an enormous amount of cash into building that expensive bunch of houses up on the mesa above Cadiz. Could be the money that bankrolled her development came from south of the border, out of Rodriguez's pocket."

"If that's true, why get rid of Rodriguez? He's the hand that feeds her."

Sprangers drank some beer while he thought about that. "Like you say, maybe she's looking for the stockpile of drugs we're all interested in. She finds it and has the contacts to move it, she's got millions. But it might also be she understands that if you throw in with a scorpion like Rodriguez, you're going to get stung eventually. Maybe she's afraid of him. If you know the cruelty he's capable of, you'd be foolish not to be scared. And maybe this, too. If we're right about her laundering money for him, we're talking big money. With Rodriguez out of the picture, maybe she has more control over what she's invested in his behalf. It's a stretch, I know, but I think it's worth pursuing. I'll put my people on that."

"There's one thing that still troubles me a lot," I said.

"What's that?"

"Somebody told both White Horse and Rodriguez about Peter's rendezvous in the desert."

"Brown," he said, as if it were obvious.

"But how did she know?"

He shrugged. "Somebody in Bisonette's organization leaked it to her."

"Maybe," I said.

"I'll work on figuring out Brown," he said. "You work on the mole in Bisonette's group. We got a deal?"

I held up my beer and we clinked bottles to seal the agreement.

CHAPTER 33

There was a long wait ahead before my meeting with Rainy and Mondragón. I ate a Reuben at the Wagon Wheel. While I sat near the front window, I watched the storm play itself out over Cadiz and move to the west. With night, the sky cleared to a sea full of stars and a few floating islands of residual black clouds. On my walk back to the parsonage, I watched the heavens above the mountains to the east begin to silver with a haze from the glow of the not-quite-risen moon.

As I passed the church, I had an overwhelming impulse to spend a few minutes in the comfort of the little sanctuary. I unlocked the door and went in. The air inside was stuffy but had been cooled significantly by the passing monsoon. In the pitch dark, I turned my cell phone on and used the flashlight app to locate the candle Rainy and Mondragón had burned the night

I first met them there. It was still sitting on the altar rail where she'd left it, along with a small box of wooden matches. I lit the candle and sat in the front pew.

Because the earth itself is one great spirit, every inch of it is sacred. Beneath the asphalt parking lot in New York City is ground no less hallowed than the ground beneath Notre Dame, or under the pines and spruce of the Northwoods. But there are places that remind us of the sacredness, and at that moment, the little sanctuary was one. I sat in the frail glow of the candlelight and closed my eyes and let my spirit connect with the calm of that quiet place.

Maybe it was because I'd stepped out of the flow of events, or maybe it was just the clarity that can come in moments of calm, but I began to make connections, to understand a little better how the threads were fitting together to form a web in Coronado County.

I heard the scrape of the old church door sliding open, and I turned. What I saw was no less surprising than if the Virgin Mary herself had been standing there.

"You a religious person? God-fearing?"

The big man came slowly into the drizzle of the candlelight, a gun in his hand, an oddly bemused look on his face. His head was shaved bald and he had tattoos everywhere. On a finger of his right hand was a big silver ring shaped like a skull.

"I think of myself more as a guy on a spiritual voyage," I said. "My religion is just the boat I happen to be traveling in."

"O'Connor. That's Irish. You Catholic?"

"I am," I confirmed. "What about you, Royal? Are you a religious person?"

"I was an altar boy," he said. "Mass every Sunday."

"Still attend?"

"Spent three years in Iraq. Killed every belief I ever had about God."

"What do you believe in now?"

"Myself."

"Nothing else?"

"Nothing else."

"Lonely world."

"I like it that way."

"What are you doing here?" I asked.

"Been waiting for you."

"Alone?"

Diggs smiled. "A little bird told me you're planning on taking me down."

"I'm going after White Horse. I understand they operate out of Paradiso. And I understand you're the big man out there."

"Mister, I *am* Paradiso."

"So, going to beat me up again?"

"This time I plan to shoot you. Just get rid of your nosy ass."

"You might want to hold off on that."

He stood like a big, square chunk of boulder and waited for an explanation.

"Could be that the man who shot you in the parsonage is waiting outside to shoot you again," I said.

His free hand moved toward his side where there was a little mounding under his T-shirt, probably bandaging from the wound Mondragón had inflicted, which though clearly not lethal, must have caused him a good deal of trouble. Then he barked a laugh as if he caught on that I was bluffing.

"One more thing," I said. "You're being played. Kill me and you'll be dead, too, before you understand who's playing you and why."

The tattoo that crawled up his neck and the side of his face was a long green rattlesnake. He cocked his head, and the rattler moved as if alive.

"What are you talking about?" he said.

"You and White Horse and your ambush out there in the desert. You probably think that was only about getting rid of Rodriguez and that pesky Bisonette kid. You really had the wool pulled over your eyes on that one."

"Talk to me."

"Not while you're holding a gun."

He considered the issue. He had me by sixty or seventy pounds, none of it doughy, and stood a good five inches taller. To him I was an old man. I'm sure he figured that if he had to, he could break my spine like it was a dry twig. I figured he was probably right.

His T-shirt was black, with a white skull across the front. He lifted it and slipped the gun — a big one, maybe a Desert Eagle — into the waist of his jeans.

"So talk," he said.

"For a guy who prefers to live off the grid, there are sure a lot of people interested in you."

"Like who?"

"DEA, Border Patrol, Coronado County Sheriff, Carlos Rodriguez, Marian Brown. And that's just for starters. Some of them want to see you behind bars. Some of them want you dead. And one of them is playing you like you're her little puppet."

"What do you mean?"

"You move drugs through Paradiso. That doesn't seem much of a secret out here. Along the border in Coronado County, Carlos Rodriguez controls everything illegal that comes across. Also not much of a secret. You must have known who you were out there to kill in that desert ambush. So I ask myself, why would you shoot the man supplying you with product? The best answer I can come up with is that someone else had promised to supply you, probably more cheaply, if you got rid of the competition. So she convinced you to use White Horse to do her dirty work. How am I doing so far?"

"You got about thirty seconds before I blow you away."

"She promised you product. She must have proven that she could supply it. What was it? Cocaine? Meth? Marijuana?"

He thought about whether to answer, then, probably because he figured on killing me, he said, "Cocaine."

"Did you ever ask yourself how she was able to do that? I'll tell you how. Rodriguez has a huge stash somewhere in Coronado County, millions of dollars' worth, and I think Marian Brown knows where it is. With Rodriguez out of the way, she gets the stash."

"If that's true, why would I mind killing Rodriguez? I don't see how she played me."

"You and White Horse do her dirty work, she tosses you a few bones, but she keeps the lion's share of the profit. Like I said, millions."

"How do you know this?"

"My intel is better than yours."

His pallid blue eyes squinted, then he said, "Bullshit. How would she know about this stash, if it even exists?"

"Sylvester's been helping her locate old mining claims. You probably know that. It's why you killed his mule. Punishment or maybe a warning not to help Bisonette anymore. I think her initial interest was in controlling access to any land that might be worked when mining comes back to this area. But I think she stumbled onto something in one of those old diggings."

"The stash," Diggs said.

"And I have just one question, Royal. Why should she get all that money and you get only bones?"

I'd clearly offered him a new perspective. He kept squinting as he rolled all this speculation around in his head. "Your intel," he finally said. "Who's supplying it?"

"A variety of sources. We communicate in an interesting way."

"What's that?"

"We leave notes for each other."

"Where?"

"I'll show you."

I stood up from the pew. He loomed over me, threatening, but didn't go for his gun. I moved past him, through the gap in the altar rail and up to the altar itself. He followed me. I stood before the cross, whose brassy surface gleamed like gold in the candlelight.

"I was an altar boy, too," I said. "For me, there's still something a little mystical about being up here."

"You've never seen your friends blown to pieces."

"No," I admitted.

"Well?"

"We leave the notes under here," I said, lifting the cross with both hands. The base was heavy.

His blue eyes settled on the white altar cloth, which was empty. In that moment of his distraction, I swung the cross, base first, and caught him where the rattlesnake crawled up the side of his face. He staggered back. I swung again, and the snake spit blood. Diggs stumbled, flipped backward over the altar rail, and the back of his bald head hit the stone floor with a dull, heavy thud. He lay still, a rivulet of red blood running from his temple and glistening in the candlelight.

Royal Diggs was conscious but still a little dazed when Deputy Crockett cuffed him. Before he hauled the big man away, Crockett looked at me with what I interpreted as friendly admiration. "Good job," he said. "Must be the Indian in you." He reached up and gave a respectful little tip of that tan cowboy hat with the colorfully beaded band. Then he and Vega escorted Diggs outside to a waiting cruiser. Sprangers stayed behind, lingering with me in the sanctuary.

"What were you doing here?" he asked.

"Could be I was praying for some answers. And I think I have one."

I offered him my speculation that Marian Brown had probably found Rodriguez's drug stash and had used White Horse to get him out of the picture.

"We'll sweat Diggs," Sprangers said. "I doubt we'll get anything. But we'll also bring in Marian Brown and Sanchez. Maybe one of them will break. I'd like you there for that."

I thought about my meeting with Rainy and Mondragón. "I'll pass."

He seemed surprised but let it slide. "We'll need an official statement from you about this evening."

"It's been a long day. Would first thing in the morning be okay?"

"That'll do."

We split up outside the church, and I headed back to the parsonage. There was still half an hour before I would see Rainy again, and I slipped out the back door and walked through Cadiz to the road up the mesa to the Goodman Center. As before, Mondragón's SUV was parked in a far corner of the lot, away from the lights. When I approached, Rainy jumped out and ran to me. She threw her arms around me and laid her cheek against mine, and I smelled her hair, and, God, was it wonderful.

"Whenever I'm not with you, I worry like crazy," she whispered.

"You're with me now."

I kissed her, and the wolf of fear that had tried so viciously to chew out my gut fled in a heartbeat.

Mondragón came from the SUV, along with another figure, who was limping.

"How are you doing, Peter?" I asked.

"I'll survive." He shook my hand. "Thanks for everything, Cork."

"Where are Juan and the others?"

"Safe," Peter said.

"In one of your mine sanctuaries?"

"Figured that out, did you?"

"With a little help from Sylvester."

"We can't move them for a couple days, but they'll be safe until then."

"I don't know about that, Peter. Someone in your organization sold you out to Rodri-

409

guez. He may know all about your sanctuaries."

"I'm the only one who knows them all."

"What about Sylvester?"

"He wouldn't sell me out."

Mondragón said to me, "Have you discovered anything more?"

I told them what I knew and what I suspected.

"Laundering money through the real estate woman?" Mondragón said. "Small potatoes, comparatively speaking."

"You mean compared to the vast millions your own family has invested in the States?" I said.

"Exactly," he replied, unfazed by my tone. "So, probably there's more going on. I have certain sources here that I can tap for information. I'll get them on it."

"The authorities are going to pick her up," I told him. "They may be able to sweat that out of her."

"I could have my people do the same," he said.

"No, Berto," Rainy said in a voice hard and cold, so different from the tone I usually heard her speak in. "I can only imagine how your people would get the information."

"All right, *querida*."

"We can't use the church for notes any-more," I told them.

"Your phone? Do you believe it's safe?" Mondragón asked.

"At this point, about as safe as anything else, I'd guess."

"Leave it on, and we'll communicate that way. But sparingly. Keep an eye to your back in case you're tracked."

I looked at Peter. "You need to think hard about which of the Desert Angels betrayed you."

He shook his head. "I trust them all or I would never have brought them in."

"I've told you again and again," Mondragón said, as if speaking to a recalcitrant child. "Trust no one except family."

"A poor mantra, Berto," Rainy said.

"But clearly true." He held out his hands toward his son. "Peter wouldn't be in this fix if he'd listened to me."

Peter said something to Mondragón in Spanish that I didn't understand. Rainy laughed, and when she saw that I was confused, translated for me. "He told his father that he got all his trust genes from me, and thank God for that."

Mondragón was not amused. "You need to be very careful, Peter, or you could get us all killed."

Which, I had to admit, could well be true.

From far away rose the whine of a siren. Although it didn't seem to be coming in our direction, Mondragón said, "We need to leave. When I know something, I'll contact you, O'Connor. I expect the same from you."

"Of course." I turned to Rainy and took her in my arms once more. "*Vaya con Dios,* love."

She whispered in my ear, "Wherever you are, there I am also."

CHAPTER 34

In a pinch, it doesn't take much to be happy. Rainy and Peter and little Juan and the others were all safe. That pretty much did it for me. I walked down the mesa under the rise of a moon nearing half full, feeling relieved and remarkably hopeful and, yes, happy. In the words of Frost, there were still miles to go before I slept, but for a change I was feeling equal to the task.

Before I reached the parsonage, my cell phone rang. Frank Harris.

"Sorry to disturb you so late, Cork, but Jocko's having some difficulty. Things aren't looking so good. He'd like to talk to you."

When I arrived at the hospital, Harris was waiting for me outside Jocko's room. He shook my hand. "Thanks for coming. Jocko's been struggling for the past few hours. But I have a sense it's not so much about the beating he took as it is his worry over Peter."

"I think I can give him some good news on that front."

"Thank God." He signaled me to follow him inside.

Jocko was a big man, but his ordeal seemed to have taken a lot out of him, and lying on that hospital bed, he looked shrunken, hollowed.

"Jocko," Frank said quietly. "Cork O'Connor's here."

The old man's eyes opened slowly and took a moment to focus. He acknowledged me with a faint smile.

"How're you doing?" I asked.

"Not so good." He spoke barely above a whisper. "Think I may have flown my last plane."

"You'll fly again, Jocko," Harris said.

"Not up to you or me anymore, Frankie." He leveled his eyes on me. "I need to know if Peter's okay."

"He's okay."

"You found him?"

"I found him."

"And he's all right?"

"He's limping a little, but he's fine."

"The folks he was supposed to guide out of that desert?"

"Safe," I said and then explained about the ambush and what had happened after.

414

"I'm pretty sure the mayor of Sulfur Springs is involved in all this, and the cop there, too. Mike Sanchez. The authorities are going to pick them up. I think there's a good chance they'll crack."

"I'd love to be the one to question them," Jocko said. "Wouldn't ask gentle, if you know what I mean."

"You just take care of getting yourself better."

"Feels like a big weight's been lifted off me." He slid an arm from beneath the sheets and reached out to shake my hand. His grip was surprisingly firm. "Thanks."

"Right back at you, Jocko. You and that biplane of yours have helped save a lot of desperate people. Get well, pardner. There are still lives to be saved."

He smiled, drew back his hand, and let his eyes drift closed. Frank signaled me to follow him into the hallway.

"Is it true about Marian?" he asked.

"I know for sure she was there when I got this." I pointed toward the ugly cut across my cheek, the legacy of Royal Diggs's silver skull ring. "Everything else is speculation but based on good evidence."

"Marian Brown," he said, as if he couldn't quite believe it. "We've dealt with her in all the land transactions for our vineyards. I always knew she was a shrewd business-woman, but this?"

"Why do you grow grapes?" I asked.

He seemed surprised by the question. "I enjoy it."

"Is it about the money?"

"It's nicer to make a profit than not," he said.

"But it's not really about the money."

"No."

"With someone like Marian Brown, it's all about the money. I've seen it before. The promise of wealth, great wealth especially, can twist a person into something barely human."

"Just like Rodriguez," he said, as if it were the name of evil itself.

"Just like Rodriguez," I echoed with the same distaste. "Where's Jayne?"

"This is all too much for her. She was afraid that if she came, she might have to watch Jocko die. But, honestly, that weight Jocko says you took off him, I think it'll make a huge difference. Look, I understand that you can't give away everything, but I hope you'll keep us apprised of what's going on."

"As much as I can," I said.

"And when you see Peter, tell him how glad we are that he's okay."

"I'll do that." I glanced back through the doorway at Jocko, asleep on his bed. "Thanks for taking this watch."

"Couldn't leave him all alone, could I?"

We shook hands and I left him to his vigil.

I didn't sleep long that night, but I slept well, and I woke feeling hopeful. Until Sprangers called.

"Marian Brown's dead," he said without preamble.

I was having coffee at the kitchen table of the parsonage. The sun was shining in the window where the bullet had come through that wounded Royal Diggs. The shadow of the ragged edges of the hole in the pane lay on the tabletop, looking like the sharp, gray teeth of a wolf.

I put my cup down. "How?"

"Vega and a Coronado County deputy went out to her place this morning to bring her in. They knocked. Got no answer. Looked in the windows and saw her lying on the living room floor. Shot three times in the chest. Sheriff Carlson has a team out there right now working the scene."

"What about Sanchez?"

"Can't find him."

"Did you get anything out of Diggs?"

"Nothing useful. Have you had any con-

417

tact with your wife or Peter Bisonette or Gilbert Mondragón since we parted ways last night?"

I knew why he was asking. He was thinking like a cop, thinking that if I'd told Rainy or the others about my suspicions regarding Marian Brown and Sanchez, I'd given them motive for murder. I was thinking that, too, but only with regard to Mondragón. Although Rainy had killed a man once, the circumstances were understandable and it was long ago. She was a different person now. Cold-blooded murder was something neither she nor Peter would ever condone.

I could have lied, but I'd already started down a different road with Sprangers. I told him, "Yes." Then I said, "What about your mole? Could Rodriguez have known?"

"Like I said, Diggs hasn't broken. On my end, what you and I discussed last night has stayed with me. I haven't said anything to anyone."

Which made Rainy's first husband look pretty good to me for the killing.

Clearly, Sprangers was thinking the same thing. "I'd like to talk to Gilbert Mondragón."

"Not sure that'll happen."

"You could help."

"Let me think about that."

418

"Don't think too long. We're looking for Sanchez, but I'm guessing that if he's not already dead, he doesn't have much time left."

When the call ended, I contacted Mondragón immediately.

"We need to talk," I told him. "Now."

"I'm listening."

"All of us. You, me, Rainy, and Peter."

"In broad daylight? What about the drone that Border Patrol agent put on you?"

"He took it off."

"You'd better be sure."

"I'm sure."

"All right. Where?"

"Where are you?"

"An hour from Cadiz."

Which meant they weren't in the safe house in Nogales anymore. So where were they now?

"There's a small roadside park along the San Gabriel River south of town," I said. "Rainy knows the place. I'll be waiting."

When I was fourteen, in the dark period after my father died, I spent a lot of time with Henry Meloux, healing. He urged me to hold to the memories of my father. Memories sing to us, he told me. They're birds whose songs never fade. What I held to as I drove out of town toward the park was the memory of Tamarack County with its tall pines and evergreen-scented air and lakes where sunlight shattered on the water's surface into a million diamonds. I held to the idea that when all this was over, we would go back to what was familiar — Gooseberry Lane, Sam's Place, Iron Lake, and Crow Point, where Henry Meloux would be waiting, his ancient face cracked by more lines than dried mud and his dark, almond eyes shining warm in welcome for Rainy and Peter and me. That would be happiness. That would be home.

I parked in the small, empty lot and walked to the picnic table where, days earlier, Rainy and I had met with Nikki Edwards and then things had got really complicated. The park was hidden from the narrow highway by a wall of tamarisk bushes. The lone picnic table sat in the shade of willows and cottonwoods that grew on the riverbank. Fed by the monsoon rains, the water of the San Gabriel tumbled over river rocks with a soft, constant murmur. I thought about Nikki and about the traitor in Los Angeles del Desierto. She knew about the coordinates for Peter's rendezvous with the women and children of Guatemala and could have been the one to leak them.

But there were so many others as well. Jocko? Frank Harris? Maybe even Sylvester?

The black SUV parked next to my pickup. Rainy, Peter, and Mondragón got out and came to the table. Mondragón was watchful, his attention on the road that ran behind the tamarisks.

"Better be important," he said.

I spoke to Rainy, not Mondragón. "I just need a question answered. Did you all stay together last night after we talked?"

Rainy seemed puzzled but said, "Yes."

"Berto didn't leave you at all?"

"No. Why?"

"Yeah," Mondragón said. "Why do you want to know?"

"Someone murdered Marian Brown last night."

"And of course you thought of me," Mondragón said.

"I was thinking about motive. You certainly had one. I needed to know about opportunity."

"Why didn't you just ask me over the phone?" But as soon as he spoke he understood. "Still don't trust me."

"I trust Rainy," I said.

Rainy said, "It wasn't Berto, Cork."

"Rodriguez?" Peter offered.

"Maybe. Or maybe whoever it is that's

been feeding information about the Desert Angels to Brown and Rodriguez."

"Any closer to knowing who that is?" Mondragón asked.

I shook my head and looked to Peter.

He shrugged. "I keep racking my brain and coming up with nothing. Honestly, I trust everyone I recruited. I'd still trust any one of them with my life."

"And ours," Mondragón said sternly. He looked back at me. "I've been working with my people to find out about Rodriguez's investments on this side of the border. These are people who don't worry a lot about breaking laws. Or fingers. Seems Rodriguez has got quite a diverse portfolio. Interests in Canadian and U.S. mining in particular, a major shareholder in several exploratory enterprises."

"There's a drilling company called Southwestern Geotech that's been filing on old claims in the mountains around here. Maybe he owns a share of that, too."

"I'll have it checked out," Mondragón said.

"Something you should know, Peter," I said. "Jocko's taken a turn for the worse."

"How bad?"

"When I left his hospital room last night, he was looking pretty weak. It helped a little, I think, when he heard that you were safe."

"I want to see him," Peter said.

Mondragón and I both spoke at the same time: "No."

"If he dies and I haven't thanked him for all that he's done, it would be a great injustice," Peter said.

Rainy spoke quietly. "Do you do what you do for the thanks you'll get, Peter? Jocko's heart is full, believe me. But his body is fragile. If you risked seeing him now, his concern for your safety might do him more harm."

It was a hard truth to swallow, but Peter said, "I understand."

"Good." Mondragón turned his attention to me. "It's dangerous, meeting like this in the daylight. Don't ask again."

"Believe me, Berto, I'll be a happy man when I never have to ask anything of you again."

Mondragón and Peter headed to the SUV. Rainy and I lagged back. I held her hand.

"What do you and Berto do all day while I'm out beating the desert for clues?"

"Mostly, he's on his cell phone, delivering orders to his people, making contingency arrangements. He's very organized that way. Ruthlessly so. He talks with Peter, they argue. He talks with me. We argue."

"Do you argue about me?"

"Nothing to argue about. You're my husband. Wholly, completely, truly."

I kissed her, long and deep, and once more, we parted. After they'd gone, I got in my truck and continued south to Sulfur Springs, where I hoped I might find a few more pieces to fit into the puzzle.

CHAPTER 35

I drove to Sylvester's place on the hill above town. His truck was there, but when I knocked on the door of his odd adobe house no one answered. There may have been nothing unusual in this, but considering that his mule, Franklin, had been killed and Marian Brown had been murdered, I was concerned. I tried the knob. Locked. I circled the house, attempting to peer through the windows, but every shade had been drawn.

Inside Rosa's Cantina, I found Sierra wiping down a table. She looked up when I walked in and she frowned. "Here comes trouble."

"Not my fault," I said.

"Goes with you everywhere like dog shit on the sole of your shoe."

"Are you talking about anything in particular?"

She fisted the rag she'd used to clean the

425

table. "I heard about Marian."

"I didn't do it."

"Maybe not, but since you came here, there's been nothing but a landslide of bad. What do you want?"

"I haven't eaten today. How about a little breakfast?"

"I'll get you a menu," she said but not graciously.

"No need. I'll have the huevos rancheros."

She disappeared into the kitchen, and I sat at a table next to a window that overlooked the main street of Sulfur Springs. I could see all the way to Gallina Town, and I was struck again by the profound difference of everything south of the narrow bridge, which felt in so many ways like its own, separate community. I thought about the music I'd heard playing, the dancing in front of the taqueria, the brightness with which the homes, even the shabby trailers on cinder blocks, were decorated. Many of these people worked hard at jobs that no one else wanted and were poorly paid, I was sure. But it seemed to me that there was something resilient in their spirit, some essential quality that kept the music and the dancing and the color alive. I thought about the people of my own heritage, the Anishinaabeg, who'd been lied to and cheated and herded onto reservations, who fought against poverty and all the ills that came with poverty. But the Ojibwe I knew well, my family and those I counted as friends, had in their spirits the same resilience I saw reflected in Gallina Town. And I thought, as I had so many times before, that what's important to a human being, any human being, isn't the wealth that comes from money, but the richness that comes from community, a sense of connectedness to family and to friends and, as Rainy and Henry would probably have said, to the spirit of the Great Mystery that runs through all creation.

"Sorry I ragged on you earlier," Sierra said, setting the plate of eggs and beans in front of me. "Things have been rough here lately. Unsettled. I don't like unsettled."

"I get that. Have you seen Sylvester today?"

"No." She stood there looking down at me. "We all heard about Franklin. Should I be worried about Sylvester, too?"

"Not necessarily. But like you say, things are unsettled here. It's not a bad idea to be a little worried."

"If something's happened to that wonderful old coot, I'm taking to the warpath myself."

"Who would you go after?"

She hesitated, then said, "Mike Sanchez."

"Why?"

"There's a man without a heart or a spine. The only reason he got that badge was Marian. And now that she's gone . . ." She finished with a shrug.

"Is he involved in something a man wearing a badge shouldn't be?"

"Anything that goes on in Sulfur Springs that's not on the up-and-up, Sanchez is involved. We all know it."

"Drugs?"

"Hell, yes."

"White Horse?"

"If we had the Ku Klux Klan here, he'd be wearing a hood."

"But his heritage is Mexican."

She shook her head. "Spanish. He's very clear on the distinction."

"Have you seen him today?"

She shook her head. "Hasn't been in yet. But he will be. He always comes in."

"The sheriff's been looking for him. Can't seem to find him."

That gave her pause. She stared down at me. "Like Marian, you think?"

"Maybe."

Her eyes went to the empty street outside the window. "Is anybody safe?"

428

That was a question I couldn't answer.

Outside, after I'd finished my breakfast, I discovered a note slipped under the wiper blade of my pickup: *If you want answers call me.* There was a number with it. No name. I'd been watching my truck through the cantina window the whole time I'd been inside. No one had come anywhere near the pickup. I figured it must have been put there the night before, and I'd been so intent on other things that morning that I simply hadn't noticed it. I stood in the late morning sunlight and made the call.

"About time." The voice at the other end was surly and familiar.

"Been busy. But I'd like answers."

"Not over the phone."

"Where?"

"The El Dorado Mine."

"When?"

"Now. Come alone. I'll be watching. If you're not alone, no answers. I may even shoot you."

I got into the truck and started down the street toward Gallina Town. I hadn't gone far when I glanced in the rearview mirror and saw a dusty, little ATV swing around the corner behind me, a familiar figure gripping the handlebars. I braked to a stop and rolled down the window as Sylvester pulled up beside me.

"Is that your alternative to Franklin?" I asked.

"It don't give me the companionship that old mule did, but it gets me to the same places in these mountains and a hell of a lot faster."

"I just talked to Sierra. You've been scarce."

"Been trying to track down Mike Sanchez since I lost Franklin. Figured that like everything else rotten in Sulfur Springs, he had a hand in it. Him and Marian."

"Marian's dead."

"I heard. So that leaves Sanchez."

"I'm on my way to see him."

He shoved the bill of his ball cap up and sat back in the seat of his ATV. "You got business with that snake?"

"More like he has business with me," I said and filled the old prospector in.

"I don't know what he's got up his sleeve," Sylvester said, "but it ain't gonna be good. Could be he killed Marian and maybe he's got it in his head to do the same to you."

"I don't think so. He's scared, but not of me."

"Still, best you got backup." He dropped a hand to a leather scabbard he'd affixed to the ATV in which a lever-action rifle was nested.

"He made it clear, Sylvester. Just me."

The old man chewed on that, then said, "Take your time getting up to that mine."

"Any particular reason?"

"You'll know it when the time comes."

He swung the ATV around and headed back the way he'd come.

I drove south through Gallina Town, which felt deserted with so many of its people off working in Cadiz or wherever. Well outside Sulfur Springs, I turned onto the winding road that led up to the old mine works. I couldn't help thinking about the Guatemalans who'd been found slaughtered inside the tunnel there, and I glanced at the Winchester on the seat beside me, which I'd made sure was fully loaded before I left town. When I pulled onto the big flat where the rusting mining equipment and abandoned materials lay, I saw Mike Sanchez's cruiser, but I didn't see the man himself. I grabbed the Winchester and stepped from the pickup, keeping the truck between me and the dark mine entrance.

A few moments later, Sanchez emerged with his hands open in front of him, showing me that he wasn't armed. He came to the place where the old railroad ties were piled.

"You don't need the rifle," he called. "In fact, if you want answers, you'll put your Winchester down."

"Turn around," I said.

Sanchez turned. I couldn't see any evidence of a handgun, so I started toward him around the pickup.

"The rifle," he said. "Leave it. I know what happened to Marian. I'm not going down the same way."

I set the Winchester on the hood of the truck and walked to Sanchez.

"A bunch of badges out looking for you right now," I told him.

He lowered his hands. "They've got nothing on me. I didn't kill Marian."

"Royal Diggs is in custody. They're sweating him as we speak."

"Diggs? They'd have better luck sweating a rock."

"Did he kill Marian?"

"Doubt it. She was his bread and butter."

"How so?"

"Who do you think supplied him with the drugs he peddles?"

"I thought that might be you."

He shook his head. "I'm just paid to turn my back."

432

"Paid well, are you?"

"Was. Things are different now."

"That's why you're willing to talk?"

"I want protection."

"You think I can protect you?"

"You can help me get that protection. You've got connections with Sprangers and that task force of his."

"You know about them?"

"I'm not stupid."

I could have argued the point but saw no reason. At the moment.

"How did it work?" I asked.

"You'll help me?"

"I'll help you in any way I can."

"Let's sit," he said, indicating the stack of old railroad ties.

"Long story?"

"Could turn out to be."

There was something in his demeanor that wasn't right. Maybe it was his eyes, which kept looking everywhere except at me. Or his hands, with his fingers working themselves as if trying to rub off glue. Or his suggestion that we sit, which would have made it difficult for me to bolt if I had to. I looked behind him toward the mine entrance.

"You alone?"

"Of course," he said in a way that told me

it was a lie.

I stepped back and made a half turn toward my truck.

Sanchez leaped at me and wrapped his fat fingers around my arm. I wrenched myself from his grip, and as I did I saw three men break from the shadowed tunnel entrance of the mine. They were all dressed in black, looking like pieces torn from the dark of the El Dorado itself. They carried assault rifles. For an instant, I considered trying to make it back to the truck and to my Winchester, but between the three of them, they had enough firepower to cut me into a hundred pieces.

When they saw that I had no intention of running, they slowed their approach. Two of the men were very young, early twenties at most, Latino. The man in the lead was older, maybe thirty. They spread out in a triangle that enclosed me and Sanchez.

"O'Connor," the older man said.

"You have me at a disadvantage," I said.

"Joaquin Rodriguez."

"Any relation to Carlos?"

"My father."

We faced off in the shadow of the mountain that rose above the El Dorado, the sky overhead a clear, painful blue, a slight breeze blowing out of the northeast, the smell of creosote from the old railroad ties drifting around us. It could have been a peaceful moment, if I'd been alone.

"How is your father?" I asked.

"Doing well. Better, I think, than you."

"Better than Marian Brown, too."

"We heard about that."

I was surprised. "Not your doing?"

"Why would we kill her? We're not animals. We only kill when we have reason to."

"I did what you asked," Sanchez said. His nervous demeanor hadn't changed. "He's all yours."

"You did exactly as I asked," Rodriguez acknowledged. "Manuel, give this man his reward."

One of the young men pointed his assault rifle at Sanchez, and a burst of gunfire killed the still of the morning and along with it the only cop in Sulfur Springs. The suddenness and the sound were startling, but not really the action itself.

Rodriguez looked at me and shrugged. "We had a reason."

I'd been at the edge of dead before and had looked down at that long fall, but so far I'd always managed to keep my footing. One of the things that has happened to me when I've thought that I could see my own end has been the blessing of an odd calm. It was there in that moment, a quiet place inside me, and I spoke from it, not caring about the consequence, which was pretty obvious.

"You want to know about Peter Bisonette. You want to know where he is."

"Oh, yes," Rodriguez said. "Very much."

"Because he helps poor people slip through that greedy net you have along the border?"

"There is a much bigger reason."

I thought about it for a moment, and the pieces fell into place. "You think he has your stash of drugs."

"They are not where they should be."

"What makes you think Peter took them?"

"He filed a claim on the land. And after he took what belongs to us, he tried to kill my father."

"That wasn't Peter's doing. That was the work of Marian Brown. And if your drugs aren't where they should be, I have it on pretty good authority that she's the one responsible."

He squinted at me, and his eyebrows came together like little black leeches mating. "What authority?"

"Royal Diggs."

"Diggs." The name wasn't new to him.

"A bunch of men with badges are talking to him right now."

He turned his face from me and stared toward the desert that stretched into Mexico. There were mountains in the southern distance, looking blue and cool. I wondered if, like me, he would rather be home.

"Maybe that's true," he said, his gaze returning. "But I would still like to get my hands on your Peter Bisonette."

"I don't know where he is."

"I think I cannot take your word for that." Rodriguez laid his assault rifle against the pile of railroad ties. "Eduardo, your knife."

The man who hadn't shot Sanchez pulled an ugly-looking blade from a sheath on his belt. He stepped to Rodriguez and handed it to him, hilt first.

"Since I was a boy, I have hunted elk in the mountains of Colorado," Rodriguez said. "I remember the first bull I brought down. When my father and I had hung him from the branch of an aspen, I gutted him. It was a very cold morning. I remember how the animal's entrails steamed as they fell onto the ground. I have the head of that elk mounted on the wall in my den. Perhaps I'll do the same with yours."

We were separated by half a dozen feet. I took a step back, putting more distance between us. I was thinking that I would run, thinking with that odd calm that being mowed down by a stream of bullets would be infinitely preferable to a slow gutting.

"Grab him," Rodriguez snapped.

Before any of them could move, the still of the morning air was broken again by the sound of gunfire, and Manuel slumped to the ground. The shot had come from the north. Eduardo turned himself in that direction and brought his rifle to his shoulder. Rodriguez also looked that way. When he did, I leaped at him, grabbed the wrist of the hand that held the knife, and twisted it violently so that I felt something snap. Rodriguez cried out, and the knife fell to the ground. I fisted my right hand and slammed it into his face. He stumbled back and fell across the pile of railroad ties. I turned to Eduardo. He was no longer standing but, like Manuel, lay bleeding in the dirt. When I looked north, I saw Sylvester appear like an old, bearded angel. Instead of a harp, he carried a rifle in his hands.

I grabbed the assault weapon Rodriguez had given up in favor of the knife. He looked at me and tried for bravado.

"You shoot me, my father will kill you and everyone you have ever loved."

His arm hung uselessly at his side.

"Kill you?" I said. "I'm not an animal. I only kill when I have reason to." I lifted the rifle, the barrel level with his chest. "And I have pretty good reason now."

"What do you want?" he said, breathless and desperate.

Sylvester joined us.

"Anybody ever tell you that you're beautiful?" I said to him.

"Never anyone of the male persuasion."

"Back road?"

"Wouldn't call it a road, but it got me here quick. So, what are you going to do with him?"

"Not sure yet."

I studied the man in front of us, his eyes apprehensive and dark, his face handsome, a young man who was clearly afraid he wasn't going to get any older. I figured this was the first time Joaquin Rodriguez had ever really stood at the edge of dead. I bent and picked up the knife he'd been holding only minutes earlier.

"In Minnesota, we hunt deer," I told him. "But we gut 'em just like you did your elk."

CHAPTER 36

The trail that led into the Coronado Mountains above the El Dorado Mine was a rough one, better suited to a mule than to the borrowed pickup truck I drove. I took it slow, working over and around the rocks that littered the way. More than once, I was sure I was going to tear off the oil pan.

"You're certain about this?" I asked Sylvester, who was in the seat beside me.

"Trust me," he said.

He was one of the few in Coronado County that I did, so I kept following his directions.

"It might almost be faster on foot," I said, after twisting the truck around an especially precarious curve on a narrow shelf of rock.

"Reason Peter chose it," he said. "Not particularly welcoming to the casual traveler."

"He found this place without your help?"

"Resourceful young man. One of the

things I like about him."

We came to a flat that looked across a small desert valley several hundred feet below. A familiar black SUV was parked there, and beside it stood Mondragón, cradling his scoped Weatherby.

"Rainy and Peter?" I asked when I got out.

"Waiting in the mine," he said. "I wanted to make sure of things."

Which I understood and appreciated.

"You're Sylvester?" he said to my companion.

The old miner nodded. "You must be Peter's father."

"Gilberto Mondragón." It was said with formality and a note of respect, and the two men shook hands. Mondragón looked at me. "Rodriguez?"

After the incident at the El Dorado Mine, I'd called Rainy's first husband, and we'd discussed options. The decision had been to bring Joaquin Rodriguez to the place Peter had been calling home for many months. Sylvester knew the way. We'd bound Rodriguez with duct tape and blindfolded him and tossed him onto the hard bed of the pickup. The ride hadn't been a smooth one and, considering his broken arm and judging from his screams, must have been quite painful. Didn't bother me in the least.

I dropped the gate on the pickup bed. Mondragón and I slid Rodriguez out and stood him up. I cut the tape from his ankles, but left his wrists bound and his blindfold in place.

"So you're Joaquin Rodriguez," Mondragón said, placing himself directly in front of the man.

Rodriguez tilted his head, as if trying to place the voice.

"Gilberto Mondragón," Rainy's ex said.

Rodriguez spit at him, and Mondragón responded with a blow that sent the young man to the ground.

I helped Rodriguez up. "You're not doing yourself any favors."

"Bring him." Mondragón started across the flat.

Sylvester took an arm and escorted him on one side, while I took the other. Mondragón disappeared around a tall jumble of boulders, and when we followed, I saw the low entrance to an old digging. Rainy stood in the sunlight there. Although I'd seen her almost every day since we were married, my heart still did a little dance of joy. Peter limped from the dark of the mine tunnel and lifted a hand in greeting.

After Rainy had given me a good long hug, we took Rodriguez into the tunnel. I was amazed at how Peter had made it a serviceable headquarters for himself. Two battery-powered lanterns supplemented the light that came in through the entrance. A two-burner propane camp stove sat on a large, flat stone. A cot with a sleeping bag stood against one wall. Canned and packaged goods were stacked neatly against the other wall, along with various other necessary living and medical supplies. Next to a collapsible camp chair stood a stack of books. Two more sleeping bags had been unrolled on the tunnel floor atop a foam mattress. The bags lay side by side. Rainy and Mondragón, I understood. I wondered what had happened to the safe house in Nogales and decided it must have been abandoned because of Peter. No comfortable safe house for him. And Rainy would not desert her son. So here they all were. One big happy family. I felt the demon of jealousy trying to whisper to me, but this time, that voice wasn't so hard to silence. I loved Rainy deeply. I trusted her.

We sat Rodriguez on the floor, his back against the tunnel wall, and left him blindfolded.

"I interrogated him," I said. "Got some interesting answers."

"Interrogated?" Rainy studied the man's

face in the lantern light. "How?" she asked with a suspicious note.

"I had to cut him," I admitted.

"That's exactly what I didn't want to hear," she said, her voice stone.

"Only a little," I said. "When I threatened to castrate him, he folded pretty quick."

"You would really have castrated him?" Her eyes were as hard as her voice.

"If he didn't, I would have," Sylvester said.

"So, here's the deal," I went on. "We were right on two counts. The Rodriguez family has been laundering money through someone in Coronado County. Joaquin doesn't know who that is. Only his father and his father's closest adviser know this."

"Who's his closest adviser?" Mondragón asked.

"Since Miguel was killed, it's the son-in-law, a guy named Ernesto Rivera."

"I've met Rivera," Mondragón said. "Very smart. Educated at Stanford, the business school there. A bit of a ladies' man, considers himself charming. But with the scruples of a hyena."

An interesting characterization, I thought, especially considering that I would have described Mondragón in much the same way.

"But why him?" Mondragón said. "Why

not Joaquin? He's truly family."

Rainy frowned. "And a son-in-law isn't?"

"Only technically," Mondragón replied.

"Joaquin's father believes that his remaining son" — I looked down at the blindfolded man, who'd made it clear to me that he considered Ernesto Rivera a usurper. I thought about speaking the conclusion I'd come to myself, that a man who yielded secrets as easily as Joaquin was not a man to be relied upon, son or no. Instead I finished with — "has more important duties."

"And the other count we were correct on?" Mondragón said.

"The stash of drugs. They've been using an old mine site for a while. They create a significant stockpile on this side of the border, then fly it out in one big shipment. But the most recent stockpile has disappeared. At first, they didn't know who to blame. Then they found out Peter had filed on the old claim. Just like us, they couldn't locate him. Until someone leaked the information about Peter and the Desert Angels and the rendezvous with the Guatemalans."

"Who?" Peter asked.

"He doesn't know. Miguel Rodriguez took charge of intercepting Peter, but his father insisted on being there, too. And we all

445

know how that went down."

"How do they fly the product out?" Mondragón asked.

This news was hard for me to deliver. "They use Jocko's landing strip."

Peter looked stunned. "Jocko? I don't believe it."

"Believe it," Joaquin Rodriguez said.

There was a look of smug satisfaction on Mondragón's face when he said to his son, "How many times have I told you, trust no one but family."

Peter knelt and leaned close to Rodriguez. "If it's true, why beat him up?"

Rodriguez shrugged. "I can't say. A warning, maybe, to a man whose feet were getting cold."

"Jocko." This betrayal seemed to do a great deal more harm to Peter than anything physical he'd suffered. He stood up, looking just a little dazed. "Why?" It wasn't a question addressed to any of us.

After a moment, I said, "Marian Brown used some of that stashed product to entice Royal Diggs into recruiting White Horse for the ambush."

Rainy said, "I'd bet my last dollar that she filed the claim in Peter's name in order to throw blame on him." The tone of her voice told me that if Brown had been alive and male, Rainy might have been tempted to castrate her.

To Rodriguez, I said, "Her murder, was that your father's doing?"

"Maybe. Or maybe Ernesto. With my father recovering from his wound, Ernesto is making decisions without seeking his approval first. *Cabrón,*" he said and spit on the tunnel floor.

"The stash of drugs?" Mondragón said. "Do you know where Brown moved them?"

"No," I said.

"Maybe whoever killed her got that from her before she died," Sylvester suggested.

"You have any idea who that might be?" I asked him.

The old-timer shook his head. "So many possibilities."

Mondragón said, "We have much to discuss."

I glanced down at Joaquin Rodriguez. "Let's talk outside."

Rodriguez said, "My arm is killing me. Can you help me, lady?"

He may not have been the bravest of men, but he'd picked up quickly that Rainy was his only hope for any compassion.

It was Mondragón who answered. "Be thankful you aren't dead. *Cabrón.*"

But Rainy added in a dispassionate tone,

"Pain clears the mind and sometimes cleanses the spirit, Joaquin." Then she joined us as we headed outside.

We stood in the heat of the July afternoon. Above us, I could see clouds beginning to gather, mottling the blue of the sky. Another monsoon rain on the horizon, I figured. I thought about how tough it might be getting down off that mountain in a storm. Whatever we decided to do, we'd have to do it soon.

"I want to talk to Jocko," Peter said. "If he really betrayed me, I want to know why."

"*If* he betrayed you?" Mondragón looked coldly at his son. "How much more evidence do you need?"

"I need to hear it from him."

"That won't happen," Mondragón said.

"You're my father, but you don't speak for me."

They faced each other. I could see the father in the son, the same aquiline nose, dark eyes, firm-set mouth. In the silence of their confrontation, I heard the grating caw of a crow from somewhere above us.

To my surprise, a smile graced the lips of Gilberto Mondragón. "You know, I spoke almost those same words to my father when he forbid me to marry your mother." He stepped back and nodded. "You're right.

You are your own man."

"Can you take me, Cork?" Peter asked.

"Yes. But there are still bodies at the El Dorado Mine that have to be dealt with."

Sylvester said, "I'll take care of that."

"How?"

"I'm thinking maybe an anonymous call to the Coronado Sheriff's Office. I'm guessing they won't be much surprised to learn that Sanchez's been killed in a shoot-out with some Mexican drug hoodlums. You deal with that kind of low-life, your days are bound to be numbered."

I gestured toward the mine. "What about Joaquin Rodriguez?"

"I think it's time we dealt with his father," Mondragón said. "We have leverage now."

"What are you thinking of doing, Berto?" Rainy asked.

"We have Joaquin call his father and we meet for an exchange."

"What exchange?" she asked.

"He gets his son back in return for a promise that our son will no longer be hunted."

"You'll accept his word?" Rainy didn't hide her skepticism.

"Offering him his son is significant. And what I'll make clear to him when we meet is that if our son is ever harmed, I will see

449

to it that every member of the Rodriguez family is hunted down and killed."

"You would really do that?" Rainy stared at him. "I don't know who you are now, Berto."

Mondragón said, "Perhaps you never did."

CHAPTER 37

Hell was in the east. The clouds were gathering, black and gray armies eager for battle. I thought I'd seen some bad storms in Minnesota, but what this desert could muster felt worse, maybe because it still seemed so unnatural to me. Worse also because this was a landscape unused to the run of big water. The ground was baked so hard and dry the moisture couldn't soak in and rushed instead across the surface, etching deep channels, flooding washes, pouring itself into rivers that appeared like magic for a brief while and then vanished, leaving behind long, empty graves filled bank to bank with nothing but dust and tumbled rock. It was a land, I thought, where even what seemed to promise life could just as easily deliver death.

We came down from the mountains slowly, carefully. Peter was quiet, and the sense I got from him, from the way he sat slumped, staring out the window, was one of despair.

"Why are you here, Cork?" he finally asked.

"Strange question."

"Mom, my father, they make sense. They're my family. But the truth is, you don't really know me. I'm nothing to you."

"Not true. You're Rainy's son. Rainy's a part of who I am now. In my book, that makes you a part, too."

"Like family?"

"No, not *like* family. Family." I drove a little farther while he digested this, then I said, "But in a way, I suppose, it's the weight of history."

His face was blank. It was clear he didn't understand. Why would he? But I understood. I understood myself better than I had since I'd come to that strange land.

"Even if you weren't family, I'd probably be helping," I said. "You're one of the good people. I like to think I am, too. Good people help one another. That's what keeps all the darkness at bay."

He shook his head and set his mouth in a hard line. I knew there were demons inside him, whispering. If they were anything like mine, they were probably arguing seductively that trust only led to betrayal.

452

"I didn't see a vehicle of any kind for you up there," I said. "You always walk?"

"My Jeep's parked in Jocko's hangar. I put it there before he flew me out for the last rendezvous." His words held a bitter edge, and I knew he was considering the deep betrayal of this man he'd trusted with his life and the lives of so many others.

"Maybe Rodriguez has some leverage over the old man," I suggested.

"Maybe," he said, but it was clear he felt that justified nothing. "My father was right. Trust no one but family."

"Guarantee of a lonely existence."

"It seems to have stood my father in good stead," he said.

"Your mother would say trust your heart." When he didn't respond, I asked, "What does your heart tell you about Jocko?"

"I'm not sure anymore." He stared ahead at the restless congregation of storm clouds, at the darkness they were spreading across the land below. "I'm not sure of anything anymore."

He was not my son, not in any legal sense, and maybe I had no right to offer advice. But I'd put my life on the line for him, and I'd come to care about him deeply, so I spoke as I might have spoken if he'd been born to me.

"Do you give up that easily on all your friends?"

"Jocko." The word spoke a depth of disappointment. "He's the last person I'd expect this of."

"You don't know for sure it was him."

"It makes perfect sense."

"That's your head talking." Which was something his mother would have pointed out, had she been there.

"Look where my heart got me," he said.

"Yeah, let's look at that. You've saved a lot of desperate people from being preyed on by the likes of Carlos Rodriguez. You've helped them find sanctuary. Maybe you haven't exactly changed the world, but you've changed the lives of those folks, changed them for the better. That's where your heart has got you. Tell me you regret it."

"That's over now."

"Is it? What about Arweiler Bosch?" I said.

His shoulders had been hunched, but the name made him sit up straight. "Mom told you."

"And she showed me the photo you kept pinned to your bedroom wall all those years."

"What I do isn't about Arweiler."

"I agree with you there. You're half

Ojibwe. Do you know the Ojibwe word *og-ichidaa*?"

"Warrior," he said.

"That's one way to translate it. I prefer the more complex interpretation. One who stands between evil and his people. I think in your heart you're *ogichidaa.* I think it's what you were born to be. And whether it's Arweiler Bosch or Guatemalan refugees or God knows who, there will always be people who need your help. You have a calling, Peter, a duty that you can't turn away from."

We bounced and jolted our way down the mountain for a while, then Peter said, "And you don't give up on the people you trust."

I glanced at him, saw a calm resolve in his dark eyes. "You're going to be all right, son," I said.

We finished our drive out of the mountains in a comfortable silence.

At the hospital in Sierra Vista, we found that Robert Wieman had checked himself out.

"DAMA," the nurse at the desk said.

"Dama?" I replied.

"Discharged against medical advice."

"But he looked to be on death's doorstep last night," I said.

The nurse shrugged. "Apparently he had a dramatic turnaround. We can't keep someone here against their will. If he wanted to leave, as long as he signed a release form, we had to let him go."

"Who drove him?"

"The man who was with him. A Mr. Harris, I believe. His name's on the form, but I don't have that."

When we were back in the pickup, I said, "Maybe you've been hard on the wrong guy. What's your heart say about Frank Harris?"

"Frank's a good man," Peter replied carefully.

"But?"

"He's often been a troubled man."

"How so?"

"He has this vision of creating a world-class vineyard here, producing wines that will measure up to anything California or the Willamette Valley offers. It's been a hard road for him. He lost so many vines a couple of years ago, a lot of us thought he was done for. He's fought back, although it's taken a toll." Peter stopped talking, but he hadn't quite finished. "I've had the sense, sometimes," he finally went on, "that he and Jayne have been at odds. Not that they really fight or anything, just that they struggle. Different goals, maybe. I think Jayne hasn't been happy out here, and I think that's been troubling to Frank."

456

"A troubled man, particularly one who's struggled financially, that might be a decent target for someone looking to corrupt a few morals. I don't agree with a lot of things your father says, but I do agree that money can buy just about anything."

"Or anyone?"

"Let's find out. What do you say we head to Jocko's place?"

We were halfway there when my cell phone rang. It was Frank Harris, desperate.

"They've got Jayne and Jocko."

"Who?"

"Rodriguez," he said, the name so obviously vile on his lips.

"Where are you?"

"Jocko's place."

"We'll be there in fifteen minutes."

He was outside, pacing, and hurried to meet us as we drove up. When we got out and he saw who was with me, relief washed over his face. He hugged Rainy's son as if Peter were his own son and had come back from the dead. "God, I'm so happy to see you safe."

"What happened, Frank?" Peter asked.

"I was sitting with Jocko at the hospital this morning," Harris said. "I got a call from someone who said he represented Carlos

Rodriguez. He said he wanted to talk to Jocko. In person. I told him to come to the hospital. He said no, bring Jocko to the ranch house. When I told him that wasn't going to happen, he put Jayne on the phone. She was scared, crying. Then whoever the bastard was, he came back on and said if I didn't bring Jocko, he'd kill Jayne. And you know Jocko. He was out of that bed in a heartbeat. When we got here, the place was empty. I thought we'd been played. But then cars drove up and men with guns got out. They grabbed Jocko. One of the men, he seemed to be in charge, told me that if I wanted him and Jayne back alive, I'd have to deliver Peter or the location of the place where Peter's moved the drugs. Drugs? I asked them. What drugs? I didn't understand any of that. Didn't matter. They're going to kill them both if I don't come through."

"The man who spoke to you," I said. "What did he look like?"

"Mexican. Six feet. Clean shaven. Black hair. Forty, maybe a little more. Natty dresser."

"A name?"

"No."

"How are you supposed to contact him?"

"He gave me a number." Harris reached

458

into his shirt pocket, brought out a folded slip of paper, and handed it to me. I recognized the area code for Tucson.

"It's probably a throwaway phone," I said. "He'll use it for this transaction then get rid of it. I think we need to let your father know about this development, Peter."

He nodded his agreement, and I punched in Mondragón's number on my cell. When the man answered, I said, "Has Joaquin made the call to his father?"

"Yes," Mondragón said. "And things have changed."

"Let me guess. They told you that they have Jayne Harris and Robert Wieman."

"And someone else that Rainy says you know and care about. A minister."

"Michelle Abbott? They've grabbed her, too?"

"But we have Joaquin," Mondragón said. "If I cared about any of these people, it would be the proverbial Mexican standoff." There was some talk on the other end. I heard Rainy's voice, stern. Then Mondragón said, "I want to speak to my son."

I gave the phone over.

Peter listened, then said in a voice that would brook no argument, "We make the exchange." He listened again, and said, "We're at Jocko's ranch house." He nodded at something his father said and replied, *"Está bien."* He handed the phone back to me. "They're on their way here."

Harris looked like a man who'd just come off the battlefield, beaten and bewildered. "I don't understand what's going on."

"Let's go inside, Frank," I said. "We need to talk."

We sat at the kitchen table while I explained what we knew for sure and then our speculations.

Harris shook his head firmly. "No way. Not Jocko. I don't care if it's true they've been using his landing strip, Jocko didn't know anything about it. And I can tell you right now he's not the leak in the Desert Angels."

Peter leaned across the table. "I'm going to say something, Frank, and I need the truth from you."

Harris looked at him and understood without having to be told. "You're thinking that if it wasn't Jocko, then it had to be me, right? It's not, Peter. I didn't betray you. You've got to trust that."

I didn't know Frank Harris well, but I'd been reading people all my life, as a cop and otherwise. I didn't think he was lying. That's what my own heart told me. I guess Peter's heart must have told him the same thing, because he said, "I believe you."

I heard thunder in the distance and looked out the window of the ranch house kitchen. The fury of that day's monsoon storm was sweeping toward us.

"If Jocko was in the dark," I said, "they must have used the landing strip when he wasn't around. How would they do that?"

We all thought a bit, then Peter offered, "Maybe when Jocko flew me out to meet with a group I was going to guide?"

"How would they know when that was?"

"The leak in the Desert Angels," Harris said.

"You fed Nikki Edwards the coordinates for the crossings, so she could broadcast them," I said to Peter. "Would she also have known if Jocko was going to fly you or if you were going to drive yourself?"

"Not specifically, no," Peter said. "No one but Jocko and I would have known. And Frank." He looked at Harris.

"I didn't tell anyone. Well, Jayne." Harris's face changed in an instant. His eyes moved to the window and to the coming storm, and I could see his brain working. "No," he whispered. "Christ, no."

CHAPTER 38

Frank Harris stood at the kitchen sink, staring through the window at the storm sweeping toward us. Beyond him in the distance, the black clouds exploded in moments of brilliant white, and lightning split the eastern horizon like rips in a photograph.

"Jayne," he said, as if she were some longlost love.

I sat at the table with Peter, pieces of the puzzle falling into place for me. "You said that when your vines were killed, a lot of the other vineyard owners suffered as well and had to sell. But not you. You said Jayne's investments kept you afloat. What were those investments?"

Harris had his back to us and was slumped over, as if afraid he might vomit into the sink. "I don't know exactly. Jayne's always taken care of the business. I grow the grapes. That's the part I love." He shook his head. "She must have sold off a lot of stock or something. Everyone else had their land on the market back then, and Jayne was buying it. She had this vision that we would become the largest vineyard in Arizona. Me, I just wanted to make good wines."

Another thought occurred to me, another piece of the puzzle. "This land she bought. Who brokered those deals?"

"Marian Brown."

Brown and Jayne Harris. Two women used to handling large sums of money. Two women, perhaps, with similar grandiose visions. Maybe they were the base of a financial triangle in Coronado County, and who was at the apex of that dangerous geometry?

"Did Jayne and Brown have other dealings together?" I asked.

"They met over wine and talked a lot. I wasn't a part of that. I don't like Marian much. I don't know what Jayne sees in her."

"What did Marian and your wife talk about when they got together?"

"I don't know. Marian usually came when I was out working in the vineyards. Whenever I came back to the house, she was just leaving."

"Have their meetings been more frequent lately?"

He thought about that, then turned to me. "As a matter of fact, they have."

Then I dropped the big one on him. "Did you know that someone murdered Marian Brown last night?"

From the stunned look on his face, I could see this was the first he'd heard of it.

"Shot three times in the chest while she was standing in her living room."

He stared at me, speechless.

"The money that kept you afloat, Frank, the money you bought all that additional land with, the money you say came from Jayne's savvy investments, could it have come from somewhere else?"

Two and two were adding up in his mind, but he didn't want to accept the sum. "From Marian Brown? Is that what you're saying? That my wife was somehow in cahoots with Marian Brown?"

"I think they were both working with someone else, Frank, someone much wealthier and fully capable of murder. Someone who needed them to help launder his money."

"Who?"

I didn't answer. I just waited while he worked that one out for himself.

"Carlos Rodriguez? My wife and Carlos Rodriguez? No."

Peter was looking at me with disbelief on his face as well. "Jayne?"

"I'm just considering the evidence. Some-one leaked the information about your rendezvous with the Guatemalans, Peter. You say you trust everyone you recruited. Jayne refused to be a part of the Desert Angels, but Frank admits he confides in her."

Peter said, "If what you say is true, Jayne would have had to know the location of my rendezvous that night. Even Frank couldn't have given her that." He looked toward Harris for confirmation, but the man was silent. "Frank?"

"Jayne could have known the coordinates," Harris finally admitted.

"How?"

"You and Nikki usually sit together in church, same pew every Sunday. Jayne and me, we sit behind you."

"You what? Overheard us?"

Frank shrugged. "Enough to guess cor-rectly about Nikki using her radio program to broadcast the coordinates. But that doesn't mean Jayne sold you out to Rodri-guez."

"I'm sure Marian Brown sold her soul to the man," I said. "And she and Jayne were apparently quite tight, involved in conversa-tions that seem to have been held in a way meant to exclude you, Frank. From what I know, sounds to me like they both enjoyed handling money, large amounts especially."

Peter shook his head. "But if Jayne sold me out to Rodriguez, who killed his son in the desert that night? And how did they know I'd be there, and Rodriguez?"

"I believe Jayne told Marian about the rendezvous, and Marian used White Horse in that ambush. I think she and Jayne were trying to cut themselves loose from Carlos Rodriguez. I think they were planning on Rodriguez being killed out there, maybe even hoping for a clean sweep, both Carlos and Miguel."

"And me?" Peter said.

"You and the Guatemalans? Just collateral damage."

"No," Frank said, shaking his head and looking at me with dark, angry eyes. "Not Jayne. Hell, Rodriguez grabbed her as a hostage."

"Maybe it only appears that way," I said.

"Goddamn you, O'Connor. Who are you to be making this kind of accusation? You don't know anything about us. You don't know this land. You're a stranger here."

"Let me ask you one more thing, Frank. Jocko told me that his father and your grandfather prospected together a long time ago and mined a little. He said it was somewhere in the Sonora Hills. You know where?"

"Of course. I own the land. But I haven't gone there in forever."

"Does Jayne know where?"

"I'm sure she does. Why?"

Peter looked at me, understanding slowly coming into his eyes. "Rodriguez's stash."

"What are you talking about?" Frank said.

I explained to him about the cache of drugs that had been moved from the mine where Rodriguez had been storing them awaiting transport.

"You think Jayne moved them?" Frank said.

"Jayne or Marian or someone working with them. Your grandfather's old diggings would be a pretty good place to hide all that product. It's on private land, in a place the public isn't likely to stumble onto. Close to Jocko's strip, if plans are to fly it out eventually. And in spitting distance from the border."

"No," he said, denying it with an even more vigorous shake of his head. "I can't believe that."

"There's an easy way to find out." I looked through the window at the coming storm. "But we'll have to move fast."

We took Peter's Jeep, which he'd left in Jocko's hangar the day he went to meet the Guatemalans. Because of Peter's wounded leg, I drove. Frank directed us south several miles, then we followed a dry wash that wove into the Sonora Hills. The sky was a cauldron filled with black, and a strong wind ran beneath, bringing with it the sweet, heavy scent of rain.

We rounded a bend and Frank pointed to the right toward a fold in the hillside. I pulled out of the wash just as the first fat raindrops hit the windshield. In front of us was the opening to an old excavation.

"Granddad called it the Jezebel," Frank said. "He told me it kept teasing him but never gave him much in the end."

We got out of the Jeep as the rain began to come down in earnest, and we ran for the mine. We'd brought flashlights, and inside, we thumbed them on. There it was. Wrapped bricks rising like a false wall from tunnel floor to tunnel ceiling, God knew how many layers thick. I guessed it was cocaine, millions and millions in illegal product.

All this illicit wealth, I thought, and men

like Rodriguez still preyed on the poor who were trying to get to freedom, still stole from them what few pesos they had left.

In the backsplash from the flashlights, Frank Harris's face was as expressionless as a dead man's. "It's true then," he said. "It's all true." He continued to stare, but silently, because what more was there to say?

Outside, the storm poured down rain and lit the Sonora Hills with brilliant, blinding flashes of lightning. I stood looking through a steady stream that cascaded down the hillside above and formed a ragged waterfall over the mine entrance. The wash we'd driven was no longer dry. We needed to get to the ranch house to meet Rainy and Mondragón, who would be bringing Joaquin Rodriguez with them, but I could see that we wouldn't be going back anytime soon, at least by that route.

"Is there another way back to the ranch house?" I asked Harris.

He seemed not to hear.

"Frank," I said.

He shook his head. "Walking, I suppose. It would be hours back to Jocko's that way. Best just to wait."

I pulled out my cell phone. In the cover of the cave, I got no reception. "I'm going to make a run for the Jeep, try to call Mondragón."

I looked at Peter, then nodded toward Harris, who seemed so lost. Peter gave me a nod in return.

I sprinted to the Jeep, jumped inside, and checked my phone. Two bars. Not great, but enough. I punched in Mondragón's cell phone number. On the other end, his phone rang and rang and finally went to voice mail.

"It's Cork. We're not at the ranch house. Give me a call when you get this message."

I returned to the mine and told Peter and Harris what was up.

"I don't like that he didn't answer," I said.

"Maybe out of cell phone range?" Peter offered.

"Were you ever completely out of cell phone range when you were exploring the Coronados?"

He shook his head. "One of the reasons I wanted to set up sanctuaries there."

Harris walked to the entrance and stared into the rain.

"Maybe Rodriguez got them, too." He spoke in a dead voice.

"I'm going to wait in the Jeep, in case Mondragón calls back," I said.

"Why don't we all wait there together?" Peter suggested.

Peter and I made a dash, but Harris came

slowly, oblivious to the downpour. When he reached the Jeep, he was like a man who'd taken a shower fully dressed. He sat slumped in the backseat and, just as he had in the mine, simply stared at the rain.

"I hate just sitting," Peter said.

"Have you ever hunted?" I asked.

"Never."

"Just sitting is a lot of what you do. You learn to be patient."

"I'll kill him," Frank said quietly at our backs.

"Kill who?" I asked.

"Rodriguez."

But I knew Rodriguez wasn't to blame for Frank Harris's misery.

My cell phone rang. I didn't recognize the number.

"Mr. O'Connor, this is Deputy Crockett. One of our Border Patrol picked up your wife, and Gilbert Mondragón, on the Old Douglas Road. They asked that we notify you."

"Where are they?"

"On their way to meet you at Wieman's ranch house. Agent Sprangers is with them. They should be there soon."

"We're not at the ranch house."

"Where are you?"

"Until this rain lets up, stuck in a mine in

the Sonora Hills. What did my wife and Mondragón tell you?"

"Just that there's a hostage situation. Sheriff Carlson's working on pulling together a team for that. We assume you have Joaquin Rodriguez."

That surprised me. Why wasn't Rodriguez with Rainy and Mondragón?

"We'll get to the ranch house as soon as we can. There are some things Sheriff Carlson and Sprangers should know. Have them call me."

"I'll see what I can do."

"What's up?" Peter asked when I'd ended the call.

I explained things to him and to Harris, who seemed to be coming around now.

"We need to get to Jocko's," I said.

Peter looked at the brown torrent that was gushing through the wash and shook his head. "Going to be a while."

And it was. We waited an hour for the storm to pass and then more time for the run of water in the wash to ease enough to risk driving the Jeep out that way. Hunter though I was, I found myself growing more and more impatient, and finally I decided we had to leave.

"Buckle in," I said. "We're going."

But before I had a chance to move, a big

black crew-cab pickup truck with wheels like those I'd seen on earthmovers came crawling up the wash. The grille was high above the water, which swept around those great wheels as if around the legs of a dinosaur. The truck swung out of the current toward the Jezebel Mine and the place where Peter and Harris and I sat in the Jeep. I couldn't see through the windshield.

"Hand me the Winchester," I said to Harris.

He passed it up to me, and I chambered a round. The truck parked facing us, the grille like a huge, skeletal grin. The back door on the passenger side opened and a man got out. Hispanic, tall, muscular, dressed in black, with an automatic rifle in his hands. He walked to the other side of the truck and opened the back passenger door. He reached up with one hand and helped someone down from that raised chassis. I recognized Michelle Abbott. Her hands were bound behind her back with duct tape, and a strip of tape was across her mouth as well. Next came Jocko, bound in the same way. The man said something to them, and they walked forward a few steps then stopped, with the man directly at their backs. The driver's side door opened next, and another man got out. He kept his back to me and I couldn't see him clearly. He walked to the other side of the truck, opened the door, and helped Jayne Harris down. Like Jocko and Michelle, she was bound with duct tape. The man walked her to where the others stood and placed her in the front line with Jocko and Michelle, then took his place behind them along with the other man.

The first man, I didn't recognize. The second man I knew well. He was wearing a tan cowboy hat with a colorfully beaded band around the crown. Deputy Crockett.

They stood facing us, with the storm behind them in the distance still battering the land.

CHAPTER 39

Deputy Crockett. The mole. It made perfect sense. The task force had been trying for some time to intercept Rodriguez's shipments, always in vain. With someone like Crockett on the inside, with the knowledge of where the Border Patrol agents stationed themselves and when and where the rolling checkpoints were to be set up, it wouldn't be difficult for Rodriguez to move his product through Coronado County. In the Santa Margaritas, he'd been the one to make the call on the sat phone for backup just before Rodriguez's men fled from the Jesus Lode. He must have called Rodriguez at the same time. Probably the only reason they'd been there in the first place was because Crockett had relayed the report from the Border Patrol helicopter that had put me in the area. And when Marian Brown had come under suspicion, he must have relayed that information, and the next thing you know Brown is dead.

"Let's get out slowly," I said. "Put the Jeep between us and those guys." When we were out and positioned, I called, "So what now?"

"Now we negotiate," the first man called back.

"Ernesto Rivera?" I said.

"Corcoran O'Connor?"

"Talk to me."

"It's very simple. You hand over Joaquin Rodriguez and we give you these three. Three for one, quite a bargain."

"What about all the drugs in the mine?"

"I don't care about the drugs. You want them, take them. Believe me, there is so much more where that came from. Where is Joaquin Rodriguez? In the mine?"

"Jayne!" Harris called suddenly. "Jayne, are you all right?"

"She is perfectly fine, Mr. Harris. And she will stay that way so long as we settle our negotiation."

"Jocko!" Peter called. "You okay?"

In truth, Jocko looked in pretty bad shape, swaying a little as he stood, but he gave a nod, exaggerated so that we could see it clearly.

"You okay, too, Michelle?" I called.

She nodded.

"A requirement in our negotiation,

O'Connor," Rivera said. "Put down your rifle."

"And lose all my leverage?"

"Leverage? You have no leverage. Because this is what I'm going to do if you don't put that rifle down. I will kill one of these three people. And then I will ask you again to put your rifle down, and if you do not, I'll kill another. And then we'll repeat that process one more time. And then, if we have to, we'll use our rifles on the three of you. I understand that you're good with the Winchester. But I'm sure you realize your antique is no match for a couple of American-made M16s."

"Kill any of us and you'll never get Joaquin Rodriguez alive."

He smiled, broadly enough that I could see his white teeth, and for a moment, that look of satisfaction confused me. Then another piece of the puzzle fell into place. No matter what happened here, Joaquin Rodriguez would never make it back to Mexico alive. I heard from a great distance the continuing rumble of thunder, but the sky above us was clearing rapidly. In the wake of the storm, a kind of peace had settled. Once again, I felt the calm that, in the past, had come to me as I stood at the edge of dead.

"You've been the money handler, haven't you?" I said. "The man behind the laundering, behind diversifying the Rodriguez holdings. An upscale housing division in Cadiz. Major investments in mining interests. A silent partner in what was to become the biggest winery in Arizona. And that's just in Coronado County. God knows what you've arranged in other places."

He didn't reply. He seemed, in fact, to be enjoying this recounting of his activities.

"But that wasn't enough. You wanted it all. So you arranged for the ambush that you hoped would kill Carlos Rodriguez and his son Miguel. You used the people you'd bought in Coronado County to do your dirty work. People like Deputy Crockett there, and Marian Brown."

Part of the reason I was talking was to lay it all out, finally to put the pieces together in a way that made sense. But another part of the reason was that I was stalling. I had no plan, no idea how, with a single, old Winchester rifle, I was going to save any of our asses.

"Sending Joaquin into Coronado County, now that was genius. You'd hoped, I'm sure, that he would bungle things, just as he did, and get himself killed. That way, once Carlos Rodriguez was out of the picture,

478

you'd be set to head Las Calaveras yourself. You're not here to negotiate for his return. You're here to see that he doesn't go back at all."

He continued to look pleased with my assessment of his accomplishments. But I was sizing him up in other ways, wondering if he'd ever stood at the edge of dead.

That's when Frank Harris tried to leave the cover of the Jeep, to go to Jayne. Peter grabbed him and wrestled him back. He shook himself free and stood staring toward his wife, as if not sure who he was seeing. "Cork says you're involved in all this, Jayne. Is it true? Have you thrown in with these thugs?"

The question was left hanging in the air for a long while, until Rivera broke the spell. He took a knife from his pocket, opened the blade, and cut the duct tape that bound Jayne Harris's wrists. Once freed, she pulled the tape from across her mouth.

"Frank, you have to understand."

"Understand what? That you climbed into bed with the worst kind of people?"

"Climbed into bed," Rivera said with a laugh. "You don't know the half of it, Frank."

"How do you think I kept your vineyard alive?" she said. "You were ready to fold up and walk away. I found the money. I bought the land. I was doing it for you."

"Found the money?" Harris said. "You make it sound like it was just lying there waiting to be picked up."

"She has made some wonderful investments for us, Frank," Rivera said. "And made you wealthy in the process."

"And the drugs in the Jezebel? Are we getting rich off that, too, Jayne?"

"Go ahead," Rivera said. "Explain to your husband our financial relationship."

I was beginning to hate his smile.

Jayne opened her hands toward her husband. "Frank, I did what I had to. But it was for you, for us, don't you see?"

"And killing Marian Brown?" Rivera said at her back. "Was that for him, too?"

She turned. "You bastard."

Rivera laughed and waved the barrel of his rifle toward Frank. "Tell your husband exactly how easy it is to go from money laundering to murder."

"Murder, Jayne?" Harris spoke like a man in shock.

She turned, looking desperate. "Frank, please. You have to understand. They knew about her. She would have spilled everything eventually."

"Joaquin Rodriguez," Rivera demanded,

that irritating smile finally fading. "Where is he?"

It was clear there was no way to negotiate out of this situation. I was sure that from the get-go Rivera had planned to leave us all dead at the Jezebel. No witnesses. Simply another slaughter in the war along the border. My attention had moved to Deputy Crockett. He might have been a man who'd faced death before, and that made him, in many ways, more dangerous than Rivera. I eased the barrel of the Winchester in his direction. But he stood directly behind the hostages, and there was no way I had a clear shot.

"Crockett," I called. "Have you thought this through?"

He tilted his head, said nothing.

"Do you think Rivera intends to let you leave here alive? You know his plan now, this whole scheme he's hatched to take over Las Calaveras. Do you think he's going to trust you with that?"

"I warned you, O'Connor," Rivera said. "Give me Joaquin Rodriguez. Now."

"Why did he bring only you, Crockett?" I went on. "Why not a whole bunch of Rodriguez's men, make certain this thing went down right? While you're busy getting rid of us, you better believe that M16 Rivera is holding is going to take care of you."

"Enough," Rivera said, with a note of what could just as easily have been desperation as anger. "Now someone dies."

When he pulled the trigger, Jayne Harris jerked, as if she was a rag doll in a child's tantrum. She dropped to the ground, her blouse a pale white field where what looked like red poppies had suddenly bloomed.

"Jayne!" Frank screamed.

This time Peter could not hold him back. Harris darted from behind the Jeep, and Rivera cut him down with a burst from his automatic rifle. But Frank Harris wasn't dead. He crawled through the mud toward the body of his wife.

"Who will be next, O'Connor?" Rivera called in a high-pitched voice. It was like an animal howl, as if the killing had triggered something primordial in him.

Crockett must have heard it, too, or maybe what I'd said about Rivera and that M16 had finally sunk in. While Rivera was focused on the Harrises and me, Crockett began to back away, cautiously retreating toward the big black truck they'd come in. Rivera didn't seem to notice.

"What about Joaquin, O'Connor? Three seconds and the next one dies." Rivera sounded positively hungry for what was ahead.

I prayed for Jocko and Michelle to drop to the ground, for them to give me a clear shot at Rivera. Because in a few seconds, one of them was going to die and I had no way to stop it. I opened my mouth to scream out that directive, the only chance I thought I had to keep them — maybe all of us — alive.

Before I could speak, the shot came as a surprise. The right side of Rivera's head exploded in a crimson spray, and like an empty feed sack, he folded to the ground. I looked toward Crockett, thinking the deputy had bought my logic and decided to sever his relationship with Rivera. But Crockett seemed as astonished as everyone else.

"Deputy Crockett, drop your weapon."

Although I couldn't see him, I recognized Sheriff Chet Carlson's voice. It came from somewhere in the wash.

"Over here, Jocko," I hollered, and he and Michelle dashed to the Jeep and crouched behind it with Peter and me.

Crockett maneuvered to put the big truck between himself and the direction from which Carlson's voice had come. I sent a round from the Winchester into the grille near Deputy Crockett, then turned the barrel directly on him.

"Squeeze play, Crockett," I called. "The sheriff tags you or I do. Either way you're out of the game."

"Now, Crockett, or I take you out!" the unseen Carlson hollered.

Crockett wavered a moment more, then set down his M16 and laced his fingers across the back of his head.

"On the ground," Sheriff Carlson ordered. "Away from the rifle."

Crockett prostrated himself and waited.

The men, Carlson, Sprangers, and Vega, wet and muddied, came loping from the wash. Sheriff Chet Carlson was in the lead, a scoped rifle in his grip. When he reached his deputy, he stopped and pulled out cuffs. Agents Jamie Sprangers and Jesús Vega jogged to Ernesto Rivera and checked him. Vega stayed there, but Sprangers moved on to where Frank Harris lay with his arm across the body of his wife. The agent pulled out a cell phone, punched in a number, and requested assistance. Finally, he looked up at Jocko and Michelle and Peter and me. "You folks okay?"

CHAPTER 40

Justice isn't always about the law. Full disclosure doesn't always reveal the deeper truth. And so, in my interview with Sheriff Carlson and Agents Jamie Sprangers and Jesús Vega there at the Jezebel, I didn't tell them everything. Nor did Peter, who was the only other one among us who knew all the facts. We didn't tell them, for example, what we knew about Officer Mike Sanchez and the two other dead men at the El Dorado Mine.

"We got an anonymous call about the bodies out there and that one of them was Sanchez," Carlson explained. "Crockett told me he wasn't feeling well. Puked, in fact, in the office wastebasket. Said he needed to go home and lie down. Hell, O'Connor, you were a sheriff. A call like that comes in, you're not going to let an upset stomach keep you from going to the scene. Besides, he wasn't looking sick before that. Agent

485

Sprangers had shared with me your concern that one of the task force might be leaking intel to Rodriguez. I gave him a call."

Sprangers looked at me and shrugged. "I had to trust someone. You know that drone I put on you? We decided to put it on Crockett."

"Few hours ago, we spotted him picking up Kong at his house," Carlson said.

"Kong?"

"What he calls that monster truck of his. Another man was with him. They came out this way. The drone followed them, we followed the drone. There was no way we could come up that wash in our truck, so we hoofed it. Arrived in time to see Rivera gun down Frank Harris. That's when I . . ."

Carlson eyed his rifle. He was drained of color. He'd just killed a man, someone he'd trusted, had thought was one of his own. I suspected the killing was a first for him. I wasn't versed in the protocol in Coronado County, but in most law enforcement, a thing like that would require time with a shrink. Maybe a priest, too, or a minister.

I looked where Michelle Abbott sat comforting Frank Harris. Because of his work with refugees in the desert, Peter kept basic medical supplies and blankets in his Jeep. In her years as a Marine, Michelle had been cross-trained as a medic. She'd done what she could in a rudimentary way while we awaited the chopper that had been called in to medevac Harris to the hospital in Sierra Vista.

Jocko sat in the Jeep. For an old guy who'd been through hell, he seemed to be holding up pretty well. After we'd all given our initial statements, I joined him. He seemed to be nodding off but opened his eyes at my approach.

"How're you doing?" I asked.

"Haven't had this much excitement since the war. But I could do with some rest."

My cell phone rang. I recognized the number.

"Where are you?" I asked.

"At the ranch house where we were supposed to meet," Mondragón said. "Where are you?"

"Can't talk right now," I said.

"Police?"

"I'll explain when I see you. Stay where you are."

"Rainy's okay, by the way. Rodriguez probably needs his arm looked after."

"Thanks," I said and ended the call.

I headed back to Carlson and the two agents, who were talking to Peter.

"I think Mr. Wieman could use some

medical attention," I said. "We've given you what we can. Is it okay if I get him out of here?"

Carlson said, "I need formal statements from everybody."

"Tomorrow morning?"

"Is that a promise?"

"Solid gold. Your office. Nine a.m."

In his way, he looked as beat up as Jocko, and he gave me a weary nod of approval.

Vega said, "One thing, O'Connor. Your wife and Gilbert Mondragón?"

"They had nothing to do with this," I said.

"They're safe?" Sprangers asked.

"They're safe."

"Any way you could convince them to accompany you tomorrow?"

"I can try." I waited a moment. "Not thinking of putting that drone on me, are you?"

Sprangers smiled, slowly. "Still don't trust me? After all we've been through together?"

I walked to Michelle and sat down beside her. Frank Harris was lying quiet, his eyes closed. He seemed to be out.

"How is he?"

"Lucky Rivera fired low. Leg wound. Missed the arteries, but might have hit bone. Peter had some morphine in his medical supplies. That'll help keep him comfortable until they get him to Sierra Vista."

"Peter and Jocko and me, we're leaving. Want to come?"

"I think I'll stay with Frank until the chopper arrives."

"Thanks for everything."

"Me? I just loaned you a pickup."

"Semper fi," I said.

"Vaya con Dios," she replied.

On our way out of the Sonora Hills and back to Jocko's ranch house, we met several vehicles belonging to Border Patrol and the Coronado County Sheriff's Department speeding toward the wash that would lead them to the Jezebel. The storm was long past, and the gush of water had diminished to little more than a trickle. The sun was low in the sky, breaking golden through scattered clouds, and the air that rushed in through the Jeep windows smelled fresh and promising.

The black SUV was parked in front of Jocko's ranch house. As soon as we pulled up, Rainy rushed out to meet us. I think our senses must be hardwired to our hearts. When I saw Rainy, she was more beautiful to me than anything I'd ever seen before, and although she hadn't been able to shower or wash her hair in days, when she nestled her head against my chest, she smelled better to me than any flower I'd ever come across.

She hugged Peter and Jocko, too, and we went into the ranch house together. Mondragón waited inside with Joaquin Rodriguez, who was looking far worse than the last time I saw him.

"Get me to a doctor," he insisted. "My arm is killing me."

"It could be worse," Mondragón said. "I could be killing you."

I explained to them all what had gone down at the Jezebel Mine. When I finished, Rodriguez spit on the floor. "*Cabrón*. He deserved to die."

"You see?" Mondragón said to Rainy with great satisfaction. "Trust no one but your own flesh and blood."

Rainy's response was a glare as cold as steel in winter.

"What do we do with him?" Peter asked, nodding toward Rodriguez.

"Let me go," Rodriguez said. "I can talk to my father, explain things. I am all he has now. I am the one he'll trust."

"Let's talk outside," I said to the others.

The sun had settled on the tops of the Coronados in the west. We stood with our shadows long across the ground, all of us

490

except Jocko, who sat on the porch steps, looking beat.

"If we turn him over to Sprangers and Carlson, it won't take much for them to break him," I said. "He'll tell them everything about the shootings at the El Dorado."

"You sound like that's not a good thing," Rainy said.

"It means Sylvester gets dragged into things officially. You never know about the legal system. Even when you think you've got a slam dunk, it can be unpredictable."

"Whatever they charge his son with, Rodriguez will buy his freedom, *querida,*" Mondragón said. "The jury, the judge, the prosecuting attorney, someone will have their price and Rodriguez will pay it. And Sylvester and your precious Cork are the only witnesses. Carlos Rodriguez would never let them live to testify. He's crude and cruel. I can guarantee they wouldn't die quickly. Or alone. I don't really care about Cork, but you, Rainy, I would worry about greatly. And you," he said to Peter.

"If we return Joaquin to his father, he can explain things," Peter said. "Once Carlos Rodriguez knows the whole truth, he might see things differently."

"Maybe." Mondragón glanced toward the ranch house. "I trust Joaquin like I would

491

trust a scorpion. Me, I'd just kill him, leave his body in the desert for the vultures, then I would kill Carlos Rodriguez and his whole family."

"We're not going to do that," Rainy said.

He gave a simple nod in acquiescence. "I can guarantee that no matter what his simpering son says, if Carlos Rodriguez wants revenge, Carlos Rodriguez will seek revenge. And he won't stop until we're all dead. Or he is."

Rainy said, "I think we should turn Joaquin over to the authorities, let them deal with him and with Carlos Rodriguez."

I looked at Mondragón and he looked at me, and I could tell that a rarity had occurred. We were in agreement.

"That creates more problems than it solves, Rainy," I said. "Things could get really mucked up, legally. A good defense lawyer might be able to twist everything around to make us the bad guys. And, who knows, maybe Gilberto is right. A judge or jury or prosecuting attorney could be bought."

"You certainly have great faith in the legal system," she said.

"This is Coronado County," I reminded her. "I have no faith in how anything operates here."

"So what do you suggest?"

"If I were a different man, I'd agree with Gilberto, that Joaquin and the whole Rodriguez family end up vulture food."

"Gracias," Mondragón said.

"But all things considered, I think the best course is to return Joaquin to his father, as we'd initially planned. We take the chance that it will end our involvement in this whole affair. We go back home and put Coronado County behind us forever."

Mondragón said, "There are problems with this, but fewer than with our other options. Who knows? Maybe there is a little something human even in Carlos Rodriguez, and returning his son to him will appeal to that. After all, Peter didn't kill Miguel and he will have helped Joaquin return home."

"All right," Rainy finally said but clearly not with a full heart.

Peter nodded his agreement.

"Jocko?" I said. "You're the one who's got to live here, a stone's throw from the border and Las Calaveras. What do you say?"

He considered, then replied, "I say live and let live whenever possible. But always sleep with a rifle handy."

"Let's go deliver the verdict," I said.

When we told Joaquin Rodriguez our decision, he didn't thank us. He said, as if we'd finally come to our senses, "A wise choice."

Mondragón bent to him, put his face inches from the young man's, and spoke quietly in Spanish in a voice as threatening and venomous as I'd ever heard a man speak. At the end, he said, *"Lo entiendes, cabrón?"*

I could see Joaquin Rodriguez struggle to maintain his composure, but his eyes, which had become huge, white pools of abject fear, gave him away. He managed a nod.

"I will drive you to Nogales," Mondragón said, speaking in English for my benefit, I figured. "Your father's people can pick you up there."

"Gracias," the young man said softly.

Mondragón turned to Rainy. "Will you be here when I return? I would like a few moments alone with you before we say goodbye."

"I'll wait," Rainy promised.

"And you?" he said to Peter.

"I'm taking Jocko to the hospital, but I'll come back."

We helped Joaquin Rodriguez, still bound with duct tape and making pained noises whenever we jarred his injured arm, into the SUV. Mondragón kissed Rainy, *"Hasta luego, querida.* You will always be the love of

494

my life."

It was the kind of thing a player might say to any woman. But I knew Rainy, and she wasn't just any woman.

Mondragón gave his son an embrace, then he turned to me. "I don't like you."

"The feeling is mutual," I assured him.

"But I believe my wife and my son are safe in your keeping. Thank you."

He reached out, and I took his hand. Then he got into the SUV and drove off toward Nogales.

Peter sat beside Jocko on the porch steps. "Well, partner, you ready to have the doctors look you over?"

"They already did. Not excited about going back."

"I'd feel better if they monitored you a little longer. And if I take you back, we can check on Frank. I know we're both worried about him. I'm sure he'd be grateful to see a couple of familiar faces."

That seemed to convince him, and Jocko rose slowly. He stood before Rainy and me, pulled himself up straight and tall. "Been a pleasure to ride with you, Cork. And, Rainy, I can honestly say, I've never met a finer woman."

She hugged him and kissed his cheek, and I shook his hand.

"You okay to drive with that leg of yours?" I asked Peter.

"Pain sometimes cleanses the spirit," he said and grinned at his mother. "I'll be fine."

Rainy said, "There's something I want to give you, Peter."

She stepped inside the ranch house and came out with a photograph, which she handed to her son.

Peter stared at the picture a long time, and I couldn't read his face. Then he shook his head. "The ones you don't save, their faces stay with you forever."

He put the photo in the pocket of his shirt, kissed his mother, got into the Jeep with Jocko, and they headed up the dirt lane.

I sat on the porch steps, finally alone with Rainy. I put my arm around her and drew her to me. She laid her head on my shoulder, and together we watched the sun drop below the Coronados. The sky was clear and pale blue, with no sign left of the storm that had earlier battered the land. The air smelled fresh and clean, and although there was not a hint of evergreen, which was the perfume of the North Country, I still felt the kind of peace I might have felt if I were home. Because I was with Rainy. And wherever Rainy was, that was home to me now.

EPILOGUE

Arizona was a dangerous place for Peter, so
he came home with us. But not for long.

All our children rendezvoused in Aurora
after our return. Stephen came back from
driving cattle in Texas and Annie came from
San Francisco. Around the kitchen table,
with chocolate chip cookies and milk, as
was our habit, we told our stories. Annie
seemed particularly taken with Peter and
his commitment to helping the refugees,
who'd come so far seeking only a place they
hoped might offer something better than
the violence and poverty they'd left behind.
She was impressed to hear that he could
make himself understood in many of the
indigenous languages of Mesoamerica. She
shared with him her own experience working with the poor in Central America, when
she'd been considering taking vows with the
Sisters of Notre Dame de Namur. Over the
next several days, they talked intently. Rainy

led them both in sweats. Henry Meloux listened and offered his well-considered two cents. And in early August, Peter and my younger daughter left together for Guatemala, where Annie still had friends working among the poor.

Life in Aurora returned to normal, blessed normal. Fall came, and the leaves turned, the colors so beautiful there were times my heart ached, it was so full of gratitude.

We learned about what happened in Mexico almost by accident, from a story buried in the Saturday edition of the St. Paul *Pioneer Press,* which I nearly missed because I wanted to get to the sports section. The article reported that there had been a massacre at the compound of the man who headed the cartel known as Las Calaveras. Carlos Rodriguez, his son Joaquin, his wife, Carmela, and several other family members were among those killed. Authorities in the United States believed it was simply part of the brutal struggle between cartels for control of territory. Rainy and I believed otherwise. The next day at St. Agnes, we both said prayers for the dead.

In news reports, we watched the wall along the Mexican border expand, the folly of a belief that what we had to fear came from the outside. I thought often about the

Guatemalan women and their children. I prayed that they'd found the sanctuary they'd come so far seeking and for which they'd risked everything. I thought about little Juan, and I hoped that someday he would pitch for the Dodgers.

Winter came and winter passed. And in April, on the first anniversary of our marriage, I presented Rainy with a gift I'd made myself. It was a frame constructed of yellow birch, which I'd sanded and varnished and fashioned. Inside the frame, on velum parchment, I'd put the Pueblo prayer my wife had long ago taught me and that had sustained me during my periods of doubt in Coronado County. Rainy loved it, and she hung it above our bed. Some nights when life has seemed particularly difficult, we say the prayer together and it gives us comfort:

Across the dark night, we are not afraid.
Our love is the star that guides us.
Through the empty desert, we do not thirst.
Our love is the water that refreshes.
On the long journey, we do not weary.
Our love is the truth that offers strength.
As the mountains rise before us, we are not
    discouraged.
Our love is the hope that waits on the other
    side.

500

When we are together, let us hold hands.
Our love is the promise that is never
broken.

ABOUT THE AUTHOR

William Kent Krueger is the award-winning author of fourteen previous Cork O'Connor novels, including *Tamarack County* and *Windigo Island*, as well as the novel *Ordinary Grace*, winner of the 2014 Edgar Award for best novel. He lives in the Twin Cities with his family. Visit his website at WilliamKentKrueger.com.